Bloodfeather Lullaby

Blood Song Trilogy 1

Amber L. Werner

Contents

NORTHERN DEPTHS
DOLN
NORWICH
MIDSPORT
GRANSEA
KINGDOM OF
DRACWOOD
MAGEHAVEN
EPRORA
OCEAN
ORDDON
OCEAN
GREENVALE
FLAMESMOAT
BOGSMOUTH
THE BOGLANDS
MIDO ISLANDS
STONESHORE
RAIMIRE
SLINAS
SALT CLIFF
SULAND
WASTE
JORIA
SOUTHERN SEA

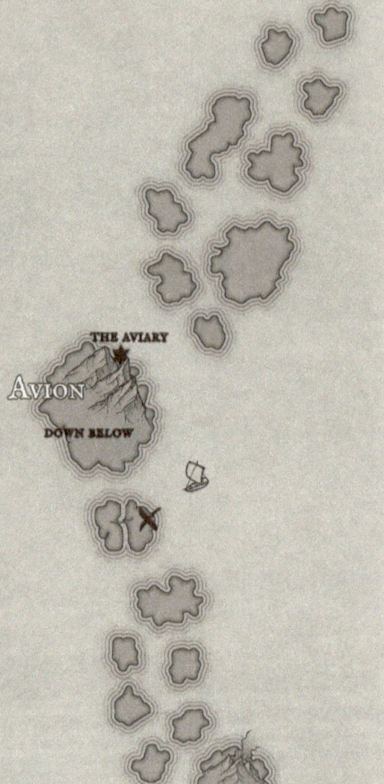

THE
STILL
SEA
THE AVIARY
AVION
DOWN BELOW
SALT CLIFF

JOLIT ISLE

Prologue

Ryon winced as he stepped into the sunlit temple, a cold breeze chilling the tears stuck in the corners of his brown eyes. He creeped in farther, birdsong echoing all around him. The glorious sound reverberated through his blood like the sweetest music, melodic and haunting.

Was he really about to do this? Did he have a choice?

Yes, and no. He could still walk out of here. Could keep his ears open to the sweet song. But he wouldn't. He needed this. He owed Rovan that much after what he'd allowed to happen.

Ryon approached the room's center, shivering as a chill whispered across his shins. The gray stone columns loomed large around him, dotted with countless holes like a basket woven too loosely, providing the perfect perches. Hundreds of eyes bore down on him, beady black orbs set into cocked heads. The shuffle of countless feathers whispered on the breeze that spilled through the stone.

Ten stilted steps brought him to the altar. Made of the same gray stone as the walls, it spread out before him in all its glory, basking in the sun that flowed unimpeded from a gaping hole in the roofless structure. Intricately carved stone birds decorated the altar's front and sides, which rose to the height of his chest.

Last year, he'd barely been able to see what lay upon it, but a recent growth spurt raised him high enough to peer at the offerings spread neatly atop the flat stone surface. Trinkets shone against the rock, scattered among piles of seeds. Ripe berries abounded, and even a few wiggling earthworms squirmed across the flat rock.

Ryon bit back a yelp as an orecoln landed atop the altar. The gull-sized bird shook out its glimmering silver feathers and cocked its neck, pinning Ryon with its gaze. It opened its sharp yellow beak and whistled. The melody sang through the air. Then the orecoln dropped its gaze to the altar, before zeroing in on him again, an expectant glint in its black eyes.

Trembling fingers reached into his pocket. Eleven years old, and this was the first time he'd ever been to the temple alone, but he still knew what to do. You didn't come to worship empty-handed. Especially not if you hoped to make a wish.

Ryon took a deep breath and slid a smooth rock atop the altar. The orecoln eyed it curiously, then opened its mouth again, gifting him another sweet note.

Was he pleased? The silver orecolns were always male. Everyone knew that. But would the offering be enough?

He'd scoured the river for days to find that one glimmering stone. Traveling farther from the comfort of his home until it appeared, like an answered prayer, right when he was about to abandon hope.

He'd raced all the way here. Not giving himself the chance to second guess.

Shimmering feathers fluttered as the orecoln hopped closer to the silver nugget. He bent his torso and snatched the rock in his beak while keeping his clawed feet perfectly still. He hefted it like he was testing its weight. The rattle of the stone inside his closed beak tickled Ryon's ears. Then he watched the bird's throat work as he swallowed the rock whole.

Eyes widening, Ryon held his breath. *Please. Please be enough.*

He dreaded going back there. His feet twitched, bloody and raw from the river stones, a hundred cuts marring the tender flesh of his aching soles. But if he had to return to searching, he would. He owed Rovan. He'd suffer a death of a thousand tiny cuts if he could turn back the clock.

The orecoln straightened from his crouch and eyed him once more. After an agonizing heartbeat where Ryon didn't dare to breathe, he tilted once again and plucked a tiny, shining, silver feather from his chest.

Ryon exhaled shakily, bowing his head and holding out his hand. When the sharp point of a beak scraped his palm and deposited something immeasurably soft onto his skin, he almost wept with relief.

He pushed aside the hem of his green tunic and dug into his pocket. His switchblade glinted in the sun as he flicked it open. This was it. He didn't give himself time to think. To reconsider. But he did close his eyes for a single heartbeat and listen one last time to the sweet song reverberating all around him.

Ryon's eyes snapped open, and he dragged the blade across his palm. He hissed at the sharp sting. But what was one more cut? Just add it to the thousands he deserved.

A tiny pool of warm red spilled into his palm. Copper stung his nostrils, but then the soft silver feather struck the blood, and a blissful warmth radiated through his skin. A smile slid across Ryon's face as he made his wish.

"You wish to be a priest, son?"

Ryon peeled his gaze from his stinging palm and met the orecoln's eyes. "No."

Feathers flapped all around as hundreds of eyes flicked to him. But where before, he'd have only heard that sweet melody echoing all around, now voices spoke out clear and—angry.

"No!"

"Heresy."

"He must be a priest."

"This must not be allowed."

He picked out a few of the louder voices, but even more spoke on top of one another, rumbling in a maddening cloud. Ryon cringed, barely resisting the urge to cover his ears. This was what he asked for. What he needed.

"Silence," squawked the orecoln on the altar.

Ryon drew a steadying breath as the clatter quieted.

"Why?" The orecoln cocked his head, twisting his neck until his silver head sat practically horizontal.

"I wish an audience with Mother Orea."

The orecoln huffed out what might have been a laugh. "For?"

Ryon ground his teeth. He might still be a child, but he knew the rules. "That's between me and Mother Orea."

The orecoln straightened, gave him one more appraising look, and spread out his wings. "Wait here." Then he lifted off the altar and flew up to the very top of the stone wall.

Flashes of gold hovered behind where the orecoln's silver wings landed, and Ryon's stomach fluttered in time with all the flapping feathers around him.

This was really happening. It was almost enough to make up for the loss of the song. Almost.

Whispers broke out, most far too quiet to distinguish, but a few reached him. Enough to have him shifting on his feet and his gaze darting around nervously.

"Is he the one?"

"Bold? No, cocksure, I'd say."

"Not a priest... it won't stand."

"Look at that plumage. It's disgraceful."

Ryon curled a hand through his short black hair. He suddenly understood why the priests grew their hair long and decorated it with feathers and shimmering gems. But he hadn't exactly planned to come here.

The flutter of silver returned, and the whispers halted. Ryon inhaled as the orecoln landed in front of him so deftly not a single offering slid off the altar.

"I've spoken to Mother Orea."

Ryon nodded gravely.

The orecoln cocked his head. "Can you be as patient as the river? As hardworking as the beaver?"

"Whatever you ask of me, I will do it."

"Then you shall have your meeting. When the time is right."

Ryon smiled, his chest swelling with hope. Glorious, wonderful hope. But then he lifted a brow. "How will I know when the time is right?"

Another one of those airy chuckles rose from the bird's throat. "Mother Orea will say when."

"All right. What do you wish of me?"

"Silver. More."

"How much?"

"That is for her to decide."

Ryon frowned, his stomach sinking.

The orecoln shifted, and one black eye bored into Ryon's gaze. "Bring what you find here, each night that the full moon rises." His gaze turned disdainful and rose to the top of Ryon's head. "And do something with that—mop." Then he lifted off, quickly disappearing within the sea of nests.

Ryon bowed his head and turned to leave.

In his heart, he knew he'd been given an impossible task. Mother Orea would keep him hunting for silver, wading through the streams and slicing his feet bloody for years. Decades. He'd seen it happen time and again.

But despite that, he couldn't wipe the smile off his face. At least now, he stood a chance. He might one day make up for his terrible mistake.

He just had to be patient and hardworking. And get used to wearing feathers in his hair. He cringed inwardly, but the thought didn't displace his smile.

He could do it. He would do it.

Merriment echoed all around Kayda. Constant chatter hummed, punctuated with peals of laughter. The aroma of fine food and sweet wine prickled her nose. A pleasant warmth enveloped her skin as the late summer sun washed over her.

If only she could watch it sinking down below the tree line; the clouds changing color, shades of rose and mauve painting the sky. A year ago, that thought would've been enough to set off a cascade of miserable longing. But now, two years after the battle that saw her vision lost, it only caused a brief twinge of regret, quickly brushed aside.

She may not have her sight, but she was still queen. The beloved savior of her country—loved even more than her grandfather had been. And at least now, she didn't have to squirm in her seat from all the eyes upon her. She knew they were still there, watching her every move at the grandest table at the head of the annual Harvest Festival. She could feel their heavy gazes upon her like a physical touch. But without her eyesight, the adoration was bearable in a way it had never been when she was just a princess.

"Ana," she called, waving a hand and waiting for a shadowy form to step beside her.

"I'm here, my lady."

"Tell me what you see, please."

Ana took a deep breath. Kayda imagined her gaze scanning the crowd, picking out details and cataloging them. Trying to determine what to mention first.

"There are blankets spread out all around, every color and pattern you could imagine. Everyone's smiling, eating, and laughing at the jugglers and tumblers you hired." A giggle escaped Ana, and Kayda wondered what had caused it.

She'd hired a dozen women from the Southmoat slums to be her eyes. Picking from the commoners—women who'd no doubt live a life of drudgery in an inn or worse—and giving them enough pay each week to ensure they'd want for nothing. Now, she always had someone at her side who helped her make sense of the shadows that were all she could see, even after trying every tonic and treatment the healers could dream up.

Ana swallowed her laughter and cleared her throat, her voice hushed. "At the table to our left, there's a red-bearded man who hasn't taken his eyes off you all afternoon."

Kayda shifted in her seat, aiming a smile in Taul's direction. She slid her hand forward to her wine glass—the servers knew by now where to leave it—on the left of her plate. She found it where it was supposed to be, the smooth glass cold beneath her fingers as she lifted it in a wordless toast and drank deep. The sweet wine slid down her throat and pooled in her belly, filling it with warmth.

Ana giggled again. "He toasted you back."

Of course he did. Kayda sighed, spinning to face forward before Taul took her toast as an invitation to come chat. The Doln warrior and his father, Clan Chief Aundrea, had been angling for a betrothal since the battle's end. But after her last disaster of an engagement, she'd not been too keen on the idea. Besides, she was only eighteen. Marriage could wait.

"A woman is walking toward you. She has blue eyes and long brown hair pulled up into a ponytail. On your right," Ana said hurriedly.

Kayda swiveled to the right. "Ereni, I'm glad you made it."

"Of course. I wouldn't miss the Harvest Festival."

Kayda waved a hand where Ana hovered beside her. "You can leave us, Ana. Thank you."

"My lady," Ana said reverently before Kayda sensed her presence vanish.

The chair beside her scraped against the dirt and grass. Ereni was silent, no doubt studying her, but Kayda felt calm in her company. She'd cultivated a familiarity with her brother's wife over the last two years that she only shared with a few choice people.

"Is Conall here as well?" Kayda asked, lifting her glass again.

"Yes." She could practically hear the smile in Ereni's voice. "He'll come chat in a bit, I expect. He stopped to show Violet the jugglers." She chuckled. "I'm surprised you didn't hear her screeching, *Stop, Dada, stop!* from over here."

"I'm glad she's enjoying herself." Kayda cleared her throat and leaned closer. "And what of that matter I asked you to look into? Is it as we suspected?"

Fabric rustled beside her, and when Ereni spoke again, her voice was hushed. "I think it's safe to say now that it is. No one has reported finding a talented child born in the last two years. But there are likely still dozens of children out there with suppressed talent, just waiting to erupt."

Kayda wrinkled her nose. Without Mage Keep there to find and teach all the young folks with talent, it would be as disastrous as it had been in the first days of humans discovering elemental magic.

Ereni's hand landed on her forearm. "I have a plan to help. Do you remember the willow that grew back in the Abandoned Lands when Lark had us all sink our magic into the ground?"

Kayda nodded. "Yes, I've heard about it."

"Well, it seems that tree has become something of a magic well. One of the mages brought her little brother to the spot to see where the battle happened, and when he touched the tree, all the potential magic he held was sucked right into the land."

Kayda bit back a gasp. "Are you certain?"

"She is a seer, like me. She watched the blue fade as he touched it. This might be the answer to all our problems."

Kayda couldn't contain her smile. Rarely did answers just fall in her lap like this. "Yes, it's perfect. I'll announce a reward. Any child with untapped magic that journeys to the willow will be awarded a tidy sum." She turned to Ereni, her smile tugging at her cheeks. "Would you and the other seers search them out, same as you did when hunting for mages to train at Mage Keep?"

"I can certainly arrange that." Ereni's voice contained a note of hesitancy Kayda wasn't expecting. "I would ask a favor in return."

"Of course."

"Violet must be allowed to keep her talent."

It was times like these Kayda wished she could still see more than anything. She pictured Ereni's face, firm and full of unwavering resolve. But if she could peer into her eyes, would she see a flicker of doubt hiding there? "Are you sure that's a chance you're willing to take?"

Surely Ereni had heard all the stories she had. Likely more, being a former mage and the daughter of the last Sade Prim. Why would she risk her daughter's safety for a handful of magic that was just as likely to wreak havoc on her life as it would help it?

The first time Kayda summoned she'd nearly burned down her own bedroom. She would've surely set the entire castle aflame had Izora not been there to help her and teach her how to control her abilities.

Ereni's next words were as firm and unwavering as Kayda had imagined her expression to be. "It's not a matter of taking chances. Violet will *need* her talent one day. I'm sure of it. If we strip it from her now..." Ereni's hand, still resting on Kayda's arm, quivered as she trailed off into silence.

"All right. She keeps it." Kayda patted Ereni's hand gently. She frowned. "Anyone else who wants to keep their talent shall be allowed to as well. Be sure to make them aware of the potential consequences. I imagine, with a large enough reward, most will see the sense in the offer."

"I'm sure you're right. And I suspect we'll be able to locate most of them easily enough. Younger siblings and children of former mages will likely account for most of them."

Kayda leaned back in her chair. "We have to send seers out to scour for the rest of them. I'll see to it they're well compensated for their efforts."

"Speaking of scouring. Has there been any word from Jayan?"

Kayda's stomach clenched at the reminder. "No. Nothing."

"I'm sorry. I'm sure he'll be back soon."

Kayda sighed. "Of course. I'm sure you're right." But though she forced a smile and a degree of lightness to her tone, deep down, she couldn't stop the prickle of unease that wormed up her spine.

It was taking so long. Would she ever see the Sul captain again, or had she sent her friend on a wild sparling chase that would be his end?

A Life Less Ordinary

A warm spring breeze blew through the grazing field and swirled Violet's yellow and white striped dress around her legs.

She sneezed and rubbed her itchy eyes. How she'd made it to twenty felt like a miracle some days, when the world was out to kill her.

Well, maybe not *kill* her—but it was certainly happy to inconvenience her beyond belief.

She sighed. Every year when the grasses sprung up like weeds and the trees bloomed with lovely pastel blossoms, she was guaranteed a few months of agony. Didn't help that she was stuck on a farm, smack dab in the middle of all that greenery.

"Violet," her mother called, her brown ponytail swaying across her shoulders as she stuck her head out the door of their modest wooden farmhouse. "Lunch is almost done. Come in and wash up."

"I'll be right there," she hollered back. She sniffed, resisting the urge to wipe her runny nose on her sleeve.

Violet lived with her parents on a simple farm. She helped them tend to the crops and herd the goats and sheep. She had it better off than most. Her parents even had connections with the queen but preferred the quiet pace of the farm to the hustle and bustle of city life. And for the most part, she did, too. But a small part of her still wished things weren't always so simple.

She had a loving family. A wonderful home and plenty to eat. Her parents had gone through so much to provide her with a life devoid of danger or strife. She would be a fool to wish for something more. To allow herself to admit to the deep yearning for a life less ordinary.

As she turned to head back inside, motion in the distance caught her attention. She squinted, then a smile spread as she realized what the blur speeding toward her was.

She waved. "Hello, Shadow."

Her father's bondmate skidded to a stop in front of her, and Violet's smile faded.

Something was wrong. She might not be able to communicate mentally with the wolf, like her father, but she could sense it from his jumpy manner and the wild flick of his golden eyes.

"What is it?" she asked, her brow furrowing.

Shadow barked.

Violet flinched at the high-pitched yelp, her eyes widening.

She could count on one hand the number of times she'd heard him bark. The last time, she'd found her father lying in the dirt with a broken leg. She wouldn't find her father injured this time; he was still bedbound, recuperating from that injury.

When Shadow trotted back in the direction he'd come from, she followed, a pit quickly coalescing in her stomach.

The delicate crunch of grass beneath her boots faded as she followed Shadow onto a well-worn footpath cutting through the woods bordering their farm. Star-shaped leaves and pink and lavender blooms abounded, blocking out the fading afternoon sunshine.

She sneezed again, twice in quick succession. Shadow jerked at the sound, and Violet aimed a crooked smile at him as she rubbed her watery eyes. Her father told her once wolves weren't fond of humans sneezing. It sounded too much like a snort of aggression, or a warning of a threat to a wolf's ears.

Normally, Shadow barely flinched when she sneezed. He must be on high alert. What would they find hiding in the woods?

Shadow's ears perked, and he tore off like a shot.

"Wait," Violet called, racing after him. Growling and snarling rent the air, and as she circled a bend in the path, Violet gasped.

Shadow had a racoon cornered beside a huge oak tree. The angry critter hissed, teeth bared, spittle dripping down its jaws.

Violet frowned. Surely Shadow hadn't led her here to watch him chase off a racoon. But the longer she stood there, catching her breath and watching the stand-off, the more it struck her as odd.

Why hadn't the racoon fled when it first spotted the huge gray wolf? Even now, the creature could simply climb that oak and be safely away where Shadow couldn't hope to catch it. Shadow drew closer, hackles raised, snapping and growling. He was easily five times the size of the tiny racoon. Surely it was a fight the critter couldn't win.

Blazes. Abnormal aggression. All that drool. Was that racoon rabid? She couldn't let Shadow get bitten.

With her heart racing, Violet snatched a massive, fallen branch off the footpath and barreled forward just as the racoon leaped at Shadow.

Crack. She landed a hit on its chest, sending the racoon flying across the path and careening into a pine tree. Violet cringed as the poor thing yelped and hissed. Pine needles rained down as it scrambled away from the trunk. She readied the stick to take another swing, but the racoon wobbled to its feet and tore off into the forest.

She spared Shadow a glance. "Was that critter headed for the farm?" Racoons didn't usually attack the sheep and goats, but they had a nasty habit of stealing their feed.

Shadow ignored her and trotted straight to the oak where they'd found the racoon. Violet followed, tilting her head as she spotted a large hollow in the trunk. A bird hopped out of the hole, one golden and white checkered wing bent awkwardly as she hobbled along in the dirt.

"Muse?" Violet knelt down beside the injured falcon. No wonder Shadow had been so determined to chase that racoon away.

It had been three long years since she'd last seen her aunt Lark's bonded falcon, but still, she would recognize her anywhere. Violet peered behind her curiously, biting her lip and holding her breath. Lark and Muse were normally inseparable. Would today be the day her aunt finally returned?

After only a moment, her heart sank. Muse was alone. Alone and hurt. Violet scanned her quickly and didn't see any blood. No scratches or bite marks that could have come from the racoon. She exhaled, and her galloping pulse slowed.

She needed to carry Muse back to the farmhouse. It was obvious her wing was damaged, but what if she had other hidden injuries? She didn't trust herself not to hurt Muse further if she grabbed her around her middle. But she appeared to be standing without issue.

Violet scoured the underbrush beside the trail—there. She dropped the huge branch she'd used as a bat and grabbed a stick, long and thick enough to serve as a perch, and settled it on the ground in front of the wounded bird.

"Hop on, Muse. I'll carry you back with me."

Muse cocked her head sideways, studying her. Then she dutifully hopped atop the branch.

Violet lifted the stick, balancing it in front of her as she spun around and headed back down the forest trail. Muse clung tightly to the makeshift perch, her head hanging wearily.

Violet's mind brimmed with questions on the walk back to the farmhouse. How long had Muse hobbled through the forest with an injured wing? What brought her here? Where was Aunt Lark?

Shadow stayed at her side until they passed the herb garden bordering the house, then he darted ahead as the side door swung open.

Her father limped into the doorway, propped up with a crutch, his broken leg stretched out stiffly beside him. He still wore his pajamas, the thin cotton rumpled, and his gray hair was tousled like he'd just jumped out of bed.

"Conall, what are you doing up?" Her mother appeared at his side, hands on her hips and a startled gleam in her blue eyes. "You shouldn't be—"

"Hush, Ereni," he said. "Look. We have a visitor."

Ereni's gaze flicked out the door as Violet arrived with her shoulders and arms screaming. She ducked past her parents and balanced the stick atop one of the wooden kitchen chairs with a sigh. Bright light filtered in the large bay window, highlighting the simple lunch of soup and sandwiches laid on the table inside the cheery yellow-painted kitchen.

"Is that Muse?" Ereni's eyes widened as she shooed Conall away from the door, then removed the white apron from around the waist of her tan frock. "What is she doing here?" She took a final peek outside, no doubt just as hopeful she'd see Lark emerging from the woods as Violet had been, then closed the door.

"I don't know." Violet rubbed her shoulders. "Shadow led me to her. I found her in the woods."

Her father collapsed on the chair beside Muse, breathing heavily. "Muse, my friend. Let me take a look at you."

Violet frowned, tilting her head sideways. "Her wing is bent. Can you help her?"

"I'll certainly try." He reached out, aiming for her wing, but Muse cocked her head and hobbled sideways on the branch. "Well, what do we have here?" Conall's hand lowered, and he smiled. "Fetch me a knife, love."

Ereni retrieved a small blade from a drawer. A moment later, Conall removed a folded piece of parchment from Muse's leg.

How had she missed that while she carried her? Violet bit back a gasp as her father unfolded the paper. "Is...is that a map?"

He smoothed the parchment on the table, squinting at it curiously. "I think so." He studied it for a moment, then he flipped it over and sat back in his chair, his eyes pinched shut and a hand splayed across his chest.

"Father, what is it?" Violet squeezed his shoulder gently.

Ereni snatched the paper off the table, her eyes widening as she read silently.

"Mother?" Violet asked expectantly.

"It's from your uncle. Lark's been... taken."

"Taken? By whom?" Violet stiffened.

Her mother's gaze danced across the page. "He doesn't say. Just that he needs help and to follow..." She squinted and shrugged. "The map, maybe? There's more here, or there was at one point, but that's all I can make out."

Violet peered over her mother's shoulder. The entire bottom half of the back of the parchment was smudged, the charcoal writing impossible to read. Whatever Muse had to endure during her flight back must've erased the message. Luckily, the inner section with the map was still intact.

"It doesn't matter what else it says. It's enough." Her father dragged a hand down his face. "If Muse is here, then it's serious. I have to save her."

He started to hobble to his feet, but Ereni planted a hand on his shoulder, pressing him back down on the chair.

"No. That's not happening. You heard what the healer said. You need to stay off that leg." Her mother's blue eyes never left her father's, but her voice gentled. "Besides. It's time."

Conall shook his head, his gaze drifting to Violet and then back to her mother. "No. She's not ready."

"And we were?" Ereni chuckled and squeezed his hand.

Conall pinched the bridge of his nose, but then he dropped his hand and nodded once. Only then did Ereni turn that sharp stare to her.

"Violet, love. There's something we need to tell you."

Violet's heart nearly stopped. She sank into a chair. The last time her mother looked at her like that and used that tone, she'd launched into a lecture about the birds and bees. Something told her this discussion would be equally monumental, though hopefully not quite so awkward. Especially not with her father present.

"What is it?" she asked.

"Well, we've told you all about fighting the Unseen. All the trials we faced with your aunts to defeat the evil plaguing Dracwood."

Violet nodded, a tiny smile curving her lips. Her family's history was like something out of a fairy tale. As a child, she'd wondered whether the story filled with dragons, magic, monsters, and an evil force determined to destroy the world had all been a clever tale crafted by her mother to entertain her before bed, but she'd learned it was all true. "Yes, many times."

"I'm afraid there's one piece of the puzzle we've left out."

Violet quirked a brow. "There is?"

"You remember how your father traveled to the Winter Witch to find Lark?"

Violet chewed on her lips. It had been years since she'd begged her mother to tell her the tale, so it took her a moment to dredge up the details from her memory. "Yeah. That's when he had the dream vision where he first spoke to the Unseen, wasn't it?"

Ereni drew in a deep breath. "I've been to see the witch, too."

Violet leaned back in her chair, crossing her arms. Why would her mother keep that part of her past a secret when she'd been so brutally honest about every other facet of her life? They'd always shared the kind of relationship where they could speak about anything and everything.

Violet's stomach clenched as she waited for the rest. And the fact that her mother suddenly clammed up, brow furrowed, twisting her hands in her lap, didn't set her mind at ease in the least.

Conall grabbed Ereni's hand. "I know we haven't kept many secrets from you, Vi. But I hope you'll understand why we thought it was best to wait to share this. Your mother and I both struggled when we glimpsed what fate had in store for us. We didn't want it weighing on you with everything else..."

His voice trailed off, and he shared a glance with her mother. Ereni appeared to gather strength from that one long look and his gentle caress on her hand.

"I was shown a vision as well," Ereni said. "About the daughter I would one day have."

"Wait, your vision was about me?"

Ereni nodded. "My father appeared to me. He told me I would bear a daughter who would one day hold the fate of the world in her hands."

Violet blinked furiously. If it had been possible for her to blanch with her pale skin, she would've surely done so now. Her grandfather had died long before she'd been born, when her mother was still a child. Had Ereni truly been given a message from the dead—about her?

"He said a day would come when you would be needed on a long journey. That you would travel far beyond the lands I've tread. And that although I would be willing and able to follow, it was something you must do without me."

Violet's gaze dropped to the map on the table.

"I begged him to tell me more, but he only told me one more thing."

Violet stared back at her mother. "What was it?"

"He said I must tell you, follow your heart song."

Violet chuckled nervously. "That's rather cryptic, isn't it?"

Her father smiled crookedly. "Dream visions often are, I'm afraid."

"So, this is it?" Violet's heart fluttered. "This is the journey I'm fated to take?"

Her mother nodded sagely. "I think it must be. But if you're not up for it—"

"No, I'm up for it. Are you kidding?" She practically squealed with excitement. Fear was there as well, buried somewhere deep down inside, but the glee bubbling up within her didn't give it room to flourish. Then a thought struck her that made her smile lengthen. "Maybe I'll find my bondmate on this voyage."

Her father smiled gently, glancing at Shadow curled up beside the hearth. "I imagine you might."

"When should I leave?"

Ereni stood, smoothing her tan dress. "Not just yet. Muse will need time to recover, and you'll need time to prepare. Run into town and fetch Breham to see to Muse, Vi. I'll see you tomorrow."

"Tomorrow? It won't take me that long to fetch him."

"I know." Ereni chuckled. "I'm off to Flamesmoat. There are a few things I need to gather before you start your journey."

Violet nodded quickly, gave her mother a hug and her father a peck on the cheek, then disappeared out the side door. It wasn't long before she sneezed. But for once, she didn't let it bother her. Her life was about to get interesting.

The Favor

N ox strolled down the servant's corridor in Kings Keep, whistling, his hands stuffed into his trouser pockets. His boots tapped softly down the empty candlelit hall. Likely, everyone was already tucked in for the night. He was headed for bed, too. After the workout he just had with the cute servant girl, Ana, he felt like he could sleep for a week.

Nox reached out with his thoughts. *"You still up?"*

"Of course. You know I prefer to hunt at night."

Nox halted, his hand outstretched to push open the door to the great hall. *"Flint. You promised."*

He could picture Flint's tail twitching angrily at that. Maybe he shouldn't head to bed after all. He couldn't have his bondmate wreaking havoc on the city. Not after last time.

"I've not broken my promise. I'm just... practice hunting."

Nox strode into the great hall. *"So, you're what? Stalking unsuspecting townsfolk?"* He eyed the back door that led outside to the castle grounds.

"I won't pounce on them. They won't even spot me."

"Flint."

A quiet snicker reverberated in his mind as he shoved open the door and strolled out into the moonlight. A black tail flicked ahead and a pair of golden eyes met his. *"You're so easy to rile."*

Nox rolled his eyes. *"Goodnight, Flint. Behave."* He sent his bond-mate a crooked smile as the huge black jagoth stretched out in a moonbeam like an overgrown house cat, his delighted purr thrumming on the breeze. Then he reversed course back into the castle, heading for the Royal Corridor.

Kings Keep was quiet as a tomb this late at night. A few coals lingered in the main fireplace, their charred scent infusing the drafty space with a campfire odor. He passed a single guardsman, decked out in his glistening metal armor, walking rounds of the silent building. But the man only sent him a nod and disappeared down the hall to the Northwest wing.

They were all used to him here at Kings Keep. His half-sister was queen, after all. She'd appointed him as her goodwill ambassador to his home country of Raimire years ago. The job meant he was a glorified messenger and spent his time split between visiting with Kayda here in Flamesmoat, the capital city of Dracwood, and dealing with the prickly Matas who led Raimire.

Nox slipped into the Royal Corridor and paced past the walls lined floor-to-ceiling with portraits of former kings and queens. He couldn't resist shooting them a playful smirk. Wonder if any of those stuck-up royals in their fancy silks and jewels ever imagined a lowly Raimish commoner sleeping in one of the fine suites of rooms reserved for the royal family?

His gaze trailed down to his clothing. He'd taken to wearing black cotton trousers, so as not to offend the Dracians' modest ways, but he still wore a sheer green luct shirt. His plain, slightly scandalous attire was about as far from the stuffy suits and dresses depicted in those portraits as it got.

But his half-sister had insisted he stay here while he was in Flames-moat. She was quick to remind him that though he might not have grown up in this castle, he still had royal blood in his veins. And what the queen wants, the queen gets.

Soon, Nox entered the Royal Corridor, leaving behind the judging eyes of his distant ancestors. He threw open the door to his chamber and gasped.

"Hello, Nox."

Clenching his chest, Nox forced a gulp of air down his throat before returning his sister-in-law's greeting. "Hello, Ereni. I'd offer you a seat, but I see you've already made yourself comfortable."

Ereni perched on the edge of a poofy chair in his modest sitting room. She'd stoked the corner fire high. Shadows danced on the pale blue walls and illuminated the scowl on her tanned face.

"You're retiring quite late." She adjusted the hem of her simple tan dress. "I searched the keep when I arrived a few hours ago, only to give up and wait here for your return."

He clicked his tongue and lounged on the equally fluffy chair opposite her. "What can I say? They run me ragged while I'm here. So many responsibilities eating up my day."

From the way Ereni lifted a single brow and crossed her arms, he guessed she wasn't buying it. But then she rolled her eyes and dropped her scowl. "Forget it. I have a favor to ask."

Nox sat up straight, his curiosity instantly piqued. Ereni had never asked him for a favor before. "I'm listening."

Ereni pulled a crumpled parchment out of her pocket. "Muse delivered this to the farm today."

The paper crinkled as Nox plucked it in his fingers and smoothed it against his thigh. Within moments, he gasped again. "Lark."

Nox's eyes slammed closed. He hadn't seen her for years. Truthfully, out of all the half-siblings he'd discovered, she was the one he'd never grown particularly close to. Not through any fault of hers, but simply out of a lack of proximity. She and her husband had a penchant for traveling, which hadn't allowed much time for bonding. Still, reading that single line—*Lark's been taken*—on the back of that map made his stomach plummet to his feet.

His eyes snapped open. "Well then, what are we waiting for?" He shoved off the cushion and jumped to his feet. "I'll pack a bag. I can meet you and Conall—"

Ereni clamped his arm, halting him before he stomped off into his bedchamber to fetch his belongings. "I'm afraid we can't go."

He stared down at her, frowning. "You can't mean that. It's *Lark*."

"I know. But Conall broke his leg last month. He needs to stay off it. And someone has to stay with him to ensure he listens to reason."

Nox's frown deepened at the news of his half-brother's injury. "Is he all right?"

"Yes, he'll be good as new in a few months, but until then, he won't be in any shape for a hard ride to the coast or sailing into uncharted waters."

"Hmm. I see. Well, you can count on me and Flint to find her." He shook off her hand and took another step closer to his bedchamber.

"Violet will go with you."

Nox cocked his head and spun around. "No, no, no. We'll have our hands full with the rescue mission as it is. I don't need to play nursemaid, too."

Ereni loosed an aggravated sigh. "Vi is twenty now. She'll be an asset to your search." From her firm unwavering tone, he sensed she wouldn't withdraw her demand.

"Is she prepared for this?" He shook the map, still clutched in his shaking fingers. The waters off the eastern shores of Dracwood were well known to be some of the most dangerous. "Are you prepared to send your daughter on a journey she might not return from?"

He'd been expecting her shoulders to slump at the question. At the reminder that no one who'd ventured on this particular journey had returned—yet. But Ereni surprised him by meeting his gaze with a determined glimmer in her blue eyes.

"I've been waiting for this day for longer than you can imagine. She's ready. We're all ready."

He nodded once. "All right. I suppose a little company won't be the worst thing in the world."

"Thank you, Nox." Ereni stood, smiling warmly and clasping his shoulder. "Make your way to the farm when you've settled whatever you need to here. I'll have mounts and supplies waiting. Goodnight."

"Goodnight."

Nox walked Ereni to the door, then leaned back against the hardwood, a thread of excitement raveling around the tension pooled in his chest.

He reached out to his bondmate in his thoughts. *"Hey, Flint."*

Flint's reply came almost instantly, even though he was likely still outside. *"Yes?"*

"Get some rest tonight. We're leaving tomorrow."

"So soon? We're not due back in Raimire for another fortnight."

Nox stared down at the map in his hand and smiled. *"We're not going home. Not this time."*

The morning came much too soon. The few brief hours of rest were barely enough to take the edge off his exhaustion. But as soon as the sun crested the horizon, Nox hopped out of bed with a spring in his step. Maybe he should feel guilty for being as excited as he was for this adventure to begin—his half-sister was missing after all—but he couldn't quite wipe the smile off his face.

He'd been too young to take part in the battle in the Abandoned Lands twenty years ago. The small part he'd played in his sibling's heroic story wasn't anything the minstrels were likely to sing about. Frankly, it was exactly the opposite. But now, he had a chance to make up for that by playing the hero for Lark. And after she saved his life back on the Mido Islands, he was certainly eager to return the favor.

With that thought in mind, he snatched the pack he'd stuffed full of clothing and other odds and ends last night and departed his rooms. Nox exited the Royal Corridor, ignoring the pointed stares of the portraits that followed him down the hall.

A quick detour to the dining hall, and then he'd collect Flint and head out. No time like the present for beginning his adventure.

The delectable aroma of spiced sausage and honey pastries greeted him as he stepped inside the expansive hall. Bright dawn rays cascaded from the skylight windows across the massive wooden table in the room's center. The table's single occupant glanced up at his approach, her red irises not quite connecting with his as she cocked her head in his direction.

"Nox? Is that you I hear? I'm surprised to find you up so early. Won't you join me?" Queen Kayda smiled behind a mug of what he suspected was likely tea, as steam coiled around her shoulder-length red curls. The freckles on her light brown skin winked in the sun, the little dots standing out brightly against her simple cream dress.

"I'd be delighted to." He strolled to the sideboard, quickly filled a plate, then settled down beside her.

"I spoke to Ereni last night." Kayda set down her cup and turned to him as he tore into a rasher of bacon.

"So, you know I'm leaving then?"

"I imagined you would be. I have a feeling half my maids will be heartbroken. And Ana, too, I suspect."

Nox chuckled. Where he came from, no one thought it unusual to share pleasure liberally. He was careful not to draw unwanted attention to his partners here in Dracwood, where attitudes were a bit more prudish, but his sister had a way of learning everything that happened under her roof without fail. "I expect they'll be fine without me. There are no hearts involved."

Kayda's brow rose at that, but she let the matter drop. "Well, all the same, I'll miss having your company. But I'm pleased you agreed to go after Lark. If things were different, I'd go with you."

"You? The whole country would be lost without you. Let me and Flint handle the rescue missions."

"It's not that I don't think you're capable. It's just—I sent her out there. Lark's been captured because she's on a mission I sent her on." Kayda reached out tentatively. Her fingers brushed the arm of the chair before she grasped his arm and squeezed. "Everyone who sails beyond Salt Cliff has a way of disappearing. Please, promise me you'll be careful."

The desperation in her tone had his stomach clenching, but he forced an air of levity to his voice when he replied. "Hey, I'll be fine. No one had a map before now. Surely, that gives me an edge over the others."

Kayda retracted her hand, a tiny smile gracing her lips. "Let's hope that's the case."

"I'll be sorry to miss the wedding."

Her shoulders tightened marginally. "Don't worry about that. What matters is finding Lark. You might even find her quickly and be back in time. The Harvest Festival is still a long way away."

"That's true."

Kayda was finally tying the knot. At thirty-six, she'd put it off about as long as she could without ruining any chance the monarchy had for ensuring the line of succession continued. He could tell the idea of marriage still rankled with his independent sister, but it appeared she'd finally grown tired of her advisors' constant calls for her to wed enough to agree to set a date at the annual Harvest Festival in late summer. With it being early spring now, he didn't hold out much hope that he'd be back by then—but who knew? Maybe he'd get lucky.

Even so, he was glad he had the chance to say goodbye. It would be hard to pause the comfortable life he led here in the palace and back home in Raimire, but he was excited for the challenge.

And beneath that, he couldn't quiet the tiny voice in his mind that whispered, *yes*. He couldn't bury the hope that this journey would put to bed the questions he harbored over the Unseen's demise. More than anyone else still alive, he had a connection to the evil force who'd nearly destroyed the world. That quiet voice continually nagged him that things were not as *finished* as everyone else seemed to believe.

Even after twenty years of relative peace and prosperity, the shadow of the days he'd spent connected to that villain still haunted him. It didn't sit right that the mystery of where the Unseen came from, and who and what he was, had never been answered. Maybe, somewhere in this new land sketched on the map folded neatly in his pocket, he'd finally uncover the truth.

He wolfed down the food on his plate and wrapped a few sausage links in a cloth napkin for Flint. Then he eased away from the table with a grin.

"I guess this is goodbye, for a while at least," he said.

"Nox." Kayda's voice held a tentative note he wasn't used to hearing. "I—Years ago, I sent another on the same quest I did Lark. I'm sure it's too much to hope you'll find him as well, but if you wouldn't mind keeping an eye out for a Sul man by the name of Jayan, I'd appreciate it."

Nox kneeled beside Kayda and embraced her quickly and tightly. "I will. I'll be back soon."

"Good luck, brother. I hope you're right."

Vibrations

R yon sank his axe into the hard-packed soil with a grunt. Sweat pooled on his lower back under his brown cotton tunic and dripped down his thighs beneath his pocketed skirt. The cool tunnel provided little respite from such sweaty work. He tugged, finally dislodging the hunk of shimmering rock he'd been working to remove all morning.

He pursed his lips, whistling sharply. "Got it."

Anyone else would hear the answering trill for what it was—birdsong. But words filtered to Ryon's ears clearly. "What did I tell ya? I knew that was where ya oughta dig."

Ryon grabbed a torch he'd left hanging on the wall behind him, grinning when the filthy rock glittered in the firelight. "You're right as usual, Quill. I don't know what I'd do without you."

Well, that wasn't entirely true. He'd likely still be cutting his soles to shreds searching in the upper rivers. A phantom ache tickled Ryon's feet within his brown leather boots as he recalled the handful of long years he'd spent scouring the river as a teen. It had truly been the ultimate stroke of luck he'd come to an arrangement with the greedy orecoln when he had.

"C'mon. Roll it out of here and break me off a chunk."

"All right, all right." Ryon rehung the torch, dug his knuckles into his sore back, then bent his knees and went to work. The huge stone had to weigh as much as a fully grown man. He huffed and puffed, slowly working it up the sloping path to the fresh air above.

Quill watched from the tunnel mouth, cocking his head to study the rolling boulder from different angles as it inched closer. "So shiny. That looks like a good one."

"I think you might be right."

"I usually am," he replied, puffing out the silver feathers on his chest. Quill was plumper than most orecolns but just as sleek and regal, about the size of a gull, with long slender legs. "What are you waiting for? Let me have a taste."

Ryon chuckled as he adjusted the top knot holding back his long black hair. "Give me a moment. I need to head back in to clean up."

Quill squawked angrily. "Can't that wait?"

"Relax. I'll be right back." Ryon rolled his eyes and reentered the tunnel. Maybe he ought to be more accommodating to the little bird, but he didn't relish the thought of creeping inside the dark recesses of the hillside once his torch guttered out.

Truthfully, he owed Quill everything. It had been eighteen long years since he'd made his first wish in the temple. On the night of every full moon since, he'd returned, bringing with him whatever silver he found that moon cycle, like the birds had requested.

The first five years had been the worst. Back then, the only place he'd known that held the precious silver was the treacherous river. He would search the banks and dredge the river bottom from sunup to sundown, often going weeks discovering nothing.

After the third time he returned empty-handed, one of the priests dragged him aside. He'd warned him not to come back without something again. Mother Orea would allow each petitioner five fruitless full moons, but no more.

That had only been the first year. One year in, and he'd been empty-handed three times already. He redoubled his efforts, squirreling away a portion of silver on the lucky moon cycles to ensure he never ran out on the bad. That minor change saw him through the next four years.

But during his fifth year, he'd gotten sick. He'd been so deathly ill he'd nearly died and was laid up in bed and unable to search. And since he'd used his backup silver for the previous two months, that meant another fruitless petition. He'd left the temple on his fourth night empty-handed, fearing the worst.

He was on his last chance. If he screwed up again, it was over. He would never get the audience with Mother Orea he so desperately needed. All his hard work, all his patience, would be wasted.

Then he met Quill. The shifty little orecoln had a nose for silver. He'd agreed to help Ryon on the condition that he share a bit of the treasure with him before bringing it to the temple. Their agreement had seen them through the last thirteen years without a single fruitless full moon.

Ryon smiled as he collected his axe, slung his pack on his back, and pulled the torch off the wall. This tunnel was one of many he'd dug in the silver-rich hillsides down below over the years. Without Quill, he likely would've never had the guts to even attempt traveling here. But it had been his salvation.

Ryon made quick work of grabbing his tools and pulling the torch from the wall. "What do you think?" he asked as he approached the cave mouth once again. "Does it look promising?"

Quill darted all around the stone, his sharp black eyes flicking this way and that. "The bottom quarter over here is not pure." He settled beside the stone, cocking his head to examine the lower portion. "Looks like mostly lead. But the rest." His eyes gleamed, excitement leaking into his voice. "It's silver all right. I think this is the biggest hunk yet."

"That's good." Ryon sighed, a massive weight lifting off his shoulders. "I'm almost out of the last batch."

"Surely not? We found the last hunk two months ago, and it was nearly as big as this one. What did you do with it all?"

"What, you mean besides the bits I fed to my greedy friend?" Ryon shrugged. "There's not much to be found in the upper rivers these days."

Quill hopped alongside Ryon as he scraped his axe against the top of the silver and broke off a few jagged hunks. Quill's gaze traced his movements eagerly. "You've been supplying the other petitioners again, haven't you? What did I tell you? That won't help you at all in the long run."

Ryon placed a shining chunk the size of his thumb on the ground, then broke it in two with the axe blade. "Here, have at it." He sighed, watching Quill snatch the first piece in his beak without delay. "I know I'd likely be done with my petition quicker if I'd bring in more silver, but I can't let everyone else fail. Not when I have the means to help them."

Ryon stretched, gazing out at the rolling hillside before him. Trees here were few and far between. Just grassy hill after grassy hill, spread out in all directions. If he squinted, he could sometimes make out a blue haze on the horizon.

Today, being clear and crisp and practically cloudless, he spotted a glimpse of the blue, and his heart clenched. Despite all the warnings of the dangers in the ocean, he'd always dreamed of gazing upon the unending blue waves. One day, he'd venture there. If he ever found enough silver to secure his audience with Mother Orea, that would be the first thing he'd do.

You would think nearly two decades of toil would be enough for a single conversation. Sometimes Ryon seethed at the injustice of it all. Hadn't he been patient enough? Weren't his long years of service enough to prove he was hardworking?

But every time he raged inside, he remembered his brother's face. Rovan. He was doing this for Rovan.

Ryon sighed and swung his axe, breaking off a few large chunks of silver and stuffing them inside his pack until it was full to bursting. Quill hopped around his feet, snatching all the slivers that went flying off the ground and gobbling them up.

"Mmm. That's some of the purest I've tasted. The priests will be pleased," Quill chirped happily.

"Good. Maybe it won't take me another decade to gain my audience then." Ryon huffed, pushing the remaining silver back into the tunnel mouth. Then he knocked the dirt around the edges loose, burying his prize.

It wouldn't do to have someone else happen upon the silver and take it for themselves. Not many villagers were brave enough to chance the climb below, but after all the digging it took to find the silver, he refused to leave it in the open.

Just as he was about to cover the top of the tunnel with soil, effectively sealing it, a noise in the distance gave him pause. It bled into the air, a great piercing rumble he sensed at the very edge of his hearing. The hair on the back of his neck lifted, and his heart slammed against his ribs.

"Quill, is that sound what I think it is?" Ryon stood perfectly still, listening intently.

Quill swallowed, quirking his head sideways. "Huh, be right back." He lifted off into the sky, shooting up so quickly, Ryon struggled to track him with his gaze.

The rumble intensified with every panicked beat of his heart. When the ground began to shake beneath him, vibrating the soles of his boots, Ryon's eyes widened, and he flew into motion. He could wait for Quill to return with confirmation, but he didn't need it. Not with the sound steadily increasing and the tremor in the earth intensifying with every passing instant.

He hefted the axe, tugging free the dirt he'd packed around the silver. He had to widen the hole. If he didn't have shelter when the tritusks arrived, he'd be done for.

A flash of silver winked in the corner of his eye, but Ryon didn't slow, using the axe and his bare hands to fling dirt from the tunnel mouth as fast as he could.

"Get inside. They're almost here," Quill warned, his voice shrill with panic.

"What do you think I'm doing?" Ryon dug, forcing himself to keep moving even as he wobbled atop the trembling ground.

He chanced a glance behind him. That was a mistake.

His stomach clenched, panic overcoming him so strongly he nearly lost control of his bladder. Hundreds of massive, four-legged, gray-furred beasts ran straight for him. Each one was nearly the size of a small cabin, and their lumbering footfalls slammed into the dirt and bounced the very earth. Three sharp tusks extended from their massive chins, glinting in the sun. The herd of tritusks raced toward him, faster and angrier than the enormous beasts had any right to be.

"Guano," he cursed beneath his breath. He was about to be gored.

Not if he moved. He swung his head back around, tearing at the tunnel mouth with renewed vigor. The hunk of silver still blocked the bottom of the entrance, but he'd nearly cleared the top. A few more handfuls, and he could squeeze through.

The rumble rattled his skull; the earth shook so forcefully he staggered more than once. But he dug and dug, widening the hole.

"Now. Jump in, now!"

Quill's insistent demand broke through the haze of fear clouding Ryon's mind. He shoved a final fistful of dirt aside and dove through the opening.

Please be enough.

In the back of his mind, he envisioned himself getting stuck, his shoulders wedging into the hole and leaving his lower body exposed. Then a tritusk would race toward him, stabbing him in the gut with those sharp horns.

But his fears jolted out of him at the same moment he crashed into the hillside cave, whacking his skull on the tunnel bottom. His head spun, and he groaned. He clutched his aching head and scooted away from the silver hunk, farther back into the cramped channel.

The ground continued to rumble, and gray shapes danced outside as the herd flew past his hiding spot. But as dirt rained down on Ryon in a cloud, his heart skittered anew.

He wasn't safe yet. One wrong step on the hilltop, and the tunnel could collapse, sealing him inside. What would become of Rovan then? Ryon frowned, realizing his brother likely wouldn't even miss him, though his mother would surely grieve him long and deep. Ryon held his breath, silently praying this tunnel wouldn't end up becoming his unmarked grave.

After a long, tense moment, the deafening rumble began to fade. The rattle of the earth quieted, and the dust and debris swirling in his face settled to the tunnel floor.

Ryon breathed out a deep sigh, a smile tugging at his cheeks. "Guano, that was close."

A sharp yellow beak appeared at the tunnel mouth an instant later. "You alive in there?"

"Yeah. Barely." Ryon crawled forward, digging at the hole to displace the loose dirt the herd had knocked down, nearly sealing the mouth again. But before long, he pulled himself free and sank down on his knees in the long green grass beside the hill.

The herd was nowhere to be seen. Only the fading echo of that maddening rumble and the crushed stalks of grass surrounding him remained as evidence of their harried flight.

"I wonder what spooked them?" Quill asked.

Ryon finally caught his breath. He rolled to his feet, frowning as he spotted his squished pack in the grass beside the hill. Luckily, the tritusks hadn't squashed his axe, but he might need to replace all the supplies in his pack. "Who knows? Could've been anything."

The tritusks were just one of the creatures that roamed the hills down below, keeping most of his people firmly ensconced in their clifftop village. Some brave hunters chanced the climb every so often, working in teams to take down the tritusks. The beasts might be ugly, but their meat was tender and highly prized.

Ryon knew the villagers thought him crazy to venture out here so often. But he'd been lucky so far. Nothing would stop him from continuing his mission. He would prove himself patient and hard-working, even if it killed him.

After reburying the tunnel, Ryon hefted his pack on his back and climbed to the top of the hillside. From this height, he had a clear view of the towering rust-red cliffs that rose in the distance. He smiled and strode toward them. "C'mon, Quill. Full moon's tomorrow. Time to go home."

Ghost Sighting

The door to the Greenvale Inn creaked as Violet and Shadow slipped inside. Her stomach churned as dozens of eyes turned to the sound.

The inn was the largest building in Greenvale, and rarely empty. Today was no exception. Rosy-cheeked villagers crowded nearly every one of the wooden tables scattered throughout the massive common room, enjoying ale and conversation in the quiet hours after finishing their daily work.

Violet had left her farm mid-afternoon. Her father insisted Shadow tag along, and he'd stayed true to his name by shadowing her down the trail to the village, keeping her safe. By the time she made it to Greenvale, dusk creeped up on the village, washing the wooden and red-brick cottages in a warm glow. She'd first stopped at the modest house Breham shared with his wife and two small children, only to learn he'd departed for the Greenvale Inn shortly before she'd arrived.

She craned her neck, scanning the noisy chamber for Breham's curly brown hair. A cursory glance made her brow furrow. Where was he? Maybe she could ask the barmaid. The rumble of chatter followed her as she strode across the room on her way to the wide wooden bar.

"Oh no," a loud voice declared, full of amusement. "I just felt a chill run down my back. What do you think that means?"

"I know. There's a *ghost* nearby." Delighted braying laughter followed that statement, echoed by his companion at the table Violet strode past.

She paused, aiming a glare at two of the boys she'd grown up with. They were young men now but clearly still immature enough to find great amusement in mocking her appearance.

"I see not much has changed since we left the schoolroom behind." Violet shook her head, hands on her hips.

"C'mon, Vi. You know we're only teasing," replied Emmer, the same idiot who claimed to be *chilled*, as he drank deeply. He clunked his mug on the round table, his green eyes twinkling in a face she would've found handsome, if not for the ugly personality she knew he possessed.

A few years ago, their teasing would've surely brought a tear to her eye. It wasn't her fault she was born albino. But after a lifetime of being ridiculed for her white hair, pale skin, and unique, reddish-tinged blue eyes, she'd learned to let the jokes wash over her—mostly.

"I could stand for a haunting." Folton reached out his beefy hand, pinched her sleeve, and tugged her toward the table. From the way he wobbled slightly in his seat and even had the audacity to wink, Violet had a feeling he'd been drinking heavily already. "Join us."

Violet opened her mouth to demand he unhand her, but a menacing growl from Shadow made the rogue retract his hand before she spat out a single word. Folton's tanned face blanched, and she barely resisted the urge to laugh at his cowardice.

She didn't understand men. They had some nerve, insulting her and then expecting her to join them. But maybe the rude fools could be useful in one respect.

She waved a hand at Shadow, signaling him to quiet. "I can't. I need to find Breham. We have need of his services on the farm. Have you seen him?"

Folton hiccupped loudly, then cocked his head at the hall beside the bar. "Yeah, he's in one of the private rooms. Got a weekly card game going with a few of the older set."

"Thanks," Violet bit out. She might not wish to be overly friendly with the pair, but there was no reason to be rude after they'd helped her.

"You need more help, you know where to find us," Emmer called as she strode away.

Violet sighed and didn't bother with a reply, even though Emmer's offer sounded sincere. It would take a monumental event for her to accept help from the two of them after the way they'd treated her. Maybe some people could stand their *friendly teasing*, but she wasn't one of them.

Violet paced through the wide hall to an open doorway halfway down. She peeked in and finally caught sight of Breham's brown curls. He sat in a chair facing away from her, at a round table filled with men she recognized from the village. Most were middle-aged or gray-haired elders.

Cards, mugs, and a few pitchers of ale decorated the table. Laughter and boisterous conversation spilled into the air, the men's faces merry and at ease. They were all dressed casually in well-worn work clothes, their jackets resting on chair backs. More than one sported glassy eyes and rosy cheeks that indicated they'd drank more than their fair share of the ale in the half-empty pitchers.

Violet poked her head in the doorway and knocked loudly on the doorjamb. The men paused their conversation to glance up at her, a mixture of curiosity and annoyance painting their expressions.

She cleared her throat in the sudden silence. "Breham? I need your help."

"I'm off duty tonight, my dear. Tell your father I'll be by in the morning." Breham didn't even turn, simply waved a hand in dismissal.

"Please." Violet twisted her fingers together, wincing at the note of desperation in her tone. "It's urgent. Can you hear me out?"

Breham spun slowly in his seat, eyeing her closely before flicking a glance beside her. He, at least, was clear-eyed, the mug in front of him still filled to the brim. "Well, Shadow appears to be fine. Which of the animals needs me so urgently? One of the goats?"

"No, it's a falcon."

That caught his attention. He cocked a brow and set his hand of cards flat on the table. "I didn't realize Conall had taken up falconry..."

"He hasn't. Muse belongs to my aunt, Lark."

Breham's eyes widened, and he pushed out of his chair. "I'm afraid I have to bow out early tonight."

The room reverberated with a chorus of goodbyes and well wishes from the rest of the men.

Breham joined her and Shadow in the hall. "All right, let's go."

They exited the inn, and after stopping briefly at Breham's house to gather his gear, they set off on the trail toward her family farm. Dusk had deepened during the time she'd spent in town, but there was still enough light to see beneath the forest canopy on the wooded trail. She'd come prepared for an evening stroll, with a delicate oil lamp and tinderbox stuffed in the pack strapped to her back, but they had some time yet before she needed to light it.

"Can I ask you a question?" Violet kept step with her companion down the trail as Shadow led the way a few paces ahead of them.

"Sure." He tilted his head sideways. A few locks of his hair fell forward and blocked his dark brown eyes from her view before he brushed them aside.

"Do you know my aunt?"

Although already married with a small family, Breham was less than two years older than she was. It seemed odd he would know Lark closely, since she hadn't lived in Greenvale for two decades. Lark had only been sixteen back then, and Breham an infant. But from the way he'd reacted when she'd mentioned her name, Violet had a suspicion there was some familiarity there.

"I don't know her personally, per se. But I've more reason than most to owe her a favor." Breham smiled and the dusky light glinted off his straight white teeth.

"What do you mean?" She twitched her nose, burying the urge to sneeze.

"Lark and her mother were the midwives at my birth. My mother told me the tale countless times. Apparently, when I was born, I wouldn't cry. My mother feared the worst. But your aunt Lark rubbed something on my chest and closed her eyes. Then the whole house shook, and I let out my first wail. She saved my life with her talent."

Violet grinned. "Wow, that's amazing."

Tales like Breham's were common before the war. Now that elemental magic was gone from the world after the Unseen's defeat, it was easy to forget that a few decades ago, healers like her aunt had performed miracles every day and mages had wielded the elements to protect the realm.

Violet often wondered what it would've been like to experience that kind of power. With the parents she had, it was likely she'd have grown into a talented mage. But she never let herself dwell on the question for long. It wasn't in her nature to focus on all the little things she wished she could change.

Even so, she was grateful to have talented family tonight. If Breham feeling that he owed Lark a favor meant Muse healed quicker, then she was happy to appeal to his sense of duty. And truthfully, his story struck a chord with her for another reason.

"You know, Lark birthed me, too?" Violet quirked a crooked grin. "Right before Southmoat fell to the scourge, she pulled me from my mother's womb and cared for me the first few weeks of my life while my mother saved my father in the bog."

With Lark's love of travel, Violet might not see her for months, or even years at a time, but the story of her birth had certainly earned her aunt a special place in her heart.

Breham chuckled in response. "Huh. I thought my birth was pretty miraculous, but it sounds like you've got me beat. I guess we both owe your aunt a favor."

"You're right about that, Breham." Violet sighed, a renewed sense of determination washing over her. They would heal Muse, and she would travel to find Lark. She wasn't about to let some strangers abduct her aunt without stopping them.

Violet fanned herself outside in the warm sunshine, taking a break from her chores. Sweat stained her plain brown dress after a long morning and afternoon tending to the animals and weeding the garden.

Breham had stayed the night but left early that morning. He'd wrapped Muse's wing in a soft towel and insisted that though the injury would keep her from flying for a time, it would heal on its own. An immense weight lifted from Violet's shoulders with that joyous news. Even more so when Breham declared the wing was Muse's only injury. They still didn't know what had caused it—they likely never would—but at least she was on the mend and expected to make a full recovery.

After a fitful night of sleep, Violet rose with the dawn and busied herself by tending to the many chores around the farm. With her father laid up with a broken leg, and her mother still away at Flamesmoat collecting the supplies Violet would need for her journey, there'd been plenty to keep her occupied.

Still, she couldn't stop her mind from wandering. What was out there in the Orrdon Ocean? Had her aunt and uncle truly found the new lands long rumored to exist beyond the small chain of eastern islands bordering Raimire?

She hadn't spent long studying the map Muse brought yesterday, but it certainly seemed to suggest they had. The knowledge sent an odd thrill through her. She was about to become one of the first people to set foot in a new land. She had the chance to do something extraordinary with her life, like she'd always yearned for. What would it be like? She was dying to find out.

But even as the excitement swelled within her, a touch of fear struck her, too. There was clearly someone out there who meant them harm, if her aunt's abduction was any indication. Did she really have what it took to stop them and save her aunt? And was what her mother claimed true? Was she destined to play some part in saving not just Lark but the world? It all felt incredibly unreal.

She'd always known she was destined to find a bondmate one day. She'd longed for it so badly. But even with the help of a bonded creature, how would she be able to conquer this? An adventure into the unknown with only a crude map to guide her. Could she become something more than an ordinary farm girl? Was that truly her destiny?

The *clip-clop* of hooves on the trail bordering their farm drew Violet from her musing. She shaded her eyes and smiled widely as her mother appeared on foot, leading a brown and white paint mare overloaded with lumpy sacks.

"Mother, you're back." Violet waved and sauntered over, meeting Ereni as she made her way toward the barn. "You certainly weren't kidding when you said you'd gather me supplies."

"It's good to see you, dear. Help me load these bags in the barn, would you?"

Ereni led the mare into the barn beside the house. The musty scent of animals wafted toward Violet as she tugged open the door.

"Let's stack them here on the bench by the door," Ereni said.

Together, they made quick work of the task, though by the time she hefted the last bag off the mare's back, Violet's arms ached from lifting the heavy sacks.

Violet sneezed. "What did you buy?"

"New bedrolls and a few essentials, but mostly food for you and the horses. You'll need to ride hard to the coast, so there won't be much time to let them graze."

"It seems a little overkill for one person traveling to the coast." Violet's eyes widened. Her mother hadn't said horse, she'd said *horses*, plural. "I'm not going alone, am I? But I thought you couldn't come with me?" She crossed her arms, staring up at her mother with a furrowed brow.

"Oh, I'm not. Someone has to stay here to look after the farm, and more importantly, your father." Ereni grinned.

"Well, then who's going with me?"

As if on cue, a new voice rose to answer her question. "That'd be me, squirt."

Violet gasped, spinning on her heel and squealing with delight. "Uncle Nox!" She raced through the doorway and thudded into his chest. "I didn't know you were in Dracwood."

"I got in a few days ago. Been staying with Kayda. I was planning to stop by for a visit sometime this week, but then your ma found me and showed me that letter…"

"And you're coming?" It was really too good to be true. With the exception of her father, there was no other man she trusted as much as Nox. And there was surely no one else more capable. She pulled free of her uncle's arms and glanced beside him, glimpsing black fur disappearing into the trees behind the farmhouse. "Flint, too?"

"You got it, squirt." Nox nudged her shoulder playfully.

Violet rolled her eyes. "Watch it with the *squirt*, would ya? I'm not a kid anymore."

Nox eyed her up and down with a pensive stare. "Huh. I guess not. Still a little thing though, squirt." He chuckled, but when she stacked her hands on her hips and sent him a hard glare, his laughter faded. "All right, Vi, don't give me that death stare of yours. I'll be good, I promise."

Violet shook her head, but a tiny smile curved her lips. She couldn't help being pleased with this turn of events. She'd been worried she wouldn't be enough to save her aunt alone, but surely now, with her uncle and his bondmate to share the voyage, their success would be guaranteed.

"When do we leave?" she asked.

The Willow

Nox flicked a glance beside him at Violet. Her shoulders slumped from her spot in the saddle of her chestnut mare, and her tan tunic was stained with perspiration. "Hey, squirt, hand over the bird."

Normally, that nickname would've earned him a glare, but it appeared Violet was too exhausted even for that. He couldn't blame her. The long days of hard travel were weighing on him, too. Not to mention the added difficulty of transporting an injured falcon with them on horseback.

Violet pulled up alongside his black stallion as he slid a leather glove out of his saddlebag and onto his arm. They both slowed their mounts to a halt to allow Muse to hop from Violet's forearm to his.

Ereni had provided them both with thick leather falconry gloves before they left, not to mention all the gear they split between the horses.

At first, Nox had been resistant to the idea of riding to the eastern coast. Growing up in Raimire, he hadn't had a chance to ride. The jungle was home to countless predators that made horse travel a rarity. Once he met Kayda and traveled to Flamesmoat, he'd enjoyed a few afternoon jaunts. But this was the first time he'd ridden a long distance.

He had to admit, it was much faster than walking. Even canoe travel through the bog would take much longer, due to the twisted, maze-like nature of the rivers and streams in the water-logged region between the northern and southern continents.

Still, it wasn't exactly the most comfortable way to travel. His back and thighs ached constantly, and his arm did half of the time, too, when he took his turn carrying Muse. He grimaced, resigning himself to a little while longer in the saddle. They'd spotted a sign for a town. He was determined to make it to an inn tonight so he could trade his bedroll for a bed for a change.

"You doing all right up there?" Flint prowled beside him, keeping to the dirt trail's edges to take advantage of the shade. Being completely covered in black fur except for the flash of yellow of his eyes and his off-white fangs, Flint habitually sought shade wherever he went.

He'd been surprised to find the horses didn't spook with a jagoth beside them. But the pair they rode had been raised with Shadow coming and going constantly and were used to co-existing with predators. It didn't seem to matter to them that they were sharing the road with a wolf-sized cat rather than the wolf they were used to.

"Just tired. I'll be fine after some rest."

"You're tired? At least you're used to being awake this time of day," Flint grumbled.

"Sorry to inconvenience you, my friend. You ought to have plenty of days to rest once we set sail."

Flint hissed in the back of his throat. *"Don't remind me. I still don't like the thought of being stuck out in all that water. It's bad enough when you make me sail through the bog."*

Nox chuckled. *"You'll be all right. And think of the bright side. You'll be surrounded by fish."*

"Hmm, that is a perk, I suppose." Flint's ears twitched. *"Won't be far now. I can hear the town already."*

"Me, too." Nox grinned. Likely, Violet still hadn't picked up on it, but he wasn't surprised. Advanced hearing was one of the many boons he'd acquired over the years.

Soon, the town appeared at the trail's end. A handful of wooden cabins sheltered together in a large clearing with a small stream cutting through the northern edge. He spotted an inn right in the town's center, planted between a somber redbrick church and a huge stable house.

"Blazes, is that a sight for sore eyes." Violet let out a hard sigh, then sneezed.

"Why don't you head in and speak to the innkeeper about readying a couple of rooms for us? I'll rent the horses a stall in the stable house. And take Flint with you. He's bound to spook the other horses."

"I'm sending Violet to rent rooms in the inn while I stable the horses. Mind keeping an eye on her for me?" he asked Flint.

"Babysitting. Fun."

Violet nodded and hopped off her horse in front of the inn, then waited for Flint to follow. Nox sighed, watching them depart, praying they didn't get themselves into any trouble.

Nox led the horses to the stable house. The scent of hay and manure hung heavy in the air. A lanky man peered out of a stall as he entered, then hustled forward to take the horses.

"How long will you be needing to stable them?" he asked.

"Just for the night. Can you have them saddled at daybreak?"

"Sure. We have a mews out back with a few empty spots for your bird, too." The man slicked back sweaty brown locks and scanned him head to toe, then backed away nervously. "You headed for the miracle tree?"

Nox shook his head. "No, to the coast."

"Huh. You ought to stop there on your way. It's a thing of beauty, that willow." The man turned away with a dreamy look in his eyes.

Nox left him to his daydream, dropped off Muse, and headed to the inn. That was the second time someone had brought up that willow to him in the last week. Before they departed, Ereni had pulled him aside and insisted that under no circumstance should he allow Violet to touch that willow.

That had been a bit of a shock. Everyone knew about the reward for talented kids who sank their talent into the ground—the lucky few who had been born before the Unseen's fall with untapped magic. He'd always assumed Conall and Ereni would've taken Violet to the tree years ago. His brother was the man responsible for ending the Unseen and revealing the lie: elemental magic had never been humanity's right to begin with but a cruel *gift* stolen from the dragons by that villain.

There could only be one reason they didn't want Violet touching that tree. Was her innate magic meant to aid them on this quest?

A brief twinge of jealousy creeped up Nox's spine. The rest of his half-siblings had been born with not just bonding talent but elemental magic, too. Not for the first time, he wondered what it would've been like to have both talents. But after only a heartbeat, he shook the feeling off with a shrug.

It didn't matter. If he'd had it, he would've surely used it all by now. Either by dumping it into the willow and claiming the reward or by performing one or two miraculous acts, only to drain what he'd been given. He'd rather never have it at all than to have such a brief taste.

The rumble of the inn met his ears as he slid into the common room. A merry barkeep waved him in with a word of welcome. Nox smiled politely at the few villagers that peered at him and made his way to a small table in the back of the room where Violet sat. Flint curled up on the floor by her side, his eyes closed and his head resting on his paws.

Violet glanced up as he drew closer, and her unusual reddish-tinged eyes sparkled brighter, now that the weariness of travel was over. "I ordered some food. They're prepping two rooms for us as we speak."

"Good. I'm starving." Nox sent her a grin as he perched on a stool across from her.

"I asked you to watch out for her. Why are you napping on the job?"

Flint's eyelids lifted lazily, and he blinked slowly in that contented way Nox had learned to think of as a grin before shutting his eyes again. *"There's no threat here. It's plain to see."*

Nox rolled his eyes. But Flint had a point. The inn was only half full, the few patrons all busy chatting among themselves and paying no mind to their table in the back, except for the occasional wary glance at Flint.

It was rare to find trouble in these small rural communities across Dracwood. Everyone was content. Pleased with the years of peace and plenty their Queen had brought them.

It was strange to think, even now, there might be someone out there preparing to upset the hard-won happiness that they'd fought so hard for. Whoever was out there, abducting Lark, might very well be a new threat to their way of life. He had a bad feeling that saving her would not be the end of the danger, but merely the beginning.

They arrived on the eastern coast a few days later. A bustling port town rested on the former site of the battle that had been fought twenty years ago. As they entered Magehaven, a pair of children rushed up to greet them. They stared wide-eyed at Muse perched on his leather gauntlet and giggled and waved as they spotted Flint trotting alongside the horses.

Nox held back a chuckle as his bondmate tensed, his tail flicking angrily. It never ceased to amaze him the reactions the huge cat attracted. Most full-grown men quaked in their boots when they spotted him stalking toward them, but somehow, children always seemed to see beneath the tough exterior to the pussy cat underneath.

"Hello, there," Violet called down with a smile for the children.

The little girl waved and smiled back, but the little boy cowered behind the girl, his lip quivering. "What's wrong with her?" he asked the girl in that blunt, loud way children had of spouting off whatever was on their minds.

Nox ground his teeth. But when Violet only pressed on, with no outward reaction, he let the matter slide. Kids could be cruel to people who were different. Surely his niece was used to the looks and jokes at her appearance by now, but he was sure, on some level, the comment stung her.

He knew a thing or two about that himself. When his bonding talent surfaced at twelve, the kids in his village hadn't exactly been kind. He could certainly understand feeling like an outcast for being different.

Nox brushed aside the painful memories. By this time tomorrow, they'd set sail and not have to worry about any backward comments.

They made their way deeper into the town, heading for the docks. All the homes here were new, built in the last twenty years. The houses lined up in neat little rows, painted in cheery colors. The streets were laid out in a radial pattern, all leading into a central location.

It wasn't long before they arrived in the town center. Nox gawked up at the massive willow. Its vibrant green leaves shimmered in the mid-day sun. A group of teens lounged beneath it, reading books and playing cards in the shade.

"Wow," Violet exclaimed. "That's the tree, isn't it? The one that sprung up when Aunt Lark healed Dracwood?"

"Yeah. That's the one."

Violet veered her horse toward the tree.

"Hey." Nox heard the hint of panic in his voice and quickly smoothed it. "I know you want to join those kids lazing around under there, but it'll have to wait, squirt."

Violet sent him a scowl, her pale cheeks flushing. "I thought I told you to quit it with the *squirt*?" But she spun her mount back toward the road, and Nox let out a sigh.

"All right, Vi. Sorry. C'mon. The docks are this way."

Did she feel drawn to the willow? It was certainly an impressive sight, even for someone like him, who'd never had a shred of elemental magic talent. But he'd managed to steer her clear of the temptation to touch it. That was all that mattered.

Soon, the docks appeared, perched at the end of the long cobblestone road. A massive wharf had been built out on the shore. Several boats floated in the deeper water offshore. The shallow depths here meant that even with the wharf, many of the larger ships had to drop anchor and ferry their wares ashore on smaller crafts.

But that wouldn't stop them. He planned to purchase one of the smaller sailboats. They'd be on their way in no time. Nox turned to Violet as she drew in a deep breath, staring out at the ocean.

"It's not too late to turn back. Flint and I can handle this alone," he offered quietly.

The statement earned him another scowl. "Are you crazy? You're not getting rid of me that easily, Uncle Nox." Her scowl shifted to a cocky smile. Then, Violet steered her mount toward the docks.

Nox followed, shaking his head and resigning himself to a long voyage with only a grumpy cat, an injured bird, and an overeager girl for company.

The Aviary

Ryon nudged open the back door to the cottage and peered inside. Seeing the coast was clear, he sauntered inside and dropped his smashed pack on the kitchen table. He'd just poured himself a cup of water from the chipped ceramic pitcher his mother always kept filled on the table when he heard her coming, the *swish* of her full skirts against the tiled floor signaling her entrance.

"I thought I'd see you today. Full moon tonight." Vera sent him a weary smile before her gaze lit on his head. "Ryon. What have you done this time?" She *tsked* softly, motioning jerkily for him to sit down.

"It's good to see you too, Mama." He drained his glass quickly and took a seat at the small table as requested.

"Oh, you know it won't do to visit the temple looking such a mess. You really ought to take better care of yourself while you're down below."

Ryon smiled benignly as she worked, taking out his top knot and smoothing out his messy black locks. It was hard for him to picture when his hair used to be short. Since his first trip to the temple, he'd only cut his hair a handful of times, and always just to trim away the split ends.

He wasn't entirely sure what the orecolns liked about human hair. Maybe it had something to do with their love of shiny things. His mother certainly always made his hair shine after she was done with it.

He'd been lucky in that respect, at least. Even before his decision to seek an audience with Mother Orea, she'd been one of the most sought out and talented hair stylists in the village. Many of the petitioners visited her on the full moon nights to make sure they were up to snuff when they brought their offerings to the temple.

He was lucky he made it home early today. If he had arrived any later, he'd likely have a line of men and women ahead of him, waiting for their chance to be seen to by his mother's talented fingers. She deftly braided all textures and lengths of hair with ease and was renowned for creating some of the most intricate and detailed styles in the village.

"Are you planning to talk to him today?" She spritzed his hair with a floral oil Ryon knew from experience would make his dark locks shiny and smooth.

Ryon sighed. "No, not today. Tomorrow. You'll be too busy to deal with the fallout."

Her hands stilled on his scalp for a heartbeat, but then she was right back at it. "I suppose you're right. But tomorrow for sure. I don't like you acting like strangers. It's not right."

"I know it's not. But it is easier." He forced a lightness to his tone, although the pit in his stomach recoiled at it. "Not much longer now, and there will be no need for all this. I'm close to being granted my audience. I can feel it."

"I'm sure you're right, son." Her voice turned sugary sweet. "Ursaline was by to have her hair braided yesterday. She asked about you."

Ryon rolled his eyes. "Uh huh."

His mother didn't know when to quit. He'd told her a hundred times already; he wasn't interested in any of the girls in the village. But that didn't stop her from pushing every pretty little thing she met under his nose every chance she got.

"Such lovely fair hair she has. The color of summer wheat. You two would make such lovely chil—"

"Vera," he said warily, stopping her before she finished.

She glared at him, no doubt offended he used her name instead of calling her *Mama* like he usually did. But then her expression softened. "I know, I know. Just think about it. If not her, then *someone*. You can't keep wasting your life away, hunting for stones." She finished his hairstyle by attaching a few spotted feathers on the sides. "There. You're ready."

"Thanks." Ryon sent his mother a grin. "No time like the present, I guess. I'll be back later."

"You're leaving already? But you just got here."

"There're a few people I need to see. Not to mention"—he waved at his pack with a grimace—"I need to replace a thing or two at the market."

His mother's eyes widened as she stared at the flattened bag. "What in the world did that?"

"Oh, nothing much." He grabbed the bag and headed for the door. "A few tritusks paid me a visit."

"Ryon!"

Ryon chuckled to himself and slipped out of the cottage with his smashed pack strapped to his back. He wasn't about to stick around for the lecture that would come next.

He'd heard it all before. It was too dangerous down below. One of these days, he was going to get himself killed. He ought to abandon his foolish quest and settle down with a wife and kids.

But what his mother didn't understand was that he'd rather die than not fix what he'd broken. Rovan deserved the chance at a normal life. And if he couldn't give that to his brother, then he didn't deserve it either.

Ryon trudged up the hill toward the temple. The Aviary loomed on the highest hillside in the far back corner of their city. Today, clouds pooled around it, making the pillar and stone tower look like something out of a fairy tale. He could picture a brave hero scaling the side, searching for a maiden to rescue.

But there were no maidens at the Aviary. Just the holy birds, catered to for centuries by his people, in the hopes of being granted a prized golden feather. He *would* earn one of them—if not today, then soon.

Ryon's hand tightened on his pack's straps as he neared the hilltop. Maybe even today, if his luck held out. He'd had an easy afternoon, swapping out his smashed supplies for fresh ones. He struck enough deals in the marketplace that he only had to part with a few small chunks of silver to pay for them.

And two of the petitioners he'd grown used to supplying had lucked into their own silver this moon cycle, leaving him with the largest offering he'd ever brought.

Two priests lingered at the temple entrance. Decked out in elaborate robes festooned with feathers in rainbow shades, they could usually be called upon for a kind ear or a helping hand. But on full moon nights, their only job was to keep watch over the petitioners. They ensured each person was afforded privacy as they brought their offering to the temple.

The priests moved aside and beckoned him forward. As he ducked between two crumbling pillars and entered the temple, Ryon smiled. Maybe today would be the day he finally received his audience.

There was only one way to find out.

Sunlight filtered in through the open ceiling, highlighting the center altar. The room had felt gargantuan to him as a youth. As an adult, it was still impressive, but with all his years spent plumbing the depths of the wide-open plains down below, it no longer seemed quite so grand.

And, of course, the beautiful haunting melody lived only in his memory now. Today, like always, voices rang around him, so many on top of another he couldn't pick out much. Only a scattered word here or there broke through the cacophony of murmuring and fluttering wings.

He strode to the altar and tugged his pack off his back. Then, among the fragrant fruit and seeds, he dropped his offering. The pile of glittering silver clinked on the rock table. Many of the pieces were smashed, far denser than normal, but a few still rolled, sparkling in the sunlight.

The voices quieted as the last piece rolled to the table's edge and halted, unwilling to tumble down with so many eager eyes upon it. Then the hush evaporated, and excited voices abounded as all the orecolns hungry gazes landed on the stones.

A flutter of silver swooped down on the altar. "Silence," the bird demanded. He cocked his head at the pile. Then he flicked his gaze up to meet Ryon's. "You are quite generous with your offering this full moon, son."

Ryon bowed his head, being sure to draw attention to his shiny black *plumage*. He'd caught his reflection in a metal pot in the market. His waist length hair gleamed, and the feathers his mother had chosen matched the amber flecks in his brown eyes.

"Wait here," the bird said.

Ryon's heart pounded. This was new. Usually, the birds offered him a simple thanks and sent him on his way with orders to bring back more silver on the next full moon. Could it be that he was actually about to hear Mother Orea speak?

But when the same silver bird returned a moment later, his heart sank. Not today then. He resigned himself to more years of toil. Endless patience and hard work. Would it never end?

The orecoln peered at him from the altar. "Mother Orea is pleased with your offering. She would ask of you a new task."

Ryon gulped, gazing at the top of the pillars where he could just make out a small flash of gold. She was back there, watching him. Awaiting his reaction.

"Anything you ask of me, I will do it."

"Good, son. We know you are no stranger to down below. You must fetch something special for Mother Orea. You will need to camp beside the ocean. Your journey will start there, within the next moon cycle."

Ryon nodded. "I can do that. What am I looking for?"

"Look for one with a gull's egg gaze, hatched in moonlight, and baptized by dusk."

His eyebrows shot up. What was that supposed to mean?

"Could you be a little more specific?"

The orecoln shook his head sharply. "You must find the one and bring it back. No matter how long it takes. Do not return empty-handed."

Ryon knew better than to ask twice. If they weren't willing to provide him more details now, then they never would. It appeared he had no choice but to head off on this fool's errand and hope the answer to Mother Orea's odd riddle became clear when he discovered whatever this *one* was.

"And when I return with your one, will I be granted my audience?"

"Yes."

Taking a deep breath, Ryon turned to leave.

"Stop."

He swiveled around, meeting the bird's steely gaze.

The orecoln opened his jaw wide and let out a single sharp trill. A rain of feathers cascaded through the room as silver birds leaped from their roosts and joined the first bird on the altar.

"This search will be fraught with danger. Mother Orea has foreseen it. Take these gifts to aid you. Use them wisely and share them freely when necessary."

As soon as he finished speaking, each of the birds reached down in unison and plucked a shining silver feather from its chest. They lifted their heads and stared at him with the tiny glittering feathers clutched in their beaks.

Ryon gaped, his stomach fluttering like all those feathers had somehow taken up residence in his insides.

"Hold out your hands, son."

Gulping, he obeyed, stretching his shaking hands out and cupping them next to the altar. One by one, the orecolns hopped across the table and deposited their feathers on his sweaty palms. When the last one finished, he closed his hands tightly around the achingly soft feathers and pressed his fists against his heart.

"Thank you." How he managed to speak was a wonder to him. The whistle came by route, his lips pursing and tongue moving without him even consciously deciding to.

The birds flew off in unison, leaving him alone again with the single orecoln who'd spoken. He spread out his wings to fly, too, but offered him a parting word. "Good luck, Ryon."

Ryon fled the temple in a daze, passing the human priests who stood guard silently. He strolled through the village streets, taking no note of the brightly painted cottages. A few neighbors called out greetings to him, but he only replied with a wordless nod. His mind worked overtime, repeating that riddle again and again to guarantee he didn't forget a single word.

He knew he ought to secret the feathers away in his pack for safe-keeping, but his fingers refused to move. When he arrived back home at the cottage and found the door slightly ajar, he was glad for it. He wasn't sure if he could force his frozen fingers to bend well enough to work the knob.

"Ryon? Are you all right?" his mother asked a few moments later when she found him standing still as a statue beside the kitchen table. She pulled out a chair and guided him to sink down on it. Then she poured him a glass of water and clunked the wooden cup on the table before him.

He desperately wanted to reach for it, to wash down the dryness in his throat along with his overwhelming sense of disbelief. Never had he heard of anyone being gifted so many silver feathers. Even Talex the Great had only been given three in his lifetime, and he was a hero of legend. His mother had told him and Rovan the tale so many times when they were boys he could recite it in his sleep.

Whatever this *one* was, Mother Orea wanted it badly enough to send him out after it with a treasure trove.

His mother bent down and tugged his clenched fists forward. The warmth of her touch broke through Ryon's daze, and he finally unclenched his fists.

She gasped. "Oh, guano." Her wide brown eyes darted back and forth from his face to his hands. "Where did you get all these? From the temple?"

Ryon nodded and dumped the feathers, now damp from his sweat but just as beautiful, on the tabletop. He grabbed the cup and drained it in a single gulp.

Vera flew to the door. She locked it with a click. "Did anyone see you?"

Ryon shook his head. "No. Do you think I'm crazy?"

Their village was small and tight-knit, but orecoln feathers were highly prized. More than that—they were coveted. If anyone spotted him with these, and word spread, it wouldn't be long before someone came looking for them. There were plenty of stories of men and women who gained the favor of the Aviary, only to have their prize stolen from them when they took too long to claim it.

"What happened?" Vera returned to his side, frowning. "Why do you need this?"

"They asked me to go down below, to bring back something special." Ryon shrugged. He repeated the riddle and told her everything else he could remember. But she was as baffled as he was about the riddle's meaning.

"That's all?" She sighed, her skirt swishing loudly on the tile floor as she paced.

Ryon stared down at the pile of feathers. He hadn't counted them yet, but there were at least a dozen. "What will I do with these? I can't keep them in my pocket. They'd be too easy to lose. But if I stick them in a box in my pack, then I'll be stuck digging for them when I need them the most. And what if I lose my pack? I wish there was some way to keep them at hand." He leaned over his elbows on the table and rested his chin atop his fists.

His mother stilled her pacing and strode up to him. She threaded her fingers in his silky hair and smiled. "I can't help you on your search, but I know what to do about the feathers."

"You do?"

Vera nodded while her fingers slid through his long locks. "Just relax and let me work my magic."

Boons

Violet stared out at the sea. They'd been floating for days on their small sailing boat, slowly trailing farther east with every sunrise. She drew in a deep breath, and the salty air filled her nose.

She hadn't expected to enjoy sailing so much, but something about the wide-open water and endless expanse of blue sky touched some part deep inside of her. Out here, with the waves rhythmically lapping against their hull and the sun kissing her skin, she felt at peace.

It helped, too, that the moment she left the forested coast of Dracwood behind, her sneezing miraculously vanished. She might spend every spring from here on out sailing, if only to spare her aching head months of sniffling and sneezing.

Nox emerged from the small cabin below deck, wearing a wide smile and a pair of brown shorts, his muscled olive skin shimmering with sweat.

The little room below wasn't good for much. It wasn't even large enough for a proper bed and was far too stuffy to sit in for long. But it afforded them somewhere to store their supplies and a spot to change, or to retire to when they needed a little privacy.

Not that her uncle cared much for dressing while they'd been out to sea. Violet had to keep reminding herself Nox grew up in a place where showing so much skin was common.

She tugged at the neck of her long-sleeved white blouse. It was rather hot. Unfortunately, with her fair skin, she couldn't be out in the sun for long without being covered from head to toe. Not that she'd want to strut around with her chest on display like the women in Raimire.

"How's the view?" Nox strolled toward the rail. He spared a glance at Flint, asleep in the sail's shade on the aft deck, before he stopped beside her and joined her, staring out at the sea.

"Still nothing," she replied.

"Shouldn't be too much longer." Nox dug in his pocket, then unfolded the crumpled parchment. He smoothed it out against the rail and jabbed one long finger down at a tiny drawing in the middle of the sea. "By my reckoning, we're nearly here by now."

Violet leaned closer, squinting. The tiny shape sat right in the middle of the red line that they'd been following out to sea on the map. Three others joined it, all of them lined up in a row on the page, following the line to their destination. "Are those oars? I must have missed it on my last look. What do you think it means?"

"I gather that's where the sea becalms."

"Becalms?"

Nox nodded, shooting a glance up at the sail. "It's the reason so few dare travel this far east. They call it the Still Sea. The wind has a habit of abandoning ships here. Leaving sailors stranded out at sea for weeks, even months, at a time."

Violet's eyes widened. "You're telling me that's about to happen to us?"

"I'm afraid so."

"And we're just supposed to row our way out?" Violet shuddered, already imagining the ache in her shoulders as she stared down at the little red line of oars on the map. They covered at least half the distance they'd already traveled. It appeared they were in for days of hard rowing to escape the still water.

"Don't worry, squirt. I've got it covered."

"Huh?" she asked.

But Nox only smiled and sauntered back down below deck, whistling to himself. He returned a little while later, munching on something. He offered her a pouch full of nuts and dried berries, but she shook her head and stared back out at the sea.

The wind still whipped through the air, billowing their sails and tangling Violet's long, white hair around her shoulders. It was baffling to think sometime soon it would abandon them.

Violet brushed her hair to one side. "I wonder how long it took Lark to find her way through the becalmed ocean?"

"Hopefully, we can find her and ask. This one certainly isn't saying anything." He pointed his thumb at Muse, perched contentedly on the bow railing. "Too bad she's not a cat. Then Flint could talk to her."

"True, but then how would she have made it back with the map?" Violet grinned at Flint. "Somehow, I can't picture Flint swimming across the sea to save you."

Nox chuckled lightly. "I don't know about that. He might act aloof, but that cat's got a heart of gold. He likely would try to swim across the ocean if I were in danger."

Violet sighed. "I wish I knew what that was like."

"Hey, don't worry. You'll find your bondmate soon." He grinned crookedly. "Believe me, having a bondmate at an early age is no picnic. You're lucky to have had some time with your mind all to your own."

"I'll have to take your word for it, Uncle Nox." She grinned back but didn't miss the way Nox's smile slipped.

It was easy to forget Nox had already lost four bondmates before he found Flint. She'd heard all the stories about his youth in the jungle. All the hardships he'd faced because of it. Was he remembering them now?

It had to be awful to form such an intimate connection with another being, only to have it ripped out of your grasp. Then to experience it again and again and again—all before he was even fifteen—she couldn't even imagine the heartache he must have felt. If that had happened to her at the same age, she would've been a blubbering mess.

Violet forced aside the millions of questions she wanted to ask. That was all in the past for him now, though from the pinched scowl on his face, it still clearly pained him a great deal. She wouldn't make him relive it all to satisfy her curiosity.

The sun slowly sank as they floated farther east. Violet entertained herself by watching the rolling waves, spotting the occasional school of fish swimming close to the surface. Now and then, dark fins broke the surface. Even from where she watched, she could see they were massive. What did the creatures look like that had such huge fins?

By mid-afternoon, the pleasant breeze billowing their sails tapered off to the occasional weak gust. After a few hours, even those gentle drafts faded, and their wooden craft slowed to a dead halt.

"What did I tell you?" Nox said. "Becalmed."

Violet wrinkled her nose, staring off at the horizon. There was still no sight of land. They were in for a long, boring trip if they didn't start moving somehow.

"Do you want me to dig out some paddles or..." She trailed off, standing from her spot in the shade. A drop of sweat rolled down her pants leg as she peeled her sticky thighs off the deck.

No wonder no one wanted to venture this far east. Not many would choose day after day of roasting in the heat and slowly rowing into the unknown—with no guarantee that the food and fresh water they'd brought with them would last—rather than turn back and return to dry land. Even with the map in their hands, she still didn't relish the long days ahead as they slowly oared their way out of this still water.

"No. I told you. I've got this." Nox strode inside the little room and returned not with an oar, but with a length of rope coiled in his arms.

"What are you planning to do with that?" Violet tilted her head.

Nox sauntered over to the bow railing. He uncoiled the rope as he spoke. "I'm surprised you haven't figured it out yet. Don't you remember what species my first bondmate was?"

Violet walked closer, watching curiously as he tied one end of the rope around the bow railing. What had his first bondmate—that was it!

She gasped. "It was a fish, wasn't it?"

"Yep, a pengreen." Nox grinned, securing the other end of the rope around his waist. "Can you guess what boon he gave me?"

Violet reached his side and leaned against the bow railing. "But wait, I thought you broke all connection with your first four bondmates when you nearly died?"

Nox frowned down at the deck. "That's true. I can't hear their voices anymore. Not the way most bonded pairs do after their bondmate dies." He met her gaze. "But their boons are another story."

With that, Nox jumped over the railing, splashing into the ocean and spraying a fine mist of droplets across Violet's face. She backed away, scrubbing her eyes with her sleeve.

But even more surprising than the face full of water was her uncle's revelation. As the boat began to move—almost as fast as it had while the sails billowed with the force of the wind—he proved with his action that his words were no simple boast.

With five different bondmates—all different species—he must have collected quite the assortment of boons. What else could he do?

"Is that—I see land!" Violet shouted.

It was nearly evening a few days after they'd broken free from the becalmed waters. She'd first mistaken the spit of dark on the horizon as a cloud, darkened by impending nightfall. Excitement pooled in her belly as she realized it was far too large and green to be anything but land.

Nox shuffled beside her, unfolding the crumpled map from his pocket, his gaze flicking between the paper and the horizon. "You're right. If we're still on track, which I think we are, then we need to swing south of this first island and find another just below it."

Violet peered over his shoulder, frowning. "You mean we can't stop here at all?"

When she met her uncle's eyes and he shook his head, she sighed. Her hopes of a few hours' rest on dry land wouldn't be answered yet.

"Don't worry. We don't have much farther to go now. We might even reach our destination by tomorrow."

Violet grinned. "Oh, I'm not worried. If I could handle all the lurching while you tugged us through the becalmed sea, I can do another day or so of smooth sailing."

"Lurching, huh?" Nox chuckled. "You're lucky I was here to lurch us along or you'd still be back there rowing."

Flint yawned noisily behind them, drawing both their attention. He'd taken to waking at dusk and patrolling the ship while they slept. His eyes snapped open, wide and alert, though he stretched lazily before rolling up on his paws.

"Did you sleep well, Flint?" Violet asked as he padded to the side rail and stared down at the clear blue water. She stopped beside him, stroking him softly on his back.

The water had become clearer and shallower each day that they sailed past the becalmed sea. Even now, with night fast approaching, she could see beneath the waves to the varied ocean life happily swimming below.

Flint's yellow eyes stared into the water, tracking a huge brown turtle nearly the size of him that trailed along in their wake.

Nox laughed aloud, and Violet turned to him with a cocked brow. "What did he say?"

Nox shook his head. "Flint's just hungry." He strode across the deck and lifted a fresh catch they'd caught that afternoon out of a bucket of water. Then he returned and dropped it on the deck in front of his bondmate.

Flint licked his chops, but he didn't pounce on the fish immediately. He watched it flop for a time, batting it around with his paws whenever it came close to the side of the boat. Finally, he snatched it up in his jaws and bit into it with a wet *crunch*.

The moon rose in the sky as the sun sank farther down on the horizon. In the last quarter hour, they'd sailed close enough to the island that Violet could make out a massive mountain rising high into the air on the far side.

What would they find if they landed there? It certainly looked large enough to support wildlife. The green grasses and sandy beaches stretched out across the entire eastern horizon. Little specks buzzed around the sky above it, likely seabirds heading inland for the night.

"I'm going to drop anchor," Nox announced. "We'll turn south in the morning."

A twinge of disappointment spread through Violet's breast. But she nodded and lay down to sleep. There would be time for exploration later. Nox was right. They had to stay on course and find Lark.

When Violet woke the next morning, the moon still lit the sky, and dawn's rosy welcome kissed the earth beyond the massive island. The urge to step foot on that beach rose again, nearly overwhelming with it painted in the sweet light of a dawning day.

She yawned, sparing a glance at Nox, who still slept on the deck, his mouth gaping open and a muscular arm slung over his eyes. Flint curled up beside him, purring contentedly.

Violet's gaze lit on the tiny craft strapped to the side of their boat. She wouldn't venture all the way to the island, but wouldn't it be nice to surprise the pair with a net full of fresh fish when they awakened? She could hop in the dinghy, find a school swimming nearby, and sneak a closer peek at the island all in one fell swoop.

Her mind made up, Violet quietly rose from her spot on the deck and began untying the dinghy. It was a small boat, kept there in case of emergency or to traverse shallow waters.

This wouldn't be the first time they'd taken the little wooden boat out for net fishing. Over the last week, she'd done the same thing nearly every day. Some days, Nox hopped out of the boat and swam with the net, chasing down schools of fish with his extraordinary swimming skills awarded to him by his boon.

But this would be the first time she'd ever gone out alone. It sent a momentary jolt of fear up her spine. Was this really a wise plan?

Muse appeared, bouncing down the rail toward her. Violet's heart lifted. Perhaps she didn't have to be alone after all.

"Do you want to come with me, Muse?" She smiled at the beautiful bird, admiring the way her golden feathers shone even in the muted light of dawn.

Muse answered by hopping inside. Soon, the two of them pushed off from the anchored boat and sailed closer to the massive island on the horizon.

Violet's eyes widened. The closer they drew, and the more daylight brightened the sky, the more details appeared on the coast. White sand beaches led to fields of lush grass. Rolling hills peppered with only a few scattered trees spread out behind the sand, giving way to that huge red-tinged mountain she'd first spotted last night, far off in the distance.

"I wish we could spend a day exploring."

Muse squawked beside her.

Violet turned to her with a lopsided grin. "I know. We haven't the time." She sighed and set down the oars. "I'll grab a few fish and head back."

She leaned over the side of the boat with the rough net clutched in her hands. This was where patience came in handy. Fish swam past in every imaginable color, with none of the huge ones they'd spotted farther out to sea. For long moments, she waited, scanning the clear water for a large enough group swimming close to the surface.

Finally, she struck. Her net grew heavy almost instantly, and she pulled it out. It was filled with a half dozen squirming silver fish about the size of her hand. She smiled. It wasn't the most impressive catch they'd bagged so far, but it would make for a decent breakfast.

A noise carried to her on the wind, and the hair rose on the back of her neck. "Did you hear that?" she whispered to Muse.

The falcon cocked her head toward the boat; her gaze glued upon it where it hovered in the calm water.

The sound returned, louder this time. Violet's heart stuttered as she recognized it. It was Flint, yowling in a way she'd never heard before—almost as if he were in pain.

Violet dropped the net, not caring if the fish found a way to jump back into the ocean. She snatched the oars back up and rowed so hard and fast her shoulders screamed. But before she even made it halfway back, a scent reached her that made her ignore her aching muscles and push herself even faster. The familiar tang of acrid smoke.

"Blazes! I have to get back there," she muttered to herself, frantically rowing harder.

By the time she pulled alongside the boat, fire encased the deck and heat wafted toward her, warming the cold tears spilling down her cheeks.

"No!" She set down the oars, prepared to leap on the burning boat, but Muse hopped in front of her, squawking angrily and blocking her path.

She could see Muse was right. She'd only end up burned if she tried to traverse through the spreading flames on this side of the ship. But maybe there was still somewhere where the fire hadn't caught yet.

Violet grabbed the oars again and desperately circled the burning boat. She didn't see any sign of Flint or Nox. Had they dived into the water already to swim to shore? If that was the case, why hadn't she spotted them yet?

If they died because she'd been foolish enough to take the emergency boat out when they needed it the most, she'd never forgive herself.

But as she rounded the side of the burning craft, coughing against the rising smoke filling the air, her blood turned to ice. She crouched low in the dinghy, praying the smoke would be enough to hide her from the second boat in the water.

A pair of men stood beside the aft rail of the retreating vessel, holding flaming arrows. Their faces were hidden behind black and white painted masks of fearsome beasts. One man's resembled a fox and the second, a hawk. They sent the arrows soaring, and both of them crashed into the mast. Fire spread from where they struck, engulfing the canvas sails in orange and red flame.

Above the crackle of fire and the gentle lapping of the tide, another yowl drifted to her ears. This one was weaker, farther away. Violet's heart thundered as she realized what that meant.

Flint and Nox were gone. They'd been taken.

The Wolf, The Spider, and The Beauty

Nox awoke in a darkened room. *"Flint. Where are you?"* Groaning, he lifted his head, his stomach woozy and the world spinning. *"Flint?"*

Nox stilled, scanning the room. Anyone else would be panicked right now—blinded in the pitch black. But Nox had been blessed with not one, but two bondmate's with excellent night vision. With their boons, he could see almost as well at night as he did during the day.

What he saw certainly wasn't encouraging. The room looked to be made of stone and was barren of furniture but not at all empty. Hunched figures crouched beside the walls or sprawled on the dirty floor, motionless, likely asleep. Snores and heavy breathing abounded, and the reek of unwashed flesh hung heavy in the air.

Maybe panic was the right call. Was he in a prison? The wide door made of barred metal, placed far too close to squeeze through, certainly seemed to suggest it. And to top it off, another maddening sensation tugged at him. Something he couldn't quite put his finger on but that nagged at him insistently. There was something decidedly *off* about this place.

Where was he? And how had he gotten here? The last thing he remembered was falling asleep on the boat and—

"Squirt?" He could hear the panic now, leaking into the single word.

One figure in the room muttered angrily in a guttural foreign language.

"Violet!" he shouted. He shoved off the grimy floor, ignoring the way his body wobbled, and stuck his face between the cold bars.

"Is that you shouting?"

"Flint! Thank the Mother. Where are you?"

"In a room close to yours, if I can hear you."

Flint must be right, though even with his night vision, Nox couldn't see him. He stuck his face far enough out until he caught a glimpse of more caged doors, stretching out on either side of the one they'd imprisoned him in.

"Is Violet with you?"

"No. I think she escaped before they came for us."

Nox shuffled sideways, trying to get a better look, and his bare foot landed in something cold and squishy. He shuddered, kicking the mystery substance off. He still wore the clothes he'd fallen asleep in, a thin pair of shorts and cotton button-down tunic. It made sense if they'd abducted him while he slept.

"Who came for us? I don't remember anything."

"I'm not surprised. They had darts with them. Whatever they stuck us with knocked you out cold."

Well, that explained the wooziness. *"They drugged us?"*

"Yes. Men in masks came. They set the boat ablaze. Whatever they drugged us with didn't work as well on me as it did you. I saw the boat go up in flames before they shot me with a third dose, and I finally passed out."

Nox's blood ran cold. How had they tracked them down? They'd not seen a single boat since leaving the coast of Dracwood. With all that solitude, he'd allowed himself to grow lax, but he should've been expecting this. He should've been more careful. Now his niece was out there all alone.

"How did Violet escape?"

"She took the small boat out at dawn with Muse. I figured they were just catching breakfast, so I didn't wake you when I saw them push off."

His stomach churned. "Better out there than here," he muttered under his breath, backing away from the barred door.

"Don't worry." Nox tried to infuse his tone with a measure of confidence. *"We'll find some way out of this mess."*

"Oh, I'm not worried." Flint's voice was excessively calm for waking up in a cage.

"You're not?"

"No. We came here to find who stole your sister. If I had to hazard a guess, I'd say we found them."

"Don't you mean they found us?"

"Same difference. I bet your sister is here somewhere."

Nox spun around, returning to the spot on the floor where he'd awoken. *"I have a feeling you're right. Try not to attract any attention to yourself. I'll see what I can find out from the other people in here."*

"All right."

He sank down on the floor but sat slightly closer to the nearest man than when he'd awoken. The man was still clearly asleep. His mouth hung open, his jaw slack.

Nox reached out a hand to shake him gently awake, but flinched back. Rot and decay—he had to be one of the ugliest men he'd ever seen. But as Nox studied the man, he realized the swollen features on his face were injuries and not deformities. He looked like he'd lost a battle with a cudgel.

Gulping, Nox scooted away, searching the darkened cell. There had to be at least a dozen men in here with him. He closed his eyes and listened, scanning the dark for signs of labored breathing. Surely someone in this crowded cell was still awake?

After a moment, he heard a breath hitch. Opening his eyes, he crawled to the sound. When he got within an arm's length of the figure he suspected was still awake, he reached out again, tentatively.

Slam. His back smashed into the hard cell floor. The man leaped atop him, swinging and punching. Yelling in that guttural language that meant absolutely nothing to him.

Nox shoved him off with all his might. The man smacked into the cell wall and stayed there. Nox scrambled away on his hands and knees, back to the center of the cell.

Maybe creeping up on sleeping men in the dark wasn't his finest idea ever. His aching jaw certainly confirmed the stupidity of that decision. But he couldn't just give up.

He scanned the room. The fight had woken some of the others. He had to try again.

"Hello?" He spoke out into the dark, whipping his head to eye all the hunched figures. "Does anyone here understand me?"

No one spoke up. At least not in words he could understand. More of that strange foreign tongue spilled into the air as the men whispered to each other.

"Flint, I think we have a problem."

"Another? Lovely."

"The language they're speaking, I've never heard it before."

Nox's heart thundered. They were imprisoned in a cage with no one who understood them. What were they going to do?

At some point, light spilled down from the ceiling. It wasn't sunlight. That much was clear. There were no windows in the cell. It wasn't firelight either, or candles. The whole ceiling illuminated out of nowhere, a warm yellow glow spilling from the tiles and lighting the entire cell.

Nox stared up for long moments, trying to make sense of it. Was some magic at work here he didn't understand? It must be, for there was no other explanation that made any sense.

Footsteps in the hall outside drew his gaze to the door. A masked man appeared, lugging a bucket in each hand.

Nox's eyes widened. A wolf mask, all black and white, covered the man's face completely. If it weren't for his muscular physique straining against his all-black clothing, he wouldn't be certain whether it was a man or woman behind the mask. But his broad chest and shoulders gave him away.

The wolf dropped the buckets and tugged a string out of his black tunic. He used the key dangling from it to open a tiny door set into the bottom half of the big door.

Nox frowned. He'd missed that last night.

The wolf hefted the buckets inside. The first one landed with a *clunk*, and he shoved it farther in with one black, gloved fist. Then the second landed just behind it. With that accomplished, he slammed the little opening shut and locked it again.

As soon as the wolf left, the men in the cell descended on the buckets like a horde of flies on a pile of dung. Food and water splashed around, and more than one fight broke out. Some of the food bucket spilled on the floor, and a pair of scrawny men eagerly licked the brown syrupy stew off the filthy stone.

Nox nearly gagged, watching the men fight over scraps. Whatever was in that stew stank so badly he could barely stomach it. He didn't even bother trying to eat. But if he was stuck here much longer, he wouldn't have a choice. How long would it be before even that disgusting stew smelled mouthwatering? And how long before he was one of them, fighting over the slop bucket?

More footsteps pounded outside. Another masked man stopped before the cell. This one wore a spider mask. The eight eyes, hairy face, and curved fangs were painted in elaborate detail. But Nox only glanced at him for an instant. His gaze locked on the woman that stopped beside him.

She was achingly lovely. He would guess she was in her twenties, but it was hard to be certain. The way she filled out her dress proved she wasn't a child. Big gray eyes with dark brows and lashes contrasted with her creamy porcelain skin. Straight, jet black hair hung to her waist. Her white shift dress flowed around her legs like a cloud as she twisted outside the bars, scanning the men within.

Her eyes landed on his, and he watched them widen. She stared at him for a heartbeat. Two. When the corner of his mouth lifted, she flicked her gaze away, continuing her perusal.

The beauty opened her mouth, spouting off words to the spider man in that odd tongue. Then she turned back to the cage and pointed. Her finger landed on five of the caged men.

Nox startled when one man she pointed at began to cry. Not a timid weep, but a hearty pained wail, as if her finger were an arrow that pierced his heart.

Then the door flew open. The spider strolled in, clutching a shining metal bar in his fist. Nox's gaze darted between him and the open doorway. Only the girl stood beyond it, her arms crossed, looking almost bored.

Could he make a break for it? Surely, he could take out one man with such a small weapon. It wasn't even sharp. He could handle a few whacks with a short pole if it meant freedom.

But the spider reached the wailer and jabbed him with the pole's tip. A high-pitched *buzz* sounded, and the man convulsed on the ground, shaking and flailing his limbs uncontrollably. The room filled with a new noxious odor as a stain darkened the back of the man's trousers.

Nox coughed, covering his mouth, his heart hammering.

Rot and decay. What was that thing?

The four others the beauty pointed at rose to their feet without having to be told. The spider grabbed the bare foot of the man who still twitched nonstop and dragged him out of the cell. Then the door slammed shut again. The spider hitched the twitcher up, slinging him over his broad shoulders, and the entire group shuffled away.

Their footsteps clattered down the hall, but not for long. Nox heard the girl talking again nearby, her voice making the guttural tones of their foreign tongue sound almost sweet.

"I know I'm pretty, but the staring is a little much," Flint grumbled.

Nox scrambled to the door and shoved his face as far as he could between the bars. *"They're looking at you now?"*

The group had halted four or five doors down. The beauty listened to the spider explaining something to her in low tones while she stared into the cage.

"Yeah, they're gawking like I'm a prized pig in a stall," Flint said.

At least he knew where they were keeping his bondmate now. Nox stilled as the beauty lifted her hand. Was she about to point at Flint? Would she order the spider to open his cage and assault him with that metal tube?

But her delicate fingers only curved through her silky black hair. She dropped her gaze from Flint's cage and strolled away, and the men followed in her wake.

Nox breathed out a sigh and backed away from the door. Where were they taking those men? Not anywhere pleasant, if he could gauge by their reactions. But with no one to speak to, he wouldn't discover answers anytime soon.

He scanned the room again, inspecting the men left behind. They were clearly beaten down. Not only their bodies—though they all carried an assortment of scars, bruises, and wounds—but their spirits, too. They were filthy, underfed, and visibly shaken by what had just happened here. Why did they fear leaving the cage with the spider? What was out there worse than this?

He considered trying again, and even opened his mouth—readying the words he'd say to convince them to explain something, anything—hoping beyond hope that someone would understand him. A sudden noise halted him, and he snapped his mouth shut. It rumbled overhead, through the ceiling. Hundreds of voices raised in unison—screaming.

What was happening?

"Do you hear that, Flint? What's with the screaming?"

After a pause, Flint replied, *"That's not screaming. Listen closer."*

A chill trickled down his spine. After a moment, the sound grew so loud he didn't even need advanced hearing to register it. It roared again, practically rumbling the ceiling with its intensity.

Flint was right. So many voices, hundreds all at once—they weren't screaming. They were cheering.

On Her Own

Violet trekked across the unending plains of vibrant green grass, a pleasant breeze swirling her light cotton trousers against her legs. Muse perched upon her forearm, her gaze constantly flicking across the island. For all Muse's dogged scrutiny, there didn't seem to be much of a need for it. They'd yet to see a single person since stepping foot ashore after watching the burning boat sink to the seafloor.

Who were those masked men? She had a sinking suspicion they might be the very same people who'd abducted her aunt. Violet quickly realized she had little chance of following them farther out to sea in her tiny dinghy. She'd decided to land on the island to seek information about the kidnappers from the people who lived here. Surely there must be someone who could help. But so far, she'd found nothing.

At least she wasn't entirely alone or completely empty-handed. It was lucky she had the forethought to toss her pack in the boat when Muse hopped on board. She had her leather gauntlet and a few basic supplies to aid her on her search, but with the boat sitting on the sea bottom, she'd lost nearly everything.

She wanted to curl up in a ball and cry. How had she ended up halfway around the world, alone except for an injured falcon?

But wallowing in misery wouldn't get her anywhere. It wouldn't save Nox and Flint. It wouldn't help her follow the map—not that she had one anymore, but after so long staring at it she had a pretty clear picture of it in her mind—to find her aunt. If she wanted to accomplish anything, she had to do it on her own.

Violet sighed. "What do you think, Muse? Are we wasting our time here? Should we return to the boat and keep sailing like the map said to?"

Muse only cocked her head, looking at her silently.

"Yeah, I know. You don't understand a thing I'm saying, do you?" Violet quirked a brow.

Muse didn't reply. Not that she was expecting her to. Her injured wing had healed a great deal on their journey, but she still wasn't flying. She wouldn't be much help to Violet, at least as far as finding food went.

It was a good thing her father had shared his love of hunting and trapping with her. There'd been countless times she'd tried to beg off his lessons in the forest. If it wasn't the sneezing, there were the bugs and the mud and the endless hiking. She much preferred tending to the animals at the farm, or even weeding the garden, to traipsing around in the woods, catching and slaughtering cute little hares.

But her father had insisted. Looking back, she had to wonder if he'd been preparing her for this. Did he know one day her life might depend on the skills he'd taught her?

For all the absence of people, there was certainly no shortage of wildlife. She'd spotted dozens of species of birds. Some were bigger than Muse. They'd swoop down from the sky to snatch fish out of the sea in their huge gullets. But there were many others much smaller, tiny little spots of color smaller than her fist. They flitted through the tall grass, chirping and singing sweetly.

The birds were only the start. Lizards and turtles sunned themselves on rocks by the shore. Every now and then, she'd glimpse fur darting through the grass, no doubt belonging to some small mammals she'd sent scurrying away with her footsteps.

And of course, there were all the fish. She and Muse had shared what was left of her net haul for breakfast before they set off on their search. At least she wouldn't have to worry about an empty stomach. But how long could she afford to stay?

Violet kept one eye on the coast as she explored the grassland. She'd tugged the little boat far past the tide lines, but she didn't want to get lost.

"Well, it's getting late. Let's head back to the boat. We'll try exploring down shore tomorrow."

She wasn't sure why she was telling Muse all this. It just felt nice to talk to someone out loud. Muse only spared her a glance, then returned to scanning their surroundings.

As she was about to turn, she spotted something ahead. Violet squinted, walking a few paces closer. Smoke. There was definitely smoke curling into the air.

Violet's heart raced. Fire meant people. She was finally onto something.

Violet rushed forward before a sudden thought slowed her pace. What if it was a camp of those masked men? She might stroll right into their clutches.

Grimacing, she crouched low to the ground. A small hill rested between her and the fire, blocking her view. It probably wasn't smart to go barreling down the hillside without doing a little scouting first.

She settled Muse on the ground and shucked off her pack. "Stay here, Muse. I'll be right back," she whispered.

Violet stretched out on her belly and shimmied up the hillside. The long grass smacked her in the face when the wind kicked up, and her nose twitched with that familiar tickle that signaled a sneeze. She clasped both hands over her nose to muffle the sound and cringed.

Blazes. Just when she was trying to be stealthy.

She shook her head and continued onward. Soon, she reached the hilltop. As long as she stayed still, flat on her belly, the long grass would keep her hidden. She peered between the blades, scanning the valley below.

A small, brown tent perched in the center of another field of long grass. A fire burned out front, but she couldn't see any people from where she hid. The angle only allowed her to see the side of the tent, but surely, someone was in there. Why else would they have a fire burning?

Should she wait here for whoever was inside to come out? Or maybe she could crawl sideways and steal a glimpse inside the tent?

She lay there for a moment, considering. But just as she'd decided to scurry backward and curve around from the side, something strange gave her pause. The ground beneath her began to quake and shudder.

"What the blazes?" she whispered under her breath.

Her eyes shot to the mountain, far off in the distance. Was there a rock slide?

A man emerged from the tent in a panic. He leaped over the fire and bolted to the top of a hill across from her. Then he turned and ran—straight at her.

Violet's eyes bulged. The man had no mask, that much was certain, but the sheer terror she sensed pouring off him wasn't exactly welcoming. What was he running from?

The man bolted down the hill and past his campsite. Then he began climbing up the hill she hid on quicker than she thought possible, racing toward her. Just as she spun sideways and heaved up on her hands and knees, the man jumped over the hilltop. His foot caught on her stomach, and he tripped, flying over her and rolling to a stop in a heap beside Muse.

"Oof." The breath blew out of her stomach. She clearly hadn't scrambled back fast enough.

He shoved thick locks of black hair off his face as he rushed to right himself. Then his gaze landed on her, laid out just above, clutching her stomach and groaning. He shouted, his words spilling out fast and frantic.

Oh no. "I don't understand," Violet bit out through the pain.

He tried to stand, but fell back down, shrieking and clutching his ankle. But after only a heartbeat, words spilled out of his mouth again, even more frantic than before. He gestured wildly behind her, then at the ocean.

The quaking in the earth had intensified. Violet lurched up, her eyes widening as she spotted the source. A herd of hairy beasts raced toward them. Stampede!

They were already almost on top of them. She glanced back at the man, then at Muse. He clearly wanted them to make a break for the ocean. Even now, with his injured leg, he inched closer to the sand.

Her gaze darted back to the threat, fast approaching. The beasts were bigger than any land animal she'd ever seen—four-legged, covered in coarse hair, with three large bony growths on their chins. If one of them collided with her, she'd be flattened.

She took a step away, wobbling precariously as the earth bounced beneath her. Could she carry Muse and the man to the sea in time? She peeked over her shoulder.

No. There was no time.

She turned and stood her ground, ignoring the way her knees buckled. Then—calling on every ounce of confidence that came from living and working with a herd of goats her entire life—she started swinging her hands wildly and screaming.

"Here, beasties. This way, get a move on."

This had better work. Tamping down the panic bubbling up in her aching stomach, she raced sideways, directing the herd to turn away from Muse and the man. This worked with goats. Maybe, just maybe, it would work with this crazed herd. She sucked in a huge breath and it was almost like her skin crackled with the flow of air around her.

"That's it. This way. Turn." She gritted her teeth as the first of the beasts spotted her jumping and waving. This was it. If she could convince the first few to turn, the rest would follow.

"C'mon, beastie. This way. Follow me," she cooed, swinging her arms.

Then, like a miracle, the huge, muscled beast spun on its heel and pivoted. Then the next, and the next. Violet bobbed on her feet as they trundled past, so close the musty stench of their fur enveloped her. She sneezed twice in quick succession.

In the space of a few heartbeats, they were gone. Violet hastened back to the spot where the man sat beside Muse, staring at her, mouth agape.

She gulped. With all the excitement, she hadn't given him more than a cursory glance, but—wow. He was strikingly handsome, so much that even his scruffy appearance and dirt-dusted attire couldn't disguise it. Shoulder-length, rope-like, locks of hair surrounded his head, and a thick beard covered his face.

Violet smiled gently. "Are you all right?" she asked, nodding to his ankle.

The man's mouth clamped shut, then he sent her a crooked grin. He hobbled up on one knee.

Violet rushed to assist him. "Hey, let me help you." She ducked beneath his arm and nearly stumbled when he rose to his full height. He was heavy. And huge. The top of her head only hit at his chin. But that made her the perfect size to act as a crutch as he settled his arm around her shoulders.

She felt the muscles in his arm tense as she helped him hobble back to his campsite.

She swallowed. The place was trashed. The herd had smashed the tent flat and snuffed the fire with their heavy footsteps. She started to realize why there were no big settlements near the beach like she'd first expected.

But then, what was this guy doing out here? She set him down beside his flattened tent and strode back to grab her pack and Muse.

"Hey, Muse. You hanging in there? Sorry for all the excitement." She crouched beside the excited bird and slipped the leather gauntlet back on her arm. "I don't think this guy will be any help. It's a pity I can't understand him. I don't know why I thought we'd speak the same language." She sighed and stretched out her arm.

Muse hopped on, and she straightened, then climbed back up the hill. The man was gone from sight, but she spotted movement beneath the tent fabric. No doubt, he was inside, scrounging around for whatever supplies he could salvage from the ruined interior.

"I'm back," she called. He might not understand her, but she didn't want him to think she was sneaking up on him either. The man might be injured, but with all those muscles, he could crush her if he wanted to.

The thought should've made her wary, but she wasn't. The way he'd immediately tried to warn her of the herd's approach when he'd fallen proved he wasn't out to hurt her. And even without that assurance, she'd always had a way of knowing when someone wasn't a person she could trust. Maybe it came with the territory, growing up looking different, being ridiculed. Her instincts were already telling her this stranger wasn't like that.

Too bad they couldn't understand each other. She didn't have time to learn a new language. As she sat there waiting for him to emerge from the crumpled tent, she made up her mind to say goodbye. She wouldn't find any help on this island. She'd be better off climbing back in the boat and making her way around the island alone, following the map in her memory.

Finally, he tore the fabric off his head and stared up at her.

Violet smiled woodenly, rubbing a hand on her neck. "Well, this has been fun, but I have to go. I hope you'll be all right, with your ankle and all."

She inched away.

"Wait. Don't leave."

Her eyes widening, she turned back to meet the stranger's eyes. "So, you do understand me! Blazes, why didn't you say anything earlier?"

He cringed. "Sorry."

She walked closer, deposited Muse on the ground, and crouched next to him, holding out a hand. "I could really use your help. I'm Violet."

He sucked in a breath. "Violet," he repeated, staring at her hand curiously.

Violet smiled. "Where I come from, it's common to shake hands when you first meet someone." She nodded to his hand. "Give me your hand."

He stuck out his hand, and Violet's smile widened until she got a good look at it.

"Oh, you're bleeding." She flung her pack off her back and dug inside. "I don't have much, but I do have some clean bandages with me."

"It's just a scratch."

Violet huffed. "All the same, let me wrap it for you." She met his eyes. They were dark brown with tiny flecks of amber scattered in the irises. She waited for him to nod his assent, but he just kept staring at her strangely.

Then she spotted something more disconcerting. "There's blood in your hair." She reached forward, raking his thick, rope-like locks out of the way, searching for a gash in his head.

He caught her wrist with his good hand. "It's nothing." He lifted his bloody hand. "I touched my hair."

Violet tugged her wrist free and grabbed his injured hand. She settled it on her lap and dug out a jar of ointment and a fresh strip of cloth.

"You need help?" he asked.

Violet nodded. She opened the jar and spread a thin layer on the gash. She thought for sure the wound would be jagged, the work of some rock or shell he'd encountered in his fall, but it was remarkably straight and even.

"I come from a land far away across the sea," she began. "My uncle and I were searching for my aunt, Lark. She's been out here exploring for years, but a few weeks ago, Muse—that's the falcon over there—came flying to my house and brought a map with her. There was a message on the back. *Lark was taken.*"

She glanced up as she wound the bandage around his palm and spotted him staring, mouth hanging ajar. "Well, no sooner did we land our boat off the coast of this island then men in masks came and captured my uncle and his bondmate. Muse and I escaped on a dinghy, but we lost our boat and almost all of our supplies. We decided to come ashore and look for help."

Violet finished wrapping his hand and ran her gaze down his body. He wore peculiar clothes. His shirt was quite normal, light brown, long-sleeved, albeit it was a little odd that the bottom hem was embroidered with detailed stitching of elaborate feathers.

No, the strangest part of his attire was the bottoms. He was wearing some kind of short skirt that came down to his knees, leaving his muscular calves exposed. Violet almost laughed at the sight of it. She'd never in all her days met a man in a skirt. But at the same time, a blush warmed her cheeks.

She scooted closer to his injured leg. "How is your ankle?" The flesh appeared slightly swollen.

He picked up his foot, wincing as he swiveled it around the joint. "It hurts, but I can still move it. Probably just a sprain." He peered at her closely. "Thank you for what you did back there. I've never seen anyone change the tritusks course like that."

Violet shrugged, and her face warmed even more. "It was nothing. I've herded goats my whole life." She met his eyes, cocking a grin. "Just promise me, if you ever meet my father, don't tell him I saved you with my herding skills. He'd never let me hear the end of it." She chuckled.

"I'll help you, Violet." He leaned closer, smiling. "It's the least I can do after you saved my life back there."

Violet bounced lightly in place as the stress of being all alone slipped away. "Great. But first, could you tell me your name?"

His smile widened, and he stuck out his hand—the uninjured one. "I'm Ryon. It's nice to meet you, Violet."

Stay Or Go

R yon kneeled down, glancing at the wet sand on the beach.

Violet used a stick to mark another line, then leaned back. "That's it." She aimed a smile at him.

He tried his hardest not to stare at her, but it was a difficult task to manage. Silvery white hair floated around her ivory skin. Her eyes landed on him, the reddish hue so unique he'd never seen the like.

She was a tiny thing, but tough. She'd stood up to those charging tritusks to save him, putting her life on the line for a complete stranger. Then she'd stayed with him and nursed his wounds.

When he woke this morning and found her gone from camp, he'd broken out in a cold sweat. But she'd returned before he could hobble after her, carting a dead gull she proceeded to pluck and cook like it was nothing. She was really something...

He shook off the thought. He was staring again.

He flicked his gaze down to the squiggles she'd drawn. "It's what?"

Her brows pinched. "The map." She jabbed the stick at a huge circle on the far side. "Here's where me and my uncle started, in

Dracwood." She traced a line in the sand, curving through what he guessed was meant to be water. "We sailed across the sea until we made it here." She marked a spot next to a smaller circle with an X. "This is where we are now." She traced a new line, circling around the small circle and approaching a third circle, this one even smaller than the last. "And this is where we need to go."

Ryon chewed on his lip. Were there really people out there, across the sea? There must be. It's not like Violet had been holed up in his village, hiding from everyone her whole life just to appear here one day with this crazy story. He certainly would've noticed her before now, if that were the case.

He had no reason not to take her at her word.

"How will we get there?" He gestured to the stick she stabbed into the sand.

"Do your people have a boat we could use?" she asked

Ryon shook his head. "No. We live in the mountains. Few of my people come down below. Those that do, stay far from the sea."

Violet cocked a brow. "Not even to fish?"

Ryon turned to the clear blue water spread out beyond them and shuddered. "No. Bad things happen to those who do. There are many stories about this in my village."

She scoffed and wrinkled her nose. "Bad things?"

"They disappear. Like your aunt and uncle."

Violet grimaced. "Oh. Well, I guess we'll take the dinghy then." She sighed. "Are you sure you want to come with me?"

His heart pounded. Should he tell her? Or would she wrinkle her little nose again and think him a superstitious fool?

Ryon nodded and settled for a half-truth. "Of course. It's the least I can do after you saved my life back there. Where's your boat?" He stood, wincing as his weight shifted on his ankle. The pain had faded a great deal after a night's rest, but it would likely be a few days before it was back to normal.

"Here, let me help you." Violet rushed to his side and ducked beneath his arm.

He sucked in a breath at the feel of her slim shoulders beneath his arm. "Thank you."

They shuffled across the hard-packed sand close to the tide line, his pack bouncing on his back with each step. Every now and then, a warm wave crashed over their feet, making their boots sink into the surf. If not for the constant ache in his ankle, it would've been the most relaxing stroll he'd ever taken.

Violet balanced Muse on her outstretched arm and allowed him to settle a bit of his weight on her shoulders. He kept his pace slow, determined not to burden her unduly with his hobbling pace.

A few voices reached his ears, too soft for him to make out what they said. He cocked his head, watching a pair of gulls hover above, on a course out to sea. Muse spun toward the sound but didn't call out a greeting. He'd yet to hear a peep out of the beautiful, injured bird of prey.

"How did you come about having a bird as a pet?"

"She's not my pet. She's my aunt's bondmate."

"Bondmate. You've said this before. What does it mean?"

Violet's pace slowed, and she gazed up at him. "Do your people not have bonding magic?"

Ryon lifted a shoulder.

"It's a special tie between two creatures. Humans, animals, dragons—a few people in my land have this talent. It allows the pair to hear each other's thoughts and share some skills."

"My people do not possess this magic." He stared down at her. "Do you have a bondmate?"

"Not yet, but I will one day. The talent runs in my family."

"How many summers have you seen?"

"Summers?" She bit her lip. "Are you asking how old I am?"

Ryon nodded.

She grinned. "Twenty."

Though he tried to keep his expression flat, he must've shown some sign of surprise.

"Why? Does it matter?" she asked.

"No. You're so small, I wondered…"

"If I were still a child?" she huffed. "I'm not." She walked a few more steps before speaking again. "How many summers have you seen?"

"Twenty-nine."

"Huh." Her nose wrinkled again. "You don't look it."

He smiled down at her. She peeked up at him with those striking eyes, and her pale cheeks reddened before she looked away.

"Here it is." She turned, trudging across the dry sand headed inland. He hobbled even more here, with the sand shifting beneath his boots. Violet stopped beside a pitiful wooden craft hardly large enough to fit both of them inside it.

"You want to go out there, on this?" he asked.

Violet nodded at the tiny boat. "We don't have to sail far. You saw the map. We can make it."

All the stories of ocean monsters flooded Ryon's mind. Great behemoths, so large they could swallow a man whole. Tides that would grab a vessel and swipe them out to sea so fast they'd lose all sight of land and be lost on the unending blue waves.

All his life, he'd heard the stories. As he got older, he'd grown skeptical, certain the tales were only clever stories invented to keep adventurous children on a leash.

But when he was still a child, a pair of brothers began bringing fish back to the village. They hadn't believed the tales, boasting that there was nothing to fear. They'd feasted on the sweet meat, picking tiny bones from their teeth and laughing at any who warned them to stay away from the sea.

Within a single moon cycle, they were gone. Disappeared just as surely as Violet's aunt and uncle—there one day and gone the next.

Was he really going to venture out there? On this little vessel, no less?

"You don't owe me anything. You know that, right? If you want to return home, back to your mountains, I won't stop you." Violet gazed up at him, frowning.

His heart clenched. She was definitely something...

He caught himself staring again and shook his head. Then he slid his pack off his back and dumped it on the floor of the boat. "Let's go."

Her answering grin spread fast and bright. She settled Muse inside the boat and started dragging it down the sand.

Ryon grabbed the side, helping her haul the boat to the lapping surf.

"Hop in. I'll drag it out farther," she said as they approached the water.

"I can do that."

She narrowed her eyes. "Not with that ankle. Hop in."

Ryon sighed. "All right," he conceded.

He sank down on the hard wooden bench. Violet tugged the boat through the waves, waiting until the surf nearly reached her waist before she hopped out of the water and climbed inside the boat. Then she lifted two wooden paddles and used them to propel them past the breaking waves out into the deeper water.

Ryon stared down into the clear water in awe, spotting dozens of colorful fish swimming beneath them. He glanced up at Violet with a grin, but his smile fell when he caught sight of her unusual leg coverings plastered to her shapely thighs.

If he hadn't believed her about coming from across the sea, her clothes surely helped sell her story. No one in their village wore anything so—indecent. Billowy skirts were worn by all in the mountains, the women's so long they covered them to the ankles. These—trousers, as she'd called them—were barely decent when they were dry. Now that they were wet, the thin fabric molded to her skin, revealing every curve.

Ryon gulped, tearing his gaze higher.

"Are you all right?" Her brow furrowed with concern. "You're not feeling sick in your stomach, are you?"

He shook his head. "No."

Violet nodded, sending him a crooked smile. "My aunt was prone to seasickness. I always found it funny she'd agree to explore the eastern seas beyond our kingdom. But I guess her love of travel was enough to convince her to deal with the discomfort." She sighed. "I hope we can find her."

Ryon met her eyes. "We will."

He hadn't told her as much, but he knew she was the one Mother Orea sent him to find.

He'd begun his search, certain he was looking for a bird. *Hatched* in moonlight—they'd said. But the first thought that had struck him upon seeing that lovely hair and pale skin was the silvery moon's rays.

He'd seen gull's eggs countless times. Their mottled shells were the loveliest blend of red, blue and violet—just like her eyes.

And her name—Violet—just like the sky at dusk.

She was the *one*. He would help her find her family then bring her back to the mountains. What else but this would be fraught with danger and require so many wishes?

She was the answer to the riddle. He would bet his life on it.

Whatever It Takes

N ox listened to the rumble of cheering for what felt like hours. Time was hard to gauge in the barren cell. That mysterious glow seeped down from the ceiling, never changing.

Wolf Mask came again at some point. With less mouths in the cage, the resulting frenzy over the buckets was less intense. Nox even gulped down a few mouthfuls of tepid water, but he still couldn't bring himself to try the sickening stew.

"Are they feeding you the same filth we're getting?" he asked Flint.

Flint scoffed. *"You're being fed? All they've brought me is water."*

Nox's stomach clenched. Were they purposely starving him? He ground his jaw so hard his molars ached. *"You're not missing out on much. I can't even bring myself to try it. Smells disgusting."*

A door clanged open. Footsteps followed. The spider was back with the men that had left earlier in tow.

Nox's brows shot up. They'd taken five away, and only three had returned. They were in bad shape, bleeding from fresh gashes, their steps stilted.

The spider threw open the door and barked at them. All three stumbled inside, then quickly collapsed to the ground. Then the cell door slammed shut behind them, and the spider disappeared.

Nox crouched beside the closest man, eyeing his wounds. His arm bled profusely from deep slashes, four lined up in a pattern that he recognized. Claw marks.

He reached out, intending on resting a comforting hand on the man's shoulder, but the fellow drew back with a hiss before his fingers connected.

"Sorry," he murmured. "I'm only trying to help."

But though he approached each of the returning men, doing his best to mime his intention of looking at their wounds, none of them wanted his help. The second snapped at him in that guttural tongue and curled into a ball, and the third shoved him away.

Nox sighed. He'd never had an easy time making friends. It had been the same story his whole life.

He'd always been more comfortable with animals, likely a side effect of his unique bonding magic. When the children in the village back home looked into his eyes, they could sense something wild inside of him.

As he'd grown older, that wildness had only grown. Some women were drawn to him, but most men he met were uneasy in his presence. Even now, while injured and in pain, none of the men wanted his help.

"I'm not sure what's happening here, but I have a bad feeling I'm not gonna like it when I find out." Nox returned to the cell bars, peering out down the hall toward Flint's cage.

"You and me both."

Sometime later, the door clattered open again. The spider was back, with that lovely vision in the white frock. The beauty chattered at the spider, her tone easy and carefree, compared to the spider's harsh grumbling replies.

Nox stilled, staring at the pair from his spot on the filthy floor. Was she about to point again, and the spider cart more men off? Would he be one of them?

The cage door swung open without the girl's perusal or pointing, and they both entered. Nox's gaze flicked to the open door. But the spider took up residence in the opening, that metal pole clutched menacingly in his fist.

What were they doing now?

The girl glided inside. She crouched beside the first man who'd returned earlier and settled a bag on the ground beside his hunched form.

A few words spilled from her lips as she opened the bag and rustled within. The man answered her, and though Nox didn't understand his words, he could sense within the man's tone both the carefully leashed anger the man tried to hide and something else just below the surface he couldn't quite put his finger on.

The beauty pulled something from her bag. Nox tilted his head and watched her open a little tube and slick a bit of a fragrant ointment on her hands, redolent with herbs and a hint of something astringent.

She slicked the cream over the man's slashes. The man hissed from the contact but remained still, allowing her to continue her ministrations.

Nox frowned. She came here to heal them?

The beauty repeated her actions with the other two. Both of the men talked to her in that same odd tone. After the third time, he finally placed what he'd failed to notice in the first man's voice. They were all clearly angry but still—reverent.

Yes. That was it exactly. They spoke to her like she wasn't merely a woman but a goddess sent to dole out punishment and reward in equal measure.

As she spun from her work with the last man and her gaze locked with his, Nox's heart froze. Rot and decay—she was stunning. A single ray of sunshine in a dank pit.

"Who are you?"

Her eyes widened, those big gray orbs flashing as Nox realized he'd muttered the question aloud. For a bare instant, she leaned forward and almost looked like she understood him—like she understood and wanted to answer.

But then the spider strode forward, barreling between them. He lifted that gleaming pole and bent down, thrusting it at Nox's chest.

The beauty jumped up and caught the spider's arm before the pole connected, and Nox's breath escaped in a gasp. She tugged the spider back, a steady stream of chatter pouring out of her throat. The spider turned, they paced away, and the door slammed shut. They departed without a backward glance, the easy flow of their conversation trailing behind them.

What was that? He shook himself, shoving aside the vision of her crouched beside him, peering at him with those big round eyes.

There was a time and a place for bedding a woman. This wasn't it. But maybe he could use her interest to his advantage. He recognized that gleam in her eye. She *was* interested. Spider had noticed it, too, or he wouldn't have come speeding across the cell, ready to break him.

But had she really understood him? Surely, someone in this place must. Why not her?

Whether she understood him or not was irrelevant. He'd find some way to use her interest to his advantage. It might be the only edge he had in this strange place.

The ceiling darkened abruptly only to lighten just as abruptly hours later. Whenever the lights disappeared, the men hunkered down, sleeping fitfully. The wolf returned like clockwork, twice each *day*, or what passed for day. With the unnatural light leaking down upon them, he couldn't be certain of the true hour.

On the third day, Nox caved. He shouldered his way between the crowd of men around the buckets and slurped up some of the disgusting gruel. It didn't taste any better than he'd imagined it would, but he swallowed the rancid slop, determined to keep up his strength. If it weren't for the hunger gnawing at his gut and the knowledge that his bondmate and sister still needed him to find some way out of this, he'd have been happy to ignore the reeking stew for the rest of his short days.

Flint didn't get off so easy. They continued to starve him, only bringing him water. Nox's gut churned with the injustice of it all.

They'd done nothing to deserve this treatment. All they'd been doing when they were abducted was sleeping on a boat, idling in the ocean. Now they'd been imprisoned like rabid dogs with no sign of reprieve. Who did these people think they were, to pluck unsuspecting people out of their lives like it was nothing?

The monotony was breaking him. The long hours sitting in his sweaty clothes slowly wore on him, with nothing to do but stare at strangers who talked around him in an indecipherable tongue. If it weren't for Flint, he'd have surely gone mad.

The thought of going mad dug at him. He, of all people, felt the fear of that future intensely. Snatches of memory rose unbidden of how he'd been trapped within his own mind as a young man; his body led around like a marionette on a string.

He couldn't face that fate again. He refused to.

On the fourth day, someone other than the wolf finally arrived. Nox sat upright and peered through the bars as a squirming, chattering man was led down the hall, his arm clenched in the wolf's fist.

The wolf barreled past his cell with the man—who, upon closer inspection, Nox realized was little more than a lad of twelve or thirteen—dragging his heels in the dirt behind him. The boy's face held an expression of genuine horror as he kept up that steady stream of chatter.

Nox didn't have to know the language to understand what he was saying. He was begging. Pleading for the wolf to take him away from this place. For him to do anything other than open one of the cell doors and toss him inside.

The boy's wish wasn't granted. Nox heard a cell door slam open and shut, and a moment later, the wolf appeared again, stalking off down the hall, alone.

"Hmm, I have a new neighbor," Flint announced, his bondmate's voice ringing clearly through Nox's mind above the sound of the boy's mournful wails.

"Did they put him in with you?" Nox asked.

"No. They threw him in the empty cell next to me. But there's a hole in the wall. I can see the little wretch clearly. Poor thing. He's nothing more than a kit. Why would they throw him in here?"

"Your guess is as good as mine."

A few moments later, a chorus of grumbling shouts rose from within his own cell, and others down the hall. The wailing stopped, and the boy quieted. Whatever threats the men leveled had done their job.

Nox leaned back against the wall, more puzzled than ever. What did these people want?

He kept hoping for the girl to return, but she didn't. He began to question the surety that had filled him upon their last meeting. Had he imagined the flicker of interest in her eyes? He'd been so certain, but clearly, he must've been mistaken.

Nox sighed. He didn't know what he was thinking. That she'd stride in here and set him free? It was a silly thought. She was his jailer—one of them, at least. She'd left this dank place behind, taking her beauty, her light, somewhere it wouldn't stand out so starkly. Gifted it to men who actually deserved it.

The monotony drug on, coiling in his spine until he felt ready to spring at one of the strangers in his cage to experience something other than boredom and hunger. When the wolf returned with the buckets later, he fought the others, thrusting them aside in his eagerness to fill the empty chasm in his gut.

A feral grin tugged at his cheeks as he hunched over the slop bucket, shoveling handfuls down his throat until the rancid sludge pooled in his belly like a sunken stone. Then he shoved away into a corner, shaking the last of the filth from his fingers and feeling like a caged animal. Just what they wanted him to feel, no doubt.

"Well. I think I'm going to like my new neighbor," Flint said, surprise evident in his voice.

"What did the lad do?" Nox asked.

"He gave me his dinner. Shoved the bucket through the hole in the wall." Flint sounded more pleased than he had any right to be about that disgusting gruel. But Nox smiled again anyway. At least he wasn't starving.

"Good. I'm glad you're making friends. Not like I've made any." He stared at the men around him, all of them eyeing him and each other warily. Their jailers weren't exactly fomenting comradery by forcing them to fight over what little food and water they dished out.

He knew he should try harder, but after the first day, he'd given up. Every time he approached one of the men, they either glared at him like an enemy, fists raised to defend themselves, or stared at him with naked fear, shrinking in on themselves when he talked.

As the light faded that night, he tried not to let the uselessness boiling in his blood overwhelm him.

"Tell me we're gonna get out of this, Flint."

"We will, my friend. Someway, we will."

Nox didn't see the beauty again for three more days. Three more days of fighting for slop and staring at the blank walls of the cage. Three more nights of lying in the dark, pretending he couldn't hear the soft sniffling from the boy down the hall.

Three long days and nights for his anger to smolder. He kept it in check somehow. He tamped down the fire boiling in his veins. Kept his fist from flying at the strangers who stared at him. He kept the animal inside his chest leashed, even when it snarled at him, begging for blood.

But that all changed when she came back.

She strolled in just after the ceiling lights blinded him in what might have been morning. Her stride was purposeful, steady. Those long legs eating up the hall as she strode past, the spider at her side.

Her voice echoed loudly down the hall, the feminine lilt so foreign after days of only guttural groans of men pounding in his ears. He heard her long before he saw her stride past. The warm melody of her sweet voice preceded her like a siren song.

The sound wound within him, setting his heart racing. He glanced around the room and spotted heads lifting, fists clenching, and the rapid breathing of nearly every man in the cage. Only the one man, still snoring in the corner, seemed unaffected.

How did she do it? Have every man in the cell awaiting her arrival, hearts in their throat? Was she coming to point her finger and drag more men in her wake? But her feet didn't pause outside their cell. Not like before. She walked past without a sideways glance.

He must've imagined it then. That flicker in her gray eyes. She hadn't been interested in a single thing about him. It was only wishful thinking born out of the confidence of years of successful conquests. What would a vision like her want with a lousy wretch like him?

Nox stood, his feet moving without conscious thought, leading him to the barred door. He slipped his head through the bars as far as he could to watch the gentle sway of her hips swish in a long red dress.

What was she doing here?

She stopped abruptly, her gaze flicking into one of the cells down the hall. The one that belonged to Flint's neighbor.

Her sweet voice stilled mid-sentence. She leaned forward, and though he couldn't make out her expression, he didn't need to. Her body stiffened, displeasure seeping into her tone when she spoke to the spider next.

The rumble of his answer didn't appease her. Not by a long shot. She dragged a hand through her silky black tresses, tugging at the roots. Her body practically thrummed with tension.

But then, like a mirage, it all washed away. She straightened and continued her stroll, only to stop again at the next cell.

Nox's breath caught in his throat. No.

She turned, the red fabric swooshing against her thighs as she went silent, staring into Flint's cage.

Nox watched her hand raise and point at his bondmate. He heard that sweet voice whisper to the spider. And something inside him broke.

"Flint! No. Leave him out of this. Take me! Take. Me," he screamed out the words, repeating them over and over until his throat was hoarse and dry.

It made no difference. The spider didn't even spin his head in his direction. He just pulled a skinny wooden tube from his pocket and lifted it to his lips.

A dart flew out. Flint yowled and hissed.

"Flint, I'll find you. Wherever they're taking you, I'll find you. I swear it."

The spider refilled the tube with a tiny, glimmering dart. He lifted it again and took aim. Another yowl.

"Leave him alone, you rotting bastard!"

"It's all right, Nox. We knew this was c-coming." The words filled his mind, each one sounding groggier than the last.

He knew it. They'd both realized it. What other reason would they have to keep him on the edge of starvation?

"Do whatever it takes. Whatever they want you to kill, you kill it, Flint. Come back to me."

Flint couldn't die. He couldn't lose another bondmate. It would break him. Throwing him in this cell hadn't been enough to do it, but that would. He knew it as surely as he knew anything.

The spider lifted the blowgun to his lips. Flint's answering yowl was barely a whisper. As soon as the pitiful noise reached his ears, Nox clenched his fingers around the bars and shook. A growl reverberated through the cell, so loud and jarring it rattled against the ceiling, setting off a chorus of gasps and whispers behind him in that guttural tongue.

From somewhere far away, he realized the sound had come from him. That the animal inside was taking over. For once, he didn't do a thing to tame it. He opened his jaw and howled, the sound more beast than man.

And when the girl finally turned to look at him, he knew she saw it, too. He watched her perfect brows shoot up into her hairline and those pretty little doe eyes widen like the full moon. She flicked her gaze away, back to the spider as he opened the door to Flint's cage and dragged his limp body out into the hall.

They wanted to cage him. Treat him like an animal. As soon as he got out of this cage, he'd show them what an animal like him could do.

Out of the Trees

Violet stirred, her head lolling against her shoulder and her body swaying. Her lashes fluttered lazily, lifting open and revealing nothing but blue water stretched out before her.

The ocean was so tranquil today. Her eyelids drooped again and would've likely closed completely if not for the whistling in her ears. She turned in her half-awakened daze, ready to chide her uncle for waking her with his noisy trilling, but her eyes widened instead.

That's right. Nox was gone. Her gaze shot to Ryon, seated across from her, his lips pursed as he worked the oars. He'd barely closed his lips when Muse chirped in response. Her sharp black gaze locked on the hulking man, head cocked.

Violet shook the last lingering wisps of sleep from her mind and sat up straight. "Do you know bird calls?"

Ryon flinched, his stare flicking to her. "Oh. I thought you were asleep. Sorry if I woke you."

She rubbed her stiff shoulders and sent him a half-smile. "It's all right. I probably shouldn't have nodded off, anyway." She split a look between her handsome companion and her aunt's bird. "So, do you?"

"Something like that." He grinned, nodding his head behind her. "I think we found the end of your map."

Violet shifted in her seat and blinked as she stared over her shoulder. A little island rose in the distance, much smaller than the one they'd left that morning. Was it really the spot they'd been seeking?

It seemed too easy to be true. Surely something was about to pop out of the water and force them off course. Her stomach churned as her uncle's face rose in her mind.

It wasn't fair at all. If this really was their destination, then they'd been so close. Barely a half-day's sail, and they would've made it to the map's end. If they'd only had one more day...

She shoved the thought aside. It wouldn't do to dwell on what might have been. She had to keep pressing forward.

"Do you mind taking a turn with the oars?" Ryon asked.

Violet nodded and crawled carefully across the wobbly boat to swap places with Ryon. It would be nice having something to keep her hands busy. Maybe then her mind wouldn't spend so much time wandering.

His rough, calloused hands brushed hers as he handed her the oars. She ignored the tingle the minor contact spread up her forearm. "Thanks."

She expected him to head to the spot she'd vacated in the front of the little boat, but he stopped in the center, right next to Muse. He crouched beside the falcon, lifting a hand and reaching toward her.

"What are you doing?" She winced at her abrupt tone, but she couldn't help feeling instinctively protective of her aunt's bondmate.

Ryon shot her a quick glance but didn't pause his reaching. "She wants this thing off." He lifted a corner of the soft towel wrapped around Muse's injured wing.

"Careful. She's not usually a fan of strangers touching her."

"I'll be fine. I'm doing her a favor."

Violet was tempted to argue further, but when Muse dutifully sat still under his touch, she brushed the urge aside.

Ryon gently unwound the towel, and Muse stretched out her gold and white checkered wings. Violet peered at her curiously. The bend in her wing looked to be healed, from where she was sitting at least. How had Ryon known it would be?

He whistled softly again, not taking his eyes off the predatory bird. Muse trilled a single note in response, then lifted off, soaring into the sky.

"Muse!" Violet's heart thrummed wildly. "Where is she going?"

Ryon shaded his eyes, watching her path through the sky. "Ahead."

"Oh." She could see he was right. Muse flew on a straight course toward the island.

"Don't worry. We'll catch up soon enough."

The island loomed ahead of them. Even from far away, she could tell it was much different from the wide-open grassland of Ryon's home. Beyond the sandy beaches, a thick canopy of trees covered this island. Birds flew overhead, flitting in and out of the greenery. The wide mouth of a river split the land in two before flowing out to join the sea.

Violet aimed for the white sand on the eastern banks of the river mouth. As they drew closer, the occasional high-pitched cry of some hidden animal met her ears, unlike anything she'd heard. It was halfway between a hoot and the pained yowl Flint let out when he'd been captured. She shuddered. What creature lurked in the forest making such eerie noises?

Soon, they pulled alongside the shore, and Violet hopped out to drag their boat through the surf. Ryon helped her tug the little craft out of the sand into the beginning of the tree line.

The trees here were strange. Much different from the tall, stately trees in the forests back home. Many appeared to bear fruit, attracting the attention of colorful birds. She stopped beside a thin trunk with papery skin dangling and peeling off in loose layers. It bore bright yellow leaves, and oblong orange balls perched in the branches.

She peered up, spotting a bug-eyed brown-haired mammal—which almost looked like a cross between a fox and monkey—reaching out a clawed hand to swipe a fruit before disappearing higher in the canopy. Its spotted tail trailed in its wake, helping it balance against the branches.

"Do your people travel to this island?" she asked.

Ryon shook his head. "Not that I'm aware of. We mostly stay on the mountain."

Violet wrinkled her nose. He had told her that already, but a part of her found it hard to believe. This island was so close to his home island; surely, they must be able to see it with their naked eyes from somewhere. Maybe even from up on that mountain. It was puzzling to think none of them would be the least bit curious about exploring.

"Well, I guess this will be new for both of us, then." She smiled and pointed up at the branches. "Could you pick one of those fruits for me?"

He quirked a brow. "Are you sure that's wise?"

Even as he asked, another of those hairy creatures hopped into view, snatching a fruit. Violet shrugged. "If those guys can eat them, they're probably fine."

Ryon took a step closer, suddenly so close she could smell him. Clean sweat, salt, and something musky and male. She sucked in a breath. What was he doing?

But then he rose on his toes and plucked one of the fruits out of the branches. He dropped on his heels and backed up a pace, offering her the fruit with a grin.

"Thanks." She plucked it out of his palm and took a sniff. Whatever it was, it smelled tangy and sharp. She licked her lips, giving the apple-sized fruit a tentative squeeze. It was so ripe and soft that a small amount of pressure sent her nails through the flesh, and a warm trickle of juice spilled down her wrist. She hurried to lick the sticky line, moaning softly when the sweet flavor hit her tongue.

A huge smile split her lips. "That's so good."

She held it out to Ryon but frowned when she caught sight of the muddled expression on his face. He looked worried and curious and something else altogether that made a warm flutter erupt in her belly. His hand hovered in the scant space between them, his gaze flicking between the fruit and her.

Violet lifted it a little higher. "Try it. It's really good."

Instead of taking the leaking fruit, he slid his fingers across her wrist, holding her hand steady. He dipped his head down and bit into the fruit with a smirk.

Another trickle of juice spilled into her palm. He retracted his hand from her wrist before the sticky liquid rolled across his fingers.

He swallowed, brown eyes meeting hers. "Delicious."

Violet's face warmed. She frowned at her juice-slicked hand. "Too bad it's so messy."

She nibbled at the ripe flesh. Her tongue darted out again to lick the juice off her finger.

Ryon made a strangled sound in the back of his throat, and her eyes shot back to his. He was watching her, his gaze glued to her mouth.

Violet's heart hammered. He was still standing so close. Why was he still so close?

The crunch of footsteps intruded on the moment. Ryon spun toward the sound, whipping out the pickaxe he wore slung against his hip and raising it to his shoulder.

Violet's heart hammered as another one of those strange cries echoed from within the island's depths. The footsteps pounded louder with every passing instant. Whatever was coming, it was almost on top of them.

Violet held her breath, waiting for some crazed beast to lunge at them from the trees. A man emerged, blond-haired and blue-eyed, wearing a wide-brimmed hat and carrying Muse on his forearm.

"Uncle Aren!" Violet dropped the fruit and rushed forward, thumping into his chest.

Aren squeezed her in his embrace for a long moment before tucking her beneath his arm and smiling down at her. "Vi, I'm surprised to see you here. Where's Conall?" His gaze slid across Ryon, lingering on his skirt and bare legs. "Who's your friend?"

Violet stretched out a hand. "Aren, this is Ryon."

Ryon tucked his axe back in the holder on his waist and raised his chin.

"Dad couldn't come," Violet continued. "He broke his leg last month. I came with Uncle Nox. We followed your map. But then yesterday, some masked men took him and set our boat on fire."

Aren's jaw clenched. "Sounds like the same people that stole Lark. Are you all right? How did you escape?"

"It was just pure luck. I was out on the dinghy fishing with Muse when they came. I found Ryon on the island north of this one. He agreed to help me on my search."

Aren's eyes popped wide, then narrowed as he swung his gaze back to Ryon. "And how did you convince him to help you so quickly when he couldn't understand you?"

"But he does understand me." Violet frowned, not at all liking the way her uncle was staring down Ryon. What did he think she'd done to convince him?

But Aren twisted to face her, his brows shooting up. "What?"

"I said, he does understand." She turned to Ryon with a smile. "Now would be a good time to say something."

Ryon cleared his throat. "I understand."

Aren jerked back as the words fell from Ryon's lips. Then a wide smile broke out on his face. "Son of a—" He shook his head. "You're the first local I've met who can understand me. All the people we've met on these eastern islands speak some different language."

Violet stilled, remembering the way Ryon had shouted at her in that foreign tongue when he first spotted her. How had he learned to speak their language when no one else could?

"There are people on this island?" Ryon asked.

Aren nodded. "Yes. This one, and others. There's a whole string of islands. Lark and I explored about a dozen before she was captured."

Violet tilted her head to the side. "How did it happen?"

Aren sighed. "It's a long story. C'mon. Let me take you back to the village. I'll tell you about it while we walk."

Violet offered Ryon a hand to help him walk, but he waved her away after selecting a thick branch off the forest floor.

Aren led them past the papery fruit tree to a worn footpath and turned inland. "We've been out here exploring for nearly three years.

After we made it through the Still Sea, we spotted these islands. We circled around them before we set foot on any and made that map I sent with Muse."

"So, you haven't explored all the islands on the map?" There'd been well more than a dozen on that small handwritten map, though she'd never counted them. Probably closer to twenty or thirty, in all shapes and sizes.

"Not yet, no." Aren sighed. "We started at the top and worked our way down. Found people on nearly every one of them. But we still haven't caught a hint of what we're looking for."

"What were you looking for?" she asked.

"Didn't anyone tell you?" Aren cocked a brow.

Violet shook her head. Apparently, there was more than one thing her parents had left out.

"We were hunting for Druturion's hidden clutch of eggs," Aren said softly.

Ryon spoke up, "Who's Druturion?"

"A dragon." Violet bit her lip. "I didn't know he had any eggs."

Aren shrugged. "I'm sorry they didn't tell you, Vi. Kayda didn't want word getting out. Imagine the hunt that would ensue if people knew there were dragon eggs out there somewhere, just waiting to be found."

Violet nodded, pushing the twinge of hurt aside. More secrets. Why didn't anyone in her family trust her? She wouldn't have told anyone. Or were her parents just eager to shelter her from this, too?

"Everything was going fine until we ran into those masked men. We were exploring this island when they came. It all happened so fast. One moment Lark was right there beside me, and the next, I was watching her being dragged off with them."

Violet crossed her arms. "Why didn't you go after her? If you saw them taking her, why didn't you do something?"

Aren sighed. "I couldn't, Vi. Not then. I tried to follow, but they destroyed our boat anchored offshore, same as they did yours. I've been building a new one, though. It's almost finished."

It didn't make sense. Why would he watch her being dragged off without doing something? Lark was the love of his life. She'd watched them together for years. They were as smitten with each other as her parents—practically inseparable.

Had something happened in the last three years that forced them apart? Something terrible enough Aren would stand back and watch strangers run off with his wife?

"Now that you're here, we'll set off after them together. I'm glad you came to help, Vi." Aren sent her a sad smile.

"Do you know where they took her?" she asked.

"Not exactly. But I'm hoping our friend here can help with that." Aren lifted the arm that held Muse.

As her aunt's bondmate, Muse would still be in contact with Lark. At least Lark had that small comfort. She wasn't totally alone.

"With any luck, Muse will lead the way to wherever they're keeping her. She can fly ahead of the ship, act like a beacon," Aren said.

"Uncle Aren, Muse was injured bringing the map to us. I'm not sure how much flying she should be doing."

Aren's shoulders stiffened, and he scanned the falcon up and down. "She was?" He shuddered. "When Lark finds out, she's gonna kill me."

"We've been wrapping her wing for weeks now. Breham looked her over back home. He insisted she would heal fully, but she had to take it easy for a while." Violet sighed. "Too bad we can't talk to her like Lark. She could tell us which way to head."

Aren frowned. "We'll figure something out."

Ryon opened his mouth, but then shut it again an instant later.

They'd arrived at the village. Long wooden dwellings lined the sides of a clearing. Four great buildings sprawled out, each three times the size of her family's farmhouse, one on each side of the rectangular clearing.

In the center, people gathered, their skin various hues of brown, tan, and olive. They wore furred clothing that covered their chests and groins but left their limbs and stomachs bare. Violet recognized the pelts as belonging to the same creatures she'd spotted snatching fruit from the papery tree.

Adults crouched in the clearing, their hands busy. Some prepared food. Others wove baskets and nets. Children sat by the adults' sides, helping with their tasks, or playing quietly with each other.

Many of the folks glanced up at their arrival, faces full of curiosity. Aren strode in, tipping his hat up and waving, then turned to the nearest building's entrance. "C'mon. I've been staying in here."

Aren ducked beneath the doorway. Violet followed, without having to duck. She blinked in the doorway as she scanned the interior of the cabin. Beds lined the walls, covered with straw mats. Fireplaces perched at the short ends of the rectangular building, neither lit.

Aren strode purposefully to the left and stopped beside a young woman lazing idly on a cot, braiding some white fiber in her hands. She smiled as Aren approached, a wide grin of pleasure that lit her whole face.

Violet frowned. The girl was pretty, with short curls framing her cheeks, bright brown eyes, and a face full of freckles. Was this girl the thing that had come between her aunt and uncle?

"Who is this?" she asked, unable to hide the hint of accusation in her tone.

Aren turned to her and smiled. "Relax, she's just a friend, doing me a favor." He turned back to the girl and raised his brows, then pantomimed a rocking motion with his arms.

The girl nodded and pointed at the floor behind her. From where Violet stood, she couldn't see anything past the cot in front of her. She circled around the cot, and her eyes widened.

Aren stopped at her side, speaking in a whisper. "I'll have to introduce you to your cousin a little later. You don't want to see what happens if you wake him from his afternoon nap early."

Violet stared down into the cradle on the floor, her heart clenching. A little boy with soft golden curls rested inside, sucking his thumb. Suddenly, it clicked. This was why Aren hadn't chased after Lark. He had someone else to protect. Those masked men hadn't just stolen Lark from her husband. They stole her away from her son.

As Violet gazed down at the sweet little sleeping boy, she made a silent promise. She wouldn't let him grow up without a mother. She would do whatever it took to find Lark.

The Dark King

None of the men in the cage would look at him after they dragged Flint's limp body out of the hall. Nox paced the stone cell, pulling at his hair, growling low in his throat. The men surrounding him stared blankly at the floors, seeming to instinctively realize he was a mere hairsbreadth away from breaking. That a single glance or word from one of them might set him off.

He almost wanted one of them to say something. To look at him sideways. He was dying for an outlet to unleash his rage.

Hours later, when the spider returned with the beauty trailing silently at his side—for once neither of them chattering pleasantly in that maddening tongue—he knew what was coming.

The girl raised her hand. It swung around the cell, landing on three men crouched listlessly on the floor. Then it swung over and pointed right at his chest.

Nox smiled.

Something passed over the girl's face. Surprise? No. It was the same look he'd glimpsed once before. Interest. Only this time, he wasn't eager to exploit it.

This time, that flicker of interest in her eyes made a riot of squirming fingers clench within his gut. He wouldn't be her toy. Her sideshow freak. Not after what she did with that finger. Pointing it at Flint. Making the spider sink those darts into his bondmate and drag him off to who knows where.

She could take her *interest* and shove it.

The beauty held his gaze as the spider swung open the cell door. Nox stared back, until the shadow of the spider fell upon him, just as dark as he was, clothed head to toe in black. The metal pole glinted in his hand; his fingers clenched around it like he was itching to use it.

A part of Nox wanted him to. He wanted the pain. If only so the ache in his body might distract him for a single instant from the unending agony of knowing his bondmate was alone in their clutches.

But Nox wouldn't give them the satisfaction of watching him writhe on the dirty floor. And beneath that lived the hope that wherever they led him, might be the same place they had dragged Flint. He stepped forward with the others, out into the hall. After they slammed the barred door closed, he followed dutifully.

They led them out of the hall, through a doorway to another corridor. More cells lined the wall here. More broken men stared out at them.

Another door. Another wall of cells. But these didn't house more haunted men. This hall echoed with the snarls and shrieks of starving animals. He caught a glimpse of a furred back of some enormous beast, crouched in the shadows. The low rumble of a pained yowl reverberated off the walls.

Nox's chest ached. He heard that cry for what it was. Not just a warning. Not just aggression and anger. He recognized the pain and the fear. The pleading note of agony begging for release.

Being what he was—a man blessed with bonding magic so rare, he could bond any species—he'd never known the obsession that came with being drawn to a certain species. He'd seen the way his brother Conall could charm any dog. Even the meanest, most vicious hound turned to putty in his hands. Lark was so obsessed with birds she could name nearly every one she spotted. And when she sang, the whole lot of them quieted to listen.

It had never been like that for him. For him, it had been all animals. He felt a kinship to every critter he ever came in contact with. He spent his childhood in the jungles of Raimire with pets by the dozens. Lizards and birds, fishes and snakes. He loved them all.

Hearing the hurt of the creatures in this cell nearly broke him again. What were these people doing? Why were they torturing these animals?

Men, he could almost understand. Just because he and Flint had been innocent didn't mean they all were. Surely, some men in those cells deserved to be caged away. He'd even spied the truth of it in some of their eyes. The guilt and shame.

But these animals were innocent. They hadn't stolen or killed—not maliciously. They hadn't broken the laws of man. Why were they caging these poor beasts? Why?

Before he could lunge at the cells and attempt to tear open the bars with his bare hands to release the helpless animals, the group turned again. They sped through another doorway, this one leading to a stairwell.

Nox lingered in the hall with all those animal cries pounding in his ears. Until the spider whipped around and banged that metal pole on the door frame. Nox spun, his jaw clenched, and he slipped past him into the stairwell.

They climbed, feet slapping on the stairs. Nox's feet were still bare. He wasn't the only one. None of the men in the cell wore boots or shoes of any kind. They all smelled awful, day upon day of sweat and stench coating their skin. The reek spilled into the stairwell, following them up like a disgusting cloud.

He didn't know how the spider and beauty could stand it. It sickened him even more every time he caught a whiff of her. He found himself drawn to her, his steps bringing him just behind her on the stair. With every step, her scent perfumed the air he breathed. Flowers and spun sugar.

He was close enough to touch her, but he kept his hands clenched at his side. It didn't stop him from imagining it, though. He didn't want to picture it, not after what she'd done. But with her sweet scent filling his nose, he couldn't stop the images from plaguing him.

She would be soft. So soft and so sweet. He could almost taste her on his tongue.

But that would never be. If he laid even a finger on her, she'd recoil. No matter what he spied in her eyes. Why would someone so perfect ever want a filthy, stinking prisoner to touch her? She wouldn't. That flicker of interest was a lie.

They arrived at the top of the stairs. Another door stood there. This one opened to a near blinding light.

It hadn't seemed so dark down in the cell, but now that he walked out here in a wide-open space, light streaming down from the top of a domed roof, he realized how dim and dank it had been. He squinted, his eyes taking long moments to adjust.

Where were they? Some kind of immense building shaped in a wide circle. They stood on the ground, on a dirt floor. All around, raised seating lined the walls. People filled the benches, hundreds of them, staring down at them as they exited the stairwell door.

That's when he heard the sound. The same sound he'd heard days ago after the first round of pointing. When five men left and only three returned.

The cheers erupted, so loud they were nearly deafening. Nox's heart hammered as he gazed up at all the faces circled around him. They were raised so far away he couldn't reach them, but he could still see their faces. Their smiles. Why were they smiling? Wasn't he a prisoner?

The spider led them to a bank of cages set on the circle's far side. Nox nearly wept when he spied what lay in one of the closed cages.

"Flint!"

He was still out of it, slumped against the dirt floor. But Nox could see the rise and fall of his chest, and a wave of relief washed over him so strongly his knees buckled.

The spider threw open the door to an empty cell. The men filed in, and Nox followed. He sank down on his knees in the dirt, staring around the enormous building as the barred door slammed shut, locking them inside.

There was another set of cages across from them on the far side of the ground level. Unlike the ones that they sat in, which were made of metal bars, allowing him to look his fill of the building, those cells were completely closed off with shining silver sheets of metal.

But he could sense something inside. Even over the roar of the crowd, he could hear the cries of the animal within. He watched those metal walls shudder and shake as whatever beast threw itself at the cage doors. And just like down in the cells, he could sense the pain and fear beneath the rage and anger. The knowledge of it burned within him, setting a fire burning in his chest.

Nox's gaze drifted away from the cages to the stands. All those smiling, clapping people stared down at them, their faces relaxed and eager. Children sat on their parent's laps, pointing their grubby little fingers down at the cages.

Scents wafted toward him from above, and his stomach rumbled. He spied men pacing the lengths of the stands, carrying boxes of smoked meat and sweet bread. Every so often, someone would wave one over, licking their lips before digging into the delicious food.

What was happening here? Who were these people being merry and eating? Watching him.

He sat there for long moments, waiting and watching. The rows of seats continued to fill until nearly every spot was taken. Every spot except for one.

At the center of the building, a box sat apart from the rest of the seats. It was lined not with hard wooden benches, but a pair of grand, carved chairs, painted gold.

"Nox?"

Nox whipped around, staring into the cage beside him. *"Flint. Thank the Mother. You're awake."*

"What's happening? Where are we?"

"I don't know. They brought us up here for something. Some kind of show by the looks of things."

Flint's gaze swung up to the stands. He studied the crowd, no doubt realizing the same thing Nox had. Whatever was about to happen here, they would do with an eager audience watching.

"I'm glad you're all right."

Flint wobbled up to his feet. *"I'll be fine. That was a nice little nap."* He yawned, stretching as he swayed.

Nox spotted movement in the empty box. He watched a door open, and a man dressed in purple and black robes strode through. His stomach recoiled at the sight of him. A feeling washed over him. One he'd felt once before, long ago.

"What is it?" Flint asked. *"What's wrong?"*

Nox shook his head, his eyes widening and mouth dropping open. It couldn't be. *"I-I... It can't be. I must be half-starved and half-crazy."*

But then the man seated himself in one of those fancy chairs and flicked his gaze down at them.

Flint stiffened in the cage beside him. *"Nox... do you feel that? What is wrong with that man?"*

Nox gulped. He felt it, too. That sickening, crawling itch slithered up his spine, and he nearly gagged from the feel of it.

"I've felt this before. When I was just a boy. It's him. The Unseen."

"No." Flint growled, low and barely audible. *"Conall killed him. It can't be."*

Nox's heart slammed against his ribs. That same sense of disbelief rose in his mind, but it evaporated like a fine mist. Deep down, he knew. He'd always known it wasn't over. He'd always sensed it in the back of his mind. Now, the proof stood right before him.

And of course, there was nothing he could do about it. Not now, as a prisoner. All he could do was stare up at him. Watch the people crowded so closely on the bench seats gaze upon him with adoring eyes. It was enough to nearly make him scream.

Then a second figure popped out of that same door. This one strode in reluctantly, shoved into the box by a rough hand on the small of her back. The spider pushed in behind her, cutting off her escape.

For half a heartbeat, he thought it was the beauty. But then his stomach dropped to his feet. The dark hair hanging around her shoulders was brown and curly, not black and straight. The girl wearing it was short, not like the beauty with her endless long legs. And her face, while just as beautiful, held an expression of utter contempt. A face he recognized.

Lark. He'd found her.

"Your sister." Flint's voice rose in his mind, full of triumph. *"I knew she'd be here."*

But when she sank down in the empty seat beside that pompous robed man, Nox's heart sank. Rot and decay. What was she doing with *him*? With *that thing*?

A final figure strode into the box. His wide stomach stuck out from his black cloak, and deep scars marred his face along one side, so deep even his thick, gray-streaked beard couldn't disguise them. He strode out from the doorway and stepped aside before closing the door. Four black crows flew in before the door swung shut and perched on the rails. As the man spun around, Nox spotted a fifth bird dangling on the man's shoulder.

Lark clearly wasn't happy about being there. Even from so far away, he could sense her discomfort. When the purple-robed man leaned over and spoke in her ear, she shuddered and pressed as far away in the chair from him as she could manage.

The man only smirked in response, flicking his long black hair over his shoulder and straightening. Then he stood and strutted to the edge of the box. As the crowd noticed, the hum of conversation died down. Parents hushed their children, and all eyes snapped to the lone man.

He straightened his robes and cleared his throat. Nox fought the urge to cower as the man's dark gaze roved over the cages. His eyes were black, or a brown so dark it was almost black. From so far away, it was hard to tell. But even at a distance, there was no mistaking his power and influence over the crowd. He tipped his square jaw up, staring down the edge of his rounded nose at the people gathered in the stands.

The hush was nearly complete when he finished his perusal, his gaze trailing across the circle of benches. If not for the slamming and grunts of the animal in the walled off box, it would've been quiet enough to hear the panicked beating of Nox's heart.

The man spoke. His voice rang out across the huge room, clear and filled with command. Even without understanding the language, he could see the way the people here deferred to him. Like he was a king.

The dark king spoke for a few more moments. Each word reverberated up Nox's spine, tingling against his skin and forcing a host of sickness to take up residence in his stomach. He felt like retching, but he shook off the desire. For once, he could be thankful for the lack of food. Surely, if he had a full belly, he would've spilled its contents on the dirt floor.

Finally, the man's words cut off. A chorus of cheers rose from the crowd. Nox had thought the sound deafening before, but he was wrong. The crowd was a living thing now, screaming its pleasure at the dark king. Eager to show him the depth of their adoration.

The dark king smiled. Even that was a terrifying thing to behold. His face split, bright white teeth gleaming, but Nox sensed the predator lurking behind that mask of civility. That man was more than he seemed. He *knew* it.

Then the dark king spun on his heel and sank down on his throne. The spider and man with the crows watched from the back of the box, standing silently. And Lark just sat there, looking as nauseous as Nox was.

Nox's stomach churned. If that really was a throne up there, and he really was a king, then what did that make Lark?

He wasn't sure he wanted to know.

But then the spider strode to the front of the box. He knelt and lifted some kind of contraption. The great glass jar shone in the light.

It was shaped oddly, wide at the top and bottom and narrow in the middle, like it had been pinched. The bottom was filled with what looked like grains of sand.

"What do you think that is?" Flint asked.

"I'm not sure."

The spider didn't say a word. He settled the jar on the box's railing and flipped it. All the sand started to rush down to the empty bottom, but with the shape of the glass, only a trickle fell.

Nox didn't have long to speculate what it all meant. As soon as the first grain of sand fell, the door to his cage—to all the cages—opened. The crowd roared. And as a massive beast burst out into the ring, Nox's heart plummeted to his toes.

Now he understood why those men hadn't returned. Those people were here to watch them be slaughtered by the caged beast.

Nox shoved his shoulders back and turned to Flint with a grimace. *"I think they mean to kill us."*

"No. They just want blood. Let's give it to them." Flint burst out of his cage, hissing and snarling.

Nox jumped up, past the men cowered on the floor in their cages, and followed his bondmate into the ring.

The Raft

Ryon stared in awe at the long log building he stood in while Violet chatted with her uncle.

It was all so unexpected. To think, all this time people had been living here, a mere half-day's sail across the sea. And if Aren was to be believed, there were people living all over, lined up in islands north and south of his home.

Why did everyone in his village work so hard to keep them away from the ocean? Was there something out here they didn't want found?

The people here looked no different from the folks in his small village. Sure, they were clothed strangely in their animal furs, but beneath that, they were just the same. He'd even caught a few snatches of conversation as he reached the village. Enough to know that the language they spoke was similar enough he could speak with them if he wanted to.

After a few moments of whispered conversation, their voices low to avoid waking the sleeping child who looked to be around two,

Violet and Aren withdrew from the bedside and headed for the cabin entrance.

Ryon trailed along, trying not to let the fact that they'd practically forgotten him bother him. Violet had to be overjoyed at finding her uncle. It was only natural they'd want some time to catch up.

Perhaps he should find something else to keep himself occupied with for a while? He let his gaze travel around the central clearing as they strode back out into the forest. Maybe the people here could answer some of the questions he had.

But then Violet turned and met his eye. "Ryon, are you coming?"

"Hmm?"

"Aren offered to show me the boat he's been working on. Would you like to join us?"

His fingers flexed around the stick he'd been using as a crutch. He really ought to rest, but he said, "Sure."

When she asked so nicely, he couldn't resist tagging along. Besides, if she wanted to be rid of him, she'd say something. Violet didn't seem like the type to hide her feelings.

They traipsed through the forest on a western course. Birds chattered all around him. He frowned, careful to keep quiet. The last thing he needed was to be swarmed by a curious flock of feathered critters.

There were many other animals he couldn't understand, scampering through the underbrush and leaping through the treetops. It was so much different here than the grasslands of his home.

Soon, the scratching of critters in the canopy was joined by rushing water in the distance. But the sound was different from the ocean. A sound he recognized from his years scouring for hidden stones.

They emerged on a river's edge. The channel was large, nearly twice the size of the big buildings in the village clearing. A wobbly rope ladder stretched across the banks, swaying in the breeze.

Aren set his course straight for it.

Violet gulped, staring down into the deep water. "We have to cross?"

"If you want to see the boat, then yeah. Don't worry, it's perfectly safe. I've been crossing every day for weeks now." With that, Aren set off, crossing the bridge at a fast clip. He turned around on the other side and yelled over the sound of the rushing water. "C'mon, Vi."

"You want to go next?" Ryon stared at the narrow bridge. He'd offer to walk with her, but the space was far too narrow for it. It was clearly designed for foot traffic and nothing more.

She tiptoed to the edge, a frown firmly in place. "I-I don't know. It doesn't look stable."

"Your uncle made it across. He has to be twice your size, at least."

Violet shook her head. "I don't think I can do this."

"C'mon," Aren yelled again. "You got this, Vi."

Violet turned her wide eyes to meet Ryon's. "Aren't you going to tell me to go, too?"

Ryon shook his head, his stomach clenching. He'd badgered someone who wasn't ready to face their fears once before. Never again. "No. Go or not; it's up to you. I'll stay with you either way."

She stared up at him, and her expression shifted. Her brows pinched together, and she clenched her jaw. "No, I got this." She took a deep breath and her first shaky step across.

Ryon smiled. Yeah, she was tough. Even in the face of her obvious fear, Violet strode across the bridge, her fingers locked on the handrails. Within a few moments, she made it to the other side, and her uncle slapped her on the back as a relaxed grin crossed his face.

Ryon had no such problems. He'd learned to overcome his fear of heights early in life. And with all the climbing he did, traveling down below and back up the mountain every moon cycle, he had plenty of experience dangling over precipices, one wrong move away from plummeting to his death.

In comparison, this was easy. If he fell here, he'd even be guaranteed a soft landing in the river. The rope ladder swung and swayed, dipping close to the water's surface. The blue-green liquid chugged beneath him, loaded with brightly colored fish and long skinny serpents that whipped past, chasing the fish.

Soon, he'd traversed the bridge and stared at more trees nearly identical to the forest on the other side. "Why did you build the boat over here and not across the river?" he asked.

"Boat building has been a bit of a learning experience." Aren rubbed his neck and motioned for them to follow him down river. "This raft I'm about to show you, it's my second try. The first time I tried using the ploom fruit logs."

"Ploom? What's that?" Violet stared into the forest, her brow scrunched.

Aren pointed at one of the trees they'd stopped at when they first landed. Ryon licked his lips, remembering that delicious flavor on his tongue. And Violet, so sweetly offering it to him.

"Those orange fruits," Aren explained. "They taste great, but the wood is not the best for sailing. I barely made it to the river mouth before the damn thing collapsed on me."

"Oh." Violet chuckled. "I'm sorry I wasn't around to see that."

Aren grinned. "Yeah, laugh it up." He chucked her gently on the shoulder, then pointed again. "See those trees?"

Ryon followed his finger. A thick tree stood off to their left, its bark a dark blackish-brown with hints of purple.

"Those trees grow on this side of the island. After I took my spill into the river, one of the villagers bade me follow him until we stopped directly in front of one and handed me an axe. I got the message."

"How long have you been staying with the villagers here?" Violet asked.

"Since the day we arrived here, actually. These people are the friendliest we've encountered. I count my blessings every day that we didn't end up on a different island when those masked animals stole Lark. Not all the people we've found have been so welcoming."

Ryon drew back. Maybe that might be why his people forbid sea travel? Had they run into some of the less friendly islanders in the past?

"Ah, here we are." Aren strolled up to a curve in the riverbank, quickening his pace. He brushed aside a few wide palm fronds off the ground, revealing a wooden raft perched on the banks.

Ryon lifted a brow. Hadn't he said it was almost done? A pile of logs sat on the riverbank next to the skinny raft. A few were lashed together, but it would clearly take a lot of work until the craft was finished.

Violet cleared her throat. "You made this all on your own?"

"Pretty much." Aren shrugged. "The villagers were nice enough to let us stay with them, but none have been eager to help me, though the village children are happy enough to sneak over here and gawk." He chuckled. "But now that you two are here, we'll get the raft seaworthy in no time."

"You're right. We'll help as much as you need, won't we?" Violet aimed a smile at Ryon.

Ryon nodded. "Of course." When she smiled at him like that, how could he say no?

They returned to the village at dusk. After hours of chopping wood and lugging logs through the forest, Ryon was ready to collapse. Even with all the work they'd done, the raft would still require a few more days to complete.

Back in the village, he was prepared to climb into whatever cot the villagers gave him. He strolled back into the clearing and approached the closest man he could find.

"Excuse me, do you have an empty bed for my friend and I?" he asked.

The man—a skinny old grandfatherly type with white hair and wrinkles so deep his tanned skin gathered in big folds and bunches—gaped at him in response.

"Ryon…" Violet said his name on a gasp.

"Yes?" He turned to her, noting her wide eyes and tense shoulders.

"Can you talk to these people, too?"

He shrugged. "Yeah. They speak a lot like we do back at home, only with a bit of an accent."

"Where did you come from, boy?" the old man asked. "How do you speak both tongues?"

Ryon grimaced. He should've probably spoken up when they'd first arrived.

Aren slapped him on the shoulder. "Well, I'll be. You are full of surprises, huh? What luck! I can finally figure out what these folks have been saying."

"What's your name, boy?" The old man tugged his sleeve, demanding his attention.

Ryon frowned. Maybe he looked like a boy to this old geezer, but he was nearly in his thirties. "I'm Ryon. This is Violet. Aren is her uncle."

"Good, good. I am Balun. You will come by the fire. I have much I've been wanting to say to the pale foreigner."

A sigh spilled out of Ryon's lips as the old man hooked an arm through his elbow and towed him across the clearing. His plans to crash on the closest cot would have to wait.

Villagers crowded around, an air of excitement bubbling up around them. A smiling woman shoved a wooden plate heaped full of roasted meat and more of that ploom fruit into his hands while children skipped through the clearing, chattering excitedly.

The freckled girl they met earlier appeared with Aren's son on her hip. She wasted no time plopping the smiling toddler on his father's lap. The boy busied himself snatching bites off Aren's plate.

Ryon took turns chewing and making introductions. Nearly every villager made an appearance around the fire, popping out of the large wooden buildings, everyone appearing eager to be included. But by the time he scraped up the last bite of his dinner, Balun called for a hush.

"Ryon." Balun slung a casual arm over his shoulder. "You say these two come from far across the sea, but not you, yes? Which island do you hail from?"

"You're right. I live on the island just north of this one."

More than one gasp sounded, and all the villagers stared at him curiously. A few women across the fire leaned close together, speaking in hushed whispers behind their hands.

"Do you live on Bloodfeather Mountain?" The old man's eyes gleamed in the firelight as his gaze raked over his attire.

Ryon sensed from the way the man stared he'd met others from his home before. He wouldn't get away with lying about it, even if he'd wanted to. "I've never heard that name before, but I suppose it's fitting. Yes. That's where I hail from."

"And do you have any?" Balun asked.

Ryon gulped. Ah, so that explained the glint in his eyes. Greed. Balun didn't have to name it for him to know what he was asking for.

"No, I don't."

"I hope you don't mind if we make sure." Balun crooked his finger at two beefy men on the far side of the fire. "Search him."

He shucked off his bag and surrendered it to one of the men, then stood while the second patted him down.

"Ryon..." Violet tilted her head and rubbed her palms down her trouser legs. "What's going on?"

Ryon sent her a crooked smile. He'd not translated any of Balun's questions about his homeland. This had to make a peculiar picture. "Nothing to worry about. Just their way of greeting. Like your handshakes."

Violet frowned. "That's the oddest greeting I've seen."

He sat back down with a grin a moment later when the men finished their search, sighing inwardly. He owed Mama a big kiss the next time he saw her. Without her unique hiding spot, he'd have surely lost all his feathers by now.

"Funny. They never greeted me that way," Aren said.

Ryon shrugged and went back to translating. Balun shared a brief history of the island they were on. Aren asked a dozen questions that had been puzzling him and shared a few stories from their lands across the sea. The conversation stayed light and easy until the subject of the masked men came up.

"Bah, you can't go after them," Balun declared. "I'm sorry for your wife. Truly I am. But if the masked invaders took her, then she's lost."

"What do you mean *lost*?" Aren asked. "Please, tell us what you know. Impossible or not, we will find her."

Balun leaned back, stretching his wrinkly legs out by the fire. "They come here hunting. Mostly for the girboon in the depths of the jungle, but sometimes they take people, too. There's only been one among us who was ever taken and returned."

Aren's eyes lit up. "Who? Can we speak with them?"

Balun shook his head sadly. "I'm afraid not. This happened many moons ago, in the time of my father. The man who escaped is long dead."

Ryon translated, his mind reeling. If that were true, then whoever these people were, they'd been stealing people for decades. Maybe even centuries. Who were they? Inhabitants of some other island? How had they operated in secrecy for so long? How many people had they taken, and for what?

"Can you tell us the story of the man who escaped?" Violet leaned forward, her words rushed. "Anything at all could help us."

"I will share what I know." Balun rubbed his chin. "It's not much, and an odd tale at that. Not everyone here believed him. Some claim he must've struck his head and dreamed it all up, the tale is so bizarre."

Aren chuckled, but his laughter was humorless and dry. "I've seen some strange things in my day. Let's hear it."

"Long ago, in the time of my father, there was a man named Dumas who was taken by the masked men. He'd been out in the forest harvesting ploom fruit when they came. He watched them sink their darts into a family of girboons and tried to hide. But they caught him anyway."

Aren scratched his temple. "Girboon. You said that before. What are they?"

Balun cocked his head and cupped a gnarled hand around his ear. "Listen. Those wails you hear come from the girboon. They're great furred apes that live in the deepest parts of the forest."

Violet wrinkled her nose, turning a pensive stare on Balun. "Apes? What do the masked men want with them?"

"Until Dumas was taken, we never knew. If he's to be believed, they turn them into fighting creatures. They starve them near to death and force them to battle men for sport."

Ryon shuddered. "That's awful," he couldn't help but whisper before he continued translating.

"Is that what happened to Dumas?" Aren cocked a brow. "They made him battle the girboon?"

Balun nodded. "He claimed to have been taken to a great city. He was imprisoned with a great many men, all of them forced to battle all kinds of beasts and each other. Dumas thought he would die there. He nearly did."

"How did he escape?" Violet asked.

"He was on the verge of death, bloodied and battered in one of the matches. The masked men must've thought him too far gone. They set him free, and against all odds, he managed to survive and return."

Aren's blue eyes widened. "Did he see where they were?"

"That's the strange part." Balun sighed. "The part that will make your search impossible."

They all leaned forward as Ryon translated, eager to hear the rest.

"The masked men do not hail from an island." Balun rubbed the back of his neck and pursed his lips, almost as if he wasn't sure if he should continue. Finally, he said, "If Dumas is to be believed, they live on a great ship beneath the sea."

Violet gasped. "Under water?" She shook her head and stood abruptly, heading for the cabin her uncle was staying in.

Aren frowned, watching Violet retreat. "I better go make sure she's all right." He lifted his son in his arms and followed his niece.

Balun spoke up before Ryon had a chance to translate. "It's been a long day. I'm sure you will all need rest. Take two of the empty cots in that cabin. There ought to be a few available."

Ryon nodded, bade a quick goodbye to the folk still gathered around, and entered the cabin. Crackling fires in the corner hearths dimly illuminated the long room. He found Violet and Aren crowded around Aren's bed in the back, speaking in hushed tones. The little boy cooed from inside his cradle, reaching out a pudgy hand toward Muse's perch.

"You tell 'em yet?" Muse asked.

"I will," Ryon replied.

Violet cocked her head, first at Muse, then at him. He smiled, even as the corners of her mouth turned down and her brows sank. But she didn't address him, just returned her gaze to her uncle and continued speaking.

"How can you be so sure? Even if Muse has the strength to lead us there when the boat is finished, if the city is underwater, then what chance do we have?" Violet let out a weary sigh.

"I think I can help with that," Ryon said.

Aren's brows shot up. "You can?"

Ryon glanced around. A few villagers lounged on beds nearby, but none of them could understand what they were saying. Even so, he had to be cautious. If these people knew about the bloodfeathers, then he couldn't risk talking about them openly. But he had to tell them something. He couldn't let Violet walk around with that devastated expression, thinking all was lost. Not when he knew the odds were not quite so dire.

"I don't just know bird calls. I can talk to them, understand them."

Violet's eyes widened, the red in her irises looking more violet in the dim fire-lit cabin. "You—that whistling—you've *really* been talking to Muse?"

Aren scrubbed a hand down his face. "Truly? I've never—Lark can speak to her, but they communicate in their thoughts. You understand her whistles?" He crossed his arms. "Ask her to tell me something you couldn't possibly know."

Ryon nearly rolled his eyes. But it was only natural to want proof when presented with a skill so uncommon.

He turned to Muse, pursing his lips and whistling, "Aren won't believe me unless you tell him something only you would know."

"Oh, loverboy." Muse shifted on her perch, her feathers bristling. "Tell him the first time he kissed Lark he was red as a lobster."

What? Of all the things the silly bird could've chosen to say, *this* was what she chose?

Ryon held back a chuckle. "She says the first time you kissed your wife, you were red as a lobster. And she called you *loverboy*."

Violet didn't hold back her laughter. It bubbled up around them, and Ryon grinned. Even if they didn't believe him, at least he got her to smile.

Aren flushed, turning a little red right then and there. "Well, I'll be... It's true. I had an awful case of sunburn that day." He shook off his embarrassment with a shrug and stared at Ryon, his blue eyes burning with intensity. "Ask her if she's still in contact with Lark. Are they still speaking?"

Ryon whistled again, and Muse shook her head as soon as he finished relaying the question. "No, I haven't been able to speak to her since the day she was taken. There's something blocking our bond. But I can still sense her out there. The closer I get, the more I can feel her. I can find her."

Aren's shoulders stiffened when he relayed Muse's answer, and he let out a weary sigh. "That's so strange. Their bond has never been blocked before..."

"I agree it is peculiar. But at least Ryon can help us direct the raft." Violet's smile fell. "But I still don't see how we'll find her underwater."

"I can help with that, too," Ryon said.

"But how?" Aren asked.

Here's where he had to be careful...

"To explain that, I need to show you something, and I can't do that while we're here."

Violet bit her lip, then her mouth dropped open. "That wasn't a greeting earlier, was it? They were looking for something."

Ryon sent her a lopsided smile. "You're right. But trust me, I have something that will help us." He grabbed her hand. "We can still save your family."

Violet gazed back at him with those lovely gull's egg eyes and smiled. "I do. I trust you."

Aren slapped him on the back. "All right. We're back on track. Let's get some sleep so we can work on the raft in the morning."

True Defiance

Nox's heart lodged in his throat. The roar of the crowd filled his ears, almost as loud as the roar of the beast across from him. Almost, but not quite.

The huge ape opened his mouth and bellowed again. His jarring cry was so full of rage and hunger it sent a shiver up Nox's spine. The massive beast's furred head reached nearly to the height of the lowest benches curving around the massive ring. He set his attention there first, reaching up a beefy arm to swipe at the spectators.

Masked men tore into sight, bounding in front of the seated people and stabbing the beast's hands with long poles that had more of those small metal cylinders strapped to the ends. Loud buzzing droned as they connected with his hairy fists, and the ape jolted back. He slammed to the dirt floor with a *crash,* and the ground rumbled beneath Nox's feet.

"What's the plan, Flint?" Nox studied the ring, searching for something to use as a weapon. There was nothing. How did these people

expect them to survive? He couldn't fight that thing with his bare hands.

"Just stay out of the way, my friend. I'll take care of this." Flint hissed, darting forward and crouching low to the ground, his black tail flicking angrily behind him.

Nox didn't like that plan one bit. But what could he do? Without a weapon—

The floor beside the cages cracked open, and a weapon rack ascended from somewhere below. Nox darted for it. There wasn't much to choose from, but now wasn't the time to be picky. He snatched a worn javelin from the rack and whirled around in time to watch Flint leap atop the ape as he lumbered up from his fall.

Flint landed on the beast's chest and scraped his long claws down, drawing blood.

The ape yowled. Big brown eyes widening with shock and pain, his hairy fist clenched around Flint's tail. He yanked the huge cat off like he was a mere kitten and flung him away.

Flint crashed into the ring wall and smacked down atop the dirt.

"Flint!" Nox raced to his bondmate's side. *"Are you all right?"*

Nox's hands tightened around the javelin, ready to defend Flint while he lay dazed in the dirt. But the beast shifted away from them, spotting a man at the weapon rack.

"Ow, that smarted." Flint shook his head.

Nox exhaled in relief. *"He's busy for the moment. Take your time getting up."* Nox kept one eye on Flint as he staggered to his feet and watched the ape barrel toward the man at the rack with the other.

The man saw the beast coming. He snagged a longsword and jumped back just before the ape collided with the rack.

Metal clanged against the stone walls. The ape yowled again, shaking the arm he'd bloodied flinging the weapons aside.

The injury only seemed to infuriate him more. He rounded on the man, smacking the longsword away like it was a twig. Then he clutched the screaming man around the middle with both of his massive fists.

The man shrieked in agony, his eyes bulging. The *crack* of bones resounded in the ring. The ape crushed him to death in only an instant. Then the beast dropped him to the ground and ripped into his belly, pulling out his innards and feasting on them.

Nox resisted the urge to heave as the crowd roared around him. His gaze jerked up to the stands. Though a few women and children turned away from the gory sight, most clapped and cheered.

It was sickening. How could these people root for this?

He spared a glance at the central box. That glass jar still rested on the ledge, sand covering the bottom now in a shallow layer. The dark king smirked, his stare glued to the ape as he shoved the dead man's intestines into his mouth, biting down with a wet *crunch*. Lark's gaze was just as focused, but her face held an expression of pure horror, her hand loosely covering her mouth, her hazel eyes glossy with unshed tears.

That man was there one minute, fighting for his life, and gone the next. That ape ended him in the space of a heartbeat. If Nox wasn't careful, he or Flint might be next.

The two remaining men creeped out of the cage while the ape was busy. They scrambled to the downed weapon rack, then hurriedly pulled weapons from the wreckage.

Nox could see their mouths moving, but couldn't hear what they said over the slurping of the ape and the roar of the crowd. Not that he would understand them, could he hear anyway. But the pair appeared to be coordinating an attack.

"Should we have another go at the beast while he's distracted?" Flint stretched beside him.

"Are you sure you're up for it?" he asked warily, eyeing his bondmate for injuries.

As they hesitated beside the ring wall, the men put their plan into action. Seems they had the same thought. They leaped atop the ape in tandem, stabbing their blades into his back.

The ape roared, dropping a handful of viscera and whipping around. He smacked the first man aside.

The man's sword clattered to the ground, and he slammed into the dirt in front of the cages. The second man backed away warily, his blade lodged in the ape's back and his hands raised in front of him in submission.

But the ape opened his massive jaw and roared again. Spittle and flecks of blood sprayed all over the shaking man's face. Then the ape clutched the man's skull in his massive fist and lifted him by his stringy black hair. He smacked him into the ground, over and over.

Bones cracked and blood exploded from the poor man's body, spraying across the dirt. The front row of spectators shrieked and backed away from the rain of red splattering their clothes.

Flint's ears pulled back flat against his skull as he watched the carnage. *"I still think I can take him. I just need to snag my jaws around his neck. Can you distract him so he doesn't see me coming?"*

Nox gulped. He watched the ape fling the limp body of the man aside and return to his meal.

The crowd was wild now, frenzied with bloodlust. Men screamed encouragement at the ape while children looked on, watching the ape tear into the dead men like this was nothing unusual. People were still eating, smiling around their mouthfuls of food.

Nox opened his mouth, ready to agree to Flint's plan. They had to finish this. Sooner rather than later.

But that was when the beast glanced up and met his gaze. Nox stared into the ape's big brown eyes, and something inside his soul screamed, drowning out the crowd. Their eager cheers faded, and the world stood still.

"No." He lurched up from his crouch beside Flint. *"Wait here. Trust me."*

Nox walked, his steps measured and sure. After one step, he let the javelin fall out of his clenched fist. It thunked into the dirt, instantly forgotten.

"Nox, what are you doing?" Flint's panicked voice reached him, but it was a mere whisper in the back of his mind.

"It's all right," he whispered back. *"I know what I'm doing."*

Nox took another step, his gaze still locked with the beast's. Those big brown eyes widened as he drew closer. His fist stopped moving. He stopped shoving the dead man's guts into his mouth and stared back.

"I'm sorry, my friend," Nox said soothingly as he approached.

The ape rumbled in the back of his throat at the sound of his voice. But he made no aggressive move toward him.

Nox held the ape's gaze. He was nearly upon him now. Another step, and he would be close enough for the beast to snatch him up and end him. And though that thought should've sent fear scrambling up his spine, it didn't.

Nox took that step. And then another. He marched right up to the ape and laid a comforting hand on his bloodied fist.

"It doesn't have to be like this. We don't need to fight. We don't have to give them what they want," he whispered, holding the ape's gaze.

Nox could see it in the beast's eyes. He was a prisoner, too. An unwilling participant in these bloody games. If not for the crippling hunger and a drive to live, he'd have never attacked those men. He wanted out.

They were the same. They were *exactly* the same.

The crowd fell silent. Everyone gaped, jaws slack, looking at each other and shaking their heads as if to confirm what they were seeing was actually happening.

The ape sat on his haunches in the dirt. One massive arm curved out, and he wrapped it around Nox's back.

"Nox!" Flint bent back, ready to leap to his defense.

"No. Stay there. It's all right," Nox insisted.

The ape clutched him close, wrapping his arms around Nox and hugging him to his hairy chest. The animal's pungent musk and the bright tang of copper filled Nox's nostrils. But the beast's hold was not crushing. Not in the least. The ape clutched him like a child would his mother, soaking up all the comfort he offered.

The ape's body trembled around Nox. The beast was scared. Just as scared as he was furious. Just as full of regret as he was hunger.

The realization burned in Nox's gut. This ape didn't want to be a killer. He wanted to be free. To be loved. He could sense it in the depths of his soul. The frightened animal inside called to him, and all the aggression Nox had been hoping to expend in the ring, all the rage boiling inside of him, simply evaporated.

These people wanted blood. But in that moment, he knew this was the true defiance. He wouldn't give them blood and gore and destruction. He would show them the depths of love he felt for this animal. And maybe, just maybe, some of the fools watching would understand how deeply wrong all this was.

They were not meant to be enemies. They were kindred souls.

Nox clutched the ape and whispered soothingly. "It's all right, my friend. I'm here. We're the same."

He held the ape for long moments, listening to the panicked beat of his heart slow. The crowd remained silent, the people staring wide eyed, perched on the edges of their seats.

Finally, a voice boomed from the stands. The dark king stood at the edge of the box. He eyed Nox clutching the ape, and though he tried to conceal it with a stoic expression, Nox glimpsed surprise in his dark eyes.

He gestured beside him at the glass jar. All the sand sat on the bottom now. The dark king spoke again, and his voice bore a note of warning.

Movement near the cages drew Nox's gaze. The lone man remaining scrambled to his feet and raced for the cages. What was he in such a hurry for?

But then the ground rumbled. A spark shot up from the dirt, spearing Nox in his bare feet. Dull pain radiated up his legs. The ape pulled his arms back and stood, trembling and growling.

"*Ah, what is that?*" Flint yelped behind him.

Nox was still staring at the man in the cage. He alone appeared unaffected by the painful blasts. They continued to pulse through the floor, increasing in intensity with every breath he drew.

"*Quick, back to the cages,*" Nox yelled.

Soon, he barreled into one of the empty cages, and the shooting zap in his feet disappeared. Once they had all returned, and the ape lumbered back to his metal cage on the far side of the ring, the doors slammed shut, and the *buzz* in the ground halted.

What now? Nox crouched beside Flint, his chest heaving as he fought to catch his breath. At least he'd leaped into the same cage as his bondmate. They better not separate them again.

The dark king spun around and sat back down. Then he leaned over the arm of his chair and spoke in Nox's sister's ear.

Lark shivered, clutching her arms tightly around her chest. Then she rose and strode to the front of the box.

Nox hadn't had much time to study her, what with everything happening in the ring. She looked healthy and well fed, dressed in a floor-sweeping dress similar to the ones the beauty wore, but in a shade of light blue.

Had she recognized him as he fought? She didn't give any sign as she stood there, but Nox had a feeling that was by design.

As her half-brother, their resemblance wasn't so strong that the people here would suspect they were related. But even though they'd been raised in different countries, they spent enough time together in their later years that she would know him. And Flint was kind of hard to miss. He wasn't aware of any other man who'd bonded a jagoth.

Why was she ignoring him? Was she afraid to draw attention to him?

More importantly, what was she doing at the front of the box?

He didn't have to wait long for that question to be answered. Lark opened her mouth and started to sing. Her voice rang out, so lovely and sweet, around the notes of a song he didn't recognize. It was clearly something she'd learned recently, for it was the same language all these people spoke.

The crowd stared at her with adoring eyes. He couldn't fault them for that. Lark's voice was beyond compare. Like the beauty, she made the guttural tones of the puzzling tongue sound lovely. The melody wrapped around him, and for a short time, Nox almost forgot about the enormous heap of trouble he was in.

As the song drew to a close, Lark's eyes trailed over the cages. She only spared him a quick glance, but the moment her eyes connected with his, he saw the recognition there. He sensed the depth of emotion hiding behind her eyes. He heard it in her voice as she sang that foreign song.

Just like the ape, Lark was afraid. His sister was terrified.

But she didn't allow her gaze to linger. She turned back to the crowd, looking into the smiling faces of the folk crowding the stands. And as she sang the last lines to the beautiful tune, the crowd erupted into a deafening thunder of cheering and applause.

The crowd continued to hoot and holler before rising to their feet to leave. Lark spun around without meeting his gaze again and disappeared through the back door. She followed the dark king, who spoke quietly with the man surrounded by crows. The spider trailed behind and slammed the door closed.

And though Nox should breathe easy now that it was clear the trial was over and everyone was leaving, his heart refused to quiet.

It was that single look from Lark. Deep down, he knew. She wasn't afraid for herself. That terror he'd glimpsed in her eyes was all for him. The knowledge made goosebumps break out across his flesh and a deep pit clench in his belly.

That look in his sister's eyes confirmed what he'd feared as soon as the cage door slammed closed. He hadn't survived the last of the danger. It had only just begun.

Out With It

Violet leaned down, staring into her cousin's big hazel eyes. The dawn sun shone in the open windows, highlighting his springy blond curls as he bounced in the crib. They were alone in the cabin, with only her Uncle Aren for company. Ryon had left with Muse as soon as the first hint of dawn rose, likely to scrounge up some breakfast.

"Vi-lit," Dylen cooed, reaching out with his tiny fingers, a bubbly grin stretching across his face.

"Hey, buddy." She lifted her cousin from the crib, unable to still her own smile as the little boy clutched her tightly.

They'd been working on the raft for over a week. Last night, Uncle Aren finally declared the vessel seaworthy. This morning, they would set sail, following Muse's instructions out to sea. All of them except for the little boy she cradled in her arms.

"Do we really need to leave him?" She turned to her uncle, shooting him a glare as he stuffed his pack full of his belongings.

"I don't want to leave him either, Vi. But who knows how danger-ous this journey will be? And the raft is not exactly the safest spot to keep a little boy still learning how to walk. Dylen will be much safer here. We'll come back for him after we find Lark and Nox."

Violet sighed. "I know you're right. I'm just gonna miss the little guy."

"Vi-lit, bye-bye," Dylen said, clearly used to watching the three of them leave every morning to work on the raft. Aren had already tried to explain they would be gone for longer, but at his age, it was unclear how much he understood.

"Bye-bye, Dylen. Vi-lit loves you." She tweaked his tiny nose, smil-ing when he giggled. Movement drew her gaze as the freckle-faced girl who'd volunteered to watch Dylen appeared in the doorway.

"Here, let me have him." Aren held out his arms, and Violet reluc-tantly handed her cousin over. Aren strode across the cabin, whisper-ing softly to his son. After planting a loud kiss on the little boy's cheek that had him laughing uproariously, Aren handed him over to the girl and returned to packing his things.

Violet settled down beside her cot to finish packing. "I'm still not sure why you and Aunt Lark decided to become parents out here."

Aren chuckled. "We didn't exactly plan it."

"I would've thought with Aunt Lark being a healer, she wouldn't make that kind of mistake."

"Normally, you'd be right. But we were becalmed in the Still Sea for quite a while. She ran out of the herbs she needed for moon tea before long."

"Huh. And you didn't think to return to Dracwood? Weren't you afraid to have a baby out here all alone?"

"That was the plan, actually. We had every intention of returning home before Dylen's birth. But just before we'd planned to leave, we discovered an island with a group of people nearly as welcoming as these folks are. They had a midwife who offered to help with the birth. So we stayed."

"That was lucky. And then what, you went right back to exploring, only with a baby in tow?"

"Yep." Aren grinned. "Sure, it wasn't ideal, but we'd made a promise to Kayda, and we wanted to see it through. Honestly, it wasn't much more trouble after Dylen was born. He loves being at sea. There's nothing quite like a rocking boat to soothe a colicky baby."

Violet offered her uncle a wan smile as she stood and cinched her pack closed. "Well, let's go rescue his mother, shall we?"

Aren grinned again. "Thanks for this, Vi. I'm glad you came."

"Me, too."

They exited the cabin, quickly spotting Ryon and Muse surrounded by a circle of villagers beside the central firepit. Old Balun sat beside Ryon, chattering away in that baffling language.

Ryon looked up as he approached and met her eyes. Violet's belly fluttered. She'd hoped the more she grew to know him that odd reaction to his presence would fade, but if anything, it had only gotten stronger.

"You ready to sail?" Aren called out.

Ryon patted Balun on the shoulder, spoke a few more words, and then rose. "Let me grab my bag." He jogged past with a quiet, "Good morning, Violet."

Violet blinked, and warmth flooded her cheeks. "Good morning," she called after him.

Aren cleared his throat beside her, sending her a knowing look.

"What?" she asked.

"Nothing." Aren chuckled and let the matter slide. Then he waved goodbye to all the villagers crowded around the firepit and whistled for Muse, who flew up and landed on his gauntleted arm.

Ryon reappeared, and they set off through the forest. Violet's mind wandered during the trek, her thoughts flitting around and setting off a mess of anxiety in her belly.

What would they encounter on their voyage? Did they have any chance of finding the underwater city? Did it even exist, or had the lone survivor been too addled from his experience that he'd imagined it?

It certainly seemed far-fetched. She'd never heard of any people surviving below the sea for more than a few moments, let alone a whole city remaining hidden for decades—even centuries.

Her gaze settled on Ryon. His broad back bent as he ducked beneath a low-hanging tree branch on the path ahead. What secret was he hiding that would help them? She'd tried asking again while they'd been away from the village working on the raft, but whenever the subject came up, he would shake his head and stare off into the forest like he was certain he was being watched.

But once they were out on the open sea, he'd have no more reasons to hide. That, more than anything, drove her forward, even when that familiar rush of fear settled over her as she strode across the rickety old footbridge spanning the river.

Soon, they made it to the raft and strapped down their supplies. Then all that was left was to shove off.

"This is the moment of truth." Aren's smile broadened. "Here's where we see if we'll be completing our journey today or taking a swim."

Violet knew her uncle was joking. The raft was sound. They'd tested it already, and it floated well, with no sign of decay like he'd reported with the papery ploom fruit tree logs. Still, as she sat and waited for Aren to shove the raft in the river, her heart sped up all the same.

This was it. One step closer to finding Nox and Lark.

Splash. Water droplets splattered her trousers. The raft slowly picked up speed, rushing along the wide river.

They departed while the tide was out, trusting the single sail mounted in the raft's center to push them out to sea. They'd crafted a pair of oars to bring along and a big wooden trunk to store their things. Other than that, the raft was practically bare except for the wooden perch Aren secured for Muse on the front of the flat structure.

It would be an unusual experience, living, eating, and sleeping on the raft. They'd made certain to build it oversized, with plenty of room for Nox, Lark, and Flint once they found them. Still, Violet couldn't help but worry about what might happen if they crossed a bad storm or if a nightmare sent her tumbling off the edge in the middle of the night.

"You all right?" Ryon sat beside her, cross-legged, his skirt spread out across his knees.

Violet smiled. "Yeah. I'm fine. Just wondering what comes next."

"We'll find out, together."

Violet waited until the island faded into the early morning dew before she asked the question burning in her mind.

"Out with it now. What do you have that will help us?"

Ryon grinned. "I'm surprised you waited this long to ask."

Aren shuffled over, abandoning his spot at the mast. "I'm dying to know, too."

"Where I come from, there live beautiful birds called orecolns. If you gain their favor, they will reward you with one of these."

Violet peered at Ryon closely, watching as he curled a hand through the thick locks of his shoulder length black hair. What was he doing?

He grabbed one of the locks and began prying it apart. After only a moment, he frowned and pulled a knife off his belt. A small slit in the lock revealed a flash of silver.

"What is that?" Violet's eyes widened as he tugged the tiny shining item from his hair. "A feather?" She supposed that made sense if he'd gotten it from a bird. "How will a feather help us find an underwater city?"

But Aren gasped. "A feather... I heard something about feathers long ago. Conall and Kayda spoke of them, at the battle in the Abandoned Lands. Something about wishes?"

Ryon nodded. "You're right. Silver feathers, like these, grant the person one wish."

"Really? That's incredible." Violet held out her hand. "May I?"

"Sure, just don't drop it. And don't bleed on it." Ryon slid it on her palm. The whisper soft feather tickled her skin, glimmering in the sun.

"Why would I bleed on it?" she lifted a brow.

"That's the only way to get your wish. They're called bloodfeathers."

"Bloodfeathers," Violet repeated, staring at him curiously. Her gaze fell on his hand. The gash on his palm had healed, no longer requiring a bandage. But the ghost of the wound remained, a shallow scar painting his hand in a neat, even line.

His bloody palm... The blood in his hair... "Is that how you learned to speak our language?"

Ryon nodded. "Yes. Silver feathers will give one person one wish. But there are limitations."

Aren scratched his jaw. "What limitations?"

"The silver feathers can only change the person making the wish. And whatever change you wish for is permanent, so you have to decide carefully. Many of my people learned the hard way that what you wish for may one day become your greatest regret. There are often unforeseen consequences that you must learn to live with."

Violet twirled the lovely feather between her fingers. "How many wishes have you made?"

"Just two, so far. The orecolns require any who wish to be gifted feathers, first make the same wish. That one I made when I was still a boy."

"What's that?" Aren asked.

But Violet suspected she already knew. "They want you to know how to speak to them, don't they?"

"Yes."

She wrinkled her nose. "What consequences came with that?"

"Like I said, it's permanent. Now, whenever a bird sings, I don't hear their song, I hear their words." He sighed. "The orecolns song, it's a thing of beauty. So achingly lovely that not many in my village are willing to make the sacrifice. Not even for the chance at more wishes."

Aren scratched the blond scruff on his chin. "How many wishes do they give you once you can talk to them?"

"See, that's the thing. There are no guarantees. It's been almost two decades since I made that first wish, and in all that time, I wasn't given another feather. Not until recently."

Aren leaned over, gazing at the feather clutched between her fingers. Then he shot a look at Ryon's head. "How many do you have now?"

Locks covered his head, the rope-like strands swaying gently with the motion of the raft. "Before I left the mountain, they gave me thirteen."

Violet's eyes widened. "Thirteen? Nothing for so long, then thirteen all at once? Why?"

Ryon grimaced. "Mother Orea sent me on a quest."

"Mother Orea?" Violet repeated.

"What quest?" Aren asked at the same time.

Ryon drew in a deep breath. "Hold on, I'll explain. Mother Orea is the rarest kind of orecoln. The silver orecolns are always male. There are nearly a hundred of them at any one time. The female orecolns are typically born a dull gray, and their feathers are still lovely, but they hold no magic. Once in every generation, a female orecoln is born with golden feathers. She becomes Mother Orea until another golden female is born to replace her."

"What do golden feathers do?" Violet asked, her mind whirling with all this new information.

"Golden feathers grant a single wish, the same as the silver—but the golden feathers allow you to change one thing about *someone else* in exchange for a personal sacrifice."

Aren shivered. "That must be the feather Dru had. Kayda said he saved her life with magic that required a sacrifice."

Ryon smiled. "This Dru must be very lucky. Golden feathers are incredibly difficult to come by. I've been trying to earn one my whole life."

Violet stared at him. She wanted to ask him why he needed a golden feather so badly, but Aren spoke up before she could blurt the question out.

"You still haven't told us what quest they sent you on."

"Before I left, the orecolns presented me with a riddle. They told me to wait by the shore down below and to look for one with a gull's egg gaze, hatched in moonlight, and baptized by dusk."

Violet stared at the feather between her fingers and let the strange words sink in. It meant nothing to her. But when she glanced up and met Ryon's gaze, her heart picked up speed at how closely he was watching her.

Warmth spread across her chest and heated her pale cheeks. "What? What does it mean?"

"I think they wanted me to find you."

"Me?" She scoffed. "Really?"

That couldn't be true, could it? Some birds she'd never even heard of knew she'd been coming and sent Ryon out after her? It was too bizarre to be believed. She thrust out the feather toward him, trying to hand it back.

Ryon shook his head. "You can hold on to that one. I have more."

Aren blinked. "So that's it? That's all the birds asked of you, to wait by the sea?"

"They asked me to find the one who fit the riddle and bring them back to the mountain. No matter how long it took. And then they gave me the feathers. They said I'd need them and to share them freely. That the journey would be fraught with danger."

Aren peered at Violet curiously. "I've never seen a gull's egg before... What do they look like?"

Ryon smiled. "They're lovely. A blend of blue, red, and purple."

Violet's stomach flipped. That did sound an awful lot like the color of her eyes.

"All right. Say we believe you." Aren frowned. "That means you aren't doing all this out of the kindness of your heart. You want to bring Violet back with you. Back to your mountain."

"Yeah," Violet squeaked. "When were you planning to tell me that little detail?"

Ryon cringed. "I guess I should've mentioned it sooner."

"What will they do with her when you take her there?" Aren asked.

"I honestly don't know," Ryon admitted. He shifted away from Aren and directed his words to her. "If you don't want to go, I won't force you. But I've never known the orecolns to harm anyone. Think about it. If you're at all curious to learn why they want you, I'll be happy to take you after we find your family."

Violet crossed her arms and stared back at Ryon. A part of her wanted to be angry at him for keeping this from her. She'd believed he was helping her because he wanted to. Because she'd saved him back on his island and he wanted to repay her. But now, learning he had his own agenda all along... It certainly made her look at him in a different light.

But still, she couldn't help being curious why these magical creatures wanted to meet her.

"All right. I'll think about it," she said finally.

Ryon grinned. "Good."

Muse whistled loudly from her perch at the front of the raft.

Ryon cocked his head, listening intently. He whistled back, a single sweet note, and then he turned to Aren. "Muse says to turn south."

Aren nodded. "She still can't hear Lark?"

Ryon whistled again, then waited for a reply. Muse only shook her head, back and forth rapidly.

"No. She still hasn't spoken to her since she was taken."

Violet's heart sank at the news. But surely Muse wouldn't be able to sense where her aunt was if she weren't still alive. Just because they couldn't communicate currently didn't mean they had to fear the worst.

Sooner or later, they would learn the truth. Violet stared out at the blue expanse before her and sighed. Next stop, the city under the sea.

Pity or a Test

Nox crouched in the cage, watching silently as all the spectators trickled out. Most seemed eager to be off, filing out in a fast and orderly queue. A few couples lingered, too caught up chatting to rush out. A little boy wandered away from the adults and creeped up to the edge of the seating to stare down into the cages.

Flint flicked his tail at the boy and bared his teeth. The little boy laughed, baring his own teeth and showcasing his gap-toothed grin.

"What is the deal with these people?" Flint asked.

Nox frowned as the boy's father scooped him up and headed for the exit. *"I don't know. If we could find Lark, maybe she'd be able to explain."*

The last spectators disappeared, and a door slammed across the ring. The spider strolled in with the beauty at his side. Smiling and chattering at the spider, the beauty's hands swung at her sides as her long red dress swished around her legs.

Nox's heart sped up when he spotted what the spider was carrying. *"Get behind me, Flint. He's got that rotting dart blower."*

Nox didn't wait for them to finish their stroll. He hopped to the front of the cage, gripping the metal bars tightly. "Don't shoot him with that thing again. I can keep him calm. I promise. Flint will follow wherever you lead."

The spider ignored him. He stopped before the cage and aimed his mask directly at Flint. He was close enough Nox could've reached out through the bars and grabbed his black tunic had he wanted. But Nox kept his hands firmly locked around the bars.

"Please. He listens to me. We're bondmates," he pleaded.

The beauty stopped at the spider's side, her head cocked. She slid her gray gaze over Nox, then squinted behind him, no doubt sizing up Flint.

Nox wouldn't get anywhere with the spider... He was already raising the dart blower to the mouth-hole of his mask. But the beauty... It was likely just his imagination, thinking she understood him, but maybe she could be swayed.

He stared directly at the girl. "I swear, Flint will do you no harm." He let go of the bars and shifted within the cage to block the spider's shot. "Leave him alone. Please."

The beauty laid a hand on the spider's sleeve and spoke to him quietly. The spider tensed and shook his head, replying harshly. They chattered back and forth, their voices rising in volume until the spider dropped the dart blower.

The beauty smiled triumphantly, then backed away, turning her gaze back inside the cage. She met Nox's eyes again and nodded once, lifting a slim brow.

Nox grinned. "Thank you! Thank you, you won't regret this."

The spider shoved the dart blower in his pocket, but when his gloved hand reappeared, it wasn't empty. He lifted that metal pole again, and he waved it in the air, making sure they saw what he held.

"I get it. We'll behave." Nox backed away from the bars and kneeled beside Flint.

"I thought they couldn't understand you? How did you manage that?" Flint asked.

Nox shrugged. *"The beauty took pity on us, I guess."*

"Or this is a test." Flint's ears flattened against his skull as the door slammed open. *"I saw what that pole can do."*

"Me, too. Don't give the spider any reason to use it."

The spider barked at them, gesturing for them to leave the cage. Then he strode sideways and threw open the door beside theirs.

"C'mon. I told them you'd behave. Don't make me a liar."

Flint bared his teeth again and cocked his head—his version of a smirk. *"I'll be a good little kit, don't you worry."*

They inched out of the cage, making it out at the same time as the only other remaining man. Even with his step wobbly and dried blood caked to the side of his head, the man jumped to comply, lining up behind the beauty with his gaze set on his feet.

Nox and Flint followed suit, though they both kept an eye on their surroundings instead of staring numbly at the floor. With the place deserted, the vast ring echoed with the sound of every footfall as they strolled toward the stairwell.

A keening wail from the metal cage made Nox's step falter. What would become of the ape? Likely, the beast would be starved again, forced to slaughter more men for his next meal. One day, perhaps even killed by some man who got a lucky hit in.

Would the beauty creep into the ape's cage and rub that cream on his wounds, like she'd done with the injured men? Or would she leave the poor beast to suffer? He bet it would be the latter.

The spider barked a word in warning and smacked the metal pole against his leg.

Nox tore his gaze from the metal cage. Clearly, they didn't want him to stand there and gawk. He forced his feet to move, though it tore at his heart to leave the creature there to his unknown fate.

The spider led them back to the stairwell.

"Do you know where they're taking us?" Flint asked as they descended.

Nox blinked. Flint must have seen none of this, since he'd been unconscious when they brought him to the ring. *"This leads back to the cages. We came this way earlier."*

Flint's tail whipped through the air. *"I suppose it was too much to hope they'd free us after that little performance."*

"Yeah, I don't think so."

Soon, they arrived at the bottom of the stairs and entered the first hall. Flint's fur bristled as the animal cries reached his ears.

"All these animals... Remind me again why I have to behave? I can have my jaws around the man's neck, and you can subdue the—"

"Stop, Flint. We can't." He met his bondmate's yellow eyes and inclined his head down the hall. *"They're never alone. See?"*

Flint might have missed the men stationed at the end of each corridor, but Nox surely hadn't. They stood like statues behind their animal masks, but he had no doubt they'd leap into motion at the first sign of violence.

Flint's tail twitched before curling between his legs. But he followed without further complaint. They left the hall with the animals, their angry voices and pained calls disappearing with the slam of the heavy door behind them.

Countless cages filled with men and the occasional beast dotted the next corridor. And the next. So many. All of them were no doubt forced to compete in those sick games. Nox walked silently, his fists clenched at his sides. He concentrated on the gentle aroma of the beauty wafting around him to keep his rage in check.

Soon, they were back in front of Flint's empty cage. The spider threw open the door and halted beside it, head cocked expectantly.

"Go ahead, Flint. Stick close to the spider. I'm going to slip in behind you."

Flint sauntered forward, and Nox darted in at the last moment.

The spider shouted, his guttural words full of anger. He stepped forward, the pole raised.

The beauty spoke up, and she set a hand on the spider's arm. They argued again, but if earlier was any indication, the beauty would win.

Nox hid the grin that fought to spread.

Whoever this girl was, she called the shots. The spider might not like it, but he deferred to her decision.

The door clanged shut. Nox sank to the floor as the spider and beauty led the last remaining survivor back to his cage.

"We're lucky that worked," Nox admitted.

Flint nodded, then stalked to the hole in the wall. *"The boy. He's not here."*

"Maybe they moved him while we were gone." Nox frowned, sensing his bondmate's distress.

Flint had formed a bond with the lad during the long days they'd spent as neighbors. The boy continued to feed him, and though the foul stew had not been enough to satisfy him, it kept him from starvation. If not for the boy's kindness, Flint would be weakened and near mad with hunger by now.

"I didn't see him in any of the cages we passed. Do you think they set him free?"

Nox didn't want to destroy the glimmer of hope he heard in Flint's voice. *"Yeah, maybe,"* he replied, though deep down, he had a feeling that hope was far-fetched.

"At least I have you here with me now. You'll share your slop with me, won't you?"

Nox grinned. *"Sure, buddy. My slop, is your slop."*

But it wasn't long before his smile fell. Would they even feed both of them? Or had he signed himself up for days of starvation by shoving into the cell with Flint?

He nudged the morbid thought aside. Either way, they'd find out soon enough.

Footsteps echoed down the hall. Nox leaned sideways, staring out into the dim corridor. Was that the wolf with their dinner already? It had been hard to tell the passage of time with all the adrenaline pumping through him, but it hardly seemed long enough when breakfast had been served just before they took them to the ring.

But the first thing he glimpsed was a flash of red fabric. The beauty then. She must be back with her cream to see to the wounded man down the hall.

Nox leaned away from the hall. She wouldn't be visiting them, that's for sure. He'd escaped the ring without a single injury, and Flint was free from gashes, though he might have a lump or two on his thick skull after walloping into the wall.

Imagine his surprise when the beauty passed his former cell and strode right up to his and Flint's cage. The spider was with her, as always, and a third man trailed behind them.

He was undeniably handsome. So much that even the thick layer of grime on his tattered clothes and the thick beard covering his face couldn't fully disguise it. His hair and beard were both plaited neatly, one thick braid for each that appeared at odds with his ratty clothes.

His brown shorts and dirty tan tunic had so many holes it was a marvel they still functioned as clothing and didn't slip off his thin, dark brown limbs.

What was most surprising was that this man—this prisoner—was smiling and chatting comfortably with the beauty, like they were old friends and not jailer and captive. But when they stopped outside of Nox's cell, the man peeked inside, and the spider began opening the door, the tone of the conversation shifted quickly.

The handsome fellow shook his head violently, backing away. A steady stream of words flew out of his lips, and Nox didn't need to know the language to realize he was pleading. Same as the boy had so many days ago, this man begged his jailers for release.

No, not for release. Simply to be jailed elsewhere. The fear in the man's eyes as he stared at Flint was unmistakable. He wanted no part of being housed in the same cell as a jagoth.

Nox couldn't blame him. Few men were immune to the fear that came from facing a massive cat as big as a wolf.

But it was soon apparent the man's pleas fell on deaf ears. No matter how chummy he'd been with the beauty during their stroll, she didn't lift a finger to help him when the spider threw open the cell door and ordered him inside. And though he kept up his barrage of pleading, the man shuffled inside, flinching when the door slammed closed behind him.

What were they doing, throwing another in the cell with them? Did they mean to drive Flint to murder?

Nox leaned sideways, peering beyond the cage door while the man tore at the metal bars, still screaming his pleas into the hall. He caught a single glimpse of the beauty with a gentle smile on her lips as she strode away.

"Dirty dust eaters, the whole lot of you are!" the man yelled, before falling silent.

Nox jolted where he sat, his heart thrumming to life. "What did you just say?"

The man stilled. Then he swiveled on the balls of his feet and stared down at him with brown eyes. "Ha." He laughed uproariously, the maddening sound bouncing off the walls and setting off a cascade of prickles on Nox's back. "Oh. I see what she did, that little minx."

"You can understand me?" Nox exhaled, a grin splitting his face. "Thank the Mother. I've been going mad in here. Who are you? What is this place? Who are these people? How do you speak both tongues?"

The man's laughter finally died down, and he shot a wary glance at Flint. "I'll answer your questions, but only if you keep that animal away from me."

Nox waved a hand. "Oh, that's Flint. He's my bondmate. He won't harm you. I promise."

Just to be safe, he spoke to Flint as well. *"This man understands me. Don't make any sudden moves. He's afraid of you."*

Flint curled up in a corner and laid his head on his paws. *"I'll rest over here. Get him talking."*

Some of the tension in the man's shoulders lifted when Flint lay down. He blew out a shaky breath, sat beside Nox, and leaned against the wall. He stuck out a hand. "My friends call me Iggy."

Nox gripped his hand and shook. "Iggy. I'm Nox."

Iggy split a look between him and Flint. "Hmm. A jagoth for a bondmate, and you're thanking the Mother. You must hail from Raimire."

Nox grinned. "I do. You've been there?"

Iggy sighed. "Not for a long time. I'm from Joria, myself, but I've been a prisoner here for so long, I can't even say. Years. Decades, more likely."

Nox's heart sank. Decades? There really was no chance of being set free then, was there?

"That's how I learned their tongue. Time aplenty for it, with no one else to speak to. You're the first man I've met from back home since I got here."

All those years Iggy spent here and there'd been no one else? Though he couldn't say it was too surprising. The Still Sea was enough of a deterrent to keep boats from making the voyage. Really, it was stranger that Iggy had ended up here at all.

"How were you captured?" Nox asked.

"My family controls one of the major trading companies in Joria. I was out on an expedition searching for a new trade route to Dracwood when we stumbled upon these people. Well, they stumbled upon us, is more accurate. There was an old geezer here at the time who could speak both tongues. I convinced them to make a deal with my family for my release, but it ended up falling through."

Nox's brow wrinkled. "There was a revolution in Joria twenty years ago. None of the families who were in power then still are."

"Well, that explains it, I suppose." Iggy picked at a hole in his shorts. "I can't say I'm surprised. My brother would've stopped at nothing to get me back. He must be long dead."

Nox's heart clenched. It couldn't have been easy on him, being forgotten here all these years. Why hadn't these people let him go when it became clear his family wasn't planning to seek his release? If what he said was true, he was just the same as he and Flint. Innocent of all but sailing the ocean.

"Who are these people?" Nox asked. "Why do they keep so many beasts and men as prisoners?"

"They call themselves the Thalass. They live in this city, ruled over by Jurdan the Supreme, their great king."

Could that be the man he was thinking of as the dark king—the one that made that disgusting sensation creep up his spine? "Is he the man with the long black hair and fancy robes that sits in the central box?"

Iggy nodded. "Yeah, that's him. He rules with an iron fist. He sends any who commit crimes to live out their lives here in the cells."

"And those sick battles with beasts? How often do they hold them?"

"It depends." Iggy shrugged. "Some weeks, nearly every day. Other weeks, only once or twice. There's no rhyme or reason I can see behind it."

"I can't believe these people have been here all this time with no one back home realizing it."

Iggy chuckled. "That's the thing. If the other prisoners are to be believed, they weren't always here."

Nox cocked a brow. "What do you mean?"

"They have a legend about Jurdan the Supreme. Long ago, the Thalass were said to live in another land. One rife with monsters far crueler and more vicious than the creatures in the fights. Their life was a constant struggle. Food there was scarce, and dangers lurked around every corner. But Jurdan delivered them from that land and brought them here, centuries ago."

"Hundreds of years ago?" Nox frowned. That couldn't be right. He'd be long dead. "Are they talking about the first Supreme? This one's great-great-grandfather?"

"No. They speak about him like he's a god." Iggy's hand trembled. "From what I can gather, they might be right. If what you told me is true, then I've been here twenty years. In all that time, Jurdan hasn't aged a day. He looks the same today as he did the first day I set eyes on him."

Nox's stomach churned. How could that be? But even as disbelief washed over him, he pushed it aside. The Unseen. If Jurdan the Supreme was connected to that vile creature, then surely it was possible. Conall had told him of the promises he'd been offered when he destroyed the creature he'd found living under Dracwood. He'd offered him eternal life.

But if his brother really destroyed the Unseen twenty years ago, then how was this possible? How was this king—this god—here ruling over these people for centuries?

Nox kept at it, questioning Iggy for long hours, but all he had was rumors and stories passed down from the men he'd talked with in the cells. Who knew how much of it he could believe?

One thing was certain. He'd found an ally at long last. Two, even. Maybe he shouldn't read so much into the beauty's actions, but he wanted to. No matter that she was his jailor and he was a captive.

He'd gone to the ring wanting nothing to do with her after the way she rounded up Flint with the spider, but surely, her actions after could be interpreted as friendly. She'd trusted him to walk Flint through the halls. She'd sided with him when the spider wanted to tear him out of the cage with Flint. And then she'd brought him someone who could talk to him.

When he looked into her eyes, he sensed something far different from when he stared at Jurdan the Supreme. A softness behind her interest that did funny things to his insides. He would count her as a friend, if only in his own mind. And if that made him a fool, then so be it.

Wishing

R yon stared down into the dark water. They'd sailed for a full day and night before Muse called for a halt. The waters here, south and east of his island home, were far deeper and darker than the clear shallow seas they'd first sailed.

"Are you sure this is the spot?" Ryon whistled quietly.

"Yes. This is where she is. I can feel it," Muse replied.

"The island is somewhere below us," Ryon announced.

Aren nodded and tied down the sail.

"What's the plan now?" Violet asked. "Do we all use one of those feathers and wish to swim like fish?"

"You two are going without me," Aren said. "Someone needs to stay up here to make sure the raft doesn't float off course. I would ask you to do it, Vi, but I don't think you'd have the strength to man the oars."

Violet turned to him with a frown. "Are you sure, Uncle Aren?"

"Yeah. I've thought it through. If something has happened to Lark down there, I don't trust myself not to rush in after her and get myself captured. And like I said, someone has to man the oars. We don't have an anchor, and the water here looks too deep for one, even if we had one." Aren loosed a long, low sigh. "Besides, if what your mother told you is true, then you're meant to do this, Vi. I don't want to mess around with fate. Not when Lark's life depends on it."

Ryon sensed there was more to it than that. From the looks of the blond man's tense shoulders and the way he violently knotted the rope around the folded mast, he wanted nothing more than to go after his wife.

Aren was likely thinking of the little boy back on that island. As much as he loved his wife, he loved his son just the same. If something went wrong in the underwater city, he wanted to ensure Dylen didn't grow up an orphan.

Ryon could certainly respect that decision, even if Aren didn't want to voice it. Duty and loyalty to family was one thing he understood intimately.

Violet walked to her uncle's side and clasped him in a tight hug. "We'll find her. We'll find them all."

"I know you will." Aren offered her a pinched smile, then swung his gaze to Ryon. "Keep her safe."

"I will," Ryon vowed.

Violet pulled free from her uncle's embrace and crossed the raft to his side. She dug into her pocket and withdrew the shining silver feather he'd given her. "You're sure this is going to work?" she wrinkled her nose, staring down at the soft feather on her palm.

"It will." Ryon reached into his hair with his knife and slit one of his dreadlocks. He pulled free a feather for himself.

After they used these, that would leave him with ten. Not a lot, considering the wishes had to last them long enough to escape with Violet's family. They'd likely need three more just to ensure the others could survive the swim back to the raft. That only left him with seven to overcome whatever challenges they'd face freeing and escaping with everyone.

He buried the thought. It would be enough. It had to be.

Ryon twirled the feather in his fingers. "I've been thinking about what to wish. We have to be careful not to say anything that will lead to unforeseen consequences."

Violet's brow furrowed. "What do you mean?"

"Well, we could wish to breathe underwater, but that might leave us dependent on breathing water and not air."

Violet shuddered. "That could happen?"

Ryon shrugged. "Maybe. I've never heard of anyone wishing for anything like it."

"So, what will you wish for instead?" Aren asked.

"I plan to wish for the ability to breathe water as well as air," Ryon answered. "I think that wording will suffice. What do you think?"

Aren tipped back his hat. "Sounds like it might work."

Violet nodded and inhaled deeply. "Let's give it a shot."

Ryon flipped the knife to his hand and pricked his palm. He winced at the sharp pain, but he only cut a small slice. It was a tiny pinprick compared to the huge gash he'd given himself when he had to be certain his blood would soak into his hair.

"As soon as your blood touches the feather, that's when you make your wish. You remember the wording?" He wiped the blade on his skirt as a few droplets of warm blood pooled in his palm. Then he flipped it over and offered the hilt to Violet.

"I remember." She grasped the blade and nicked her own palm. She breathed in sharply but showed no other sign of pain. Then she met his eyes as a matching pool filled her cupped palm.

He took the blade back from her and slipped it on his belt. "Ready?"

Violet nodded. Together, they dropped the feathers on their hands. Warmth tingled across Ryon's skin. He closed his eyes and made his wish.

Then he watched Violet, staring at her own palm, her mouth slack and fingers trembling. "Is that it? I felt warmth race up my arm, but then nothing. Did it work?"

Ryon grinned mischievously. "Only one way to find out." With that, he turned and leaped into the ocean. The jump sent him barreling below the surface. Before long, instinct tugged at him, begging his body to surface. He ignored the sensation and opened his mouth beneath the sea.

Cold water rushed into his lungs. The flooding sensation burned, and panic tore through his veins. But after half a heartbeat, the pain lessened, and his body adjusted to the odd sensation. Ryon stared down at the water in front of his face. He watched the current flow in and out of his mouth and nose and smiled.

He surfaced a moment later. Panic spread through him again as the water spewed out of his lungs in a huge gush. So much water. He choked, coughing and spraying the salty brew out endlessly. But finally, the stream subsided, and he sucked in a breath of fresh air.

He stared up at Violet's concerned face. "It worked." He grinned. "Takes a little getting used to at first, but the wish worked." He treaded water on the surface, spreading his arms out by his sides. Lucky for him, he was a strong swimmer after all his years scouring the mountain rivers.

But Violet... he suddenly realized he'd never asked her about her own skills. "You can swim, can't you?"

She huffed, crossing her arms. "Of course, I can. You think I'd agree to this fool plan if I couldn't?"

Ryon smiled at her indignation. "Then what are you waiting for? Hop in. The water's lovely."

Violet turned around. "You're sure you'll be all right?"

"Yeah, Muse and I will be fine," Aren said. "Go. Bring them back. I believe in you, Vi."

Violet nodded once, then spun around to face Ryon. She splashed into the water beside him, quickly surfacing with a sputter.

"Liar." She shivered. "It's cold."

"You'll get used to it." Ryon shrugged and grabbed Violet's hand. "When you go under, open your mouth and breathe in the water. It will feel like your lungs are burning at first, but it will pass after a breath or two."

Violet's eyes widened, but she sucked in a breath and ducked beneath the sea. Ryon followed her down.

He inhaled a breath of water, ignoring the burning sensation. He still clutched Violet's trembling hand, and he could see that despite his advice, she was reluctant to take it. Her fingers shook, her mouth still clamped tightly shut.

Ryon grabbed her hand and settled it on his chest. Violet's gaze zeroed in on him as his chest rose and fell against her fingers. Finally, she exhaled and sucked in a breath of water. Her wide eyes flitted around, and she tried to tear her hand out of his grasp and push to the surface.

Ryon held her steady. Soon, she abandoned her struggles as her chest, too, began to rise and fall with each intake of water.

Ryon tugged Violet's hand and dove deeper. Muse insisted Lark was down here, but for all they could see, she could be anywhere. After they swam down a short distance, the dim light afforded by the sun beating against the surface faded, and they were left swimming in an unending blue-black gloom.

But just as Ryon made peace with the idea of searching for the city by feel alone, a light appeared beneath him. Then another.

An enormous school of strange fish, more reminiscent of clouds than the finned creatures he'd spotted in the shallow coastal waters beside the islands, lit up the ocean below them. They exuded a yellow glow, bright enough to stave off the worst of the darkness.

As they swam closer, it became apparent the glowing clouds were condensed around two huge objects. The first was almost directly below them. Ryon stopped in his tracks. He gazed in awe as the school parted around it and more of the massive structure became visible.

This had to be what they were searching for. The oval structure was as long and wide as his island, if not bigger. It looked large enough that it could fit the mountain he'd grown up on within it. The cloud fish swam around it on all sides, making it clear the structure was not attached to the seafloor, but floated within the ocean.

Ryon's heart sped up. It certainly didn't look like a city. It looked more like a rock than anything, the sides smooth and shining beneath the fish's glow. He tugged Violet's hand, intending to head for what must be the city under the sea, but she didn't budge.

He swiveled in the water to study her. Her gaze wasn't locked on the immense city, but on the second structure. This one was farther away, and impossible to make out any finer details, but the shape was clear enough with all the cloud fish floating around and through it. It was a gargantuan ring, large enough it could fit the submerged city and another, just like it, through the open center.

Ryon tugged again, harder. Violet jolted, then turned her wide eyes to him.

He pointed down at the city. She nodded. They set off again, swimming through the water toward the massive shape.

Soon, they approached the husk of the massive structure. It shone even brighter the closer they got, and Ryon amended his earlier assessment. It wasn't rock. The floating island appeared to be made of some kind of metal, yet it held no hint of rust or even any debris or sand, but was unnaturally smooth.

He and Violet swam around it for a long while, searching vainly for an entrance. He'd begun to think the task would prove impossible, forcing them to give up and swim back to the surface, when he finally spotted something.

There was an indention in the smooth exterior. He swam for it.

Was it a cave? No. The hole in the casing was far too uniform for that, shaped like a perfect square.

He approached the edges, spotting nothing more than the same shining metal inside. Violet swam in ahead of him. The square dwarfed her, so massive, they could fit fifty more people inside with them.

She turned to face him after she hit the back wall of the square, but her eyes slid over him and landed on the wall.

Ryon followed her gaze and spotted a small box, the same metal again, but raised with a lid. He swam toward it, meeting Violet beside it.

Cautiously, he peeled back the lid. He half expected something to fly out and stab him when he slid it open, but nothing happened. There was nothing inside, either. Just another square of smooth metal hiding within.

Ryon frowned and started to lower the lid, but before he could shut it, Violet stuck her hand in and pressed down on the metal square.

A sheet of metal slammed down over the opening to the cave, sealing them inside. Light illuminated the space, streaming down from the ceiling, massively disorienting after the dimly lit sea.

Violet shook her head violently and pounded on the square, again and again.

Disoriented from the light, Ryon tore off, heading for the new wall. He slammed his hand against it, then dropped to the floor, digging his nails between the wall and the floor.

Guano. It was no use. The metal wouldn't budge. Wherever they were, they were stuck.

A great *whoosh* sounded. Ryon scrambled backward, bumping into Violet. Her wide eyes found him, and she grabbed his shoulders, clutching him tightly.

It took a moment before Ryon realized the water in the room was quickly draining. Within the space of a few heartbeats, the water level fell enough that their heads were above water.

Ryon coughed, tilting his head sideways while water spewed out of his lungs. Violet wasn't so quick to turn aside, and she caught him in the chest with a blast of water as it exploded out of her mouth. He was too busy gagging on salty water to be mad about it. Finally, the choking sensation faded, and air flooded in and out of his chest once again.

By the time they both adjusted to breathing normally, the water had receded completely. Then the wall opposite the new one that slammed down, dropped.

What in the...

Ryon blinked, flicking his sopping locks out of his eyes. A vast chamber spread out beyond them, filled with tiny replicas of the huge city they'd just entered. That was to say, tiny compared to the city. The metal ovals were still far bigger than he was, large enough that a dozen people could fit inside.

He strode forward cautiously, but it was soon clear the chamber was empty except for the metallic ovals.

"I've never seen anything like this," Violet exclaimed.

Ryon turned to her with a grin, then walked up to one of the ovals. "Me either. What do you think these are? Mini versions of the floating city?"

"Maybe they take these out when they leave to gather people? Though when they nabbed my uncle, they were on a normal sailing ship that floated above the waves."

Ryon squinted at the ceiling. "Look at that light. Where is it coming from?"

Violet shrugged. "Magic?" She raised her hand toward the ceiling. "It doesn't give off any heat."

Ryon frowned at Violet as water dripped from her drenched clothes. He was in the same state. All the supplies they'd brought with them would no doubt be equally sodden.

"We should look around. Try to find some clothes. If anyone sees us looking like this, they'll realize we don't fit in."

Violet nodded. "Good plan."

Ryon ducked behind the closest oval, searching the massive room. Tables and drawers perched along the far wall. Tools, some familiar but most utterly foreign, hung from the walls, everything neatly in place. He stopped in front of a large cabinet and began opening and closing each drawer.

Ryon finished with the first set of drawers and moved on to another. "We're lucky no one's spotted us yet. I'm surprised there weren't a bunch of those masked men waiting for us when that door opened."

"I doubt they've ever had anyone sneak in from that doorway before." Violet giggled. "Who else could sneak in but us? Those glowing fish?"

Ryon chuckled. "I guess you're right."

Violet swung open the door to a metal closet taller and wider than she was. "I found something."

He shoved closed the drawer he'd been searching and strode toward her. With the door open between them, all he could see was her shapely backside peeking out from behind the open door as she leaned over.

"What is it?" He cleared his throat, surprised at his gruff tone. Was all that sea water affecting his voice?

Violet straightened and peeked out from behind the closet door. "Do you want to be a wolf or a dragon?" She lifted two black and white masks in her hands, painted with fierce expressions of animals ready to strike. "There's plenty more here. Come take a look."

Ryon rounded the door and kneeled beside her. A box sat at the bottom of the closet filled with masks. Some of the animals he recognized, while others were new to him. He pulled out a mask shaped like one of the tritusks on his island. Violet chose one that resembled Muse when she was on the hunt, beak spread open menacingly.

Black clothing hung on hooks above the masks. Another box held simple black leather shoes and a third, stacks of gloves and balled-up socks.

"Looks like there's everything we need here to blend in." Ryon smiled. He gathered clothing from each section, taking the largest sizes he could find. "I'll head to the other side of the room to give you some privacy."

Violet nodded, her cheeks reddening. "Thanks."

Ryon swerved around one of the big metallic oval ships—if that's what they were. The big ship blocked Violet and all but the very top of the closet from his view. It didn't stop him from picturing her peeling off those tight, wet pants, though.

His heart hammering, he shoved the mental image of her bare legs out of his mind and set to work tugging off his own wet clothes. Soon, he was changed, covered head to toe in black. The shirt even had a hood, allowing him to fully cover his hair.

It was a good thing they'd happened upon these clothes. He wasn't sure how else he and Violet would've managed blending in. With his unusual hairstyle, and Violet's distinctive pale coloring and striking eyes, they both stood out more than most.

He'd have to suffer wearing trousers. Ryon adjusted the smooth black fabric around his legs. Far too confining for his taste, but he couldn't chance wandering around in his wet skirt.

As he fitted the tritusk mask to his face, he wondered again about the people they'd find inside. The only people the islanders had ever seen were these masked men. Would all the people here wear masks, or only some? Or were there so few masked that even with their disguises, they'd be noticed instantly?

That was a chance they had to take. At least until they got a look at what awaited them once they exited this room.

Ryon cleared his throat again. "Are you finished yet?"

"Yeah, you can come back around."

Ryon grinned as he spotted Violet, unrecognizable in her black getup and falcon mask. But she was still clearly much smaller than any man he'd ever met... He had to wonder if that difference would end up getting them caught.

"What?" she asked. "Do I look awful?" Her voice came out muffled behind the mask, but clear enough, he noted the tremor in it.

"No, you look fine. It's just you're... rather small."

Violet tensed, then shrugged, nodding back at the closed closet. "They had clothes my size in there. There must be someone using them."

Ryon sighed. "Well, that's actually reassuring." He grinned behind his mask, wondering what expression was painting Violet's face now. With the masks in place, it was impossible to tell. Even the eye holes were covered with a thin layer of a strange glass that made it impossible to see within to the person below, but he had no trouble looking out.

He headed to one of the drawers he'd spotted earlier. "Here, let's stash our wet stuff in here. We can come back for it later." Violet nodded and tossed her things in with his. With that out of the way, all that was left was to leave.

"Are you ready?" He strode toward a large set of doors at the far end of the chamber.

Violet drew in a deep breath and squared her shoulders. "Yeah. Let's find my family."

A Different World

iolet's heart pounded as the door swung open. She followed Ryon out into an empty hallway.

The magic light that seeped down from the ceiling lit the space in a warm glow reminiscent of a spring morning. She'd been expecting more metal walls here, like in the last room, but stepping inside the hall was like entering a different world.

Her stolen shoes crunched down on blades of grass. The walls and ceiling were painted a tranquil blue. Flowers, herbs, and vegetables of all shapes and sizes abounded, bursting out of planters hung on the walls.

When the first person rounded the corner, Violet was thankful for the mask so they didn't catch her gaping in awe. She stiffened beside Ryon, but the pretty young lady wearing a brown frock paid them no mind. She flitted between the planters, a spray bottle clutched in her hands.

Ryon snagged her elbow and led her away from the girl down the opposite end of the hall. More plants greeted them with every step, the smell so fragrant and lush it was impossible to miss, even with the mask covering her face. It was almost like being outside, except for the absence of any breeze, though the temperature was so pleasant she didn't mind. That was until that familiar tickle itched her nose.

As they turned a corner and encountered another person—someone dressed as they were, all in black, with a mask shaped like a reptile she didn't recognize with massive teeth—the tickle became too much to bear.

Violet sneezed.

The masked man said something. Violet stopped in her tracks, her skin prickling with gooseflesh. Was she supposed to respond? That was going to be a problem. She didn't understand what he'd said.

The man cocked his head and spoke again.

Blazes. She might not know what he said, but she couldn't mistake his angry tone. She readied herself to be found out. The masked man would tear off her mask, and the mission would fail before she got a single glimpse of her aunt and uncle.

Ryon spoke up. He chatted with the man back and forth for a moment, then turned to her. Staring straight at her, Ryon barked a series of sharp words, none of which she understood.

What was she supposed to do now? She nodded and bowed her head, hoping the men would interpret her silent action as contrition for whatever slight she'd unknowingly committed.

They chatted back and forth again, then the man sauntered off. Violet sighed, shooting a look at Ryon. He tugged her elbow, past a group of plainly dressed people gathered by the wall, plucking ripe black berries with stained fingers.

When they were finally alone, he slowed to a stop and leaned close. "That was lucky. They speak the same tongue as they do in my village."

"What happened back there?"

"He was offended when you didn't respond after he wished you good health when you sneezed. You're supposed to say thank you. I'll teach you how to say it in case it happens again."

"Seriously? That was all?" Violet clenched her fists. "I was afraid he was about to unmask me right there."

Ryon shrugged. Then he chuckled. "He thought you were my son. I guess those small outfits are for boys in training."

Violet bristled. "Your son?" She was used to being talked down to for the way she looked, but this was the first time anyone had mistaken her for a boy—although the clothes were rather baggy, and her feminine curves weren't as prominent as some. She sighed.

"C'mon. You better let me do the talking. Stick close to me and act like you're learning."

Violet followed, trailing after Ryon down more plant-covered halls. It was certainly lucky he spoke the same tongue as the people here. Did that mean they had some connection they were unaware of? It seemed a little odd they'd speak the same language when they were cut off from each other.

As they rounded the next corner, all thought of foreign tongues fled her mind. Lark. There she was!

The hallway let out into a massive room about the size of the one where they'd found their clothes and masks. But instead of being empty, this room was packed with people. Masked men stood silently, stationed along the walls. Plain-clothed people—men, women, and children of all ages—sat at tables, eating, drinking, and talking pleasantly with each other.

Ryon took up a spot standing silently against the wall, clearly doing his best to fit in with the rest of the masked men. Violet followed beside him, but when he stopped, she grabbed Ryon's sleeve and tugged frantically until he bent his head beside her.

"The woman at the center table. That's Lark," she whispered, careful not to draw too much attention in the crowded hall.

Almost every table was full of people, but somehow, she'd spotted Lark almost instantly. She sat alone, swathed in an exquisite silver gown, stoically staring down at the plate in front of her. She ate methodically, chewing and swallowing like the food—which looked and smelled delicious from where Violet was standing—were as tasteless as sawdust.

Violet stiffened, unable to tear her gaze off her aunt. What was she doing there, alone, among all those people? She had to find some way to help her. To free her from this place.

But no matter how much she longed to go to her, she knew that would be unwise. At least not here and now, with so many people watching.

Violet was so intent on staring she didn't notice the masked man approaching until he was practically on top of them. She tried to appear relaxed while the shark-masked man struck up a conversation with Ryon.

They chatted long enough she could pick out the slight variations in their accents. A tremor spread through her belly. Would the shark notice it, too?

Violet's hands moistened beneath her black gloves. She was certain the masked man would toss off Ryon's mask and reveal them for the imposters they were. But after exchanging a few more stilted words, the shark slapped Ryon on the shoulder and strode away.

Ryon waited for the man to walk out of earshot before leaning close to her. "We're in luck again. That guard spotted you staring. He offered to swap details so you can shadow her through the city."

Violet practically hummed with excitement. "Really? I don't believe it." But she spotted the tension in Ryon's stance. "What is it?"

"The shark, he didn't call her Lark. He called her the diva."

Violet sucked in a breath. "What does that mean?"

"I'm not sure." Ryon straightened. "C'mon, she's leaving."

They strode off after Lark, dodging tables until they reached her side. Lark spared them a glance, then dismissed them, continuing on without a word. It was clear she was used to being shadowed. She didn't balk when they fell in behind her and followed her across the packed dining hall.

They stayed a few paces behind as she wandered down a corridor leading away from the route they'd taken to get there. After several turns down crowded halls bustling with people tending to more flowering planters, Violet's stomach churned.

She was hopelessly lost. Every passage in here looked the same as the last, only the plants changing from hall to hall. With their winding route, she had no clue where they'd come from or how to retrace their steps.

What would they do when it was time to leave? Hopefully, Ryon remembered the way, or else they might be stuck inside this mysterious city for good.

Violet kept her eyes peeled, but she saw no sign of Nox or Flint. These people appeared to not keep pets or animals of any kind. Or if they did, they didn't allow them free reign of the halls. She certainly didn't smell any evidence of them. Only the sweet perfume of all the flowering greenery filled the air, so thick it was cloying.

The urge to sneeze washed over her, again and again, but she did her best to bite it back, not wanting to attract any more well wishes. Ryon still hadn't shared the proper response with her, and if she did blurt it out, surely someone would realize the voice within the falcon mask was far too feminine to belong to a boy in training.

Lark strolled calmly, her steps measured. People stared at her as she slid past, gawking at her fine gown. Children waved, spouting out what might be greetings in their foreign tongue. Lark smiled benignly, but whenever Violet glimpsed her hazel eyes, she noticed the haziness clouding her expression.

They walked for so long Violet's feet began to ache, pinched uncomfortably in her borrowed shoes. Finally, Lark stopped before a door set into one of the endless halls. She swung the door open and strolled inside, then quickly turned, her hand perched on the knob to shut it.

Violet slipped past her before she had the chance to slam the door closed. They were alone. The room was small and opulently furnished, but she only gave the fine décor a brief glance before whirling around to stare at her aunt.

Lark cleared her throat loudly, eyes widening. "Excuse me. You're clearly new, but guards don't usually follow me in—" She cut off mid tirade, seeming to realize that she was speaking in the wrong language. She spun toward Ryon and uttered a single word in the foreign tongue.

But Ryon only stepped in and tore the door out of her hands, swinging it closed after a quick look in at the empty room. "We can't leave. Not until we speak to you."

"Who are you?" Lark crossed her arms, her gaze flitting between them both.

Violet reached up and removed her mask. "Auntie. It's me."

"Violet?" Lark squealed and closed the distance between them in an instant. "What are you doing here?"

"Isn't it obvious? We're here to save you." She wrapped her arms around her aunt and smiled.

When Lark pulled back enough to gaze at her, tears glimmered in her eyes. "I don't understand. Aren, Dylen—are they all right? What about Muse? How did you find me? Nox, was he with you? I saw him and Flint in the games."

"You've seen Nox? We got separated. We've come to save him, too." Violet sighed. "It's kind of a long story. Can we sit down? My feet are killing me."

Lark nodded, leading her farther into the room to a cushioned tan bench. Ryon seated himself across from them on the edge of a massive bed, swathed with silky sheets and a thick golden comforter. But when he tugged his mask off, Lark frowned.

"You two ought to leave those on. I'm not afforded much privacy here. Someone could burst in at any moment."

"What is this place? Why are you here?" Violet fixed her mask back in place. This wasn't what she'd been expecting when she'd learned her aunt had been taken prisoner. Fine art of delicate flowers decorated the walls, and a closet bursting with more gorgeous gowns hung open in the far corner. It looked more like a room fit for a princess than a prison cell.

"I'll tell you everything, but you first."

Violet conceded, quickly relaying the events of the last few weeks. Lark sat patiently listening, the relief washing over her at the story evident. By the time Violet finished, the cloudiness in Lark's eyes had lifted, and a brilliant smile lit her face.

"Blazes. Thank you, Vi. I'm so grateful for all you've done." Lark squeezed her hand and let out a deep sigh.

"We're not done yet. We need to get you out of here." Violet turned to Ryon. "Do you remember the way back to the room we swam in from?"

"No." Lark spoke up before Ryon could answer. "I'm sorry, but we can't leave. Not yet."

Violet's head snapped back to her aunt. "Are you crazy? We can't keep this up forever. We need to sneak you out while we still have a chance."

"No, you don't understand. There's something I need. I've tried to get it on my own, but I can't. Now that you're here, we can get it together."

Ryon leaned forward. "What do you need, and where do we find it? We can hunt for Nox while we're searching, and then all leave together."

"No, you can't. I need Nox where he is. He's the only one who can win the map."

"Map? What map?" Violet asked.

Lark sighed. "Let me explain. I attracted the attention of Jurdan the Supreme with my singing. That's why they set me up in this blazing room, so he can show me off like a damn doll whenever he wants."

Violet drew back. "Jurdan the Supreme. Who is that?"

"The sick freak who runs this place. The people here treat him like a god."

"Are you all right?" Violet scanned the huge bed Ryon perched on. "Is he—"

"No." Lark shuddered, catching her meaning without her having to ask. "It's nothing like that. But he has a map leading to Dru's eggs. I was there when the spider brought it to him."

Ryon tilted his head. "Spider?"

"Another of the masked men. He's like a second in command here."

Violet's brows shot up. Lark had said one word in the foreign tongue, but how much could she really have gleaned in her short time here? "How did you even understand what they were saying to know that the map you saw will lead to Dru's eggs?"

Lark leaned closer. "I heard everything that day. They weren't speaking in their tongue. They were speaking in ours. Jurdan, the spider, and a few other of his trusted advisors speak it already. They use it like a secret code, talking among themselves when those they don't want overhearing are present."

"And they don't mind you overhearing?" Ryon asked.

Lark shrugged. "Jurdan told me plainly no one has ever escaped from here before. I guess they don't consider me a threat."

Violet's nose twitched, making her mask shift slightly. "I don't understand. How will Nox get the map? Where is he? You said you saw him in some kind of game?"

Lark shuddered. "Yes. All the people they abduct are forced to take part in the games. Anyone here who commits crimes, too. There's only two ways to escape. If you catch Jurdan's eye, he can give you a pardon—"

"I take it that's what happened to you?" Ryon interrupted.

"Yes. But we need Nox to try for the second method."

Ryon cocked his head. "What's that?"

"He has to win. Anyone in the games can challenge the reigning champion to a match to the death. If they win, they are guaranteed a boon from Jurdan. Whatever they ask for is granted. They always ask for their freedom."

"But Nox will ask for the map instead? Then what?" Violet asked.

"Then you can save us, like you planned." Lark shrugged. "We can't leave here without that map. Can you imagine if these people got their hands on dragons? And I promised Kayda. Please, Vi. We're so close."

"But a death match... what if Uncle Nox loses?"

"We'll just have to make sure he has an advantage so he can't lose." Ryon tugged his knife free from his belt and reached inside his hood for a lock of hair. With a few sure strokes of the knife, he pulled a silver feather free and crossed the room to place the shining feather reverently in Lark's hands. "We'll need to leave you for this plan to work. Take this."

Lark's eyes widened. "I didn't realize you had more."

Violet squeezed her aunt's hand. "You remember how to use it?"

Before Lark could answer, the door to her chamber swung open, and a lovely woman strolled in. She stiffened at the sight of them, Violet clutching Lark's hand with her gloved fist. Ryon standing over both of them so closely.

A string of foreign chatter spilled out of her lips. Violet could gather from her tone alone, she wasn't pleased.

She retracted her hand from Lark's and stood. Then she and Ryon shuffled back toward the door. Ryon murmured at the woman as they hurried away, his tone thick with appeasement.

They swapped spots with the woman. She strode farther into the room as they closed in on the exit. It all happened so fast, Violet didn't get a close look at her, except for the impression of loveliness and waist-length black hair. Her floor-length cream dress rustled across the carpet as they passed.

Ryon hustled her out into the hall, tugging her elbow.

"Are you all right?" someone asked behind her as the door slammed shut.

"Did you hear that?" she whispered frantically. "I think that woman could speak—"

"That's not important," Ryon said in a rush. "Not now. We need to go."

"What? Where?"

"That woman just told me another one of those games is about to start. We have to find your uncle, fast."

Scum Like Us

Nox waited for the mini door in the cage to slam closed before he headed for the buckets. With just the three of them, there'd been no fighting over the slop. It still wasn't nearly enough to be satisfying, especially for Flint, but with them sharing peacefully, no one was forced to lick the dredges off the filthy floor.

He wrinkled his nose at the first bite. "What do they put in this stuff?" he asked around a chunk of spongy meat.

Iggy chuckled. "Fish mostly. They throw in whatever vegetables are close to rotting, too, but never the herbs and spices. Those are far too dear for scum like us."

Nox leaned back, raising a brow.

Iggy shrugged. "There was a cook in here once. He didn't last long, but it was long enough for him to cry over his lost herbs and spices."

Nox leaned back from the bucket. "I've had enough."

Iggy took a final bite and leaned over the water bucket. "Me as well."

Nox nodded, then hauled the food bucket back to the cage corner. *"Hey, what did I tell ya? My slop is your slop, buddy."*

Flint's tail swished weakly. *"You're too kind."*

Nox frowned. Flint had been sleeping far too much lately. He had to conserve his energy with so little food and the specter of battle looming at every turn. Hunger, ever present, gnawed at Flint's gut. The scant bit of stew they saved for him at each meal was barely enough to take the edge off it.

Though Flint tried to hide the ache growing within him, Nox could sense it through their bond, increasing every day. How much longer until it broke him? Until his predatory nature arose and forced him to make a kill?

As Flint lifted his head off the floor and dug into the bucket, Iggy flinched, his wide brown eyes watching the huge cat's long canines scrape against the wood.

His new cellmate was still uneasy around Flint. Nox couldn't blame him. It had only been a day they'd been together, and Flint had made no aggressive moves toward him, even so, few men would be eager to ignore a predator within reach.

Nox returned to Iggy's side and took his turn with the water bucket. The lukewarm liquid did little to wash away the lingering taste of the foul stew coating his tongue, but it was welcome all the same.

"Did you want any more?" he asked Iggy.

Iggy shot a sideways glance at Flint. "No. I've had my fill."

Nox lugged the bucket to Flint. *"Here, drink up."* Then he sank down beside Iggy, leaning back against the cold stone walls.

"Twenty years is a long time to be stuck here. What else can you tell me about this place?"

Iggy busied himself picking at the dirt beneath his nails. "What do you want to know?"

Nox sighed. That was a loaded question if there ever was one. So many questions swirled through his mind, he hardly knew where to start.

"How did you survive in here so long?" Nox shot a look at his companion. Long, lean muscle dominated his lanky frame, but his body had far fewer scars and bruises than the men in his former cage. "Twenty years of weekly battles doesn't seem like a feat anyone could survive."

Iggy's face split into a wide grin. "Ah, that's the thing. I haven't fought nearly that often."

"What do you mean? Do they keep you out of the ring?"

"No. I've had my share of performances."

"Performances?" Nox tilted his head.

"The folks up there, they don't care how they're entertained, just that they are *entertained*."

Nox bit back a gasp. "They don't make you battle?"

"Only when I can't get them to laugh." Iggy smirked.

Nox rubbed his brow. "What?"

Iggy explained, "I had a stranger introduction to the games than most. You remember I convinced them to arrange for my trade? Well, I watched as, one by one, the men who'd been captured with me were taken to compete above. It wasn't until my family stopped communicating with Jurdan that they forced me to take part. It was long enough for me to notice a pattern."

"A pattern?"

Iggy nodded. "The first time, no matter who you are, they test your mettle by making you battle a beast. But if you survive that first encounter, they give you an opportunity to entertain before unleashing the beasts in the cage with you."

Nox shuddered. Did that mean Lark had to battle a beast before showing the crowd she could sing? "What do you do instead of fighting? How do you make them laugh?"

"I guess you could say I'm the resident storyteller." Iggy shrugged. "I always had an ear for stories. Growing up well off in Joria, I had more opportunity than most to listen to traveling performers. By the time I was forced to join the games, I'd learned the tongue spoken here. I told them all the tales I remembered from back home. When I ran out of stories I recalled, I made up new ones, each more fantastical than the last."

"And that works?"

"Most of the time. There's been a time or two the tale was a dud. I've had to rely on my fighting skills those nights when they unleashed beasts."

Nox pinched the bridge of his nose. "That's good for you, my friend. Too bad Flint and I aren't the story-telling type."

Iggy leaned closer. "You have no skill you can show off for the crowd? I've heard the men whispering about what you did in the cage. Taming that ape." He cocked a brow. "I imagine that had to be an impressive sight."

Nox's hand fell slack in his lap. "I suppose that's true. But I have no idea if that will work again."

"You're better off trying something new, anyway. You calming the ape was shocking while it was unexpected, but if you rely on it too much, they'll tire of it. I tried repeating a story once. That didn't go over well."

That settled it. He needed to think of something before he and Flint were forced back into the ring. Violet was still out there, somewhere, searching for them. He had to survive long enough to give her a shot at finding them. Or, barring that, figure out a way to escape on his own. Maybe he could still convince the beauty to help him.

"Who's the girl?" He stared at Iggy's profile beside him.

Iggy went back to digging beneath his nails, not turning to meet his eye. "Forget about her. She won't help you. I've been trying to gain her favor for years."

"You two were acting awfully chummy when she brought you here."

"And that didn't stop her from tossing me in, did it?"

Nox scowled. But he was right. The beauty was their jailer. He needed to stop imagining he could sway her to help.

"What's the deal with the masks? Do they ever take them off?"

"Not that I've ever seen. It's some tradition of theirs. I'm not sure what drives them to cover up head to toe. From what I can gather, they start training as teens, always hiding behind those masks, and they keep the same mask for their whole life. The spider who shadows the girl has always been a spider. Always that same voice behind the mask."

Nox opened his mouth to ask for more details, but Iggy's hand shot out and gripped his shoulder.

"Do you hear that?" Iggy whispered.

Nox's mouth slammed closed. He listened carefully, but noted nothing unusual. Just the same quiet murmuring of voices speaking in those guttural tones.

"I don't—" he started, but then a door banged open down the hall. Footsteps followed.

Iggy retracted his hand and curled up in a ball on the floor beside him. Nox stared out the barred door as the footsteps grew louder.

Surely, they weren't coming to gather men for another game... It hadn't even been a full day since the last ended.

But even as the thought crossed his mind, the swish of a pale cream dress joined the soft tap of footsteps before halting outside the cell. The beauty and spider stood outside, staring in. The beauty raised her hand and pointed at him and Flint. The spider dug in his pocket, but before he pulled the blow gun out, Nox rushed forward to the door.

"You don't need to shoot Flint. He'll listen, like last time." Nox turned back to Iggy. "Tell them. Translate for me."

Iggy's brows shot up, but he hurried to comply, not moving from his ball on the ground.

The beauty nodded and tugged the spider's arm away from his pocket. He uttered a few angry words but moved to open the door.

"Remember what I told you, Nox. Entertain them and you won't have to fight," Iggy whispered hurriedly.

Nox nodded somberly. "I remember. I'll see you soon."

Flint stretched, yawning lazily before joining him, waiting for the door to swing open. *"Another fight, already?"*

"Perhaps not." Nox smiled wryly down at Flint. *"Iggy's been filling me in on the games."* Nox relayed his last conversation to Flint as they followed the beauty and spider out of the cage and down the hall. By the time they reached the stairwell, Flint was caught up.

"So, if we can entertain them some other way, they won't make us fight. What are we going to do?" Flint asked.

Nox frowned. *"I'm not sure. I was hoping you'd have some ideas."*

"Me? When have I ever needed to entertain humans?"

"You do today." Nox sighed, his bare feet slapping on the steps. *"There's still time. I'll think of something."*

A pair of masked men atop the stairwell drew Nox's eye. One of them was much shorter than his companion, wearing a black and white falcon mask. It struck him as odd until he remembered Iggy's words. This must be one of the teens in training.

The boy stiffened at the sight of him and Flint climbing the stairs. He'd seen grown men run screaming at the sight of a jagoth approaching. Poor lad must be shaking with fear behind that mask.

But from the beauty's reaction to the pair, he gathered they shouldn't have been there. A frown crossed her face, and she barked out a command that had the pair retreating ahead of them at a fast clip. The boy in the falcon mask turned back to gaze at them once but scrambled up the stairs after the horned-masked man with him tugged none too gently on the lad's elbow.

Something tickled the back of Nox's mind at the sight of the boy, but he shoved the notion aside. He had to think—and fast. He and Flint couldn't end up in that ring with another beast. There was no guarantee that the trick he'd used with the ape would work again with a different creature.

But what could they do? He was no entertainer. Lark had spent years living and working with a traveling show, but he'd received no such education. His heart sank as the door to the ring flew open, and the roar of the crowd boomed around him.

The spider led them across the dirt ring to the open-air cages. The heavy gazes of all those eyes descended upon him once again. A shiver tingled up Nox's spine, and he swiveled around, knowing before he even set his eyes on the lone box that Jurdan the Supreme would be there watching.

His intuition was right. Jurdan perched in the fine chair, swathed in those same dark robes, staring down at the ring. For a single instant, their gazes locked, and Nox nearly gagged at the sensation that accompanied a direct look into his black eyes.

Vile. That man was vile. Nox shuddered and broke the stare, physically unable to keep contact with him any longer.

Lark was seated beside him once again, and Nox let his gaze trail over her. She met his eyes for a fleeting instant, with that same fear he remembered flooding her gaze, before she looked away.

The man with the crows was there, too, standing silently in the back of the box with a bird on each shoulder.

The spider barked at him, and Nox faced forward. Soon he was forced to crouch down inside the cage with Flint to await his turn inside the ring.

Flint perked up. *"My old neighbor, he's here."*

Nox spotted the boy crouched alone in one of the cages lined up beside theirs. Tears streamed down his cheeks, and his shoulders shook uncontrollably, but he was there and he was alive.

Nox sighed. How long that would last was a different matter. He turned away from the frightened boy to eye the stands. Spaces were filling swiftly. It wouldn't be long before the dark king rose to call for the games to begin.

Across the ring, something rumbled, followed by a low hiss. Nox's skin prickled.

"Tell me that's not a snake…" Flint shuddered, crouching low with his tail between his legs. *"I hate snakes."*

The sound reverberated again, and Nox realized it was more like a rattle than a rumble, followed by an even louder hiss. *"I'm sorry, my friend. But I think you're right."*

"Had any ideas yet?"

Nox shook his head and closed his eyes. *"Not yet."*

What could they do? He thought back on all the performances he'd watched over his life. Growing up in Stoneshore, a remote village in the Raimire jungle, traveling shows had been few and far between. But once he learned of his father's true lineage and began traveling to Kings Keep, he'd witnessed more than his share of performances.

He'd never yearned to be the one putting on the show. Still, there might be one thing he and Flint could pull off together...

"Do you remember last year's Harvest Festival?"

"What about it?" Flint asked.

"Do you remember the players during the evening meal on the last day?"

Flint stiffened. *"You can't mean... those idiots. What of them?"*

"They got a ton of laughs. Shall we give it a try?"

A disbelieving chuckle rumbled in Nox's mind, then Flint let out a strangled noise when he spotted his expression. *"Rot and decay. You're serious?"*

"What do we have to lose?"

"How about our dignity?"

"Don't act like you were dignified before. I've seen what you do with your tongue when no one's watching."

Flint hissed. *"At least I'm clean. Have I told you lately how much you stink?"*

Nox chuckled, but then his stomach dropped to his feet. He whipped around as the familiar sickening itch spread across his skin at the same time Jurdan the Supreme's voice rang out through the massive space.

Bile burned the back of his throat. How could the people here stand it? His gaze darted around the seats. Only Lark seemed to be affected by Jurdan's presence the same way he was. That and... the boy.

That boy from before on the stairs was stationed at the front of the stands. For some reason, Nox's gaze was drawn to him. The boy stood beside the same man who'd tugged him away earlier, but whereas the hulking man in the horned mask stood easily, the boy's hands quivered around his long pole, his falcon mask aimed directly at Jurdan as he spoke.

As Jurdan finished speaking and stalked back to his seat, the boy shook off his reaction. Nox leaned back, frowning. Was he simply too young to have gotten used to the dark king's presence, or was something else at play?

The spider strode forward and raised the sand-filled glass high. Nox abandoned the thought of all else as the glass slammed down on the box edge, and the door to his and Flint's cage opened.

"Showtime. You ready to give it a shot?"

"Fine," Flint bit out. *"But when this ends badly, don't blame me."*

"Such a pessimist. We've got this. Stop in the center of the ring and follow my lead."

Flint trotted out ahead of Nox and halted dead center. Nox breathed in deeply, then took off running.

With his boons, jumping and balancing were child's play. If anyone could make this act a hit, they could.

The crowd let out a collective gasp as he barreled toward Flint. Flint played along, acting oblivious. But just before Nox slammed into the huge cat's backside, he leaped into the air, tucking his legs close to his body and rolling.

Like a cat, he landed on his feet. The crowd roared their approval.

"Act like you're pissed," he said as he performed an exaggerated bow for the crowd.

"It's not an act," Flint grumbled. But from the gasps and fingers pointing behind him, Nox knew Flint was playing his part. It was his turn to act oblivious. He blew kisses into the stands, winking at ladies and grinning as if he couldn't get enough of their adoration.

"Duck," Flint yelled.

Nox bowed again, avoiding a blow from Flint's claws as he leaped over him.

The crowd *oohed* and *ahhed* as they kept up the ruse, leaping and jumping over each other. Flint kept acting like he was trying to kill him, and Nox like he was barely avoiding each hit—all while remaining oblivious to the danger.

The crowd ate it up, chuckling and cheering louder with each tumble.

Nox spared a glance for the lone box. Lark's eyes twinkled with barely leashed humor, her hands loosely covering her smiling lips. But Jurdan the Supreme gazed on with a flat expression, seeming bored. Sand trickled down into the glass, almost covering the bottom fully. But Nox sensed if the dark king got bored, they'd still be in trouble.

"Time for one more trick. Do you remember what they did for the finale?"

"Ugh. Yes." Flint reared back into position. *"Here goes the rest of my dignity."*

Nox smiled broadly, then leaped again, twisting in an intricate spin. But instead of landing cleanly, he fell, rolling to land just in front of Flint.

Gasps echoed all around. Nox lay on the ground, clutching his head, acting dazed. He didn't look at Flint to see what he was doing, but from the shouts and yells coming from the crowd, he imagined he had to be acting plenty menacing. Children who'd spent the last few moments giggling at his antics pointed and shouted, clearly urging him to leap to his feet.

Nox stayed put, waiting.

"Roll, now," Flint demanded.

Nox didn't hesitate. He rolled out of the way as a spray of urine blasted the dirt beside him. He hopped up to his feet, his expression aghast as the crowd exploded with laughter at his close call.

Loud clapping sounded from the box. Jurdan the Supreme strolled to the edge, his manicured fingers reaching out to clasp the glass jar. He barked out the same rough order Nox remembered from his last round in the ring.

"*Run.*" Nox tore off, back to the cage. It all happened so fast—Flint's leg was still lifted high in the air, the gush of urine slowing to a trickle. He rushed to finish his business and race back.

As Nox landed on the dirt inside the cage and spun around, the door slammed closed. Flint smacked into the cage wall with a resounding *crack* and ricocheted back into the dirt.

"Flint!" Nox yelled. "Let him in." He scrambled to the cage door, tugging uselessly at the bars. "Open the door. He did what you wanted. Let him in!"

But the next cell to swing open was not his own. Nox shook his head in disbelief as the lad creeped out to join Flint on the dirt ring.

"*Flint.*" Nox's voice warbled in his mind. "*You have to survive. Please.*"

Flint backed away from the cage, glaring warily at the spectators in the stands. He'd hit the cage door hard, and Nox could tell he was still rattled from the blow. He saw the moment Flint glimpsed the boy in the ring with him.

Flint slunk back. "*No.*" He shook his head. "*He's just a kit.*"

Tears stung Nox's eyes as the weapon rack rose from the ground. "*Flint. Please.*"

"*No. You could ask me for anything, and I'd give it to you. But not this. Not this.*"

Nox tore at the bars, a wordless bellow tearing out of his chest. The boy scrambled for the rack and plucked a worn javelin free.

Cheers erupted from the crowd, and Nox nearly vomited at the bloodthirsty lust gleaming in men's eyes. Those same men who'd laughed so hard they'd doubled over at Flint's comical antics screamed for his blood.

And his bondmate stalked out to the center of the ring and sat on his haunches. Proud and defiant to the end, he turned to the dark king, opened his jaws, and hissed deep in his throat. The sound rumbled across the ring; a menacing threat laced with pure venom.

The boy inched forward cautiously, egged on by the guttural shouts of the crowd.

Tears spilled down Nox's cheeks. He tried to scream again, but his voice cracked, agony pouring off of him so thickly his throat clogged.

He watched it all transpire in his mind's eye. The boy would stab Flint with that javelin, again and again. And Flint would just lay there and take it, unwilling to harm the lad who'd shown him kindness when he'd been all alone. Who'd fed him while he'd been wracked with hunger.

His bondmate's inherent kindness would be his downfall, and there was nothing Nox could do to save him.

Terror And Anguish

Ryon stared down into the ring as the massive black cat hissed. The sound sent a flurry of shivers up his spine—and it wasn't even directed at him.

Violet practically quivered beside him. He shifted closer to her, wishing he could take her in his arms. But that would be sure to draw attention. He could do nothing but stand silently beside her as she watched her uncle's bondmate face death in the ring.

Why was the cat not fighting? The lone boy stalking toward him with that pitiful, worn javelin hardly seemed a threat to a creature with such massive teeth and wicked claws.

But the black cat just sat calmly on his haunches, watching the boy advance.

Was he luring him in, waiting for the last moment to pounce?

Tension coiled in Ryon's belly. He watched Nox tear at the bars to his cage, screaming his bondmate's name, cursing the games, pleading over and over for Flint's return. Even over the roar of the crowd—the screams and shouts of men in the stands begging for blood—Nox's voice reached his ears, full of terror and anguish.

The boy glided closer, eyeing Flint warily. He lifted the javelin high over his head and ran, a war cry ripping out of his chest. The cat just sat and watched. Not a single muscle on the predator coiled to strike. Only his tail moved, flicking lazily. At the last instant, the boy dropped the javelin. He flung his arms around Flint's neck, his shoulders heaving as he burst into tears.

A stunned hush enveloped the crowd, followed closely by excited murmuring. The contented rumble of purring rose from the ring as Flint comforted the scared boy. Nox finally gave up tearing at the cage, his tense shoulders slumping.

The dark-robed man jerked up from his seat in the lone box. Where he and Violet stood, they could see and hear him clearly. Ryon hadn't needed anyone to tell him this was the man Lark had dubbed Jurdan the Supreme. The way the people in the stands hung on his every word confirmed it.

Violet shuddered as Jurdan's voice rang out. "Enough of this. Beasts in my ring will fight like beasts." He sneered down at Flint and the boy, clearly displeased with their show of friendship. "Release the serpent."

The walled-off cage across the ring slammed open. Ryon's heart skipped a beat as a massive snake, twice as long as Flint, shot into the ring.

The snake slithered out, its skin a deep tan mottled with orange and brown dots. It would be at home in the sand, camouflaged completely. But this beast didn't seek to hide. It zipped out to the center of the ring, hissing and waving its rattling tail menacingly.

The boy spotted it coming and released Flint. He snatched his fallen javelin and scrambled away. The snake whipped around, zeroing in on the boy's movement and racing straight for him. Struggling under the weight of the weapon in his hands, the boy tripped over his own feet. When the snake reached him, he sprawled out flat in the dirt, the javelin rolling away from him uselessly.

Ryon's heart slammed against his ribs. The snake coiled back, ready to strike. The lad screamed.

Then Flint struck. He snagged the snake by the tail with his powerful jaws and whipped him away from the boy. The serpent emitted a horrid, pained screech before tangling with the cat.

They rolled through the dirt, a tangle of scales and fur, moving so fast they were hard to track. But then the snake stopped moving. Flint bit down on its neck and shook. Blood pooled on the ground and dripped down his fangs.

The crowd cheered, finally rewarded with the blood they'd been craving. But beside him, Violet's knees buckled.

Ryon steadied her by her elbow and spotted where her gaze was locked. She wasn't watching Flint. Her stare was locked on her uncle.

The expression on Nox's face was one of pure anguish. He gaped at his bondmate, his jaw trembling, tears streaming down his red cheeks, mouth moving but no sound escaping.

Ryon turned back to Flint, his mind whirling. He'd just won, hadn't he?

Ryon spotted blood dripping from twin puncture wounds on the cat's haunches. Flint dropped the snake out of his jaw and collapsed to the dirt.

Nox spoke then, but the sound that emerged from his lips couldn't be called words. Nor a scream. If he hadn't seen for himself that the sound came from a man, he would've never guessed. It was a roar of pure anguish, ripped from the depths of Nox's soul—raw, primal, and animalistic.

Ryon shuddered. And when Nox renewed his attempts to tear at the bars with his bare hands, he wanted to weep. But one look at the other masked men, all standing stoic and unmoved, and he knew that would be a mistake.

He tightened his grip on Violet's elbow instead, wishing he could do more to comfort her. Her skin trembled beneath his fingers, and he sensed she was barely holding it together.

Jurdan leaned close to the spider and whispered something in his ear. The masked man spun on his heel and departed the lone box without a word.

Nox's wails continued to rain down. The crowd muttered excitedly. Most of the spectators looked on without remorse, though a few women and children turned away from the gory spectacle in the ring.

The boy recovered from his fumble and sprinted to Flint's side. He petted the massive cat's hide as Flint trembled with convulsions in the dirt.

Ryon's stomach clenched. Flint was still hanging on. Whatever venom that snake injected him with had not yet done its job. Was it too much to hope that he'd recover? Perhaps some antidote would be administered?

But that thin shred of hope tore apart when Flint opened his jaws and vomited out a great bout of blood. Far too much to be just from the contents of his stomach.

Though he hadn't imagined they could, Nox's screams increased in volume and ferocity at the sight. Blood coated his hands and dripped down his arms, his knuckles and nails torn to shreds from his barrage on the cage.

The spider emerged from a side corridor into the ring.

Ryon stiffened, mentally preparing for anything. Would he attack Nox for daring to show his grief? Kill the boy for showing kindness to the dying beast that saved his life?

The spider strode up to Nox's cage and pulled a tube out of his pocket. Nox turned his venom on him, his screams finally yielding words Ryon could understand.

"I'll kill you. I'll kill you all for what you did to Flint." He bared his teeth, his gaze flitting over everyone assembled in the stands before landing squarely on Jurdan. "You're dead. All of you are de—"

His tirade ended when the spider's dart hit him square in the neck. After a few wobbly steps, Nox crumpled to the ground.

Violet gasped, her intake of breath clearly audible. Luckily, dozens of others in the crowd had the same reaction, so it didn't stand out so starkly.

The spider strode across the dirt to where the boy crouched beside Flint. He stepped over the snake's carcass and leaned down to the boy. Whatever he said made the lad scramble away, racing for his cage.

Flint shuddered, his body overcome with death throes. Despite his obvious pain, he raised his head weakly and hissed at the spider gazing down at him. But that was clearly all he could manage. After a single hiss, his head flopped listlessly to the dirt.

The spider lifted his dart gun again and took aim. Darts embedded in the cat's flesh, three times, in quick succession. Finally, Flint's eyelids closed, and his body stilled.

A bark from the box beside him drew Ryon's gaze from the dirt. Jurdan glared at Lark, his gaze filled with disdain. "Sing," he screamed, heedless of the tears streaming unchecked down her cheeks. He gripped her forearm in his fist and shoved her up out of her seat. "Sing, or you're down there next."

Lark lurched to her feet. She forcefully tugged her arm from Jurdan's fist and scrubbed at her cheeks. She strode on shaky legs to the edge of the box.

The spectators watched her, their gazes lit with interest and adoration.

And though her chin quivered, Lark opened her mouth and sang.

Ryon immediately understood why they called Lark the diva. Her voice was transcendent. In all the years since losing the ability to listen to the orecoln's song, he'd heard nothing that could compare to his memory of their haunting melody. Not until now.

But it wasn't the pure sweetness of Lark's voice that made a shiver tingle up his spine. It was the song. He recognized it instantly.

She sang a song he knew intimately. His mother had sung this same song to him hundreds of times. It was the story of Talex the Great and his fateful end, saving his one true love at the cost of his own life.

How had Lark learned the same song he'd begged his mother to sing to him as a child? And more strangely, why did these people react the same way he had, as if they instantly recognized it?

They all spoke the same language, and now this... What did it all mean? Were these peculiar, bloodthirsty people some long forgotten kin with his own?

But then as he gazed at Lark, singing so sweetly in her elegant silver gown, he remembered how she'd gotten here. Traveling from island to island, searching each. Meeting the people there.

Perhaps she'd learned this song on her travels? As soon as the idea took root in his mind, a wave of relief washed over him. Of course, that was it.

The people here were merely affected by the song itself and Lark's lovely voice singing so sweetly. The lyrics, about a man valiantly giving his own life to save someone he loved, were so moving after watching

Flint's sacrifice that women and children openly wept. Even the men were affected. Dozens of them scrubbed at their cheeks and shook their heads sadly, staring at Flint's unmoving body in the dirt.

The spider disappeared from the ring, leaving the two beasts to lie there, bloody and broken. Ryon's stomach churned, and tears pooled in his eyes beneath his mask. It was such a waste. Why did these people insist on watching that brutality play out before their eyes?

Jurdan looked on, his dark gaze unmoved where he sat behind Lark in the box. Not a dash of sadness was written on his face, but the slight hint of something more sinister lay behind his eyes as he watched the people reacting to Lark's song. A smirk tugged at his cheeks, and he stared at her like a greedy boy would a favorite toy he was showing off in the schoolyard.

But soon the song ended. Applause roared through the stands. Lark bowed her head and backed away, her tear-stained cheeks a direct contrast to Jurdan's dry face.

As one, the spectators rose to their feet and moved to depart back into the city. Ryon tugged Violet's arm and cocked his head to the side, hoping she would follow him without complaint. Of all the times not to see someone's face... She had to be hurting after seeing her uncle's bondmate killed. Hearing her aunt's heartfelt song.

He would lead her away from this dreadful place, find somewhere private to pull her aside so she could mourn in peace before they put the rest of their plan into action.

If only they'd found Nox in time and not happened upon him while he was already within the spider's clutches...

But as they closed in on a stairwell exit, a masked man approached. He hustled over, his voice labored beneath his serpent mask.

Ryon flinched reflexively. It was far too soon for him to face a man disguised as a serpent after what he'd just been forced to witness. But it appeared he had no choice.

The man didn't seek to move past them but stopped directly before them and barked out a greeting. "Ho. What is your shadow doing? He should be fast asleep with the rest of the trainees by now."

Guano. This wasn't good.

Ryon rubbed a hand on the back of his neck, trying for nonchalance. "Oh, my boy's a huge fan of the diva's. I didn't see any harm in letting him have a listen."

The serpent chuckled. "Yes, the diva is worth the trouble. All the same, it's time to turn in, boy." He directed his last words to Violet, and sweat collected on Ryon's brow beneath his mask.

He jumped in, "Don't worry, that's where we're headed."

"No need. Thank you for taking him under your wing. You can pick him back up in the morning. The boy can shadow me back to the dorms. I'm heading there now." The serpent stood there expectantly, staring Violet down. From his tone and body language, it was clear he expected to be taken up on the offer readily, like being saddled with a trainee was a task most men would happily be rid of.

"Of course. If you mind, I need a private word with the boy first," Ryon insisted, praying the request wouldn't see them both unmasked.

If the serpent was taken aback, he showed no sign. He simply nodded and strode off to wait by the door to the hall.

Ryon leaned down and whispered quietly in Violet's ear. "He wants you to follow him. Said I can collect you in the morning."

Violet tensed. "What? You can't expect me to go with him all on my own... What if he wants to talk to me?"

Ryon frowned beneath his mask. "I'll tell him the battle has you overwrought. I suspect if I deny him this, it will make us stand out.

Just follow along and try to blend in until I find you." He clasped what he hoped looked like a friendly hand on her shoulder and felt the slight tremble beneath his fingers. "I'll find you, Violet. I promise."

She nodded.

He led her back to the serpent and leaned close to him, conspiratorially. "I wonder... could I ask you for a favor, friend?"

"Depends. What is it?" the serpent returned dryly.

"The lad is a bit overwhelmed after..." He gestured in a wide circle behind him. "All that excitement. See that he heads straight to bed, would you? We have a long day tomorrow."

"Will do."

With that, the serpent walked away, clearly expecting Violet to fall in line behind him. Ryon nodded to her as she followed and prayed he hadn't just made a huge mistake.

Going Mad

Violet trailed the serpent-masked man's heavy footsteps. They trod through the plant-covered halls, making so many turns she soon lost all sense of direction.

Her nerves went haywire. The serpent might round on her with a barrage of questions at any moment. Questions she had no means to answer.

How could Ryon leave her? He was off doing who knew what while the serpent herded her away like a misbehaving youth. What happened when it was time to sleep and they made her take off her mask? She would be found out, forced to compete in those wretched games like Nox.

The thought of him wrenched her heart. And poor Flint. She nearly stumbled when she let herself picture him as she saw him last, lying still in a pool of his own blood. Blazes. How could they all sit back and watch that happen?

All those people perched in the stands—they hadn't just watched passively. They took pleasure in Flint's pain. They screamed for his blood. And they weren't the least bit ashamed when he lay in the dirt, his life fading before their eyes.

Lark's song had brought out the softer side in some. Tears fell. Faces filled with regret. But what about tomorrow? They'd be right back at it again, no doubt. Watching some other poor man or beast torn to shreds at the whims of that vile *Supreme*.

Violet shuddered at the memory of his presence. Something was *wrong* with him. She could sense it the moment she drew close. Her skin suddenly felt two sizes too small. Like squirming insects had wormed their way underneath and were fighting for room within her flesh.

The serpent stopped suddenly. Violet halted behind him, leaning sideways for a peek at what rested beyond the bulky man's torso.

He twisted open a door that looked the same as all the rest. With all the uniformity in this city, it was a wonder everyone didn't spend their lives lost. But the serpent didn't hesitate. He strode right in, like he knew exactly where he was heading.

Violet gulped and followed him inside. She gazed around at the passageway beyond. This one was like all those they'd just traversed in size and shape, but that was where the similarities ended.

Unlike the cheery sky-blue outer corridors with their endless greenery, this hall was drab and dull. Gray paint dominated the walls, and doors perched in a line down the inner wall. Most were closed, but a few hung open.

Standing at the very end, an open doorway led to another chamber. From so far away, she couldn't discern much except for the bright light that seeped out into the dim hallway, shining so strongly she was certain the room was much larger than the narrow corridor she stood in.

The serpent turned in that direction and halted before one of the open doorways. Violet strode up beside him and peered inside. A single cot took up most of the space, along with a tiny table and chair. Crisp white sheets and a black wool blanket covered the cot. A bowl filled with water sat on the table, next to a neatly folded set of towels.

The serpent bit out a few guttural words, then gestured inside. Violet gulped again. Clearly, she was supposed to go in.

She stepped inside.

The serpent whirled away from her as soon as her feet crossed the threshold. He walked to the next open door and disappeared inside, slamming the door closed behind him. The quiet *snick* of a lock clicked in her ears.

Violet heaved out a sigh and closed her own door. Perhaps she wouldn't be found out after all. The people here must value their privacy. Her door locked, too—from the inside. If someone wanted to come in, she'd have time to don her disguise.

Understanding what they said was another matter... but for now, at least she had a quiet place where she could think, a bowl of water to wash up, and a warm bed to sleep in. It was likely more than her uncle had—and not quite as comfortable as the room Lark had been given.

The room was so small that, were her arms a little longer, she'd have been able to touch both walls at once, and only long enough to fit the single bed and tiny table. The lack of personal effects inside suggested these rooms were shared.

She strode to the table, pulled out the chair, and bent beneath it. She trailed her hand along a stack of folded black clothing, in various sizes, stacked neatly on a single shelf she found beneath the tabletop. But there was nothing else. No parchment for writing. Just the bowl of water and towels, and the clean clothes.

She paused, catching the glint of something shining. A single hook hung above the table, set into the otherwise bare gray walls.

Had something hung there at one time? A painting perhaps?

But as her eyes trailed down, she spotted a few flecks of black and white ringed around the hook.

She tugged the mask from her face and hung it. The hard edges clattered on the wall as it settled, right next to the paint specks.

Were these lonely rooms the only place where these men could take off their masks? Curiosity burned within her. It was all so odd. Why wear the masks at all? It almost made sense that they donned them when they left to snatch unsuspecting people and beasts, but wearing them through the halls was a degree stranger. Who were they hiding from—within their own city, no less?

She stared at the bed. It looked soft and warm. It would be so easy to crawl in it and let the weariness deep in her bones wash over her. To let the oblivion of sleep creep up, so she forgot all the devastation she'd just witnessed.

But a quiet part inside of her screamed—not yet. This might be the only opportunity she had to learn more about these people. Anything they learned could be the difference between a successful mission and failure.

Violet hefted the mask off the wall and slid it back into place. Then she tiptoed to the door and opened it as quietly as possible.

She slid back into the empty corridor. At the very least, she could find out what lay at the end of the hall. A few moments of poking around, and she'd sneak back to her room and go to sleep until Ryon came to collect her in the morning.

Creeping silently, she made her way past a dozen closed doors and three open doorways. In each of the open rooms, she peeked inside, spotting cots and tables identical to the one she'd just been in.

She considered trying the knobs on the closed doors, but the last thing she needed was to attract attention. If there were men in each of those rooms sleeping, surely, they wouldn't expect to be disturbed. And really, what could she glean from peeking in at them? It wasn't like she could ask them any questions.

Soon she made it to the end of the hall. Her instinct was right. Bright light seeped down from the ceiling in the large chamber and reflected off shining black furnishings. Long, cushioned benches upholstered in smooth black fabric lined the rectangular walls. There was enough seating for a few dozen men.

The center of the room was open, with countless scuff marks dotting the bare floor. Shining poles hung from the walls, much like the one that had been shoved into her hands when she and Ryon took their places at the front of the stands during the games.

She suspected this was a training room. It was empty now, but during daylight hours, the men and trainees likely gathered here, whacking each other with the practice poles and scuffing up the floors.

A doorway rested on the far side of the room. Violet edged up beside it and peeked inside. Another corridor, drab and gray, like the one she'd exited, stretched out before her. There were more rooms, no doubt housing more sleeping masked men. She decided to turn back and examine the training room more closely when a door slammed. Violet flinched, then froze in place as footsteps clattered down the hall she'd come from.

What was she going to do?

She glanced at the room behind her. There was nowhere to hide in there. She could sit down on one of the benches, or act like she was getting in some extra training...

That wouldn't look weird at all. She cringed, then made a beeline for the closest open doorway in the new hall.

Luckily, there was one open right next to the training chamber. She slid inside and shut the door as the footsteps halted and voices rose, loud enough for her to realize there was more than one person out there.

A male and a female spoke, their voices echoing noisily—and use-lessly—around her. She cursed under her breath, wishing for the hundredth time she spoke their language. Why hadn't she insisted on Ryon giving her another one of those feathers? If he'd used it to learn her tongue, she could use it to learn theirs, too.

But a heartbeat later, the voices changed.

"We should speak carefully. The walls in the dorms are thin," the man said.

"You're too suspicious. No one would care if they knew what we're doing here," the female answered.

Violet tugged the door open a tiny sliver, just enough to peek through. She spotted the muscular back of a masked man hovering over someone in a cream-colored dress, only the bottom half of her visible from where Violet stood, as she bent down and dug through a drawer.

Was it the same woman who'd barged into Lark's room? From the sound of her voice, she guessed it was, but it was hard to be sure. She'd not gotten a close look at her before, and now, all she could see was her long legs and her bottom waving in the air as she continued shoving things aside inside the low drawer.

Violet held her breath, determined not to make a peep while she listened in on the strangers' conversation. This was too good of an opportunity to pass up.

"All the same." The man let out a heavy sigh. "I still don't see why you tend to them. They're bound for death. You should leave the healing cream here for the men who deserve it."

"There's more than enough to go around," the girl replied matter-of-factly.

"You know *he* wouldn't like it."

Violet didn't miss the emphasis the man put on the word he. Who were they talking about?

The girl scoffed. "Well, maybe I don't care what *he* thinks."

"You should."

The woman straightened, a small jar clenched in her hands, and spun to face the masked man. It was the woman from earlier. Violet was almost certain. That curtain of long, black hair definitely looked the same, at least.

She frowned up at her companion. "If I don't do something, I'll go mad. I-I have to do *something*." Her voice cracked, and her lip quivered, the pale skin on her knuckles turning white around the jar.

The man's broad shoulders twitched. "Fine. I'll go with you."

"Thank you." She smiled.

"And no chatting with the new fellow."

The girl shrugged. She unlatched one hand from the jar and swept her long hair over her shoulder. "Why do you think I left Iggy in there? He'll fill me in."

"At least that joker is good for something."

The girl stuck the jar in her dress pocket, then leaned back down to dig into the drawer. "Are you ever going to clue me in on why you hate him so much?"

"No." He shifted from foot to foot. "Are you ever going to explain your fascination with the new prisoner?"

"Suit yourself." She straightened again, this time with a roll of what looked like bandages in her hand. "And isn't it obvious? He's from out *there*. I want to learn what I can before..." She shuddered slightly instead of finishing her sentence. "You know what he's planning. I might not get another chance."

Violet's heart seized. What was that supposed to mean?

It appeared she wouldn't learn anymore tonight. The pair strode off together, still chatting, but their voices quickly faded and became lost beneath the sound of their retreating footsteps. Soon, a door banged again, and silence returned to the hall.

Violet glided out of the dorm, through the training room, and back down the hall to the room she'd been given. When the lock clicked shut behind her, she exhaled wearily, and her racing heart finally slowed.

That had been stupid. She'd almost been caught. But still, she'd learned something. How much of it would come in handy remained to be seen, but it was more than she'd known when she first arrived here.

She pondered the girl's words as she removed her mask again and settled it on the hook. Who had they been talking about? She suspected the *he* they were both so worried about might be Jurdan the Supreme. What was he planning that made the girl want to defy his wishes?

And who was *she*, if she could traipse in here to take what she wanted, barge into Lark's room when she saw fit—and from the sounds of things—visit the prisoners, too... Perhaps she was one of the advisors Lark had mentioned. She knew their *secret* language, after all.

Violet grinned. If she wished to defy their ruler, then maybe others did, too. Maybe they could find enough of them to help find a way out of this strange place.

But all that would have to wait until morning. Violet checked the lock one more time and curled up on the bed to wait.

Guard Duty

After Violet wandered off following the serpent, Ryon trailed after them, hiding within the crowds of spectators leaving the games. When he was certain he'd memorized the plants surrounding the door she'd disappeared beyond, he went exploring.

It hadn't been difficult to locate the prison level. He walked down countless halls brimming with plants and dotted with doors until he came across a group of masked men chatting together. He lingered nearby, pretending interest in a fruit tree until he overheard something that piqued his interest.

A man wearing a wolf mask started grumbling about heading back down for prisoner feeding duty. When Ryon spoke up, offering to tag along, the wolf seemed happy for the company. As they descended to the bottom level, he could see why.

The place was a far cry from the brightly painted, fragrant halls up above. It stank of feces and sweat. Men and animals moaned in pain or screeched with anger when they passed.

How anyone could stand it down here, he didn't understand.

"Not many guards want on this duty," the wolf said. "I don't recognize you. What detail are you normally on?"

Ryon gulped, thankful the fellow couldn't see him cringing beneath his mask. "I go out on the boats."

The wolf nodded, appearing to buy the lie. "Let me guess, you waiting for a peek at the little missus?"

Ryon chuckled dryly. He had no idea what he was talking about, but it made sense to play along. "Was it that obvious?"

He let out a low whistle. "She's a fine one. It's the highlight of my night when she comes swaying on past. I swear she does it just to give these scum a taste of what they're missing. She may be pretty, but she's cold as a dead fish."

"You'd know better than me, I expect."

The wolf turned to assess him, his mask sinking, then lifting as he eyed him up and down. "All right then. Follow me. The guy that got hurt tonight is over here."

They strode down two more halls, each identical to the last. As they entered the third, the wolf stopped him in the doorway.

"We're in luck," he whispered. "Looks like she's already here." He nodded to the cage ahead of them.

A man in a spider mask stood watch in the open doorway, his gaze glued inside the cell. Ryon leaned forward to peer around him. He immediately spotted Nox sprawled out on the floor of the cell. He was obviously still under the effects of whatever they'd drugged him with in that dart. One of his legs was bent at what looked like an uncomfortable angle, and a line of drool dangled from his open mouth down to the floor.

He suspected his arms would have been in a similar state of discomfort if not for the woman in his cell. Ryon bit back a gasp when he recognized her. It was the same dark-haired girl that had reprimanded him in Lark's room. And then once again on the stairwell.

What was she doing here tending to Nox's wounds? She laid one of his bloody, torn fists in her lap as she sat on the floor beside him. Tenderly, she rubbed some kind of ointment against his skin before wrapping his hand in a long length of cloth.

"You've hovered back there long enough. Out with it already."

Ryon stilled. For half a heartbeat, he thought she was speaking to him. Who else would understand her when she spoke in Violet's language, instead of her own?

But a moment later, a handsome dark-skinned man clothed in rags strode out of a darkened corner of the cell.

The spider tensed, his hand clenching around the short pole in his fist.

The prisoner paid him no mind. He stopped beside the girl as she finished with Nox's first hand and reached across his body to grab the other.

"I'll tell you everything I've learned so far. It's a lot, too." He nodded down at Nox, a sly smile on his lips. "He shared his entire life story with me once he found out I could understand him. But what do I get out of it?"

The girl rolled her eyes. "What do you want?"

"I want out of this cage, for starters. I've seen how that cat eyes me when he's not looking. I don't care how trained Nox says it is. Won't be long before it decides to eat me for breakfast."

"The cat won't be coming back," she announced.

Ryon thought that news would appease the man, but it only seemed to make him more anxious. His breath caught, and he inched closer to the cell door, before catching sight of the spider and creeping back toward the girl.

"Even more reason to leave. If Nox lost his bondmate, I don't want to be here when he wakes. You don't either... trust me." He shifted nervously, then stared pointedly at the girl's lap. "Hurry with that and let's go."

"Bondmate. He said that before." The girl didn't hurry her ministrations. If anything, she slowed down, her gaze flitting curiously to stare at Nox's face. "Did he tell you about that as well?"

The prisoner's head bobbed up and down, shaking his neatly plaited braids wildly. "He did. He told me all about it. And I'll tell you as soon as we get out of here."

"Don't look so scared, Iggy. That dart will have him sleeping till morning." The girl chuckled sweetly and even squeezed Nox's hand. "See?"

She went back to work. She'd finished with the ointment on Nox's second hand and dug through her dress pocket to gather more bandages. "If I let you out of here now, then who will talk to him more?"

Iggy's gaze darted around nervously. "Send me back in a few days, if you must, but we have to get out of here now."

The girl scoffed. "Really, Iggy. You're being redicu—"

Her words cut off, strangled right out of her throat. Nox! His hand shot up, snagging the girl's neck. He'd woken up and immediately grabbed her, cutting off her air.

Ryon raced forward when the wolf did, both of them flying on instinct. But they needn't have bothered. The spider bent down in a flash and stabbed Nox with that metal pole at the same time the girl clamped down on Nox's wrist.

A loud buzzing rent the air. Nox dropped the girl's neck and convulsed on the ground.

Guano. What was that thing?

Ryon's hand flew to his belt, where a matching pole rested against his waist. He and Violet had been handed the weapons when they took up their spots *guarding* the rows of spectators in the ring.

He had no idea it could do this.

Ryon halted outside the cage as the prisoner and the girl spilled out. Iggy held the girl's arm, tugging her out while she fought to catch her breath, a hand clutched against her reddened throat.

The spider backed out of the cage and slammed it shut, leaving Nox to writhe in the dirt. Nox spun to stare out through the bars, and Ryon nearly gasped when he looked at his eyes. Torment and agony burned in their depths so strongly it sent a shiver down his spine.

"C'mon," the girl croaked out, swapping back to the tongue all the commoners here used. "Leave him. He's suffered enough." She set a hand on the spider's wrist, and it wasn't until she did Ryon noticed the spider clenched his blow gun in his hands once again.

Even after Nox nearly choked her to death, she was still sticking up for him... How peculiar.

"Back to your post," the spider barked as he turned to leave.

Ryon and the wolf returned to their place stationed at the end of the hall as the three of them shuffled off in the opposite direction.

The wolf sighed as he stopped and leaned back against the wall. "Well, that was about all the fun we'll be having tonight. I'm afraid it's mostly just standing around being bored until it's time to swap."

"I'm sorry to hear that."

"I suppose you'll be wanting to leave now."

Ryon bit his lip beneath his mask. Really, he wanted to stay. He desperately needed to talk to Nox—alone. But if he insisted on sticking around, it was bound to look suspicious.

"Well, if there's not much else to do, then yeah." He snapped his fingers casually. "Say, do you need a break to grab a snack or take a leak before I go? I'll stand watch for you. It's the least I can do after you let me tag along for a peek at the..." What had he called her? "Little missus."

"Don't mind if I do." He could practically hear the grin in the wolf's voice. "You sure you don't mind?"

"No. Go ahead." He leaned back against the wall, acting like he was getting comfortable. As soon as the door to the next hall slammed behind the wolf, Ryon pushed off, heading right back to Nox's side.

He stared at him within the bars. His eyes were pinched shut. Was it pain from that freakish weapon or the agony of losing his bondmate? Likely both.

The stench from within wafted toward him. Ryon cringed and turned around. A few moments later, he returned with a change of clothes and a bucket of water.

When he slid open the lock on the small door at the bottom of the cage door, Nox's eyes shot open. He scrambled to right himself and eyed the folded fabric and bucket warily. "Leave." His voice cracked, and his eyes pooled with tears.

Ryon drew a deep breath, his heart breaking at the torment contained in that single word. "I'm afraid I can't until we talk."

Nox blinked repeatedly and his mouth dropped open. "You can understand me? I heard them talking just now, but I thought it was a dream..."

"They were. And I do." Ryon leaned down to shove the bucket and clothes inside. "We don't have much time. The wolf will be back any moment. Here."

"Th-thanks." Nox grabbed the bundled clothes and snagged Ryon's wrist in the process before he could retract it. "Who are you? Why are you helping me?"

"I came with Violet."

Nox dropped his crushing hold to rub his head. "Violet. She's here?"

Ryon pulled back his hand and shook his wrist, burying the urge to wince. "Yes. We came to save you, and then we got separated. But that's not important. Lark needs you to do something before we can leave."

"You talked to Lark?" Nox rubbed his head more forcefully, his lashes fluttering, looking like he was moments away from passing out.

Guano. Would Nox even remember this conversation when he left?

But then Nox grabbed a handful of water and splashed it on his face. "Tell me. What did she say?"

"The leader here has a map to Druturion's eggs. She needs *you* to get it."

"Me?" He spread his arms wide, then rolled his eyes. "Not likely." He tugged off his soiled clothes with a grimace and got to work scrubbing himself.

Ryon averted his eyes. "Lark said anyone in the games can challenge the reigning champion. If you win, Jurdan will give you a boon."

"And I'm supposed to ask for this map?"

Ryon nodded. "Then we'll sneak you both out."

Nox chuckled as he finished washing. "Sure. I'll get right on that." He tossed the wet cloth down on the dirt floor with a *plop*. "Doesn't she realize how impossible that will be? Maybe when I had Flint..."

"For what it's worth, I'm sorry," Ryon said quietly.

"Yeah. Sure." Nox pulled on the new clothes, a pair of black pants and a plain black shirt, like Ryon and all the guards wore.

Ryon glanced around, his ears perked. Still no sign of footsteps returning. There was time.

He reached into his hood and withdrew a lock, then tugged his knife from his belt. "Here. This will help. Add at least one drop of your blood on the feather and make a wish. You'll be able to change one thing about yourself." He eased the feather through the bars.

Nox's brow wrinkled. "Wishing feathers? Now I've heard every-thing."

"It'll work. Trust me." Ryon sighed, sensing Nox's continued dis-belief. "Hide it somewhere no one will find it. You'll need it."

"If you say so," Nox grumbled. But he took the shining silver feather and tucked it into the waistband of his trousers, then folded them over twice. "These pants are too big, anyway." He stumbled as he finished the task, then leaned back against the wall. "That dart they hit me with... I can't stay awake." He slid down until he sat hunched over in the dirt.

"It's all right. I have to go anyway." Ryon reached in and collected the dirty clothes and bucket. Then he closed the little opening and slid the lock back in place.

"You never told me your name." Nox yawned, then forced his eyes back open. "Violet... you're going to find her?"

"Yes. I'll find her. I'm Ryon."

Nox nodded in response, then his eyes fluttered closed and his head tilted, lolling against his shoulder.

Ryon just had enough time to dump the water and stash the dirty clothes before the wolf returned.

"Hey. Thanks for the break. You can go now."

Ryon nodded and turned to leave.

"Wait..." The wolf grabbed his arm, his mask aimed at Nox's cell. "Did you give a *prisoner* some of our gear?"

Ryon stiffened. Was he about to be unmasked?

He forced an affronted tone to his reply. "That disgusting pig shit himself. I wasn't about to stand here smelling it. You ought to thank me or you'd be stuck with it all night, too."

The wolf's fingers tightened on his arm for an instant. Then he laughed uproariously. "Yeah, you sure don't get this detail often, do ya? It happens enough here that you don't even notice it after a while." He dropped his arm and shoved his shoulder. "Go on, then. I'll see you around."

"See you around," Ryon echoed. Then he strode away and slipped through the door before the wolf even finished laughing.

Crack Thump

Violet swam through the dark sea. Water chilled her bones and flooded her lungs, whooshing in and out of her chest. Fish glowed all around the massive ring, their peculiar cloud-like bodies hovering through the water lazily.

How had she ended up back here?

The question flitted through her mind, there and gone in the space of a heartbeat. For the very next instant, the most wondrous sound captured her attention completely.

A melody whispered on the waves. A song so sweet—so breathtakingly lovely—her eyes closed of their own accord to focus on it more clearly.

What was that song? Where was it coming from?

She opened her eyes and swam closer to the massive underwater ring. The closer she came, the louder the song played in her ears.

The structure looked the same as when they'd passed it on the way to the underwater city. Made of a gleaming substance that somehow deflected the bits of flotsam and sand in the water, to remain smooth and shining.

The circle loomed over her as she approached. So huge, it was practically unfathomable that anyone could have made this. It reminded her of the stories her mother told of the Palisade. A wall so high it towered over the tallest tree and stretched across the eastern coast of Dracwood.

The Palisade had been conjured—not made. Was this ring made by magic as well?

She swam closer and closer to the yawning chasm in the center. It was as if an invisible rope wound around her very being, pulling her forward.

The water beyond the ring stretched out, dark and endless. But somehow, she knew if she swam through, she wouldn't find more ocean on the other side.

The song wrapped around her limbs, leaving her feeling weightless within the water.

She had to go through. She had to see what lay beyond...

Rap, rap, rap.

Violet gasped, jolting up on her cot.

Someone jabbered out in the hall in that language she was growing to hate. What did they want?

She dragged herself out of bed and plucked her mask off the wall hook. Within moments, she was at the door.

Rap, rap, rap.

She flinched, then set her shoulders, unlocked the door, and threw it open.

A man, unmasked and in plain clothes, stood in the hall, holding a steaming bowl. He chattered at her pleasantly, then thrust the bowl into her hands.

Violet took the bowl and bowed her head, her palms sweating beneath her black gloves.

Why hadn't Ryon taught her how to say thank you, yet? She was certain she was about to be caught, but the man only nodded in response and moved onto the next door in the line.

What was she supposed to do now? She stared down into the bowl of unappetizing brown mush and grimaced. But then the aroma snuck beneath her mask. It smelled divine, redolent with exotic spices and something sweet she didn't recognize.

The man in the hall tapped on the next door as she stood there sniffing, and the door opened. A gloved hand reached out and snagged the bowl, then the door slammed shut so quickly she almost missed it.

Well then. They must want her to eat in her room.

She shut her own door and locked it with a *click*, then sat down at the little desk to dig into her breakfast. She lifted the first spoonful with trepidation, then smiled as the sweet, spiced mush hit her tongue. It was just as delicious as it smelled, and she was famished.

These people's strange customs were certainly coming in handy. She'd been positive they'd be caught before the day was through, but somehow, she'd blended in through a whole day and night.

But the solitude made her even more curious about the masked men. Were they never allowed to remove their masks in front of others? *Ever?*

That would certainly make it difficult to find a wife. But perhaps they didn't have any... Customs varied, even within her own part of the world. The nuances of relationships here were a mystery she wasn't likely to solve in the short time she had before saving Lark and Nox and escaping.

Violet's stomach turned as that thought crossed her mind. Would they save her family? Or was she destined to be caught and spend the rest of her days battling beasts in the games?

She had no idea where she was within the city. She'd been cut off from Ryon and had no clue where to find Nox.

As she spooned up the last bite in her bowl, Violet sighed. She certainly had her work cut out for her.

A feeling washed over her as she sat there. She couldn't help but worry she was forgetting something. Something important...

A new commotion rose in the hall. Someone was out there, barking out what sounded like orders. Within mere moments of the first words, locks clicked, and doors slammed open. So many doors it was clear the command was being obeyed by all. All—except for her.

Blazes. Violet's heart slammed to life. She scrambled out of the chair and slid her mask over her face. Then she raced to the door and threw it open.

She peeked down the hall and spotted nearly every door open, with black-clothed masked figures lined up in the doorways. The masks stared back at her, each one fiercer than the last, with countless animals she knew and a handful that she didn't recognize.

Judging by height alone, most were fully grown men. But there were a handful that clearly hadn't finished growing, and even a few who were shorter than her, which meant they were likely twelve or younger. In her experience, most of the boys around Greenvale towered over her by the time they were thirteen or fourteen.

She stood tall, waiting for whatever came next.

In the center of the hall, one man strode confidently, eyeing all the men in the doors. Something about him screamed he was in charge. He wore a mask crafted like a spider, and Violet flashed back to the games.

He was the same man who'd stalked out to skewer Nox with a dart when he was going berserk after Flint... She shuddered, flinging the thought aside before tears welled in her eyes.

The spider strode past and stopped at the door to the hall. He whirled around and barked out instructions.

Her heart raced, and a tremor spread down her spine. How much longer could she sneak around without someone realizing she didn't know what she was supposed to be doing?

As the spider finished speaking, men began moving. They exited their doorways in a flurry of activity, some heading up the hall, some down, with no rhyme or reason she could discern. She nearly jumped into one of the lines of men before she noticed something peculiar. Not one of the shorter figures had moved from their doorways. They all waited, watching the flurry of men parade past.

Should she stay or go? Her heart hammering, Violet held her position, praying it was the right decision.

It only took a few moments for the trail of men to disperse. Only one taller man lingered behind, much more muscular than the rest of the boys in their doorways. He strode out into the hallway as the door to the outer halls slammed closed behind the last man, and adjusted the fit of his mask—a bear, its mouth wide open and sharp canines on display.

The bear chattered for a moment. His voice was calm and almost pleasant, but it still contained a note of command. As he finished speaking, all the boys stepped out of their doorways.

Violet drew a deep breath and stepped in line with all the rest. Unlike the men, all the boys headed in the same direction. The bright light down the hall grew closer with each step. As the bear reached the threshold to the training room and halted, waiting for the boys to file past, a sick feeling spread in Violet's gut.

This wasn't good. Was she about to be thrust into a training session with all these boys? Her heart, already racing, sped so fast she grew dizzy.

She reached the end of the hall and stepped inside the training room. To her relief, she spotted the boys ahead of her, already seating themselves on the black cushioned benches lining the walls. A second stream of boys filed in from the hall on the far side of the room.

Violet chose a seat on the end of a bench, next to a lanky boy wearing a mask fashioned like a carnivorous fish. Within moments, the room filled up with boys. Some spoke in hushed tones, but most sat staring expectantly.

The bear strode into the room's center. A second man joined him from the other hall, wearing a shark mask. As soon as they were both front and center, all the boys' chatter instantly ceased.

The bear began speaking while the shark stood silently beside him. It reminded her of her years at school in Greenvale, listening to her teacher lecture on reading and writing. But she suspected whatever this man was teaching had nothing to do with writing.

Violet's stomach churned with every word. There had to be close to fifty boys in the room. It was easy to blend in with that number. With the matching clothes and masks, she looked like all the rest.

But how long would they stay seated silently? What if they called on her to answer a question?

The bear halted abruptly and strolled over to the wall. He pulled two wooden poles down. They were the same size and shape of the pole she'd been given while they'd been stationed in front of the spectators yesterday.

The weapons looked different today. They didn't have the metal short pole attached to the end. Instead, they were topped with a wooden pole, identical except for the color.

What were those metal poles? She'd been made to return her whole weapon at the end of the game last night, whereas Ryon had been allowed to keep the metal attachment. The bear and shark each carried one strapped to their belt, but none of the boys seated with her appeared to have one. Some weapon they were awarded when they completed their training, perhaps?

The question faded from her mind a moment later as the bear tossed one of the poles to the shark. The pair circled each other, and within an instant, they collided together. Their poles whooshed through the ring and struck each other with the loud *crack* of wood on wood.

The fight only lasted a few moments before the bear shuffled sideways and maneuvered his foot behind the shark and shoved, knocking him to the ground. He helped the fellow up while chattering at the crowd. Then he repeated the move at a much slower speed, talking all the while.

Violet's heart pounded. Oh no. She had an awful feeling she was about to be made to practice knocking someone down.

To her horror, the shark and bear finished their instruction and handed their poles off, seemingly at random. The selected boys took the poles and strode into the room's center.

Violet's eyes widened beneath her mask. It was clear, even to her untrained eye, they were not evenly matched. They'd set a beefy boy—almost as thickly muscled and tall as the instructors—up against a gangly lad who might be shorter than she was.

Crack, thump. The smaller boy dropped in a tangle of limbs, falling much less gracefully than the shark had. A few chuckles echoed from the benches until the bear's head spun sharply to the sound, his displeasure evident by his clenched fists. The bigger boy reached down, clasping the smaller boy's hand and tugging him back for another round.

Crack, crack. Thump.

Blazes. What would she do if they matched her up with a bruiser like him? She was skilled with a bow, thanks to her father, and could throw a knife with deadly precision, but hand to hand combat had never been her strength...

Apparently, three times was the limit for a single boy's humiliation. After a third bout that ended as fast as the last two, the instructors collected the poles and selected another pair of boys.

These two were of equal size, and the fight lasted for a few moments before one of them went down. They squared off again, and the opposite boy dropped to the ground. Their third battle lasted the longest, with neither gaining an advantage.

There were so many boys here. Surely, if even some matches lasted this long, there wouldn't be enough time in the day for everyone to take a turn. Maybe she might squeak through without having to fight.

But after the boys traded another dozen whacks with each other, the bear shoved between them and ended the match.

Violet's nerves jangled. And when the bear grabbed the pole from one of the boys and walked toward where she was seated, her stomach jumped up her throat.

Pick someone else... Please, pick someone else.

The bear thrust the pole in front of her face.

Of course, he'd picked her.

She grabbed the pole and rose, striding out onto the floor. The shark was still wandering past the seated boys and hadn't made a selection. She closed her eyes briefly, praying they would pair her up with someone her size.

Her prayers were not answered. When she opened her eyes, it was to watch a boy who was not far off from being a man stand with the second stick in his hands.

She cringed. This was about to be embarrassing.

Violet stood her ground, mimicking the stance the other boys had used when they started fighting.

It was probably better this way. If they'd stuck her with a smaller boy, and he beat her easily, that would've looked suspicious. But surely no one would expect her to beat a boy so much more advanced than she was. At her size, they would assume she was still a growing lad.

The boy she faced didn't have a lot of growing left to do. He was a full two heads taller than her, and his clothes weren't nearly as baggy around his muscular physique. His mask was a bird, like hers, but one she didn't recognize.

He squared off in front of her, and as soon as the bear spoke, he struck.

Crack. She blocked his first hit, but the blow was so strong it rattled up her arms and nearly threw her off balance. His second hit glanced off her shoulder, and she groaned in pain. Then, before she even realized what was happening, her feet swept out from beneath her, and she slammed hard into the floor.

She stifled a second groan as a delighted wave of muffled laughter floated around her. Bird boy puffed up his chest and preened. With a cocky tilt of his head, he leaned down and offered her a hand up.

Violet fumed. She knew if she could see his face, there would be a cocky smirk plastered across it.

She was sick of men laughing at her because of her size or the way she looked. As she hopped back up to her feet, and the laughter died, she squared her shoulders, ignoring the ache, and got ready for round two.

Bird boy returned to his spot casually, his step slow and easy. He lifted his pole lazily, as if the next round were over before it even started.

The bear barked again, signaling the start.

Violet backed away, her gaze locked on the bird. She forced a shake in her step and held her pole loosely, like she was afraid to use it.

Bird boy advanced, his pole raised high to strike.

At the last instant before he swung, Violet dropped her pole and ducked beneath his arm. She came up behind him, hooked one foot behind his leg, and using both hands, shoved with all her strength.

Smack. Bird boy went down hard.

Shocked silence reigned, then excited murmurs broke out as she stuck a hand out to help the bigger boy off the floor.

He gripped her hand with crushing strength and staggered to his feet. Violet winced, her heart squeezing nearly as tight as the boy's grip on her fingers.

Why did she have to do that? Bird boy was pissed. She didn't have to see his face to realize that.

He finally released her and strode back to his starting position.

The bear handed her the dropped pole with a few quiet words. She sensed from the tone he was pleased, so she nodded. She held her breath, half expecting him to bark out angrily when she didn't speak up in response, but he stepped away.

Oh, that was beyond stupid. She was supposed to be blending in, not sticking out.

She returned to her starting stance. She needed to lose the next round. That's all there was to it.

The bear barked. Bird boy struck. And it was clear she shouldn't have worried about winning again. In his anger, bird boy was unstoppable. She blocked a single blow that reverberated up her spine so strongly it was clear he'd been holding back before. But he wasn't holding back now.

She spun away, hoping distance would help, but quick as a hare, he darted after her. Two more hits rained down, rattling her bones when she blocked them. Then she was in the air, flailing helplessly before slamming into the ground once again.

She couldn't hold back the groan this time. Pain exploded across her face and chest. Her attempt to spin away shifted her body so that when he knocked her down, she landed on her front instead of her back. The mask dug into her cheekbone, hard enough to bruise.

Words echoed behind her, then a pair of strong hands slipped beneath her arms, grasped her chest, and tugged her off the ground.

Her head swam as the world righted itself. She expected to turn around and find bird boy helping her up, but when she craned her neck sideways for a peek, it was the bear who stared down at her.

His hands were still wrapped tightly around her chest. As the fogginess cleared from her mind, she registered pressure there. He squeezed her flesh once, then shoved her aside.

Words tumbled out of his mouth. Angry, unknowable words.

The boys rose to their feet and scattered.

Violet moved to leave with them, but a huge hand clamped down on her shoulder, keeping her in place.

Blazes. She was in for it now. It hadn't been her lack of words that got her caught after all, but her damn breasts! What was she going to do?

The Challenge

Nox faded in and out of consciousness, plagued with unrelenting nightmares. One by one, he watched his bondmates die. There were so many. Not just Flint, but all the ones that came before.

Even Chumy, the scourge, who'd been forced to turn on him in his last moments—through no fault of his own. Nox relived the burn of his claws slicing through his neck. Then he felt the cold weight of Chumy's sodden, drowned corpse cradled in his arms and woke with a gasp.

He awakened filled with a grief so intense it flooded through his veins and morphed into an all-encompassing rage. Every time, the drug pulled him back under. Forced him to relive the death of one of his treasured friends.

Bonding magic was a gift—and a curse. It created a bond between creatures so close that when one of the pair died, the surviving member could still hear their thoughts in their mind.

Nox kept waiting to hear Flint. Each time he woke, he reached out for him. But every time he was met with only silence.

It wasn't right! When he was struck catatonic in his youth by the immense grief of losing so many bondmates, the only thing that had saved him was a near death experience. That finally erased the voices of his previous bondmates from his mind.

But he hadn't almost died now. He'd merely been drugged. He *should* be able to hear Flint. Did that mean... Was there still a chance he might be alive? Was he in a cage somewhere, fighting to regain consciousness, just like he was?

He missed him. It had only been hours since Flint fell—most of which he'd spent barely conscious—still, each time he woke, the loss of his bondmate washed over him anew.

They'd been together for nearly twenty years. After so long with Flint's voice in his mind, his own thoughts didn't feel the same. He was incomplete.

"Flint, where are you?"

Still nothing. Nox shoved off the cold stone floor, his entire body aching. A sharp pain throbbed in his shoulder and another on the back of his wrist. Light streamed down from the ceiling, allowing him to see that he was alone.

His head swam, but he blinked furiously, attempting to push back the last of the drug's haziness from his mind. His black clothes billowed around him as he stood, the pants and shirt both a size too large.

What the—? Nox's brow furrowed. Where had he gotten new clothes? He racked his brain, trying to recall...

Violet! She was here. They needed him to do—something.

He grabbed the bars to steady himself. Cloth crinkled from the bandages he couldn't recall receiving, and he closed his eyes. The conversation he had with the fellow who gave him these clothes was hazy, but if he concentrated enough, maybe he could remember it all.

Footsteps pounded down the hall before he could recall anything else. With his heart racing, he peered out of the bars of his cell.

Within moments, the spider appeared with the beauty and Iggy in tow. They marched closer, each of them silent. The spider, unreadable behind his mask, the beauty wearing an aloof stare, and Iggy, looking like he was a heartbeat away from pissing himself.

When they reached his cage and stopped outside, Iggy turned to the beauty with pleading eyes. He chattered at her rapid fire, his hands linked and clutched against his chest.

But the beauty didn't respond. She only nodded at the spider, who strode forward to unlock the cage.

Seeing them here, carting Iggy around against his will, made the rage within him smolder to life.

"What is wrong with you people?" he spat, glaring at the pair. He opened his mouth to say more, but the spider grabbed that metal stick, and the memory of being stung by it flooded back. The pain in his shoulder intensified, his body signaling a warning. Nox shuddered involuntarily and backed away.

He locked eyes with the beauty. "Where's Flint? Please, tell me where he is." The anger faded from his tone, chased away by the depth of his anguish.

Her expression softened before she looked away. She stared down at the floor and shoved her hands into the pockets of her black dress. Her cheeks flushed, drawing his attention down to the column of her neck where a purple bruise stained her pale skin. The sight of it sent a shiver down his spine and made the rage reignite.

Who had done that to her?

The spider threw open the door and barked at Iggy. Iggy scrambled in, his hands held up in surrender and a sheepish smile plastered on his face. Soon, the door slammed closed behind him, and the footsteps retreated down the hall.

Iggy backed away from him. "You're not planning to hurt me, are you?"

Nox's eyes widened, and he rubbed his forehead. "Why would I hurt you?"

Iggy shrugged. "I didn't think you'd hurt her either, but that didn't stop you from trying to choke her last night when she was wrapping your hands."

"*I* put that bruise on her neck?" Nox sank down on the cell floor. "I-I don't remember. Not clearly."

"I'm not surprised. That's one effect of that sleeping tonic they coat the darts with. Makes your memory hazy at first, but it should come back to you, eventually."

Nox cradled his aching head in his hands. "I just want Flint. Did they tell you what happened to him?"

Iggy frowned. "They only told me he wouldn't be returning. I'm so sorry."

Nox's heart clenched. It was all too much. Flint was gone, yet still absent from his mind. He could barely think straight. And to top it all off, he'd... He shook off the thought, not even wanting to imagine it. What was he thinking? If he were in his right mind, he would have never...

He flashed back to his first day here. The other cell filled with men. The wary way they all stared at him. How defensive they were. Had he attacked them, too? Guess that solved the mystery of why no one wanted to befriend him.

That toxin in those darts... It was just like when he was connected to the scourge. Led around like a puppet at someone else's will. He wouldn't suffer through that again. He'd die first.

Death... Why was that a comforting thought now?

A memory struck him, and he blurted out the question that rose from it before his mind convinced him it was all a dream. "Can we challenge the champion to a match? Is that possible?"

"Oh no. You don't want to do that." Iggy shook his head and sat gingerly opposite him, leaning back against the bare wall. "Where did you even hear about that?"

"A guard told me while you were gone."

"A guard?" Iggy cocked a brow. "Is that where you got those clothes?"

Nox nodded and winced when the throbbing in his head intensified. "He said if I win, Jurdan will grant me a boon."

Iggy frowned. "Sure, that's true. In theory. But you don't want to try it. There's something off about the champion. He's unnatural. And in all the years I've been here, he's never lost. Not once."

"Who is he?"

"You've likely seen him and didn't realize who he was. He's always up in Jurdan's box, watching the games. Waiting to be challenged."

Nox shuddered, knowing instantly. "The man with the birds."

"They call him Crow. I don't know his real name. If he ever had one."

"How do I challenge him?"

"You don't. Not unless you have a death wish."

A wish... Nox smiled. "How do I challenge him?"

Iggy sighed. "Just yell at him the next time they take you up there. He'll accept. He always does."

Who knew when that would be? He might be stuck down here for another week before they put him in the games again. Violet couldn't hide forever. The longer he took to make a challenge, the greater the chance of her being found.

"What if I don't want to wait?" He lurched to his feet. His legs shook beneath him, but held. "Hey, come here," he yelled to the guard stationed at the end of the hall.

"What are you doing?" Iggy hissed.

"I'll snag his attention, and you can translate for me. Let's see if we can't get this show over with."

"Nox, are you insane?" Iggy muttered. "You can barely stand. Wait until the sleeping tonic is fully out of your system, at least."

Nox shook his head. He was done waiting. He'd waited and watched and played it safe already. Rather than fight, he'd made a rotting fool of himself. Look what that had accomplished; Flint was gone. He had to escape this place before he went mad, in truth.

"Hey, get your ugly face over here," he yelled.

Iggy groaned.

"What? They don't know what I'm saying." Nox shot him a crooked grin.

The masked man finally slunk closer. He'd not been able to see who it was from the angle of his cage until he strolled closer. The wolf.

Nox nudged Iggy with his elbow. "Tell him I wish to challenge the champion."

Iggy's jaw was clenched so tightly he imagined he could hear his molars grinding. Then Iggy complied, unleashing a stream of words that meant nothing to him.

It obviously meant something to the wolf. He scanned Nox up and down, then strode off without another word.

Nox shoved his head out of the bars and screamed at his retreating back. "Hey! Aren't you going to take me up?" He turned back to Iggy. "What happened? I thought you said I could challenge Crow?"

Iggy backed away warily. "You can. He can't take you out of here on his own. He'll have to fetch them."

Nox swallowed and forced his expression to soften. "Fine. It's fine." Then he sank back down on the floor.

"Well. I guess this is goodbye," Iggy said. "I'm sorry it had to end like this."

"Don't be so sure. I've gotten out of crazier binds than this before."

Iggy fell silent at that, and Nox closed his eyes.

He was still so weary. His body ached, and his muscles trembled; whether a side effect of the drug or the pole, he couldn't be sure. He still couldn't remember all that had happened, but the pain from that device stood out so clearly he could recall the agony of it like a ghostly memory.

It was no surprise the prisoners here were so docile, if that was what awaited them when they stepped out of line. The pain had been so jarring and intense, spearing his shoulder and zipping through his body, stabbing the back of his wrist. He'd lost all control of his bowels. If that guard—who wasn't really a guard—hadn't been there, they'd have left him sitting in his own filth, no doubt.

Nox slid a finger beneath the folded fabric of his waistband and sighed when he brushed the soft feather hidden there. So that wasn't a dream either. He had to hope that feather would be the edge he needed to win.

He must have nodded off. He awakened to the most glorious sound in his mind.

"Nox? Are you there?" Flint's voice reached him, muted but unmistakable.

"Flint! Thank the Mother. I thought I lost you for good."

His eyes popped open. He was still in the cage, with light flickering down on him. He shook out his arms and found them marginally better. The constant throbbing had dulled to a warm ache deep in his muscles.

"Where are you, Flint? Are you still—" He couldn't force out the word. Really, he didn't need to. He didn't want to believe it, but he already knew.

"Alive? No. I'm afraid not. I tried to hold on, but in the end, I just couldn't."

Nox cradled his head in his hands, his lower lip quivering. That must explain his absence. He was holding on to life, trying to stay with him, even though it must've pained him greatly. *"What will I do without you?"*

Flint's answering scoff reverberated in his ears. *"You're going to live, of course. And I'll be here whenever you need me."*

Nox blew out a shaky breath. People had been driven mad by the voices of their dead bondmates in their mind. He used to be one of them. But what was worse was being alone. Those few hours when Flint wasn't there when he called, the loneliness had been worse than the pain, bleeding into every fiber of his being and leaving desolation in its wake. Now, with Flint back—even if only his voice and not his presence—that emptiness seemed a little less complete.

He would live, defeat Crow, and save his sister. That's all there was to it.

"Flint, you're gonna laugh when I tell you what happened while you were gone."

"What kind of trouble did you get yourself into now?"

"Nothing much. Just a death match so I can steal a map from Jurdan."

"What? I can't leave you alone for a moment, can I?"

"No, you can't, buddy. You really can't." Nox smiled.

Consequences

Ryon breathed a sigh as he finally relocated the hall he'd committed to memory last night. He'd spent a sleepless night trawling the green-laden corridors, searching rooms in an effort to locate supplies that might help them on their rescue mission. The process had been dull and often fruitless, but he managed to retrace his steps back to the room with the sea entrance and stash a few odds and ends inside the drawer with their clothes.

Once the halls—which had remained lit ceaselessly but held few people over the *night* hours—bustled with activity again, he abandoned his search in favor of returning for Violet. Luckily, his searching had helped him draft a mental map of where he'd been in the city, though he'd likely only scratched the surface of the structure in his single night of wandering.

Ryon strode to the door and drew in a deep breath. His stomach clenched, the same way it always did when he opened a door in this strange city. Would this be the door that led him to being discovered?

Would someone be waiting just over the threshold to unmask and detain him?

Like each time through the night, he shoved the anxiety aside and pushed open the door. He had to trust that his mask and his ability to speak to these people would disguise him. Violet was counting on him.

A hall filled with masked youngsters greeted him. They barreled past, heading for the door he'd just stepped through. A few chatted amiably among themselves, but most sped by, seeming eager to escape the boring gray corridor into the bright blues and greens outside.

He craned his neck while he calmly paced forward, searching for Violet's falcon mask and slim build in the crowd. The smaller masked figures, clearly all boys and teens, parted around him respectfully, many sending him gentle nods as they passed.

Where was she?

A snatch of conversation reached his ears.

"I can't believe that tiny hawk knocked down the phoenix. He hasn't gone down in months."

Ryon's skin prickled, and he halted in place.

"Ha. Yeah, serves him right," a boy replied.

At the same time, another piped in, "That wasn't a hawk mask. Was a falcon."

Their voices faded as the boys walked out of earshot.

Ryon's gaze darted around, searching vainly for Violet's mask. But he had a feeling he wouldn't spot it. Not here.

He had to find her. Those boys hadn't mentioned anything about her being unmasked, which surely would've been the only thing they would focus on had it happened, so maybe there was still time for him to save her from whatever trouble she'd gotten herself into.

Hustling down the hall lined with endless doorways, he approached the far end where a bright light seeped into the corridor. By the time he neared the entrance, the last of the boys had departed into the outer corridor, slamming the door behind them with a loud *bang*.

Once the echo of the door closing receded, Ryon picked up on voices again, coming from the room ahead. He slowed down and pressed his back against the wall. Maybe if he slid closer slowly, whoever was inside wouldn't notice him approaching.

"They're gone now. Tell me why you stopped classes early. We should've gone for another three matches, at least," a gruff voiced man demanded.

Ryon inched closer and spied two men, one in a shark mask, the other wearing a bear mask. And when he spotted the figure between them, head bowed so he couldn't fully see their mask, his blood ran cold.

Violet. He knew even before she raised her head to peek up at the men towering over her that it was her. Guano.

"We have an imposter in our midst, that's why," the bear answered. His voice was calmer than the first, and his tone suspiciously pleasant despite his damning words.

The shark startled, and his whole body went rigid. "Impossible."

"You don't believe me?" the bear extended an arm toward Violet. "Give the lad's chest a squeeze."

Ryon fumed. He'd heard enough.

Violet just stood there, oblivious to what they said, clearly not comprehending that one of these brutes was about to manhandle her breasts.

As the shark thrust out his arm toward Violet, Ryon reached into his pocket, digging out one of the new toys he'd found on his search.

He slotted the blow gun into the mouth hole of his mask, took aim, and blew.

For a heartbeat, he feared the shot would miss its mark. He'd aimed for the fellow's neck, but the dart flew much lower. When it finally sank, it was into the flesh of the shark's calf.

Shark yelped, retracting his hand before it reached Violet's chest and twisting around to stare down at his leg. The bear spun toward him, peppering his companion with questions while the shark wobbled on his feet.

In the chaos that ensued, Ryon strode across the room in a few long strides and slammed a second dart into the bear's neck.

That got his attention. Bear whirled around, first clutching his neck, then reaching for the short pole on his belt. But the darts worked quickly. Before the bear's fingers clenched around the pole, they fell slack at his side. Soon, both men slammed into the ground—out cold.

"Ryon. Am I glad to see you!" Violet collided with him, her arms locking around his waist.

He chuckled. "Do I want to know what happened here?"

Violet pulled back, and stared up at his mask. "It's a long story." She turned to survey the men on the ground. "C'mon, we better hide these guys before someone spots them."

Together, they lugged the huge men into one of the tiny rooms out in the hall. Violet filled him in while they worked, explaining how she'd spent the night and morning in anonymity before landing in a battle where the bear hauled her off the ground by the chest.

Ryon locked the door behind them after they dropped the second man on the ground. He peeled off his mask and rubbed his beard, feeling so much lighter without the hard covering. But when Violet tugged hers off, revealing a dark purple bruise staining her cheek, all that lightness faded.

"Are you all right?" He closed the distance between them and gently traced the curve of her cheek. "Are you hurt anywhere else?"

Violet sucked in a quick breath, and her lovely reddish-blue eyes locked onto his. "I-I'm fine."

Ryon sensed she wasn't being entirely truthful. Her shoulders trembled gently, her chest rising and falling more than he'd expect, even after forcibly hauling two huge men down the hall.

Was she stricken with terror after her close call and putting on a brave face? Or hiding more injuries so he wouldn't demand she wait somewhere safer while their plan played out? He wouldn't put either notion past her.

But as he stared down into her face and spotted her quick intake of breath as his hand hovered near her lips, all those worries faded from his mind. She was safe. That was all that mattered. Safe and right there, looking up at him with those gorgeous eyes.

He leaned down and kissed her.

She immediately stiffened. Ryon was so lost in the sweet softness of her lips he barely noticed. Then something shifted. The tension in her limbs loosened, and she bobbed toward him. The gentle pressure of her fingertips landed tentatively on his chest.

One of the men groaned.

Violet gasped and backed away. "Are they about to wake up?" She scrambled to replace her mask.

Ryon frowned. "I doubt it. I think that stuff lasts for hours."

All the same, he slid his mask back on, too. It was better that way. Better to stave off the temptation of tugging her back in his arms.

He grabbed a sheet off the cot and quickly tore it into strips. "We should tie them up. It probably won't gain us much time once they awaken, but we might need every moment we can spare."

Violet grabbed the strips he offered her and slung them over her shoulder, but she didn't move to tie up either man. She paced the tiny room instead, wringing her gloved hands. "Hours. We only have hours to save them."

Ryon kneeled beside the shark, yanking his arms roughly as he remembered what he'd been trying to grab. "If all goes to plan, hours will be all we need."

"All goes to plan?" Violet halted, hands on her hips. "How can you say that? We don't even know where Nox is, much less how to clue him in on the plan."

Ryon smiled behind his mask. "I took care of that while you were busy sleeping."

Violet dropped her hands from her hips and bounced on her toes. "You did?"

"Yes. He's agreed to Lark's plan. And from what I overheard in the halls on my way here, news of his challenge has already filtered up from the prison through the rest of the city. Practically everyone I passed on the way here was gossiping about it and predicting a new game would be called for today."

Violet settled beside the bear and started tying his wrists. "That's incredible, Ryon. I-I don't know how to thank you."

He flicked a glance at her, but of course, her face was hidden behind her mask. "Don't thank me yet. We still need to sneak out of here in one piece."

"Tell me, what happened when you spoke to Nox? Is he all right?" Her voice warbled on the last word, and he glimpsed the pain she tried to hide with her steady tone.

Ryon sighed. "He's... hanging in there. I think giving him something to focus on will be good for him right now."

"You're probably right. I can't even imagine what he's feeling. Poor Flint."

A pang of sympathy tore at Ryon's heart. He'd never know exactly what it was like to have a bondmate, but he did have Quill. Over the years, he'd developed a closer friendship with the greedy orecoln than he shared with anyone else. If he had to watch Quill dying before his eyes...

He buried the thought. He couldn't even stand to picture it.

Ryon finished tying up the shark's feet and moved onto the bears.

Violet tugged a knot tight around the bear's wrists and turned to Ryon. "What do we do now? Leave them here and wander the city?"

Ryon shrugged. "Yeah. Hopefully, it won't be long before they call us all back to that ring for the fights."

Violet stiffened beside him.

"Nox will be all right. He'll win."

"No. It's not that." Violet slid the mask off her head. "The ring. I dreamed about it."

Ryon cinched the knot on the bear's ankles and pulled off his mask, too, so he could meet her eyes. "I'm sorry. The fighting had to be—"

Violet shook her head. "No. Not that ring. The ring in the water."

His brows pinched together. "What about it?"

"I'm not sure. But I can't help feeling like it's important." She rubbed her gloved hand across her face. "Is that crazy?"

"No. I know exactly what it is."

"You do?"

He sighed. "Consequences."

Her face scrunched up. "What?"

"Remember, I told you that wishes have unforeseen consequences? That's all this is. You being drawn to something in the water. It must be brought on by our wish."

He rose from his crouch and curved his hand through his sweaty locks, his fingers tangling among the remaining hidden feathers in his hair. That had to be what had caused her fascination.

Violet didn't look like she believed him. In fact, her expression had shifted from confusion to something else entirely. She stood and faced him, planting her fists on her hips. "You never told me. What words did you say when you wished to speak to me?"

Ryon flinched.

"What consequences came from that wish, Ryon?"

He looked her straight in those lovely eyes and told her the truth. "I wished I could understand you."

When her hand rose to hover over her lips, he knew exactly what she was thinking.

He stepped toward her, his voice a whisper. "Violet, I—"

Bang, bang, bang. Loud knocking on the door made them both jump.

"Hey, wake up in there," called a voice from the hall. "All hands on deck. A game's been announced."

He opened his mouth to explain, but Violet shook her head and jerked her mask back on, then strode to the door. Ryon sighed, following suit.

They waited for the echo of footsteps to fade down the hall before opening the door and exiting the little room. Ryon shut the door, hoping no one would be back to check the rooms again for hours, with everyone *on deck* at the games.

Violet trailed behind him, shadowing his movements. It had to be hard for her here, not knowing what was said, what to expect. At least he could listen to snatches of conversation as they strode closer to the stands.

On second thought... It might be better that she didn't know. Even from just a few scattered comments, it was clear the champion was favored to win.

People crowded the halls, all heading in the same direction. They rode the wave of spectators, only breaking off from the pack when they entered the enormous chamber. Ryon squinted, taken aback once again by the bright light and the overwhelming hum of voices chatting excitedly.

So many people. There had to be thousands. How could an underwater city remain hidden with so many people? Before this, he'd never seen so many gathered together before. His little mountain village was tiny in comparison.

"You know the drill," said a man in a fox mask as they approached a rack lined with wooden poles.

Ryon nodded and selected a pole with a short stick already latched atop it to hand to Violet. Then he tugged the short pole off his belt and attached it to an empty stick.

The fox peered around them, scanning the stands up and down. "Head for the gap by the thrones." He nodded toward the box that would soon hold Lark and Jurdan. For now, it was still unoccupied.

"Got it." Ryon tugged Violet's elbow and led the way. They veered around a few bouncy children gawking over the railing to station themselves beside the box and waited for the stands to fill. It wouldn't be long. Folk already crowded the benches, nearly full to bursting.

The spectators in the stands opposite them grew excited, all peering at something in the ring. Ryon followed their gaze and spotted Nox being led across the dirt by the spider. Another man walked beside him. Iggy—the same fellow who had begged that woman to leave Nox's cell last night.

What was he doing here with Nox?

A noise from the box beside them drew his attention. The back door swung open, and out strolled Jurdan, his straight black hair and purple robe trailing behind him. He smiled broadly at the folk in the stands and strode straight for the railing.

Lark appeared in the doorway next, wearing a floor-length gown in a stunning shade of pink. She glared at the man behind her as he shoved her forward through the doorway.

It was that odd, scarred fellow who'd lingered in the box's corner last time. He had another pair of crows perched on his shoulders, and a trio of birds flew in behind him and settled on the box railing.

Jurdan waited for Lark to sit down in one of the fancy chairs and for the scarred man to join him at the railing before he spoke. "I've been told someone wants to challenge our champion. Step forward, brave, foolish scum, and speak your challenge freely."

Ryon's gaze shot back to the ring. He'd been so focused on watching the box that he hadn't noticed the spider stop in the center of the ring with Nox and Iggy. They all stood there, staring up at the box.

Iggy turned to Nox, speaking quietly. Ah, so he was acting as a translator.

Nox nodded and spoke confidently, his voice booming through the stands. "I challenge the champion."

Iggy repeated his words much more tentatively. The spectators erupted in noise, everyone chattering excitedly with their neighbors.

"Do you accept?" Jurdan's voice boomed out from the box, but his stare was fixed on the man beside him.

So, that strange man was the champion. Ryon eyed him again, more circumspectly. The birds on his shoulders certainly gave him a menacing air, but he was portly and aged. Judging from the gray streaks in his hair and beard, he was nearly twice as old as Nox. Surely, Nox would best him easily.

"I accept," the champion agreed.

The crowd roared their approval, and Ryon prepared to watch the fight commence.

Blood

The roar of the crowd buzzed in Nox's ears. Blood. They wanted blood, and this time, he was eager to give it to them.

He waited impatiently for Crow to descend and the battle to begin. His veins thrummed to life, the raging beat of his pulse speeding through his body and setting him afire. Every emotion he'd shoved aside rose to the surface, churning through his core and begging for release.

He'd release it all soon. All the rage and pain and fear. All the heartache. The desolation. He would give it free reign. He'd let them all see what happened when they pushed a man past his breaking point.

Iggy shifted beside him and set a gentle hand on his shoulder. "They're telling me to leave now." He gestured behind him, to the weapons rack slowly ascending from the dirt floor. "As the challenger, you choose which weapon you both use. Good luck."

The spider barked a few harsh words at Iggy, and then they retreated to the door to the underground cells. But though he was finally alone, he didn't move to the rack. Not yet. His gaze was still glued to the box.

Lark perched on one of the golden carved thrones, chewing on her nails. Jurdan glared down at the ring, disdain and amusement clear in his expression. Crow smirked beside him, and his bevy of birds fluttered around the box, cawing angrily.

The sight of the animals made the rage boiling his blood spike to a fever pitch. Flint. Flint should be here with him.

"I am here," the voice in his mind said soothingly. *"I'm always with you. You are not alone."*

That reminder alone kept him from growing crazed by the rage. *"And I, with you."*

Nox strode to the weapon rack and stood, considering his options. The selections today were much more varied than his last battle with the ape. Swords, javelins, axes, nearly anything he could've dreamed up, with the exception of any ranged weapons. He'd trained a fair share with nearly all of them, but only one drew him.

He grabbed a pair of knives the size of his forearm. Growing up in a jungle teeming with thick greenery around every corner, he'd learned how to fight in close quarters. And judging from how out of shape Crow appeared, he was betting that wasn't one of the brute's strengths.

His mind echoed with Iggy's warning. Crow was unnatural, he'd said. He never lost.

Nox hadn't forgotten. He wouldn't make the mistake of getting cocky before the battle had even started, even if the fellow looked like he hadn't trained in decades.

Gasps exploded from the stands.

Nox whipped around, his brows raising. What had them all in such a frenzy?

Crow balanced atop the rail of the box, limber and steady despite his round girth. With a final smirk at the crowd, he leaped down.

When he landed easily in a crouch, Nox nearly gasped as well. The box stood easily at the height of five stacked men. No normal man could make that jump without breaking his legs.

But Crow popped up without delay and sauntered over to the weapon rack. He selected a matching pair of daggers. As soon as he'd made his selection, the rack retracted back into the ground. Then he spoke, raising his voice to be heard over the din of the crowd.

Of course, Nox couldn't understand. But when laughter rained down from the spectators in response, he knew enough.

"Let's get this over with." Nox faced Crow head on and lifted his blades.

The world slowed around him. Nox waited an eternity for Crow to whip around and face him. When he finally did, he flew at him at a speed that belied his aged, fat body.

Without the boons he possessed, that first strike would've surely been the end of Nox. But almost reflexively, he stepped aside at the last instant and struck aside Crow's blade aimed at his neck.

The second blade caught his side. A glancing blow that sheared through his tunic and sliced his stomach.

Nox hissed in pain. But he ignored the sting, certain now the distraction would mean his end if he focused on it.

Even with the world slowed down around him, Crow moved wickedly fast. It was all Nox could do to dodge each blow. His feet moved without thought, his body swaying and spinning.

Crow was abnormally strong, too. Each strike that Nox parried with his own blade reverberated up his arm, each blow so strong his teeth rattled in his skull.

Nox couldn't keep this up much longer. Sweat poured down his brow and slicked his skin beneath his clothes. He wasn't sure how long they'd been at it, but it felt like ages. Something had to give.

"Patience. Wait for him to make a mistake," Flint urged.

Nox held on, knowing it would be the only way he could win. Iggy was right. There was something wrong about Crow. Unnatural.

But Nox wasn't entirely natural either. He took advantage of every boon he possessed from his old bondmates.

When a blow sought to knock him off his feet, his cat-like balance saved him. When Crow kneeled down to cut at his heels, he jumped as fast as a meekrous leaping from tree to tree in the jungle. And when the bastard flung dirt in his eyes, seeking to blind him, his ability to navigate by feel in the dark warned him, so he turned aside before the blade aimed at his ribs sank into his flesh.

As he blinked the dust aside, he saw his opening. Crow's swing for his ribs left his own stomach undefended. Nox jabbed, and his blade wedged deep into Crow's belly.

Eyes bulging, Crow backed away, his inhuman pace finally slowing. He took Nox's blade with him, leaving him with only one knife.

The surprise on Crow's face almost made the loss of one of his weapons worth it. That and the astonished gasps from the crowd. From the sound of the excited chatter in the stands, one might think that he'd just accomplished the impossible.

The fight wasn't over yet. Nox pounced forward, his remaining dagger held aloft, ready to end it.

But when his blade slashed down, it met only air. Crow retreated with speed across the ring, so quickly Nox had no hope of catching him.

Crow halted and tore Nox's blade from his belly with a grimace. Blood spurted from the wound and pooled on the dirt, but Crow paid it no mind. He tossed Nox's dagger aside and thrust out an arm. One of his crows settled on his outstretched palm.

Before Nox made it two paces across the ring, the crunch of bones rang in his ears.

Rot and decay! The bird was dead, crushed to death in Crow's fist.

And even more strangely, his wound stopped bleeding. Nox caught a glimpse of the puckered wound beneath his torn black tunic, re-forming before his eyes.

The Unseen. This was the same sorcery he'd used during the battle in the Abandoned Lands. The same foul *gifts* he'd given to Tarquin and the escaped convicts who'd fought against his sisters.

Despite himself, Nox smiled. Once again, he possessed a boon that would allow him to survive where surely anyone else would've fallen. The healing ability made Crow look invincible, but he wasn't.

Nox knew how to kill him.

Hope swelled in Nox's heart at the advantage his knowledge gave him. But would he be able to handle the task with only one dagger? He'd barely held Crow off with two...

No. He would prevail. He spared a glance for his sister, her eyes round with horror as she watched from her spot beside the dark king.

This was for her. For all the unsuspecting people snatched from their lives, forced to perform for these people's sick amusement. For all the innocent animals they'd turned into mindless killing machines. And especially for Flint.

Rage swelled up within him again, so strongly it burned. With a scream, he ran, barreling into Crow with his blade flashing. He sought any flesh he could find, stabbing and cutting like mad.

His blade connected once, twice, three times, slicing shallowly across Crow's arms and back. But the fiend would heal from those wounds. He needed a killing blow.

The sight of Crow's blood unlocked some deep reservoir of brutality within him. The Nox from earlier, the one constantly on the defensive, was gone, replaced with an aggressor who gave no quarter.

It was the birds that nearly ended him. A pair of crows flew at Nox. The first raked his back with his claws at the same time another slammed into his face. His blade slashed through feathers and flesh, sending the poor bird in his face to his death. The first flew away, but not before giving its master the opportunity he needed.

Crow's boot slammed into Nox's stomach, knocking him off his feet. Nox smashed into the ground, dropping his blade. Crow stomped over while Nox was still dazed and kicked the fallen blade across the ring, where it impaled the wall with a resounding *thwack*.

No. It couldn't end like this.

"Get up," Flint demanded.

Anger burned in Nox as Crow turned his back on him where he sprawled in the dirt and threw his arms out wide, basking in the crowd's roar. He obviously thought the match was won.

Nox had to admit, victory felt beyond his reach. Without a weapon, he couldn't possibly defend himself. His eyes lit on his first blade, cast aside in the dirt. By some miracle he might manage to grab it, but with Crow between him and it, even that seemed farfetched.

Nox's back and side burned from his wounds. His stomach ached like he'd been whacked with a sledgehammer. But none of it could match the volume of his rage.

"It's not over. Get up, Nox!" Flint screamed, his voice thick with desperation.

"If only I were like you, my friend. Then I could take this anger and make him choke on it." Nox heaved up on his elbows, determined to die on his feet. *"I wish it were so."*

The words had barely formed in his mind when a gentle warmth bloomed across his belly. Then a sharp pain struck him. Nox stared down at his hands and groaned as agony tore through his fingers and radiated up his arms and down his spine.

He lifted his hands to his face and nearly doubled over in shock. What in the—

Then his gaze caught on his waistband. The folded fabric was soaked through with blood dripping down from the wound on his side.

The feather! The rotting bloodfeather worked!

Quick as a cat, Nox leaped to his feet. He stalked across the ring to where Crow still showboated for the crowd, oblivious to his transformation.

Then Nox took his hands—hands with nails that now looked and felt just like a jagoth's claws—and he slashed Crow's throat.

Blood spurted out of his neck in a flood of red. Crow's eyes bulged, his mouth gaping open like a fish before he collapsed to the dirt.

Nox stood over him, his chest heaving. As the pool of blood slowly spread, his anger seeped out with it.

Nox should have felt triumphant in that moment. He'd done what he'd set out to do. He'd won, completing Lark's plan. They were one step closer to getting the map and leaving this awful place.

But instead of joy and relief, a bone deep weariness washed over him. The cheers of the crowd roared in his ears, and numbness consumed him.

As the anger faded, so, too, did the claws. His nails retracted, and his hands returned to the human shape he knew so well.

Nox didn't have long to linger over what that meant. Jurdan stood at the front of the box, and his voice boomed over the noise of the crowd.

The door to the prison stairwell swung open, and the spider shoved an astonished Iggy out into the ring. Soon, they stopped beside him and Crow's fallen corpse.

Iggy gulped. "Jurdan demands you announce what you claim for your boon."

Nox stared up at the man, and that revolting sensation washed over him afresh. "I want the map to the eggs."

Iggy blanched. "What? Fool! Claim your freedom. This is your only chance," he hissed.

"No. Tell him."

Iggy spoke up. Jurdan flinched. The crowd fell silent, their gaping faces swinging wildly between the ring and their leader.

Jurdan snapped his fingers. An attendant swung open the door to the box and rushed forward. Jurdan spoke to the man quietly. The fellow hustled off at a run, back through the door.

Murmurs flooded the stands as everyone waited impatiently. Finally, the attendant returned with a parchment clenched in his fist. He handed it off to Jurdan.

Jurdan plucked the yellowed paper from the man with a sneer. He unfolded it, and gazed upon the map.

Behind him, Nox spotted his sister's face lighting up as she spied the map. She nodded slightly without meeting his eye.

So, it was true then. Jurdan would grant whatever boon the new champion asked for.

Nox strolled forward, his hand outstretched toward the box. Jurdan leaned over as if to drop it. At the last instant, he tore the map into a dozen pieces. Only then did he let them flutter down to the dirt ring.

Nox glared up at that man. That *thing*. He stooped to pick up the pieces. Iggy helped, cringing as he grabbed a few of the fragments that drifted down into the pooled blood.

Then the spider strode forward, brandishing that gleaming pole and gesturing for the door to the cells.

Nox sighed as he followed, clutching the pieces of the map in his fist. Whatever else they had planned, this rotting map had better be worth it.

What The Blazes

Violet stood stiffly, shock reverberating through her core as she watched her uncle collect the scattered map pieces off the dirt.

That fight—she shuddered, pinching her eyes closed to stave off the images of brutality she'd just witnessed—she'd never seen anything like it. It had lasted so long she'd feared Nox would tire and make a deadly mistake.

But somehow, he'd prevailed. When his fists morphed into claws, she'd known then that Ryon had a hand in his victory. Only one of his bloodfeathers could have brought on that change.

She stole a glance beside her. Ryon stood steadily in his tritusk mask, watching Nox head for the exit down below. Warmth spread through her chest. How could she ever repay him for all the help he'd given her and her family? Without that wish, Nox would've surely been struck down, instead of felling that trickster champion.

Was it the magic of those same feathers that compelled him to help her? That led him to *kiss* her, even? Her cheeks heated at the memory, and she fought the urge to squirm.

That kiss... it had certainly taken her by surprise. But at the same time, it had been amazing.

Her stomach flipped. If not for his wish, would he have even wanted to kiss her? Or was he just drawn to her, the same way she was drawn to that mysterious ring in the sea?

The door slammed closed behind Nox. Then movement in the box beside them made Violet shove all the questions in her mind aside.

Jurdan strode away from the railing and over to the thrones. With an icy expression, he hooked Lark's elbow roughly and hoisted her out of her seat.

Lark shot him a murderous glare and tugged her arm free. Then she straightened her shoulders and hurried to the railing.

Violet expected Jurdan to seat himself then, but he stomped off to the door at the back of the box. He disappeared into the hall, and a pair of masked men filed in after him, their gazes glued on Lark, clearly intent on ensuring she completed her performance.

Strange. Why was Jurdan leaving early, when he'd been so keen to lord his power over *the diva* at the last game?

Even Lark appeared to be shocked by his departure. Her eyes widened as the door slammed closed, but she quickly schooled her expression and turned her gaze back to the stands.

As Lark's beautiful voice rang out, it was like the entire assemblage let out a shared exhale. The lyrics were indecipherable—to her at least—but even so, the melody wrapped around Violet, calming some part deep within her that still thrummed uncomfortably from all the violence she'd been forced to witness.

As the first verse went on, her mind wandered again. Worry swamped her, nearly suffocating.

Nox had the map now—no matter that it was torn and filthy, it was still within his grasp. No doubt Jurdan was confident enough to allow it, knowing no one ever escaped this place.

But escape, they must. How would they pull it off? She had no time to discuss any further plans with Ryon before they'd been hustled off to watch this match. How many of his feathers would it take? Would they even manage it?

It all seemed so unlikely. The city was so crowded, filled to the brim with masked men. Surely, someone would catch on that they didn't belong.

In fact, they already had. When the bear and shark awakened, they'd better be gone or they would be out of time. At the very least, they had to find new disguises. Maybe they could try to blend in as regular citizens for a while if they ditched their masks. If they changed their hair, maybe they could make it work...

Violet's thoughts were so consuming that she didn't notice at first when the song changed. It took Ryon gently nudging her with the bottom of his staff and tilting his head toward Lark before she concentrated on the lyrics.

She could understand what she was singing! Lark still sang in tune with the same song, but she'd changed up the lyrics.

"Cover your ears," she sang, over and over.

What the blazes?

Violet peered forward carefully, examining her aunt closely. Lark sang on, her gaze trailing over the stands, a slight smile on her face. She looked exactly as she always did when she sang, giving nothing away to the gathered crowd, though a few crooked their brows and cocked their heads, no doubt wondering what the unfamiliar words meant.

But Lark's hands were busy. From her vantage beside the box, Violet could just make out the slight repetitive movement of her wrists, flicking quickly back and forth in a constant motion. She was careful to hide her hands between her body and the rail, ensuring that the guards behind her and the people before her didn't notice what she was up to.

Violet's eyes widened behind her mask as she realized what Lark was doing. She was scratching the same spot on her wrist with her nails, over and over. Digging into her own flesh to draw blood.

Was she readying to use the feather Ryon had gifted her—now?

Beside her, Ryon tucked his pole in the crook of his elbow and stuck both his hands inside his black hood.

Violet hurried to do the same. She balanced the heavy pole against her arm and slid her forefingers inside her ears just as she caught a tiny flash of silver emerging from the sleeve of Lark's dress.

She was making a wish! But for what?

Violet squeezed her ears closed tightly until the song was hopelessly muffled and all she could hear was the heavy pounding of her own pulse within her skull.

She kept her eyes wide open, watching her aunt as she continued to sing. What was she up to?

The guards behind Lark crumpled to the floor of the box. Violet gasped as the masked man stationed beside her fell, too, nearly toppling into her. All around, everyone in the entire stadium appeared to be equally affected.

Anyone standing collapsed, falling to the ground and staying down. The seated people were not spared. Children curled up in balls on their parent's laps. Heads bobbed, mouths fell slack, and eyes drifted closed.

Violet spun back to face her aunt. Lark turned to her and Ryon with a wide smile and motioned for them to remove their hands.

"What did you do?" Violet unplugged her ears. "Are they..." She trailed off, a sick feeling spreading in her gut.

"Relax, they're only sleeping," Lark announced.

"Good work." Ryon tugged off his mask. "What did you wish for?"

"I wished that anyone who heard me sing would sleep until dawn wakes them." Lark sighed sadly.

"Oh, Lark." Violet tugged off her own mask. "That's... Your voice. You'll never be able to perform again."

Lark shook her head. "It's all right. I've had enough performances here to last a lifetime. I just want to go home."

"We will." Violet weaved around the men sprawled out, sleeping in the aisle. "C'mon, let's get out of here."

Lark nodded and hitched up her skirts. "I'll meet you out in the halls." Then she strode past the thrones to the exit in the back of the box.

Ryon and Violet hurried to their own exit. All around, sleeping spectators snored gently, all of them appearing to be in a deep sleep.

The hall was deserted when they emerged. Ryon tugged his mask back on and shifted his pole in his hand. "You better put your mask back on, too. It looked like most of the city was in there with us, but there might be some stragglers out here in the halls."

Violet nodded and secured her own mask when a door slammed somewhere to their right. She whipped around, tracking the sound. Her hand clutched tightly to her pole, and her heart jumped in her throat.

Lark rounded the corner, and Violet's pulse settled.

"There you are," Lark said. "C'mon. Let's find Nox before they all wake back up."

"Sounds like we have hours before that happens, if your wish works the way it should." Ryon led the way, following one of the long, bright blue walkways away from the games. "If the people here base their sleeping and waking hours on dawn and dusk outside, then there's plenty of time before dawn rolls around again."

"That's true, but I don't think our friends bear and shark will be sleeping that long," Violet said.

Ryon flinched. "I almost forgot about them."

"Bear and shark? What did I miss?" Lark flicked her long brown curls over her shoulder.

Violet sighed. "We ran into a few problems. Long story short, there might be a couple of angry masked men searching for us in a few hours once they untie themselves."

Lark chuckled. "Since we're in a hurry, I won't ask. But do tell me the long version later. It sounds like it'll be a good story."

They arrived at a crossroads, and Ryon turned left without hesitation.

"You know where you're going?" Lark asked, a hint of disbelief in her tone.

"I found Nox last night. If they brought him back to the same spot, then he'll be that way." Ryon nodded back the way they came.

"If he's that way, then why aren't we going there?" Lark lifted her skirts, hustling to keep up with Ryon's long strides.

Ryon stopped in front of a closed door and gestured at Lark's sweeping floor-length gown. "You can't go down to the prison level dressed like that." He pushed the door open, and Violet breathed out a sigh as she recognized the room within.

"You found it again. I thought we were hopelessly lost." Violet smiled and slid into the gargantuan chamber. It was as deserted as the last time they'd been inside, except for all those strange curved whatever they were, all lined up neatly in rows.

Ryon headed straight for the large closet they'd found their disguises in. "I spent the night stashing things we might need in this room." He flung open the closet door and beckoned Lark over.

Lark picked up a dog mask, wrinkling her nose. But then a smile curved her lips. "Well, it will be nice to be back in a pair of pants for a change."

"Funny, I was thinking the opposite," Ryon grumbled.

Violet giggled. She grabbed Ryon by the arm and pulled him away from the closet. "We'll give you a moment to change," she called out to her aunt and moved behind one of the big lumps on the floor.

Ryon stopped beside her and tugged off his mask. "Violet, are you all right?" he asked quietly, his eyes flooded with concern.

She slid her mask off, too, and stared up into his eyes. "Sure, why wouldn't I be?"

"Watching that all play out with your uncle. That had to be tough to witness." His brow furrowed. "I could see you trembling."

Violet shook her head. "It's not that. Well, not entirely. Jurdan, their leader—there's something vile about him. I don't know how to explain it. When I'm near him, it just feels *wrong*."

Ryon frowned. "I didn't feel anything."

Lark piped up from the other side, fabric still rustling. "I could feel it, too, Vi. You're not alone."

"Why does he feel like that?" Violet shuddered.

"I'm afraid you won't like the answer." Lark heaved out a weary sigh, then barreled on. "I've felt that same feeling once before. Back when the Unseen still lived."

"No." Violet leaned back against the hard lump for support, her legs suddenly too wobbly to hold her steady.

Ryon's frown deepened. "I don't get it. Who's the Unseen?"

Violet stared up at him. "The year I was born, there was a huge battle in our lands. The Unseen was the one behind it all. He controlled an army of vicious beasts and nearly used them to destroy everything before he was stopped." Violet turned to her aunt as she walked into view, now clothed in all black and wearing the dog mask. "Is it really the same feeling? What does that mean?"

Lark shook her head. "I'm not sure. It's the same... but different somehow. I can't explain it. All I know is we have to escape. We need to tell Kayda. I just know that if we don't get word back home that these people are out here, we'll live to regret it."

Ryon strode forward. "All right then. Let's go find Nox and leave." He slid his mask back on.

Violet replaced her mask and followed. But though they were one step away from finding her uncle and escaping, she couldn't shake off the sinking sensation in her stomach. They might leave this city, but she had a bad feeling that their troubles had only just begun.

They returned to the halls, and Ryon led the way once again. Before they made it more than a handful of steps, Violet spotted a problem.

"Um, Aunt Lark. I don't know if this will work."

Lark startled, her head whipping around to stare at Violet. "What? Why not?"

Violet pointed at her aunt's chest. "The clothes in our size are given to teen boys in training. You're the right height to pass for a boy, but I don't know if you can hide your curves."

Ryon shook his head. "Huh. I think you're right."

As she spotted Ryon staring at Lark's chest Violet had to forcibly unclench her jaw. She was grateful for the mask for once, so they didn't see the sullen look that likely painted her face.

Lark only shrugged. "I'll just have to slouch and hope no one looks too closely." She hunched her shoulders, which disguised her figure somewhat.

"It's darker down there. With any luck, we'll be all right." Ryon stopped in front of another door before long, and they descended a stairwell and through another door.

The stench struck Violet as soon as the door opened, and she nearly gagged. Then the cries and groans of animals and men in pain reached her ears. Her eyes watered with tears.

So many. There were so many poor souls imprisoned in this city. Why? Surely so many couldn't be guilty of the kind of heinous crimes that would merit imprisonment. She wanted to cry from the injustice of it all.

But she spotted a pair of masked men stationed, unmoving, at the end of the hall. She couldn't give in to the tears, not without attracting attention they couldn't afford.

Ryon strode purposefully down the hall and through another door. She kept pace with him but hovered slightly behind Lark, doing her best to hide her from the men watching. She needn't have bothered. The men didn't move from their spot or even slow their conversation. They only waved them on lazily, appearing bored with their task.

It was much the same in the next hall. And the next. None of the men stopped them. Some of them even looked to be dozing beneath their masks. Violet's heart lifted. Maybe they would manage this after all. Maybe they could use the guard's disinterest to their advantage and simply walk Nox out without issue.

They stepped through another door, and Ryon finally slowed. A man in a wolf mask perked up as he spotted him entering. He chattered at Ryon for a moment, then thumped him lightly on the shoulder.

Ryon chattered back, good-naturedly. Could the man make friends anywhere? She didn't know what they were saying, but it was clear they were chatting amiably, like they knew each other.

She paced away, doing her best to look like a curious child, eager for a peek at the prisoners. Lark strolled with her, her shoulders hunched and doing the same. They stopped outside a cell halfway down the hall.

The handsome dark-skinned man who'd acted as translator was inside, peering back at her.

She turned back, peeking up the hall at Ryon and the wolf. They were both still chatting loudly, seeming engrossed in their conversation. Could she chance a word?

She leaned close to the bars and whispered, "Hey. Can you tell me where Nox is?"

The man jolted like he'd been struck when he heard her voice. He craned his head up and down the hall, staring beyond her at the men down the hall before he hissed back, "What's it to you? Who are you?"

"We're friends," Lark whispered. "Please. Nox is my brother. Where is he?"

At the sound of Lark's voice, his brows shot up on his forehead. "I know that voice. You're the diva!"

"Yes." Lark grabbed the bars. "Please help us. We need to find Nox."

"He's not here. The spider dumped me back here after the match and hauled him off somewhere else." He shook his head sadly. "I'm sorry, Diva. If I knew where he was, I'd tell you."

Violet's stomach dropped. He could be anywhere. Time was running out, and her uncle was lost in this massive city. If Nox wasn't here, then where was he?

Unwanted Gifts

Nox trailed the spider through empty halls, shadows and silence their only companions.

When they'd returned below to the prison level, the spider shoved Iggy into the cell alone and bade Nox to follow. He'd been certain the gruff man would only lead him to a different cell. Force him into isolation as punishment for his bold demand. But he'd been wrong.

They'd left the dank cell block behind and ascended a different stairwell. The spider led him through a section of the city he'd never seen before. Bright blue walls shined down at him, and grass crunched beneath his bare feet. Plants in all shapes and sizes grew unhindered, their sweet scent finally banishing the rank stench that clung to his nostrils.

But it wasn't long before Nox's body protested. Even with the gorgeous greenery distracting him, he didn't know how much more trekking he could handle. The wounds on his side and back still oozed blood. His step slowed, his mind woozy.

All he wanted was sleep. He considered stopping and sinking down into the fresh grass. How much longer would the spider lead him?

Nox pushed the notion aside as the spider threw open a door halfway down the hall. He trudged inside, praying that was their final destination.

His eyes widened as he crossed the threshold. This was not at all what he'd been expecting.

A tall, circular room spread out before him with banks of metal cabinets lining the walls, glittering with hundreds of buttons and dials. A whirring pulsed through the room, emanating from a gleaming cylindrical pillar in the center. The towering metal monstrosity was as wide as he stood tall and stretched from the floor to the ceiling inside the cavernous chamber.

And in the middle of it all stood Jurdan, his eyes closed as if in deep concentration. His hands hovered beside the pillar, and a stream of crackling power surged from his palms outward. The tower pulsed from it, sucking it up like a greedy whirlpool.

Nox's skin prickled all over, and a wave of revulsion crashed into him hard, nearly making him gag. As he watched the stream of energy flow from Jurdan into the ship, something tickled the back of his mind.

What was he witnessing? Something inside screamed its importance, but with his body weary and his mind dimmed from the loss of blood, he couldn't quite grasp it.

After a moment, Jurdan stopped. The flow of energy cut off, and the crackling in the air dimmed.

"Ah." Jurdan's eyes popped open, and he stared straight at Nox. "My new champion. I'm so pleased you could join me." He dropped his hands from around the pillar and strode closer.

Nox stepped back instinctively, but the spider was right there behind him. He smashed his fist against Nox's shoulders and shoved him roughly forward.

He nearly heaved again, the awful roiling discomfort of being in this man's presence too strong to ignore. But then curiosity overwhelmed the panic blooming within him.

Jurdan hadn't spoken in that guttural foreign tongue. He'd recognized his every word.

"Have you understood me all along?" Nox asked.

Jurdan stopped before him, brushing his long dark hair off his shoulder. "Finally catching onto that now, are you?" He spared him a disdainful glance, then dismissed him, turning to the spider. "What say you, spider? Is this wretch deserving of my gifts? Or would he just squander them?"

Nox frowned, beyond confused. Why were they talking around him? What *gifts*?

"No," the spider said simply, and the sound of Nox's language on his lips made his fists clench.

Had they all understood him all this time? A cloudy memory rose at the thought. The sound of his language in his ears from another. Gentle hands on his, squeezing, wrapping his stinging knuckles.

He nearly groaned as the realization washed over him. The beauty, too. They'd known what he'd been saying all the while but chose to ignore him. He felt like a fool.

But one thing was immediately clear. He didn't want anything that vile Supreme offered.

"I don't want your gifts. Take me back to my cell."

Jurdan whipped around, a snarl curving his lips. "I make the demands around here, scum." He cocked his head, his stare turning pensive. "Why the map and not your freedom?"

Nox patted his pocket, the crinkle of the torn parchment flattening against the pressure. "That was a dirty trick, tearing it to pieces," he said instead of answering.

"No matter. Keep it. You don't think I've had copies made?" Jurdan chuckled. "Fat lot of good it will do you, sitting in a cell."

Nox choked on a laugh. Maybe it was the blood loss, but suddenly the situation seemed hilarious. Then a door on the far wall slid open, and all the humor drained from him in an instant when he saw who stepped inside.

"These could use a new charge," the beauty announced, her gaze intent on the bag she carried. Then she looked up, and her step faltered. Her hold on the bag loosened, and one of the short metal poles spilled out and rolled across the floor.

"Set them down and leave us." Jurdan bent to pick the rolling pole off the ground as it settled beside his foot.

Those gray doe eyes wide as saucers, the beauty nodded once, set the bag on the floor, and disappeared out the same door she'd entered.

Nox sighed wearily. It was true, then. The whole time they could have spoken to him but kept silent. To what end?

Jurdan paced over to the bag. He dropped the pole in his hand into the pile, and it landed with a loud *clink*. "You are an odd one indeed," Jurdan mused while scanning him, his gaze lingering on his clenched fists. "I've never heard of a bonded pair sharing so many attributes."

Nox narrowed his eyes, fighting to stop himself from wobbling on his feet. Blood trickled down his side, tickling his skin. How long did he have to stand here and listen to this? "If you knew anything about bonded pairs, you wouldn't have forced Flint to fight that match."

"That was rather entertaining. Pity your cat wasn't stronger."

"He was stronger than you'll ever be," Nox hissed, anger bubbling up inside him. His hands tingled strangely.

Jurdan chortled gaily, like the very notion of someone being stronger than him was laughable. Then his laughter cut off, and he aimed those dark eyes straight at him. "You will change your mind about my gifts in time. Mark my words, the next time we meet, you will beg me for them."

Nox scoffed. "You're delusional."

Jurdan only smiled, a contented smirk that made his ageless face even more vile. "I grow tired of this. Take him out of my sight."

The spider's powerful hand clamped down on Nox's shoulder, and he forced him to turn. Within a few heartbeats, he'd opened the door and shoved him back out into the bright hall.

Nox stumbled, the short grass tangling his feet. As he righted himself, he spotted the beauty lingering beside the door.

She strode up to them, a frown marring her lovely features. She started chattering at the spider in that awful tongue.

"You might as well give it up. I know you can understand me now," Nox bit out wearily.

The spider shoved him roughly, forcing him down the hall, back toward the stairwell.

He expected her to ignore him. To keep talking to the spider in her own language. But the beauty surprised him. "I'm coming with you. He needs to have his wounds bandaged."

The spider stiffened. He didn't switch languages, only barked back at the beauty angrily in guttural words. They both ignored Nox, arguing among themselves.

Nox was sick of being ignored. A wave of anger washed over him so strongly it coiled against his spine, bleeding into his veins and bursting through his body. His fists burned.

He stared down at his hands as the claws returned, less painful this time but just as shocking to behold.

His reflexes sharpened, and his ears picked up on the sound of footsteps approaching. This might be his only chance.

He took it. He grasped the beauty and tugged her in front of him, his claws held at her neck.

"Drop it, or she's dead," he told the spider as his hand slid to the pole on his waist.

At first, it looked like he might ignore the command, but then the pole thudded dully into the ground, and the spider backed away with his hands in the air.

Nox scanned the hall. What now?

The beauty quivered in his arms. He instantly regretted his actions. His fingers rested right on the purple bruise he'd put there. She had to be frightened half to death, certain he would finish what he'd started in the cell the last time he'd wrapped his hands around her neck.

He was the only one who knew he would never kill her. The thought of killing a woman made his stomach clench and his throat burn with bile. But *they* didn't know that. He just needed a moment to think.

A trio of masked figures rounded a bend in the hall behind the spider.

Rot and decay. Now he was outnumbered.

One of the figures gasped and threw off their mask. "Brother."

"Lark?" Nox asked incredulously.

She raced forward, but the spider reached out and caught her.

Lark struggled, fighting and kicking like mad. For half a heartbeat, he thought she might break free. She knocked the spider's mask loose, and he rushed to right it before gripping her shoulder and slamming her head into the wall.

"Let her go!" Nox yelled, tightening his grip on the beauty. She hissed as one of his claws split the skin on her throat, and a tiny trickle of blood spilled down her neck.

"A trade." The spider demanded, his hand still clenched around Lark's shoulder, holding up her dead weight. "I'll give you the diva, and you give me Mariun."

Dimly, Nox realized he'd finally learned the beauty's name. But then he spotted the other masked men creeping up on the spider. The taller of the pair lifted a blowgun in his fist and took aim.

The spider whipped around and spun Lark in front of him like a shield. "No tricks." He nodded his head and barked. "Get over there where I can watch you."

The two hustled over, and Nox realized who they must be. But the thought hovered in the back of his mind, his focus caught by the spider holding his sister in his clutches.

"I'll trade. Hand her over."

"You first," the spider sneered, jiggling Lark's unconscious body.

Mariun spoke up. "Relax now. We can handle this." She nodded at Ryon. "You go grab her." She nudged her shoulder into Nox's chest. "When he has her, you'll let me go, won't you?" She stared at the spider straight on. "If he doesn't, then you can snatch her back."

They all nodded in agreement. Ryon slid the blowgun in his pocket and walked over to the spider. When Lark was safely within his arms, Nox released his grip on the beauty's neck.

Her head held high, Mariun strode forward with purpose. In a few quick strides, she reached the spot where Ryon had carted Lark away from the spider.

Quick as lightning, her hand shot into Ryon's pocket. Before any of them could do more than gasp, she lifted the blowgun to her mouth and blew.

The dart sank into the spider's chest. He stiffened for a moment, gripping his chest, his mask bobbing down as he stared dumbfounded at the spot where the dart pierced his flesh. Then, he collapsed to the ground with a *thump*.

Violet was the first to move. She rushed forward, helping Ryon with Lark. "Uncle Nox, are you all right?"

Nox wobbled where he stood, the anger he'd been holding on to evaporating in the face of his shock. His hands tingled again, and he gazed down at his fists in time to see the sharp nails detract and his hands take on their human shape again.

"What did you do that for?" Nox glared at the beauty, his brows pinching together.

She slid the blowgun in the pocket of her dress before answering. "You won't make it out of here without my help. You're taking me with you."

"What?" Nox's voice quavered with disbelief. "No."

She stood her ground, planting those long legs firmly and crossing her arms. "You want out of here? Well, guess what? So do I. Take me with you, or I'll scream so loud every guard in this city will come hunting for you."

Violet quirked up a grin. "They would if they were awake."

"What's that supposed to mean?" Nox grumbled. He spared a glance for his niece. She'd started walking, helping Ryon cart Lark down the hall, back in the direction they'd come from. Nox trailed after her, hoping she knew where she was going.

"Haven't you wondered why the halls are so deserted?" Violet grunted, huffing under Lark's weight. "Lark put them all to sleep. Everyone who was back there at the game after you left."

Mariun barreled up beside him. "She did what?"

"It's fine. They'll wake with the dawn," Ryon stated.

"All the same, we better hurry. There's still guards awake on the prison level. And more elsewhere, surely." Violet stumbled along, tugging Lark with her. Then she paused, raking her gaze over Mariun. She tilted her head back to Nox. "Are we taking her, too? She did help us back there."

"Are you crazy, squirt?" Nox shook his head. "No. She's one of them."

Mariun huffed. "I'm right here, you know."

"Not fun having someone talk around you, is it?" Nox speared her with a sour glare.

Mariun rolled her eyes. "You know what, you're right. I am one of them. I know exactly what will happen when they find you missing and come after you. Don't you think that knowledge will come in handy?"

Violet shuffled forward again. "She makes a good point."

It didn't matter how much the beauty helped them now, he couldn't spend another moment with her. Violet didn't know her like he did. She didn't watch her point her little finger at Flint and...

Nox hardened his heart and turned to tell her to take her help and shove it.

But when he stared into her eyes, something stilled his tongue.

"*Take her,*" a voice whispered in his mind.

And though he knew he'd likely live to regret it, Nox listened.

"Fine. You can come. But as soon as we're safely away from here, you're gone. Got it?"

Mariun's eyes lit up, and a smile flashed on her face, so vibrant it sent a bolt of lust straight through his belly. Nox shook off the feeling with a grimace and hustled off after the others.

Rot and decay. He was definitely going to regret this.

Not Kidding

R yon shoved open the door to the massive room. Finding it empty, he loosed a sigh, then drug Lark's dead weight inside.

"Here, we can rest her against one of these things," Violet said with a grunt.

"I take it the two of you are not real guards." Mariun strolled up beside them as Nox closed the hall door.

"No." Ryon set Lark down gently, carefully leaning her against one of the metal monstrosities. Then he flung off his stifling mask, happy to be rid of it. Violet quickly followed suit.

Mariun frowned and kneeled next to Lark. Violet scooched closer to her aunt's side, clutching her arm protectively.

"I know a thing or two about healing," Mariun said. "Let me take a look."

Violet sighed and nodded.

"If you're not from here, then how did you find us?" Mariun lifted one of Lark's eyelids gently and cocked her head to stare into her eyes.

"We swam." Violet pointed at the wall beside them where they'd entered yesterday. "Came in right there."

Mariun bristled. "You swam?" She chuckled nervously. "You're kidding, right?" She moved on to Lark's neck, placing her fingers gently on the sides. Ryon's gaze flickered between the women and lingered on the dark bruises on the new woman's neck.

His stomach clenched. Was that what had her so eager to leave with them? Was someone here hurting her?

He didn't trust her. Not in the slightest. But he wasn't about to argue to send her back to whoever hurt her—not after she helped them take down the spider in the hall. He only hoped that decision wouldn't come back to haunt them later.

"She's not kidding," Ryon piped in. "We'll need to swim out, too. Do you both know how?" Ryon shifted, turning so he could address the question to Nox as well.

Violet chuckled. "You don't have to worry about Uncle Nox. Swimming is one of the things he does best."

"I can swim, too," Mariun announced. She frowned down at Lark. "But I don't think she can. Not now, at least."

"What do you mean?" Violet squeaked.

"She's out cold." Mariun pinched Lark's arm. "That blow to the head... She likely won't wake for hours."

Ryon frowned. If Violet's aunt didn't make it, she'd never forgive herself.

"We don't have to swim." Mariun stood and paced across the room to another of the huge cylindrical shapes lined up on the floor. "We can sail."

Nox crossed his arms. "Sail? I don't see any boats lying around."

"No?" Mariun aimed a teasing grin at Nox. Then she set her hand on the vessel beside her. A quiet *hum* filled the air, followed by a great *whoosh*.

Just like it had when they'd entered outside, a doorway appeared as if out of nowhere.

Violet gasped. "Those things *are* ships?"

"Kind of." Mariun shrugged. "They're not meant to travel long distances. We use them to ferry people up and down from Thalassia."

The place they were in finally had a name. Ryon filed it away in his memory and strode forward, peering into the vehicle. The inside was bare, just a wide oval with bench seats and straps lining the walls. It looked large enough they would all fit inside with room to spare.

Nox rubbed his forehead. "You want me to get in that thing?" He shook his head. "I think I'd rather take my chances swimming."

Mariun scoffed, hands on her hips. "Don't tell me you're too scared?"

Nox rolled his eyes. He paused, his gaze flicking down to his feet. Then he grumbled almost to himself, "Don't act like you weren't terrified of the water."

Mariun cocked a brow. "Pardon?"

Nox threw up his hands and stomped over to Lark's side, kneeling with his arms spread, as if to scoop her up. But he grimaced as he bent, then seemed to think better of it, and leaned against the metal ship with a pained scowl. "Help me move her, would you?"

Ryon nodded and strode over to lift Lark. As he crossed the room to settle her in the odd contraption, Mariun hustled over to the bank of drawers and rustled around inside them.

"There ought to be bandages in here somewhere." Mariun slammed the doors open and closed, shoving her hands around inside and rattling through the odds and ends.

"I'll help you look," Violet offered, marching over to assist, her gaze lingering on her uncle warily.

"Bottom left drawer," Ryon said. "I stashed some there last night."

He strapped Lark into one of the seats, then exited the vehicle and returned to the drawers. Mariun held a roll of bandages in her grasp and was busy clucking at Nox, whose scowl appeared to have become a permanent fixture on his face.

Ryon shook his head and stopped beside Violet, his pulse racing at the sight that greeted him. She hunched over the bottom drawer with her shapely rear swaying in the air in her black trousers.

He tore his gaze away before he was forced to adjust his own pants.

Violet straightened and thrust a pile of cloth in his arms. "Here's your clothes. We better take everything we brought in back out with us."

Ryon nodded, his nose wrinkling at the musty stench wafting off his clothing. If not for that, he would've gladly changed back into them. He still wasn't a fan of having his legs swathed so tightly, but drying folded up inside a drawer hadn't exactly been a recipe for freshly scented fabric.

"We don't have time for this," Nox grumbled as Mariun wound the bandage around his middle.

"You'll bleed out, you fool man. Stay still."

Ryon shared a look with Violet as their bickering continued. He leaned over and whispered conspiratorially, "I don't think they like each other very much."

Violet grinned up at him, then her gaze strayed to his lips. His heart pounded. Was she thinking about kissing him?

"Rot and decay! Are you trying to kill me?"

Nox's strangled outburst intruded on the moment. Violet blinked and stepped away, her own clothing clutched tightly to her chest.

Ryon sighed. Talk about things they didn't have time for... Surely kissing qualified. He shoved the memory of Violet's soft lips from his mind and followed her into the craft.

Violet sat beside her aunt, and Ryon gave her some space, settling in a seat where he could stare out the open doorway. Nox and Mariun continued to bicker at each other for a few more moments, then they, too, entered the vehicle.

"What now? How does this thing work?" Nox asked.

Mariun pushed on a panel beside the doorway inside the strange craft. The panel slid down, revealing rows of buttons and knobs.

Violet's eyes widened. "I've never seen anything like this back home. How did your people make this?"

Mariun shrugged. "We didn't. We just found it and figured out how to use it." She sighed, shooting a glare at Nox. "It's a rather long story. I would tell you, but seeing as we're parting ways soon, I don't know that we'll have the time for it."

Ryon's gaze shot to Nox. His scowl still hadn't budged.

Was Nox really planning to send the poor girl off all on her own once they made it out of here? What had she done while he was here to make him so ornery?

The vessel jolted forward, and the question slipped Ryon's mind. He watched in awe as the craft slid toward the section of hull that had opened to allow them inside. Ryon couldn't see it from his position inside the craft, but something outside clanged, and soon, they slid back inside the little box he remembered so clearly.

Mariun left the little panel down and jumped out of the craft. Ryon's heart jolted. Where was she going?

Apparently, Nox had the same thought. "Hey, where are you going?" he shouted, lurching to his feet and traipsing after her. He caught her arm before she made it back into the outer room.

Mariun shot daggers at him with her gaze and wrenched her arm free. "Do you mind?" She stomped across the room and grabbed one of the metal poles out of a drawer. "I'm just covering our tracks with a bit of sabotage. Or did you want them to follow us as soon as they discover we're missing?"

Nox sputtered unintelligibly. Then he crossed his arms and watched her every move.

Mariun kneeled down in the doorway to the hatch. She jammed the pole in the floor, right where the wall would come crashing down.

She smiled as she rose, surveying her handiwork. Then she tossed Nox a haughty glare and hopped back into the craft.

Nox filed in behind her and sank down beside Violet.

"Here goes nothing." Mariun pushed a few buttons inside the panel. The door to the ship closed, and then another *clang* echoed outside.

The clang was quickly joined by a gurgling *whoosh* that likely signaled the dark ocean water rushing in to surround them. When the craft lifted in the current a few moments later, swaying precariously for a heartbeat before stabilizing, he figured his guess was right.

Violet spun in her seat, her wide eyes staring all around the ship's interior. "What's happening? Are we moving? How can you be sure when you can't see where we're going?"

Just like inside Thalassia, the ceiling of the craft was illuminated by a soft glow seeping down from the roof. But Violet was right. There were no windows or view ports to watch their progression through the water.

Though Ryon could sense that they were in motion, not being able to see where they went was unnerving. Sweat beaded on his upper lip, and he fought the urge to stand up and pace.

Mariun waved a hand. "It's all automated. The ship will rise to the surface, and a porthole will open in the ceiling so we can climb out." A thought seemed to strike her then, for her shoulders stiffened, and her fingers tangled nervously in the folds of her black dress. "Please tell me you have a boat out there waiting for your return. You didn't *swim* all the way here, did you?"

"We do," Violet insisted.

A quiet sigh escaped Mariun.

"A raft," Ryon added.

"A *raft*?" Mariun groaned. "Oh no. That won't do."

Ryon's stomach lurched. What did Mariun mean—a raft wouldn't do? That's all they had.

"You know what they say about beggars," Nox quipped.

Mariun glared at Nox. Then she turned to Violet with a soft smile. "If you want to escape without being recaptured, you might want to find something a little faster than a raft."

Violet crossed her arms, frowning. "We *had* a fast ship. Until your masked guards set it alight."

Mariun nodded. "Sounds like you're owed a replacement." She leaned forward. "I know where all the ships the guard sail are docked. It's not far from here."

"And we're just supposed to follow you there blindly?" Nox scoffed. "Sounds like a trap to me."

Mariun snorted, waving her arms dramatically. "Why would I go to the trouble of helping you escape to lead you to a trap now?"

Violet hummed in agreement. "She's right, Nox. Think about it. She could've just as easily helped the spider recapture us back there instead of knocking him out with that dart."

Ryon held his tongue. He could see the logic in Violet's words, but something about the dark-haired girl still didn't sit right with him.

He wasn't sure what she'd done to engender such a distrustful response from Nox, but he'd bet anything there was something neither of them had bothered to fill them in on yet. Until he knew the whole story, he was planning to keep a close eye on Mariun. Violet appeared to have taken a liking to her already, but he wasn't so quick to assume she didn't have ulterior motives.

"Let's talk it over with Aren when we reach the surface. I'm sure he'll want a say in where we go next," Violet continued.

"Fine," Nox grumbled. "Maybe he can talk some sense into you."

The vessel bobbed suddenly, then halted its upward movement. Moments later, the roof cracked open with a *hiss*. Sunlight streamed in, and the gentle slap of water on the hull grew distinctly louder.

Ryon shaded his eyes briefly, then released himself from the seat straps. He was the first to approach the yawning circular hatch in the roof. Just as he'd decided to leap up and grasp the edges to lever himself on the roof, Mariun tapped his shoulder.

"Do you mind backing up?" She pursed her lips, staring at him expectantly.

Ryon did so immediately.

Mariun tapped her foot three times on a circular floor tile he'd not noticed, then backed away hastily.

The floor cracked open, and a set of stairs ascended, reminding him of how the weapons racks had appeared in the games. He quirked a brow, watching them slowly creep up until a set of five steps rested on the ground, providing ample access to the ceiling hatch.

It was rather impressive. He had to agree with Violet. The vessels of Thalassia were unlike anything they had in his mountain village.

"If we go after those ships of yours, perhaps there will be time for your story, Mariun." Violet released her straps and strolled over to stare at the steps with curiosity burning in her eyes.

Ryon mounted the first step, and a second set of curious eyes stared down at him from above.

"Lark." Muse landed atop the boat and glared inside, her shrewd gaze flitting around and her feathers bristling as she spotted her unconscious bondmate. "What happened?"

"A knock on the head," Ryon whistled. "She'll be all right after some rest."

But though he assured the frightened falcon, Ryon wasn't altogether sure that was true. He winced as he recalled the dull thud Lark's skull made as the spider slammed her head into that wall.

Only the foulest of men laid their hands on a woman. Maybe the spider was the one who put those bruises on Mariun's neck. Would certainly explain why she had no qualms about knocking him out with a dart to the chest.

Ryon shook off the thought as he mounted the stairs and emerged into the bright daylight. The sunlight warmed his skin, and the sea breeze blew through his locks. He sucked in a welcome breath and waved at Aren, who was steadily rowing closer on the little raft.

"Ho, Ryon," Aren called. "Who else is with you?"

Violet's head popped out next. "Uncle Aren. We found them!" she shouted triumphantly.

Nox ascended with his scowl still firmly in place. "Almost all of them, you mean."

"What?" Aren blanched, and he rowed like mad.

"It's Flint," Nox amended, seeming to catch on late to what Aren had assumed. "Flint's gone."

He hadn't known it was possible for a man to look simultaneously relieved and horrified all at once, but that was what washed over Aren's face as the news struck him. "Gods, Nox. I'm so sorry."

Nox only grunted in response, his gaze locked on Mariun as she climbed the stairs with wide eyes.

"Who's she?" Aren asked. "Where's Lark?" He pulled abreast of their vessel and tossed a rope over.

Ryon caught it, busying himself by tying it fast to the open hatch door.

How did they tell the man that the love of his life had been injured and struck unconscious on their watch?

Violet ignored his first question and broke the news as gently as if she were speaking to a lost child. "Uncle Aren, Lark's inside resting. She struck her head while we were escaping."

Aren rushed to mount the bobbing craft and jumped inside. He returned a moment later with Lark cradled in his arms. Muse hovered around her, wings flapping and her head bobbing like a mother hen.

Aren settled her down on the raft. He cradled her head in his lap and gently brushed the brown curls off of her face.

But when he lifted his eyes, there was nothing gentle in their depths. "What happened to my wife?" he bit out.

Ryon shuddered from the venom in his tone.

Violet frowned. "We got her out, like we said we would, that's what." She turned to Mariun as she hopped off the metal craft onto the raft. "Do you have to tap on something to send that back?"

Violet kept her tone light, but he spotted the cagey way her gaze flicked between Aren and the craft, almost as if she were waiting for him to rush back inside and return to the city, desperate for vengeance.

Mariun slid off cautiously, tapping her boot on the raft gingerly before giving it her weight. Even so, she wobbled, unsteady on the floating raft that shuddered under the weight of so many people. Nox hopped down beside her and hooked her elbow, tugging her away from the edge before she spilled into the ocean.

Mariun extracted her arm and turned to Violet, then nodded back at the craft. "It will return once there's no weight inside it."

Ryon took that as his cue to hop off. He untied the rope from the hatch and joined the others on the raft.

Only once the metal sank beneath the sea did Violet reveal the whole story to her uncle. Ryon spent just as long whistling back and forth with Muse. Mariun and Nox sat nearby, glaring at each other, adding a word to the story here or there, mostly to lob barbed jabs at each other.

Once they'd told Aren all of it, he met Mariun's eyes with grim determination. "Where are those boats? I'm taking my family home."

Boat Heist

T he ink-dark sky winked with stars when their raft closed in on the little island. Violet shivered as she sank into the sea, the cold water soaking through her black clothes instantly.

They'd rowed ashore far above the large wharf where rows of sleek sailboats perched. But rather than beach the raft, Aren had returned to the black sea, keeping watch over his wife's sleeping form and leaving the rest of them to swim the final distance to land.

Would Lark ever wake? Violet's gut churned, anxious energy pinging around in her belly.

Surely, they hadn't gone to all that trouble to save her just to have her die in her sleep... fate wouldn't be that cruel, would it?

She shook off the worry as sand crunched beneath her boots. Now was not the time. They had to stay sharp if they wanted this theft to go off without a hitch.

Ryon caught her elbow as she staggered on the sand. "Everyone made it?" he whispered.

Beside her, Nox and Mariun nodded. Each of them dressed in black. Mariun had swapped her dress for Lark's set of guard clothes. They'd even painted their faces with a mixture of fish oil and ash, leaving the whites of their eyes as the only spot of brightness to hover within their hoods.

A soft trill echoed in the sky above. "Muse says the coast is clear," Ryan announced quietly.

Violet's gaze caught on Mariun as they trudged toward the wharf. She'd claimed the boats would be unmanned. Apparently, they only kept a skeleton crew on the island, watching over the ships. Crows acted as messengers, calling forth a boat to pick up any guards leaving the underwater city on their missions to stock the prisons with wild beasts.

When not needed, the guards here were left to their own devices. Mariun had heard rumor the place had become a bit of a wild haven. A reward given to the loyal defenders of Thalassia, rife with loose women and euphoric elixirs that numbed the senses.

If that proved true, then their mission would no doubt be brief and uneventful. But despite Muse's assurances, an odd premonition of danger lingered in the back of Violet's mind.

There was nothing for it but to push through it. She wouldn't let fear stop her. Not when they were so close to success.

The island was covered in trees beyond the white sand beaches. They snuck into the tree line, using the forest as cover. But it appeared the subterfuge was not warranted. They saw not a single soul on the long walk to the wharf.

They arrived at the wharf without issue. Sounds of merriment wafted on the air, laughter and revelry, boastful shouts in that odd tongue. But the voices were muted, and the men nowhere to be seen. A warm glow peeked through the trees somewhere inland, and Violet guessed the guards were gathered there, celebrating with their friends in the night.

"C'mon." Mariun made for the closest ship. "Not these few, they're far too big. Those two, on the end."

They followed her instruction and paced down to the wharf's edge. They'd decided to take not one, but two ships. Aren was determined to return to Dracwood with Lark and his son, while Violet and Nox would stay to hunt for Druturion's eggs.

So, as they approached the little ships—each much bigger than their raft, but small enough to be manned by two, with one on the sails and another at the helm—they split up. She nodded to Ryon as he followed Mariun into the first vessel, and she hurried with Nox into the second.

After a cursory search to determine the ship was indeed unmanned, they set about readying it to sail.

"Damn," Nox exclaimed, his gaze locked on the big yellow sail. "There's barely any wind."

Violet sighed, seeing he was right. They'd be forced to sail away at a snail's pace, praying all the while that none of the men merrymaking in the woods happened by.

Nox finished untying the boat from the wharf and turned to her with a grin. "Lucky your uncle is here to play tug boat." He grabbed the rope and strode to the bow.

Violet's brow furrowed, but then she remembered how he'd carted their boat through the Still Sea and grinned.

"I'll give our boat a head start, then swim back to help the others."

"All right. Be careful."

Violet cringed as he dove into the dark water with a splash. But only a bare moment passed before another sound had her scrambling away from the bow and searching for somewhere to hide.

Loud voices approached; a gruff-voiced man, his words loose and slurred, followed by the husky tones of a woman replying coyly.

Violet raced for the hatch to the underdeck, where a small room hid, with little more than a row of hammocks and a teeny closet that reeked of excrement. She slid into the privy as boots clattered above deck and narrowly avoided tipping over the chamber pot.

When the footsteps grew louder, she bit back a groan. Then the voices spilled into the air just outside, and the rustle of clothes being removed joined in before one of the rope hammocks squeaked.

They didn't waste any time, did they? Violet flinched as groaning started. But the two were so wrapped up in what they were doing they didn't notice when the boat started to move. Violet held still, praying they would keep at it long enough for Nox to return and save her.

Of course, her luck didn't hold out. When the boat jolted to a stop a few moments later, the amorous noises cut off, replaced with startled talking. Violet held her breath, waiting for them to climb back above deck. Maybe then she could slip out and search for a weapon...

But just as footsteps pounded on the stair, Violet's traitorous nose twitched.

"*Ah-choo*." Blazes. She had the worst luck.

The footsteps pounded back down, and the door to the privy ripped open. Violet stared up into the angry eyes of a half-dressed, red-faced man.

She knelt and grabbed the only thing she could. The chamber pot lid.

The man smacked it out of her hand before she could raise it in her defense. It landed on the wooden floor and rolled away into the outer room.

"Please," she pleaded. "Don't hurt me." She raised her hands and sucked in a deep breath, her heart in her throat. The foul air in the little room crackled around her.

The man reached in, his beefy hands aimed right at her throat. Before they connected, the strangest thing happened. He slid away, pushed as if by a great wind gust.

Violet's eyes bulged, her mind racing as she stared down at her hands. But before she could connect the dots in her mind, a girl in a flimsy pink dress smashed the chamber pot lid down on the man's head, and he crashed to the floor.

The wind cut off as fast as it had appeared as Violet stood there reeling in shock.

The girl had helped her? And had she just *summoned*?

Apparently, the waifish blonde held no love for the downed man, despite what they had been up to just moments ago. She even spat on him as he sprawled there motionless on the ground.

She started chattering, but Violet shook her head, frowning.

"I'm sorry. I don't understand you." Violet grabbed one of the hammocks and tugged it roughly from the walls. She set to work tying the man's hands. The girl grabbed another with a smile, then started roughly tying his feet.

By the time Nox returned, they were done. "Violet," he called, his voice full of alarm. "Where are you?"

"Down here," she said.

Her uncle's eyes looked like they might peel out of his skull when he spotted the disarray down below. Shattered bits of the lid lay scattered about, and blood speckled the walls.

"Rot and decay, Vi. I can't leave you alone for an instant, can I?" He chuckled, crossing his arms. "Who's this?"

Violet stared at the blonde. "I'm not sure. We'll need to fetch Ryon to translate for us."

Soon, they met up with the other ship and found Aren's raft floating beyond the breakers. They tied the boats fast, and everyone gathered on Violet's ship to decide what to do about their new friends.

Mariun stared at the shore, her eyes reflecting the fires blazing on the wharf. "Why didn't you say you were planning to burn the rest?" She glared back at Nox.

He shrugged. "What? Sabotage is only a problem when I'm the one doing it?"

Violet set a hand on Mariun's arm. "We can't have them following us either."

Mariun nodded. "You don't need to hide your plans from me. I told you I want away from Thalassia, too."

Ryon turned from his conversation with the blonde and cleared his throat. "Her name is Zoma. She wants to come with us. Says she was held on that island against her will."

Violet's heart clenched. When Zoma had clobbered that man, she'd expected as much, though it sickened her to hear it. "All right. Tell her she can stay. But she'd be better off returning to Dracwood with Uncle Aren. Or staying on the island where those friendly folks are watching little Dylen. Ask her if she's all right with that."

Violet sighed and focused back on Mariun as Ryon conversed with Zoma. She set a gentle hand on Mariun's shoulder. "You'll like it there, too. The people were kind and welcoming."

"I'd rather go with you," Mariun admitted quietly. "I know where you're headed. I've seen that map, too. I've always wanted to meet a dragon."

"No," Nox stated flatly. "We agreed."

"Well things can change." Mariun turned to him, staring up at him imploringly. "What if they come after you again? I can help."

"Oh, they're coming after you all right."

Violet gasped. "Lark!" She whipped around and spotted her aunt rolling up to sit, a hand clutched to the back of her head. "I'm so glad you're all right!"

Violet raced to Lark's side, ready to help prop her up, but Aren beat her to it. She backed away as the pair embraced, clutching each other desperately. The love they shared, their pure relief at being reunited, was so palpable everyone on board seemed to feel it. Violet inched away farther, giving them space.

"Wait," Nox butted in. "What do you mean, Lark? Why are you certain they'll come after us?"

Lark peered up from Aren's arms. But her gaze didn't fall on her brother. She stared straight at Mariun. "She didn't tell you who she is, did she?"

Violet spun to stare at Mariun.

Everyone stared at Mariun. Her cheeks flushed a deep scarlet as the next words spilled out of Lark's lips.

"Mariun is Jurdan's daughter. He'll never stop looking for her."

Violet reeled at the news. How could Mariun have kept that from them?

But one thing was instantly clear. "We can't leave Mariun on that island."

"What?" Nox shouted.

Violet squared off against her scowling uncle. "What do you think will happen when Jurdan finds her there? All those people... we can't do that to them after all the help they've given us."

"She can come with us," Aren said. "I'm sure Kayda will have plenty she'd like to ask her."

Violet nodded. It made sense. They'd have a great advantage hold-ing her hostage, should Jurdan choose to take up arms against them back in Dracwood.

But Mariun blanched and crossed her arms. "You can't take me there. Jurdan... he'll be livid. Besides, I'll be much more useful follow-ing the map. I know all about the defenses you'll encounter. Please."

Truthfully, if it were just up to her, Violet would take her. Even considering her omission. It didn't make sense completely, even in her own mind, but she had a strong feeling Mariun could be trusted. Still, it wasn't entirely her decision.

Violet turned to her aunt. "You spent more time with her than all of us combined. Can we trust her?"

Mariun stiffened at the question, her big gray eyes shifting to study Lark on the boat bottom.

Lark pursed her lips, then sighed. "Mariun was always kind to me." She shrugged. "Perhaps she has a point. Right now, finding Dru's eggs is more important than anything Mariun could tell Kayda. If she could give you the edge you need... I say take her with you."

"Take her, take her," Nox grumbled, as if to himself. He tugged at his hair, then threw up his arms. "Fine. You win." He stalked off to the back rail, muttering under his breath.

Ryon cleared his throat. "Zoma agreed to travel with Lark and Aren." He flicked a glance at Nox's retreating back. "You think he'll be all right?"

Violet nodded. "Yeah. He will. He's just so lost after Flint..." She grabbed Ryon's sleeve and tugged him aside, speaking quietly. "I don't know how much you heard just now, but it sounds like this voyage is about to get even more dangerous. You don't have to come—"

"I heard it all. And I'm in." Ryon grinned, leaning closer. "I still owe you for saving my life."

Violet shook her head. "You more than made up for that down there." She pointed back to the sea. She opened her mouth to say more, but his hand closed around hers and squeezed.

"I want to come, Violet." He met her gaze, still smiling, his eyes sparkling in the moonlight. "I wouldn't miss it."

Violet gulped. "I want to go with you, too. After we find Dru's eggs."

"Really? You'll come with me to meet Mother Orea?"

Violet nodded, and her heart hammered when his smile widened in response. Then her aunt saved her from staring at the poor man like a fool.

"Violet, can I talk to you?" Lark called. Aren had begun transferring supplies off the raft into the two boats, leaving her seated alone by the bow railing.

Violet left Ryon's side and crouched beside her aunt. "What is it?"

"I wanted to say goodbye. We can't stay latched here together forever."

"You're not mad, are you? That Nox and I are taking over your quest?"

Lark clutched her hands. "No. I'm grateful. I've been gone from home for so long. I can't wait to return." She loosened her grip. "Besides, someone needs to warn Kayda. Now, I can bring my son home knowing that you two are out here hunting for Dru's eggs."

Violet sent her aunt a watery smile.

"Are *you* fine with it? You can come back with us, Vi. Now that Nox has the map, he can handle this on his own."

"No. I want to finish this." She frowned. "I think I *need* to." She leaned even closer. "I think I just summoned."

Lark's eyes widened. "You did?" Then she clapped her hands delightedly. "Of course, you did." She grinned. "What was it?"

"A blast of air, when that man was after me." Violet cocked her head toward the hatch. "What if my magic is needed? I might be the only one left in the whole world who can summon."

Lark nodded sagely. "Believe me, I understand answering the call to adventure." Lark reached forward and tucked a rogue strand of pale hair behind Violet's ear. "Just promise me you'll be careful." Her gaze drifted back to the rail and landed on Ryon. "Lean on your friends. And Nox. Let them help you."

"I will. I promise."

Lark smiled warmly. "Violet, love, could you fetch Nox for me? I need to speak to him, too."

Violet smiled back. "All right."

As dawn broke, hours later, Violet stood at the rail and watched her aunt and uncle's boat fade into the distance. She couldn't help feeling a little sad seeing them go. But at the same time, she was hopeful and beyond excited.

Sure, Jurdan might come after them—eventually. The thought of that vile man sneaking up on them in the night was enough to make her tremble.

But there was still so much to look forward to. If everything went to plan, then they would be the people who brought dragons back from the brink of extinction.

Ryon stopped beside her. "You hungry?"

Violet opened her mouth to protest. A small part of her still worried he was only helping her because of his wish. He didn't *need* to feed her... But then her aunt's final plea rang in her ears.

She beamed up at him. "Actually, I'm starving."

He chuckled. "Then let's get you fed." He slung an arm around her shoulders, and she sucked in a quick breath.

She could definitely get used to this.

Epilogue

Lark smiled beneath the vibrant green leaves of the willow in Magehaven square. Her green and white checkered dress brushed across her legs in the gentle breeze. Spring sunlight flickered behind the wispy curtain, and dappled shadows played across Dylen's joyful smile.

"Have you ever seen anything so beautiful?" Lark trailed her fingers across the nearest branch.

Aren leaned in, bouncing their giggling son in his arms. "I have. I plan on setting my eyes on the glorious sight again later tonight in a proper bed."

Lark's cheeks flushed with heat. "Aren. Behave." But though she'd planned for her tone to come out indignant, it sounded breathless instead.

Dylen giggled again, his little fingers tangling in the willow's branches. Lark smiled indulgently, warmth flooding her chest and humming down to her toes. She was home with her husband and her son. It didn't get much better than this.

It had taken them weeks to make it back to Dracwood. They'd stopped off at the little island to collect Dylen and drop off Zoma. Then came long days, barely moving through the Still Sea.

They'd finally arrived in Magehaven this morning and spent the day buying fresh clothes and supplies for their journey back to Flamesmoat. It would be another week or two of hard riding to reach home, but she was excited for the change. She'd gladly take the long days in a saddle, rather than spend another moment sailing.

"You ready to find an inn?" Aren asked.

Lark grinned, easing through the willow branches into the bright afternoon sun. "Beyond ready."

"Lark? Is that you?"

Lark whipped around, searching the square for the familiar voice. "Taul?" She turned to greet the Doln warrior. His bald head glistened in the sunlight, and a wide smile peeked out behind his neatly cropped red beard. "What are you doing here?"

He pulled her in for a quick hug, and she clasped him tightly back, her arms sliding against his wide white tunic. Even without his customary thick furred coat, he was still too thickly muscled for her fingers to touch when she embraced him. "I could ask the same of you. Last I heard, you were off on a grand adventure with—Ah, there he is. How are you, Aren, old friend?"

"Taul." Aren stuck out a hand as he exited the shelter of the willow branches. "Small world."

"And who do we have here?" Taul's teeth gleamed, his smile widening with delight.

"This is Dylen." Aren stared down at their son's wide blue eyes. "Meet your Clan Chief, little warrior."

Dylen wasn't impressed. He hid his face in Aren's chest and clutched his brown tunic tightly.

Taul boomed out a laugh. "He's a good judge of character," he declared flatly, but he punctuated the statement with a wink, his eyes twinkling. "Well, my intended will be delighted to see you, no doubt."

Lark perked up. "Kayda's here? What a lucky coincidence. We need to speak to her."

Taul nodded. "We've been going over final details for the wedding."

Aren grinned. "We didn't miss it then?"

"Nope, still a few weeks for Kayda to come to her senses and call the whole thing off." Taul chuckled quietly.

Lark eyed him carefully. Theirs was no love match, that much was certain, but Taul was a good man. He'd sowed his wild oats in his youth and was finally ready to settle down... or so she'd thought. Could he be getting cold feet?

"C'mon. I'll take you to her. I'm heading that way already."

"Muse," she reached out with her thoughts. *"Kayda's here. We're going to meet with her. Where are you?"*

"I was sick of fish. Caught myself a hare. You want some?"

"No. You have at it. I'll meet you later?"

"Yep, later," she replied, sounding distracted.

Normally, Muse's gluttony made Lark roll her eyes, but today she only smiled. The whole time she'd been stuck in that underwater city, she'd felt the loss of Muse's voice like a gaping wound, a constant ache taking up residence in her heart. She still wasn't sure what it was about that place that blocked their bond, but she was beyond grateful to have her back where she belonged.

Taul led them across the square and down a side street to a humble inn. Lark's grin widened as she stepped inside, not at all surprised Kayda had chosen to frequent a small establishment rather than choosing the fanciest place she could find.

The inn was packed. A harried old woman bustled between the tables, and two women who looked like her daughters trailed in her wake, carting plates piled high with roast meat and dripping mugs of ale.

"Clan Chief," the woman called as soon as she spotted Taul in the entrance. Every head in the room turned to them as she hustled over. "The queen is awaiting you in the private parlor, my lord." She curtsied with a flourish, spreading her apron-swathed, brown skirts wide.

"Thank you, my dear." Taul flashed the old woman a roguish grin, and she tittered excitedly in response, her rosy cheeks flushing.

Aren leaned over and whispered in Lark's ear while the innkeeper giggled like a schoolgirl. "I'm going to see about getting us that room."

Lark rose to her toes and planted a kiss on his cheek. "Thank you. You're my hero."

Aren speared her with a heated glance. "Hold on to that thought for later."

Lark patted Dylen on the head and followed Taul across the room. She immediately knew which room Kayda was in, for there was a royal guard blocking the doorway, his metal armor gleaming with reflected light from the huge hearth.

"Lark? Is that you?" The portly man rubbed a hand across his sweat-soaked brow.

"Guard Captain Gawain. It's so nice to see you."

"And you. Let me announce you." He threw open the door and called in, "Clan Chief Taul and lady Lark are here, Your Highness."

Kayda jumped to her feet, shoving out of her chair. "Lark?" Her pink dress swished, the full ruffled skirt tangling around her legs, but she only hoisted it up and stepped across the tiny wooden chamber toward the doorway.

Lark rushed across the room and clutched her sister in a tight embrace. "Kayda. I've missed you so much!"

Kayda laughed. "Blazes, I'm so glad you're here! I didn't know if they'd ever find you." She pulled away and traced a hand over Lark's cheek, her red eyes wide open and pointed at Lark's face, though Lark knew Kayda couldn't see her. Kayda cocked her head, as if listening. "What of the others? Violet and Nox? Aren? Are they here, too?"

"Aren is. He'll be by after he secures us a room."

"And the others?"

Lark shot a glance at Taul. He was soon to be king, but she wasn't sure how much he knew...

He saved her from having to broach the subject. "Why don't I give you two some privacy to catch up?" Taul offered. "I'll go see how Aren is getting on with that old flirt of an innkeeper."

Kayda aimed a smile in his direction. "Thank you, Taul. I'd love a moment alone with my sister."

After the door closed, Lark led Kayda back to the little wooden table and took the chair across from her. Plates of food were already laid out, piled high with fresh fruit, meat soaked in a brown gravy, and loaves of brown bread. But though her stomach rumbled at the feast, Lark ignored the food.

She kept talking, bringing Kayda up to speed on everything that had happened during her travels.

"So, they have the map and are close to finding Dru's eggs... That's wonderful news." Kayda grinned, but after only an instant, her smile fell. "And this Jurdan the Supreme... you think he'll be a threat to us?"

Lark sighed. "I'm almost certain of it." She shuddered. "The way he felt, Kayda. It was vile. Just like with the Unseen. I'm not sure how, but they're connected."

Kayda went silent. Lark sensed the battle playing out in her sister's mind. She'd already burdened her with so much awful news she almost left her there to digest it all. But there was one more piece of news she *had* to share.

She reached across the table and clutched her sister's hand. "Kayda, the masked men. There's something else you need to know about them."

Kayda squeezed back and cocked her head slightly. "Yes, what about them?"

"As we were escaping, I was captured by one of them. He was one of Jurdan's trusted advisors and always wore a spider mask."

Kayda's eyes widened, and her hand trembled. "A spider..."

Lark drew in a deep breath and barreled on with the rest before she lost her nerve. "Just before he slammed my head into a wall and knocked me unconscious, I bumped his mask askew. Kayda... it was him."

Kayda gasped. "No. How? Are you certain?"

Lark shook her head. "I don't know how, but I'm sure. The spider was Jayan. He's alive."

A knock sounded at the door, and Guard Captain Gawain poked his head inside an instant later. "Your Highness, Lord Aren is here to see you."

"Send him in," Kayda announced. She took a deep breath and seemed to bury the shocking news in exchange for a wide smile.

Aren strode through the doorway, his blond hair messy, and his tunic spattered with their son's drool, but Lark's heart clenched at the sight of him all the same. "Kayda, it's so good to see you."

A whine spilled out of Dylen's lips from where he was cradled in Aren's strong arms.

Kayda perked up, sitting straighter. "Is that my nephew, I hear?" She stuck out her arms and beckoned Aren over. "May I hold him?"

"Of course, though don't be surprised if he wails. He has a tooth erupting that's paining him, I'm afraid." Aren settled Dylen in Kayda's lap. "Meet your Auntie Kayda, Dylen."

Dylen had a hand shoved in his mouth, but as he plopped down on Kayda's fluffy ruffled skirt, he withdrew it and promptly grabbed her nose with his spit-covered fist.

"It's lovely to meet you, too, my boy." Kayda laughed, her words sounding much more nasal than usual with the little boy's fist squeezed tightly on her face.

All was well for a moment, until Dylen spotted Lark across the table. "Mama." His little lip quivered, and he started wailing, just as Aren predicted.

Lark rounded the table, then grabbed Dylen out of Kayda's arms. Kayda frowned, seemingly reluctant to give him up, despite his shrill cries.

"I already tried to put him down in our room, but he won't settle." Aren sighed, rubbing his neck with a weary smile. "Poor little guy. That tooth is bothering him. He could really use a good night's rest after all the excitement today."

Lark smiled down at her son's face as he shoved his fist back into his mouth. "Well, let's see what we can do about that. Come along, Dylen. Let Mama sing you a lullaby."

About the Author

Amber L. Werner loves to write about magic, monsters and mythical creatures. She lives in Norristown, PA with her husband and two children. The Palisade Trilogy is her debut series.

Follow her Facebook page Amber L. Werner
Or Instagram amberlwerner

Sign up for her newsletter and receive a free novella.
Find it here amberlwerner.com

Also By

Binge the complete Palisade Trilogy now. An epic fantasy adventure, full of unique magic, animal companions, dragons, betrayal, and a quest to save the world.

Shadows That Bind Us — Palisade Trilogy 1
Muses That Align Us — Palisade Trilogy 2
Lines That Drew Us — Palisade Trilogy 3

Sign up for my newsletter for a free standalone prequel novella that tells the story of how the Palisade was built centuries ago.
You'll find the link on my website amberlwerner.com

Standalone Short Story
Somewhere In Between

The Blood Song Trilogy
Bloodfeather Lullaby — Blood Song Trilogy 1

Coming Soon — Spring 2024

Bloodfeather Heartsong — Blood Song Trilogy 2